JAMRACH'S
Menagerie

Also by Carol Birch

Scapegallows
The Naming of Eliza Quinn
Turn Again Home
Come Back Paddy Riley
Little Sister
Songs of the West
Life in the Palace

JAMRACH'S
Menagerie

Carol Birch

CANONGATE

Edinburgh · London · New York · Melbourne

For Budgie

Published by Canongate Books in 2011

1

Copyright © Carol Birch, 2011

The moral right of the author has been asserted

First published in Great Britain in 2011 by
Canongate Books Ltd, 14 High Street, Edinburgh EH1 1TE

www.canongate.tv

British Library Cataloguing-in-Publication Data
A catalogue record for this book is available on
request from the British Library

ISBN 978 1 84767 657 3

Typeset in Baskerville MT by Palimpsest Book Production Ltd,
Falkirk, Stirlingshire

Printed and bound in Great Britain by
Clays Ltd, St Ives plc

PART ONE

1

I was born twice. First in a wooden room that jutted out over
the black water of the Thames, and then again eight years
later in the Highway, when the tiger took me in his mouth
and everything truly began.

Say Bermondsey and they wrinkle their noses. Still, it was the
home before all other homes. The river lapped beneath us as we
slept. Our door looked out over a wooden rail into the channel
at the front, where dark water heaved up an odd sullen grey bubble.
If you looked down through the slats, you could see things moving
in the swill below. Thick green slime, glistening in the slosh that
banged up against it, crept up the crumbling wooden piles.

I remember the jagged lanes with bent elbows and crooked
knees, rutted horse shit in the road, the dung of sheep that passed
our house every day from the marshes and the cattle bellowing
their unbearable sorrows in the tannery yard. I remember the
dark bricks of the tanning factory, and the rain falling black. The
wrinkled red bricks of the walls were gone all to tarry soot. If
you touched them the tips of your fingers came away shiny black.
A heavy smell came up from under the wooden bridge and got
you in the gob as you crossed in the morning going to work.

The air over the river though was full of sound and rain. And sometimes at night the sound of sailors sang out over the winking water – voices wild and dark to me as the elements themselves – lilts from everywhere, strange tongues that lisped and shouted, melodies running up and down like many small flights of stairs, making me feel as if I was far away in those strange hot-sun places.

The river was a great thing seen from the bank, but a foul thing when your bare toes encountered the thin red worms that lived in its sticky mud. I remember them wriggling between.

But look at *us*.

Crawling up and down the new sewers like maggots ourselves, thin grey boys, thin grey girls, grey as the mud we walked in, splashing along the dark, round-mouthed tunnels that stank like hell. The sides were caked in crusty, black shit. Peeling out pennies and trying to fill our pockets, we wore our handkerchiefs over our noses and mouths, our eyes stang and ran. Sometimes we retched. It was something you did, like a sneeze or a belch. And when we came blinking out onto the foreshore, there we would see a vision of beauty: a great wonder, a tall and noble three-masted clipper bringing tea from India, bearing down upon the Pool of London, where a hundred ships lay resting like pure-bred horses getting groomed, renewed, readied, soothed and calmed for the great sea trial to come.

But our pockets were never full. I remember the gnawing in my belly, the hunger retch. That thing my body did nights when I lay in bed.

All of this was a long time ago. In those days my mother could easily have passed for a child. She was a small, tough thing with muscular shoulders and arms. When she walked she strode, swinging her arms from the shoulders. She was a laugh, my ma.

She and I slept together in a truckle. We used to sing together getting off to sleep in that room over the river – a very pretty, cracked voice she had – but a man came sometimes, and then I had to go next door and kip in one end of a big tumbled old feather bed, with the small naked feet of very young children pushing up the blankets on either side of my head, and the fleas feasting on me.

The man that came to see my mother wasn't my father. My father was a sailor who died before I was born, so Ma said, but she never said much. This man was a long, thin, wild-eyed streak of a thing with a mouth of crooked teeth, and deft feet that constantly tapped out rhythms as he sat. I suppose he must have had a name, but I never knew it, or if I did I've forgotten. It doesn't matter. I never had anything to do with him, or he with me.

He came when she was humming over her sewing one day – some sailor's pants gone in the crotch – threw her down upon the floor, and started kicking her and calling her a dirty whore. I was scared, more scared I think than I had ever been before. She rolled away, hitting her head against the table leg, then up she jumped, screaming blue murder, that he was a bastard and a fly boy and she'd none of him no more, flailing with her short strong arms and both fists balled for punching.

'Liar!' he roared.

I never knew he had a voice like that. As if he was twice as big.

'Liar!'

'You call *me* a liar?' she screeched, and went for the sides of his head, grabbing him by both ears and bashing his head about as if it was an old cushion she was shaking up. When she let go he wobbled. She ran out onto the walkway hollering at the top of her voice, and all the neighbour women came out at a run with their skirts hoicked up, some with knives, some with sticks or pots, and one with a candlestick. He dashed out amongst them with his own knife drawn, a vicious big stabber raised over his shoulder, damning them all as whores and scattering them back as he ran for the bridge.

'I'll get you, you bitch!' he yelled back. 'I'll get you and I'll cut out your lights!'

That night we ran away. Or that's how I remember it. Possibly it was not that night, possibly it was a few days or a week later, but I remember no more of Bermondsey after that, only the brightness of the moon on the river as I followed my mother bare-foot over London Bridge, to my second birth. I was eight years old.

I know we came in time to the streets about Ratcliffe Highway, and there I met the tiger. Everything that came after followed from that. I believe in fate. Fall of the dice, drawing of the straw. It's always been like that. Watney Street was where we came to rest. We lived in the crow's nest of Mrs Regan's house. A long flight of steps ran up to the front door. Railings round the basement area enclosed a deep, dark place where men gathered nights to play cards and drink strong liquor. Mrs Regan, a tall, worn woman with a pale, startled face, lived under us with an ever-changing population of sailors and touts, and upstairs lived Mr Reuben, an old black man with white hair and a bushy yellow moustache. A curtain hung down the middle of our room, and on the other side of it two old Prussian whores called Mari-Lou and Silky snored softly all day long. Our bit of the room had a window looking over the street. In the morning the smell of yeast from the baker's opposite came into my dreams. Every day but Sunday we were woken early by the drag of his wheelbarrow over the stones, and soon after by the market people setting up their stalls. Watney Street was all market. It smelled of rotten fruit and vegetables, strong fish, the two massive meat barrels that stood three doors down outside the butcher's, dismembered heads of pigs sticking snout upwards out of the tops. Nowhere near as bad as Bermondsey, which smelled of shit. I didn't realise Bermondsey smelled of shit till we moved to the Highway. I was only a child. I thought shit was the natural smell of the world. To me, Watney Street and the Highway and all about there seemed sweeter and cleaner than anything I'd ever known and it was only later, with great surprise, that I learned how others considered it such a dreadful smelly hole.

Blood and brine ran down the pavement into the gutters and was sucked into the mush under the barrows that got trodden all day long up and down, up and down, into your house, up the stairs, into your room. My toes slid through it in a familiar way, but it was better than shitty Thames mud any day.

Flypapers hung over every door and every barrow. Each one was black and rough with a million flies, but it made no difference. A million more danced happily about in the air and walked on the tripe which the butcher's assistant had sliced so thinly and carefully first thing that morning and placed in the window.

You could get anything down Watney Street. Our end was all houses, the rest was shops and pubs, and the market covered all the street. It sold cheap: old clothes, old iron, old anything. When I walked through the market my eyes were on a level with cabbages, lumpy potatoes, sheep's livers, salted cucumbers, rabbit skins, saveloys, cow heels, ladies' bellies, softly rounded and swelling. The people packed in, all sorts, rough sorts, poor sorts, sifting their way through heaps of old worn shoes and rags, scrabbling about like ants, pushing and shoving and swearing, fierce old ladies, kids like me, sailors and bright girls and shabby men. Everyone shouted. First time I walked out in all that I thought, blimey, you don't want to go down in that muck, and if you were small you could go down very easy. Best stay close by the barrows so there'd be something to grab a hold of.

I loved running errands. One way was the Tower, the other Shadwell. The shops were all packed with the stuff of the sea and ships, and I loved to linger outside their windows and hang around their doors getting a whiff of that world. So when Mrs Regan sent me out for a plug of bacca one day for Mr Reuben, it must have taken me at least a half an hour to get down to the tobacco dock. I got half an ounce from one of the baccy women and was on my way back with my head in a dream, as was the way, so I thought nothing of the tray of combs dropped on the pavement by a sallow girl with a ridge in her neck, or the people vanishing, sucked as if by great breaths into doorways and byways, flattened against walls. My ears did not catch the sudden stilling of the Highway's normal rhythms, the silence of one great held communal breath. How could I? I did not know the Highway. I knew nothing but dark water and filth bubbles and small bridges over shit creeks that shook no matter how light of foot you skipped over. 'This new place, this sailor town where we will stay now nice and snug awhile, Jaffy-boy,' as my ma said, all of it, everything was different. Already I'd seen things I'd never seen before. This new labyrinth of narrow lanes teemed with the faces and voices of the whole world. A brown bear danced decorously on the corner by an alehouse called Sooty Jack's. Men walked about with parrots on their shoulders, magnificent birds, pure scarlet, egg-yolk yellow, bright sky blue. Their eyes were knowing and half amused, their feet scaly. The air on the corner of Martha Street hung sultry with the perfume of Arabian sherbet, and women in silks as bright as the parrots leaned out from doorways, arms akimbo, powerfully breasted like the figureheads of the ships lying along the quays.

In Bermondsey the shop windows were dusty. When you put

your face close and peered, you saw old flypapers, pale cuts of meat, powdery cakes, strings of onions flaking onto yellowing newsprint. In the Highway the shops were full of birds. Cage upon cage piled high, each full of clustering creatures like sparrows but bright as sweets, red and black, white and yellow, purple and green, and some as gently lavender as the veins on a baby's head. It took the breath away to see them so crowded, each wing crushed against its fellows on either side. In the Highway green parakeets perched upon lamp posts. Cakes and tarts shone like jewels, tier on tier behind high glass windows. A black man with gold teeth and white eyes carried a snake around his neck.

How could I know what was possible and what was not? And when the impossible in all its beauty came walking towards me down the very middle of Ratcliffe Highway, why would I know how to behave?

Of course, I'd seen a cat before. You couldn't sleep for them in Bermondsey, creeping about over the roofs and wailing like devils. They lived in packs, spiky, wild-eyed, stalking the wooden walkways and bridges, fighting with the rats. But this cat . . .

The Sun himself came down and walked on earth.

Just as the birds of Bermondsey were small and brown, and those of my new home were large and rainbow-hued, so it seemed the cats of Ratcliffe Highway must be an altogether superior breed to our scrawny south-of-the-river mogs. This cat was the size of a small horse, solid, massively chested, rippling powerfully about the shoulders. He was gold, and the pattern painted so carefully all over him, so utterly perfect, was the blackest black in the world. His paws were the size of footstools, his chest snow white.

I'd seen him somewhere, his picture in a poster in London Street, over the river. He was jumping through a ring of fire and his mouth was open. A mythical beast.

I have no recall of one foot in front of the other, cobblestones under my feet. He drew me like honey draws a wasp. I had no fear. I came before the godly indifference of his face and looked into his clear yellow eyes. His nose was a slope of downy gold, his nostrils pink and moist as a pup's. He raised his thick, white dotted lips and smiled, and his whiskers bloomed.

I became aware of my heart somewhere too high up, beating as if it was a little fist trying to get out.

Nothing in the world could have prevented me from lifting my hand and stroking the broad warm nap of his nose. Even now I feel how beautiful that touch was. Nothing had ever been so soft and clean. A ripple ran through his right shoulder as he raised his paw – bigger than my head – and lazily knocked me off my feet. It was like being felled by a cushion. I hit the ground but was not much hurt, only winded, and after that it was a dream. There was, I remember, much screaming and shouting, but from a distance, as if I was sinking underwater. The world turned upside down and went by me in a bright stream, the ground moved under me, my hair hung in my eyes. There was a kind of joy in me, I do know that – and nothing that could go by the name of fear, only a wildness. I was in his jaws. His breath burned the back of my neck. My bare toes trailed, hurting distantly. I could see his feet, tawny orange with white toes, pacing the ground away, gentle as feathers.

I remember swimming up through wild waters, the howling of a million shells, endless, timeless confusion. I was no one. No name. Nowhere. Then came a point where I *realised* I was nothing and that was the end of the nothing and the beginning of fear. I never had a lostness like that before, though many more were to come in my life. Voices came, piping in from the howling, making no sense. Then words—

he's dead, he's dead, he's dead, oh, lord mercy – and the hardness of stone, cold beneath my cheek, sudden.

A woman's voice.

A hand on my head.

No no no his eyes are open, look, he's . . . *there*, fine boy, let me feel . . . no no no you're all fine . . .

he's dead he's dead he's dead . . .

there you come, son . . .

here you come . . .

And I am born. Wide awake sitting up on the pavement, blinking at the shock of the real.

A man with a big red face and cropped yellow hair had me by the shoulders. He was staring into my eyes, saying over and over again: 'There, you're a fine boy now . . . there, you're a fine boy . . .'

I sneezed and got a round of applause. The man grinned. I became aware of a huge mob, all bobbing their heads to see me.

'Oh, poor little thing!' a woman's voice cried out, and I looked up and saw her at the front of the crowd, a woman with a startled face and mad wiry hair, wild goggly eyes made huge and swimmy by bottle-bottom spectacles. She held a little girl by the hand. The crowd was like daubed faces on a board, daubed faces with smudged bodies, bright stabs of colour here and there, scarlet, green, royal purple. It heaved gently like a sea and my eyes could not take it in, it blurred wildly as if blocked by tears – though my eyes were dry – blurred and shivered and whirled itself around with a heaving burst of sound, till something shook my head awake again and I saw clearly, clearer than I had ever seen anything before, the face of the little girl standing at the front of the crowd holding her mother's hand, drawn sharp as ice on a mess of fog.

'Now,' said the big man, taking my chin in his fist and turning my face to look at him, 'how many fingers, boy?' He had an accent of some kind, sharp and foreign. His other hand he held up before me, the thumb and small finger bent down.

'Three,' I said.

This brought another great murmur of approval from the crowd.

'Good boy, good boy!' the man said, as if I'd done something very clever, setting me on my feet but still holding me by the shoulders. 'Fine now?' he asked, shaking me gently. 'Very fine, brave boy. Good boy! Fine boy! Best boy!'

I saw tears in his eyes, on the rims, not falling, which seemed strange to me as he was smiling so vigorously and showing a perfectly even row of small, shiny white teeth. His wide face was very close to mine, smooth and pink like a cooked ham.

He hoisted me up in his arms and held me against him. 'Say your name, fine boy,' he said, 'and we'll take you home to Mamma.'

'Jaffy Brown,' I said. I felt my thumb in my mouth and whipped it out quick. 'My name is Jaffy Brown and I live in Watney Street.' And at the same moment a dreadful sound rose upon the air, as of loosed packs of hounds, demons in hell, mountains falling, hue and cry.

The red face suddenly thundered: 'Bulter! For God's sake, get him back in the crate! He's seen the dogs!'

'My name is Jaffy Brown,' I cried as clearly as I could, for by now I was fully back in the world, though my stomach churned and heaved alarmingly. 'And I live in Watney Street.'

I was carried home as if I was an infant in the arms of the big man, and all the way he talked to me, saying: 'So, what will we say to Mammy? What will Mammy say when she hears you've been playing with a tiger? "Hello, Mammy, I've been playing with my friend the tiger! I gave him a pat on the nose!" How many boys can say that, hi? How many boys can go walking down the road and meet a tiger, hi? Special boy! Brave boy! Boy in ten million!'

Boy in ten million. My head was swelled to the size of St Paul's dome by the time we turned into Watney Street with a crowd of gawkers trailing after.

'I been telling you what might happen, Mr Jamrach!' shrilled the bespectacled woman with the little girl, bobbing alongside. 'What about us? What about us what has to live next to you?' She had the Scots burr and her eyes glared.

'The beast was sleepy and full,' the man replied. 'He ate a hearty dinner not twenty minutes since, or we'd never have moved him. I am sorry, this should not have happened and will never happen so again.' He knuckled a tear from the side of one eye. 'But there was no danger.'

'Got teeth, hasn't it?' cried the woman. 'Claws?'

At which the girl peeped round her mother's side, clutching onto a scrap of polka-dot scarf wrapped round her neck and smiling. It was the first smile of my life. Of course, that is a ridiculous thing to say; I had been smiled at often, the big man had smiled at me not a minute since. And yet I say: it was the first smile, because it was the first that ever went straight into me like a needle too thin to be seen. Then, dragged a bit too fast by her wild-eyed mother, she tripped and went sprawling with her hands splayed out, and her face broke up. A great wail burst out of her.

'Oh, my God,' said her mother, and we left the two fussing at the side of the road and went on through the market stalls to our house. Mrs Regan was sitting on the top step, but jumped to her feet and stood gaping when she saw the band of us approach. Everyone babbled at once. Ma came running down and I threw out my arms for her and burst into tears.

'No harm done, ma'am,' Mr Jamrach said, handing me over. 'I am so sorry, ma'am, your boy was scared. A dreadful thing –

a weakness in the crate, come all the way from Bengal – pushed out the back, he did, with his hindquarters . . .'

She set me on my feet and brushed me down, looking hard in my eyes. 'His toes,' she said. She was pale.

I looked wonderingly at the gathering crowd.

'Ma'am,' Mr Jamrach began, reaching into his coat and bringing out money. The girl and her ma were back. She'd scraped her knees and looked sulky. I saw Mr Reuben.

'I got your baccy,' I said, reaching into my pocket.

'Why thank you, Jaffy,' Mr Reuben said, and gave me a wink.

The Scots woman started up again, though now she'd changed sides and was defending Mr Jamrach as a great hero: 'Ran after it, he did! Never seen anything like it! Grabs it like this, he does,' letting go of the little girl's hand to demonstrate how he'd leapt on its back and grabbed it by the throat, 'sticks his bare hands right down its mouth, he did. See. A wild tiger!'

Ma seemed stunned and a bit stupid. She never took her eyes off me. 'His poor toes,' she said, and I looked down and saw them bleeding where they'd been pulled over the stones, and it brought the realisation of pain. I felt where the tiger had made my collar wet.

'Dear ma'am,' Mr Jamrach said, pressing money into Ma's apron, 'this is the bravest little boy I ever encountered.'

He gave her a card with his name on.

We ate well that night, no hunger sickness for me. I was very happy, filled up with love for the tiger. She washed my toes with warm water and rubbed them with butter she got from Mrs Regan. Mr Reuben sat in our room sucking on his pipe, and all the neighbours jostled at our door. It was like a carnival. Ma was tickled pink and kept telling everyone, 'A tiger! A tiger! Jaffy got carried off by a tiger!'

The tiger made me. When my path and his crossed, everything changed. After that, the road took its branching way, willy-nilly, and off I went into the future. It might not have been so. Nothing might ever have been so. I might not have known the great thing that came to pass. I might have taken home Mr Reuben's baccy and gone upstairs to my dear ma and things would have gone altogether differently.

The card sat propped importantly on the mantelpiece next to Ma's hairbrush and a jug of wispy black feathers, and when Mrs Regan's son Jud came home from work he read it to us.

Charles Jamrach
Naturalist and Importer of Animals, Birds and Shells

2

The first time I saw Tim Linver he was standing out in our street shouting up at the house.

'Jaffy Brown's wanted!'

It was the morning after my great encounter. I was standing in the room of Mari-Lou and Silky, who knew nothing of my adventure, the tops of my toes still burning and my plasters turning dirty and raggy. Mari-Lou, unlaced, fat brown breasts spilling, counted pennies into my palm for the fried fish stall, and a penny for me for going. Mari-Lou wore her hair very black with scarlet roses at the sides. Elaborate crinkles sprouted round her eyes, and a great round belly stuck out in front and carried her forward. 'Now, Mister Jaffy,' she instructed, 'no brown bits. Yah? No brown bits and a nice big pickle, and no you sucking on it.' Her rouge was faded. The mountain of silk that was Silky was sitting up in bed with her two thin breasts drooping down to her waist. They'd have their fish supper in bed and be snoring deeply in half an hour.

And the cry came: 'Jaffy Brown's wanted!'

I went to the window and looked out with the pennies warm in my hand and there he was. Older, bigger than me, different as could be, straight goldy-haired, pretty and girl-like of face. Tim Linver. It was late morning, the street thronged.

'Who wants him?' I shouted.

'Jamrach wants him,' he said. 'Come down.'

'What about our cod, Mister Jaf?' Mari-Lou's long red claws dug into my arm.

'I'm going!' I cried and bounded down the stairs.

The boy came forward. 'You him?' he asked gracelessly.

'Yes.'

'I've got to get you a raspberry puff,' he said morosely. 'Jamrach said.'

The raspberry puffs in the windows of the pastry cook's shop I walked past every day on Back Lane were beyond me. The berries bled juice through their hairs. The furrowed cream was pale gold, the pastry damp with sugar.

The tiger had opened magical doors.

'I'm running an errand,' I said. 'I've got to get fish.'

'Well, *I've* got to get you a raspberry puff and take you to Jamrach,' he said, as if that was far more important. 'Getting the special grand tour, you are. See all the wild animals?'

Mari-Lou leaned out of the window. 'Off you go and get that fish, you, Mister Jaf!'

'What's it like getting eaten?' the boy said.

'Eaten?'

'You're eaten,' he said, 'so they say.'

'Do I look it?'

'It's all around that you're eaten,' he said, 'eaten up and just your head left on the stones.'

I saw it, my head on the stones. It made me laugh.

'Just your head,' he said, 'and your hands and feet. And some bits of bone, I suppose, gnawed ragged.'

'Didn't hurt a bit,' I said.

Mari-Lou threw a bottle at my head. It missed and smashed in the gutter.

'Two ticks,' I said to the boy. 'Wait.' And I ran all the way to the fried fish stall and all the way back.

Mrs Regan was just taking up her post on the doorstep and looked disapprovingly at my filthy feet as I shot past her. 'You'll get blood poisoning, you will,' she remarked. I pelted upstairs and shoved the steaming bundle into Mari-Lou's eager red claws. Mari-Lou and Silky liked their fish drenched till it was soggy. My eyes stang from the vinegar. I'd forgotten the pickle. You'd have thought I'd robbed a cripple. I had to give them back a penny, but I didn't care. Wild animals were roaming in my head: lions, tigers, elephants, giraffes. I was going to have a raspberry puff and see the animals.

The boy was still there when I reached the street, hands deep in his pockets, shoulders high. 'Come on,' he said, and I followed his straight, insolent back down through the crowds between the market stalls till we came out on Back Lane, where he barred me from going with him into the shop with one movement of his arm and not a word. Himself, he went in and requested one rasp-berry puff to eat now please, Rose, darling, as if he was a man. I did not know then that he was only a year my senior and thought he must be at least eleven.

I could see Rose through the glass, a nice smily girl with flour dusting her eyelashes. Then he strolled out, looked up at the sky, handed me a raspberry puff nestled in a little napkin for me to hold to keep my fingers clean. Not that they were clean in the first place.

There he stood with his hands in his pockets and watched me eat the raspberry puff. The first bite was so bitterly sweet the corners of my mouth ached. So beautiful, a film of tears stung my eyes. Then the pain dispersed and there was only delight. I had never tasted raspberry. Never tasted cream. The second bite was greedy and gorging, stopping my mouth up. He had eyes like a statue. Never moved. He'd probably never had a raspberry puff himself. He was better dressed then me, shoes and all, but still, I bet he never ate a raspberry puff in his life.

'Want a bit?' I said.

He shook his head sharply and made that banning motion with his arm again, smiling a little, proudly.

The smell hit me first, a good thrilling smell, stronger than cheese. Then the noise. We came in from the street to a lobby where coats were hung, and boxes and great sacks stored, and a green parrot leaned over me and peered into my face. It looked as if it knew something funny.

'She speaks,' said the boy. 'Go on, Flo, say: "Five pounds, darlin'."'

Flo cocked her head sharply, shifting her gaze to him in a sympathetic way but saying nothing.

'Five pounds, darlin'! Go on, you stupid bird.'

She blinked. He made a quick sound of disgust and led me to an open door from which a smog of dark smoke was visibly spreading into the hall.

'Here he is, Mr Jamrach. He's had his creamy doodah.'

I followed him in. The great, red-faced Jamrach came down through the murk with a smile and cried: 'Ha! Jaffy Brown!' He punched me gently on the shoulder. 'Did you have a good supper last night?' He bent down with his face so close I could count the red veins in the whites of his eyes. The air was heavy, lush and rotting, filled with traces of bowels and blood and piss and hair, and something overall I could not name, which I suppose was wildness.

'Mutton stew,' I said. 'It was lovely.'

20

'Excellent!'

Mr Jamrach stood up and rubbed his palms together. He wore a business suit that made him look stout, and his hair was parted in the middle and slicked down with oil.

'Bulter,' he said to a pale young man scowling and picking his nails behind a very untidy desk, 'get Charlie out.'

Bulter stood, long and thin, flounced round the desk and stopped before a large cage. A wonderful, outrageous bird perched attentively, watching the dim room as if it was the most wonderful show. The bird was all colours, and its beak was bigger than its body.

'Come out, Charlie, you stupid bird,' Bulter said, lifting the latch.

Charlie danced with delight. Didn't he crawl as gentle as a sleepy kitten into Bulter's arms and nestle up against his breast with that hard monster beak and the downturned head bashful? Bulter stroked the black feathers on top of the bird's head. 'Daft he is,' he said, turned and placed Charlie in my arms. Charlie raised his head and looked into my face.

'He's a toucan,' Tim said.

'Got the touch, you have,' Bulter said to me. 'He likes you.'

'Likes everyone,' Tim said.

Charlie was a sane and willing bird. So was Flo, the parrot in the lobby. The birds that came after were not.

Mr Jamrach led me through the lobby and into the menagerie. The first room was a parrot room, a fearsome screaming place of mad round eyes, crimson breasts that beat against bars, wings that flapped against their neighbours, blood red, royal blue, gypsy yellow, grass green. The birds were crammed along perches. Macaws hung upside down here and there, batting their white eyes, and small green parrots flittered above our heads in drifts. A host of cockatoos looked down from on high over the shrill madness, high crested, creamy breasted. The screeching was like laughter in hell.

'This is how they like it,' Jamrach said.

My eyes watered. My ears hurt.

'They flock.'

'They're crying out for parrots,' Tim Linver said sagely, bobbing alongside with a loose and cocky gait.

'Who is?'

'People is.'

I turned my head. Small ones, pretty things, blue, red, green, yellow, in rows behind the wire, good as gold and quiet.

'My parakeets,' said Jamrach. 'Lovely birds.'

'In and out in no time, this lot.' Tim rocked back on his heels, speaking like a man, as if the entire operation belonged to him.

The second room was quieter. Hundreds of birds, like sparrows but done out in all the colours of the rainbow, in long boxes. A wall of bluebirds, breasts the colour of rose sherbet. The air, fluty with song, like early morning.

'Six shillings a pair,' Tim said.

The third and last bird room was completely silent. All the way up to the ceiling, tiny wooden cages piled on top of one another, in each one a bird just the right size to fill the space, all of them mute and still. More than anything I'd seen, this room bothered me. I wondered if Mr Jamrach would let me have one. I could tame it and it would fly free in our room and sing.

Out into the dazzling yard. Bulter from the office was there with another man, sweeping up outside a pen. A camel chewed behind the bars. A camel has to chew like it has to breathe. I know that now. Then, I might as well have stepped into a picture book. The animals were the stuff of fairy tales, the black bear with the white bib, the sideways-looking eye of the baby elephant, the head of the giraffe, immense, coming down at me from the sky to wet me with the heat of its flexing nostrils. I grew light of mind from the gorgeous stench. A wilderness steamed in the air all about me. And then I saw my tiger in his cage, with a lion on one side and some dog things on the other. The lion was a majestic and dreadful cat with the stern, sad face of a scholar and wild billowing hair. He looked me in the eye for a whole moment before turning away in total indifference. A thick, pink tongue licked out, carressing his nostrils. The hair stood up on the backs of the dog things. My tiger paced, rippling, thick tail striking the air. Little black fishes swam on his back. Scimitars, blades, dashes, black on gold, black on white. Heavy-headed, lower jaw hanging slack, backwards and forwards, steady:

three paces and a half – turn—

three paces and a half – turn—

three paces and a half—

'See!' said Jamrach. 'This is the bad boy. He knows he's been a bad boy, he is shamed, see.'

'Has he got a name?'

'Not yet. He hasn't found his buyer yet.'

'Who buys a tiger?' I asked.

'Zoos,' Tim said.

'London Zoo,' I said. I'd never been there.

Tim and Jamrach laughed as if I'd said something funny.

'Not just zoos,' Jamrach said, 'people who collect.'

'How much for my tiger?' I asked.

'He is a full-grown Bengal tiger,' Mr Jamrach said. 'Two hundred pounds at least.'

Tim babbled: 'Two hundred for a tiger, three hundred an elephant, seventy for a lion. You can pay three hundred for some lions though. Get the right one. An orang-utan, now that's three twenty.'

We went up a ladder to a place where there was a beast like a pie, a great lizard mad and grinning, and monkeys, many monkeys, a stew of human nature, a bone pile of it, a wall, a dream of small faces. Baby things. No, ancient, impossibly old things. But they were beyond old and young. The babies clung fast beneath sheltering bellies. The mothers, stoic above, endured.

'And here . . .' Jamrach, with some showmanship, whipped the lid off a low round basket. Snakes, thick, green and brown, muscled, lay faintly flexing upon one another like ropes coiled high on the quay. 'Snappy things, these,' Jamrach said, putting back the lid and tying a rope round it.

We passed by a huge cat with pointed ears and eyes like jewels that miaowed like a kitten at us. Furry things ran here and there about our feet, pretty things I never could have imagined. He said they came from Peru, whatever far place that was. And right at the end in the darkest place, sitting down with his knuckles turned in, was an ape who looked at me with eyes like a man's.

That was all I ever wanted. To stay among the animals for ever and ever and look into their eyes whenever I felt like it. So when, back in the smoky office with the pale clerk Bulter lolling behind his desk once more drinking cocoa, Mr Jamrach offered me a job, I could only cry, 'Oh yes!' like a fool and make everybody laugh.

'Very small, isn't he?' Tim Linver said. 'You sure he's up to it, Mr Jamrach?'

'Well, Jaffy?' Mr Jamrach asked jovially. '*Are* you up to it?'

'I am,' I said. 'I work hard. You don't know yet.'

And I could. We'd be fine now, Ma and me. She was on shifts at the sugar bakers, the place with the big chimney, and I was starting as pot boy at the Spoony Sailor that very night. With all that and this new job, we could pay our rent up front.

Tim came over and bumped me roughly with his shoulder. 'Know what that means, Lascar?' he said. 'Clearing up dung in the yard.'

Well, no one could be better suited for that than me, and I told them so, and that made them laugh even more. Mr Jamrach, sitting sideways at his desk, leaned over and folded back the white paper cover from a box next to his feet. Very carefully and with the utmost respect, he lifted out a snake, one greater than all the others I'd yet seen. If it had stretched itself out straight and stood itself on the tip of its tail, I suppose it would have been taller than me. Its body was triangular, covered in dry, yellowish scales. Its long face moved towards me from his hands. I stood three feet or so away, and it stretched itself out like a bridge between me and him, straight as a stick, as if it was a hand pointing at me. A quick forked tongue, red as the devil, darted from it a foot from my nose.

'S-s-s-o,' said Jamrach in a snake voice, 'you are joining us, Master Jaffy?'

I put my hand out to touch, but he drew the snake in sharply. 'No touching!' he said seriously. 'No touching unless I say so. You do what you're told, yes?'

I nodded vigorously.

'Good boy,' he said, coiling the snake back into its box.

'Will I be in charge of him, Mr Jamrach?' asked Tim anxiously. 'See,' he said to me, 'I know about everything. Don't I, Mr Jamrach?'

Jamrach laughed. 'Oh, indeed you do, Tim,' he said.

'See,' said Tim, 'so you have to do what I tell you.'

Jamrach told me to come back tomorrow at seven when they were expecting a consignment of Tasmanian devils and yet more marmosets. He rolled his eyes at the thought of marmosets.

That night I went to work at the Spoony Sailor. It was a good old place and they were nice to me. The landlord was a man called Bob Barry, a regular mine host, tough as nails and rumpled as year-old sheets. He played the piano, head thrown back, voice like tar banging out some dirty old ditty. Two men in clogs danced a hornpipe on a stage, and the waiter got up and did comic songs dressed as a woman. I ran about with beer all night and cleaned up the pots and mopped the tables. The ladies pinched my cheeks, a big French whore gave me bread and bacon, everything was jolly. When everyone was up on the floor dancing the polka, the pounding sound of all the feet was like a great sea crashing down.

The women in the Spoony Sailor were whorier than the ones in the Malt Shovel, but not as whory as those in Paddy's Goose, though the Goose girls were by far the swishest and the prettiest. I knew a girl there who wouldn't be called a whore, said she was a courtesan. Terrible women, some of them, I suppose, but they were always nice to me. I've seen them rob a sailor blind in less than ten minutes then kick him out bewildered on the street. Then again, I don't know if I ever saw a sailor who wasn't pretty much down on his knees begging for it anyway. The women slapped them about, but the sailors kept coming. I watched them reel about like stags, and remembered how beautiful their singing could be in the night, out over the Thames, heard from my cot in Bermondsey. Sailors from every farthest reach of the world, all the strange tongues blending and throbbing, and our own English tongue which rang as good as any.

I always knew I'd be a sailor. In my cradle, playing with my toes, I knew it. What else could there ever have been? The sailors had made my blood move before I was born, I now believe. As my mother stood one night upon the shit-smelling Bermondsey shore with me in her belly, the sailors had sung out there across the great river, and their siren song had come to the shell-pink enormity that was my listening ear newly formed in the amniotic fluid.

Or so I believe.

The air was woolly in the Spoony. The floor was slippery with the saliva gobbed out all over the floor. And yet, look up into the rafters and see the smoke curling there so elegant, while two golden girls painted like dolls sing high over a pair of keening violins. Could there be much better than this?

The place was still wild when I knocked off at midnight and went home to Ma. The streets were full and roaring. There was money in my pocket. I bought a great lump of brown sugar and sucked it all the way home. Ma was still out, so I asked Mari-Lou to make sure she told her to call me at half past six sharp for my new job, then went to bed and closed my eyes, determined to sleep. But there was so much noise out on the street, and so much singing going on somewhere in the house, that all I could do was doze and dream, all about a big black sea pushing up against the window.

'Last boy we had got bitten by a boa,' Tim said. 'Died. Foul it was, you should of seen.'

First words he spoke to me in the early morning yard. Dark and cold, fog catching the throat.

He ruffled the jet black curls that made me look like a Lascar, and poked me. 'What's this? What's this? Little Lascar, are we? Little Lascar, is it?' Ma said my dad was a Maltese or a Greek, she wasn't sure which, but anyway not a Lascar. You could never tell with her though; she said different things at different times. Tim was smiling, a sudden dazzle of big square teeth. We were waiting by the pen. Bulter, who served as keeper as well as clerk, was lounging by the gate with Cobbe, a brawny great square of a man who swept the yard and all the pens.

'These devils,' Tim said, 'these devils have got a rotten temper.'

'What are they like?' I asked again, but he wouldn't tell me. They've got great big mouths, he'd say, or: They stink; but what kind of a thing they were he wasn't telling. He enjoyed his superior knowledge, holding it from me like a dog with a bone. A marmoset was a little monkey, that I knew. I wasn't scared of a little monkey. I'd made up my mind not to be scared of any of these things, but it did help if you knew what you were up against. A devil? A devil from Tasmania, wherever that was. I pictured a thin red demon with horns and a tail, a whole cartload of them, walking on two legs with big mouths and foul tempers.

'What do they eat?' I asked.

'Fingers,' he came back, quick as a flash. 'Nothing else.'

'Ha ha,' I replied, and blew on my own.

'Cold?' said Tim. 'You got to be tough in this line.'

I laughed. I was tough. Tougher than him probably. Catch *him* getting shit in his golden locks. He grinned. My teeth were chattering. His were still. He vibrated slightly with the effort of not being cold. Our breath came in clouds.

'You just watch me,' he said. 'You won't go far wrong if you do.'

The gate creaked open and there was Jamrach with the cart come up from the dock, and the devils in a crate on the back. The cart came just close enough for Bulter and Cobbe to unload straight into the yard from its back. I heard the devils before I saw them. As soon as they felt the crate move, those creatures set up a terrible screeching and moaning like the hordes of the damned. A howling of monkeys began in the loft in sympathy. But when I saw them, they were just little dogs. Poor, ugly little black dogs with screaming mouths and red gums. They stank rotten.

There wasn't much for me to do. I stood looking on while Tim went into the pen with Bulter and Cobbe. Cobbe opened the crates. Bulter, with an air of graceful disdain, tipped those poor things out. There were six of them altogether, and they all set about sneezing as if they'd landed in a giant pot of pepper. Tim herded them down the far end where they turned, stretching out their mouths as if they'd break them at the corners. Their eyes were tiny and piggy and scared. All the big cats and dogs were howling and roaring now.

'Jaffy,' Mr Jamrach said, 'take the lantern and take the marmosets up to the loft and wait for Tim. Don't touch anything till he comes.' And he showed me two tiny monkeys with white tufty ears and large round eyes staring up at me through a grid.

'Hello,' I said, squatting down to look at them, all huddled up in the corner of a box with their arms round each other.

Tim sniggered at me through the wire of the devils' pen. 'They're not babies,' he said.

'I know.'

'Don't you forget.' He hoisted a bucket. 'Don't touch anything till I get there.'

I carried the box up the ramp, smelling the meaty breath of the lion to the right of me. It was too dark to see him, and darker still in the loft. The lantern's light swung about, here and there it caught the shine of an eye. There were tortoises all over the floor, I had to pick my way. The apes were muttering. I waited by the marmoset cage, setting down the box. They shrank into one another. Tim appeared soon, whistling jauntily up the ladder, hauling himself up with jerky grace.

'Jamrach says you can put them in with the others,' he said, striding towards me with a big bunch of keys. 'I'm to watch you and make sure you don't make a mess of things.'

Which he did, like a hawk, every movement, longing for me to go wrong. But those monkeys were on my side and treated me as if I was their dad, clinging to me with their scratchy little hands and feet, making small sad noises in their throats. No fight in them at all. 'In you go,' I said, loosening their fingers, and in they went. There was a skittering of shadows in the cage as I pushed the bar across. I would have stayed to see how they got on, but Tim grabbed the lantern and swept us along down to the cage of the big ape who had looked at me.

'Old Smokey,' he said.

Old Smokey looked at me like before, straight at me, calm. His eyes, flat in his face, were very black with two bright spots of light from the lantern. Something between serenity and caution was in them. His mouth was a thoughtful crooked line.

Oh, you lovely thing, I cried, not aloud but loudly inside.

'Do you want to go in with him?' Tim asked.

Of course I wanted to go in with him, but I was no fool. 'Not till Mr Jamrach says,' I replied.

'Smokey's all right,' said Tim. 'He's been living like one of the family with some big nobs up in Gloucester Square for years. He's just like one of us.'

'Why is he here?'

'Dunno. He's off up north on Tuesday,' Tim said. 'Wanna go in with him?'

'No,' I said.

'Go on. I've got the keys. You don't think he'd let me have the keys if it was dangerous, do you?'

Smokey and I studied each other.

'Go on,' Tim said.

'No.'

'Coward.'

He walked away, leaving me in the dark.

'Settle down!' he yelled at the restless beasts as I stumbled after, stopping and starting as my toes stubbed against the stupid tortoises, which just kept walking and walking as if they knew where they were going.

I should have hit him for calling me a coward. I thought

about it as I pounded down the ramp, but I never was one for fighting.

'All well?' called Jamrach.

He was standing by the pen of the black bear with a short stocky man in a long coat and sea boots. Smoke billowed in clouds above their heads in the queasy light from the back door.

'All well!' called Tim, then to me: 'See him? That's Dan Rymer, that is. I'm going to sea with him when I'm old enough.'

Jamrach called us to the office. The smell of coffee, rich and hot in the air, set my mouth watering as we went in the back door. A mild flutter danced along with the light from the lantern as we passed through the sparrow and bluebird room. The office was bright. Bulter was pouring coffee from a tall pot. Steam rose in slow, hot coils, mingling with blue smoke.

'Ah, good job well done there, Dan,' Mr Jamrach said, taking his seat behind the desk. 'I daresay you're home for a good while now?'

'Never enough and always too long,' said Dan Rymer, taking off his cap. His voice was as rough as sand.

Bowls of coffee filled up on Bulter's desk and I felt near fainting at the smell. But something terrible was happening in my feet.

'This is the boy I was telling you about,' said Jamrach, 'the one who sees fit to pat a tiger on the nose.'

'Does he now?' The man turned his small wrinkled eyes on me and looked very closely at me down his nose. A long clay pipe, white and new, stuck out of his mouth, and smoke from it wreathed his head. Now that I was thawing out, the pain of my feet was unbearable. Tears poured down my cheeks. The man reminded me of a tortoise or a lizard, but at the same time he seemed young, for there was hardly any grey in his wiry brown hair.

'He needs shoes,' Tim said.

Everyone looked at my feet. I looked. My feet were the flat

hardened pads of an animal, and they were blue with cold. The plasters that clothed my bloody toes were weeping.

The man sat down and took off his sea boots. He peeled off a thick pair of bright red socks, much darned, and pulled them over my frozen feet. 'My wife made these,' he said, 'and all the darnings were made by her. See. She is a genius, my wife.'

He gave me coffee.

'Soon as you get home, you wash them feet,' he said.

Of course, they were much too big, but I wore them like sacks and they had the heat of his feet on them.

I loved working at Jamrach's. I was looking after the animals. Mr Jamrach bought me boots. We swept the yard, cleaned cages and pens, changed straw and water and feed. Big Cobbe did the heavy stuff. Bulter kept the books mostly, but slouched about in the yard when he was needed, handling the beasts with practised aplomb. Too easy, his manner said. Too easy for me, all these lions and crocodiles and bears and man-engorging snakes.

Tim wrote up stock. I counted and he wrote down. Thus:

One Chinese alligator. The alligator stretched smiling beside us on the other side of iron bars, half in, half out of his water.

Four Japanese pigs.

Fourteen Barbary apes.

Twelve cobras.

Eight wolves.

One gazelle.

Sixty-four tortoises. A guess. You never could tell with the tortoises; they moved around too much.

Tim and I got along fine as long as I deferred to him in every way. He was a great one for wandering off in the middle of a job and leaving me with the worst bit to do. 'Off to the jakes,' he'd say and that would be it for half an hour. And yet when Jamrach was there he was always around, cheerfully toiling, whistling, pushing a wheelbarrow. He'd been Jamrach's lad since he was a tot, he told me. 'Can't do without me,' he said. He had a way of putting himself in front of me, talking over me, jostling me back with his shoulder. I never said anything. How could I? He was gold and tall and marvellous, and I was a little, shitty, bedraggled creature from the other shore. Rock this wonderful boat which had hauled me over the side? Never. Not when he broke an egg in my pocket. Not even when he fed me a mealworm sandwich. He taught me how to hold a monkey, how to keep frogs damp and crickets dry, where to stand so as not to get kicked by an emu, how to tickle a bear, how to breed locusts and behead mealworms. Mostly though it was mucking out and swilling down, slopping out, mashing feed, changing water. Only Cobbe and Jamrach were allowed to go in with the fierce apes or feed the big cats. I *could* have gone in with old Smokey though. *He* was gentle. But he was gone on the third day, taken out in a cart, sitting looking out of the back of the box as patiently as he'd sat in his pen. None of them stayed long, apart from the parrot in the hall and Charlie the toucan, and a particular pig from Japan that Jamrach took a fancy to and made a pet of, letting it wander freely around the yard and deposit its sticky, black droppings all over wherever I'd just swept.

Trade was brisk.

My own tiger went to Constantinople to live in the garden of the Sultan. I imagined it: a hot, green jungle of flowers and shimmering ponds, where my tiger stalked for ever. I imagined the Sultan going out for a walk in his garden and meeting him, face to face.

Friday, nearly a week after I started, he sent me and Tim over to the shop after it was shut, to muck out the birds and feed the fish and clean up a new batch of oil lamps that had come in filthy on a ship from the Indies.

Jamrach's shop was on the Highway, two big windows and the name up twice: Jamrach's Jamrach's, it said. It was a late, dark afternoon, and I was weary in those first days, all of a dream with the days and nights, biffing and banging about between the yard and Spoony's and home, and hardly ever seeing Ma because she was on funny shifts in the sugar factory. The shop was a dusty rambleaway sort of place, and it seemed unearthly as we roamed around it with a lantern casting lurching shadows, thick with presence. Every inch was crammed. The walls came in on you. In the centre by the stairs stood a mannequin, a naked woman, black hair piled on top of her head. She gave me the creeps. Japanese, Tim said. 'Look, you can move her arms and legs.' And he twisted her into such a horrible pose she looked like a demon in the jumping light.

Inwards was a warren of small rooms and steps and narrow passages, the walls crammed full of pictures: idols, devils, dragons, flowers with curious fevered lips. Mountains and fountains, palaces and pearls. All came to me dreamlike. A green god watched me from a throne. There was a room full of suits of armour, a giant gong, knives, daggers, Japanese silk slippers, a blood-red shining harp with the fierce head of a dragon with eyes that bulged. Tim showed me around with such pride you'd have thought he'd personally found and conducted home each treasure from its far-flung source. 'Stuff from all four corners!' He threw out his arms. 'Know what we had once? Shrunken heads! Human! Looked like monkeys. That's what they do in them places, cut off your head and wear you round their waist like a . . . like a . . . looka this. That's a demon's tongue from Mongolia, that is. And see that over there on the wall? That's a death mask. From Tibet. Bet you wouldn't dare put it on, would you?'

'No, I bloody wouldn't,' I said.

'Dare you.'

'No.'

'Go on. Double dare.'

'You put it on,' I said.

'I already have. I went out in it once. This old lady nearly dropped down dead on the corner of Baroda Place.'

Liar. I didn't say anything.

The birds and fish were at the back. Fish from China, orange and white and black, fat, mouthy creatures with big round eyes that stuck out like milky warts on either side of their heads. White cockatoos, cramped and patient, reasonable, amiable birds that watched with every appearance of deep interest as we went about our work. They'd been moved to new quarters and we were scouring down their old. Deeply mucky they were too, the ground caked thick with hard white droppings that had to be scraped off with a chisel. It was getting on for half past five by the time we'd finished the cages, and we still had the fish to feed and the box to unpack.

'You hungry?' Tim asked. 'Why don't I pop out and get us a couple of saveloys?'

'You ain't gonna be long, Tim?' I said.

'Two ticks,' he said, and off he went, leaving me alone there, locking me in 'for safety', he said.

It didn't take long to feed the fish. I was done with that and halfway through polishing the lamps, wondering with each one whether a genie would appear and offer me three wishes, when I felt the first creepings of fear. The lantern stood on the counter, casting a sombre glow that called up flickering shadows from all nooks and corners. Each lamp as I cleaned it joined its fellows in a small neat community on the floor. I was sitting cross-legged with my duster beside the box, reaching in for the next lamp and

35

thinking bad thoughts about Tim Linver. Suddenly, the hairs on the back of my neck came very slowly and coldly to attention, a sensation not unlike a thin finger drawing itself from the centre of my skull down to the top of my spine. It surprised me. I had not been feeling particularly afraid. The shutters were pulled down over the front windows and I could hear the ordinary early evening sounds of the Highway going on outside. I looked around. Only the softly pulsing shadows. What had I expected? Nothing. Nothing I had ever experienced in life up to this point had led me to believe in ghosts. I never thought of them. Even now I don't think Jamrach's shop was haunted, but something happened to me there that night.

The first thing was that time stopped. I remember looking across and seeing that woman with black hair at the foot of the stairs, stark naked with her arms going backwards and one leg dislocated at the knee and pointing upwards in a horrible way, and realising suddenly that I had no idea how long Tim had been gone and no idea of what the time might be. The street was quiet, a strange thing in itself, and yet I had a queer sense of having just been woken up by a loud noise, even though I hadn't been aware of sleep. And indeed, how could I have slept? Unless I slept sitting upright, cross-legged. Where the hell was Tim? The woman's eyes were dark, merry slits in a white face, her mouth the merest dot. The lantern made movements pass over her face. I saw that the Eastern lamps were all cleaned and arranged in two straight rows along the counter, though I couldn't remember having put them there. The box was set down at the side of the counter behind a great creel of fantastical shells, all spikes and whorls and smooth, pearly, opening mouths. I thought the light was going down. So the darker edges grew darker still, blacker and thicker, furry, and the shells appeared to writhe so gently it made a small pulse throb in the vein inside my left elbow. I stood up and looked stupidly at the lantern. We had lamps from all over the world, but there wasn't one of them I could have kept alight.

Where was he? Surely he would not leave me here alone all night? I wondered if I'd lose my job at Spoony's. Surely I should have been there ages ago? I liked Spoony's. I was the best pot boy they'd had in ages, Bob Barry said. They were good to me there. Better than here, I thought. He's done it on purpose, gone off and locked me in to frighten me. Why was the street so quiet?

A lump was growing in my throat.

I don't know why I didn't get up there and then to go and bang on the front door as loud as I could, and shout through the letter box at the top of my voice for someone to come and get me out. But I didn't seem able to move. My mouth was dry and when I tried to lick my lips, my tongue was thick and sticky. I wondered if I was getting ill. It was quite cold. Somewhere deeper in the shop, somewhere in one of those crowded little rooms, one of those narrow passages, something fluttered. I felt a feather tickling my throat. A dense bank of darkness concealed the open door that led into the first small passage, off which was the musical instrument room. I looked into that darkness, and the flutter came again.

Of course. The birds. I longed for others. I thought it would be nice to be in the company at least of those cheerful white birds in the back room. Even the pop-eyed fish would be better than nothing. Surely Tim would be here soon. I took up the lantern very carefully and walked step by step towards the darkness, which retreated gracefully before me. Strange and beautiful, a dragon's face appeared, a golden throat gleaming for a second. I turned a corner to the right and felt the left-hand turn open a gaping mouth upon my back. Down there were the tall Ali Baba jars, the vases from Nineveh, the fierce curved blades and delicate sets of china with cups with such tiny golden handles you couldn't imagine anything but a fairy holding one. Before me were demons and idols, carved gods and sacred gongs, bamboo pipes, poisonous darts. My light threw up the tremendous horns of a buck. Left at the top and I'd reach the good old birds, but I must take care as I turned the corner not to look to the right where I knew I would see the suits of armour standing to attention with their visors hiding God knows what.

Just before the turn, I saw a ship. The raised lantern revealed a painting of a curious vessel that reared up tall out of the sea at either end, a high-shouldered, many-turretted, floating castle of a ship, a thing upon which in a dream you might embark and sail away to the ends of the earth.

The light went out.

I did not panic. I stood there holding my darkened lantern in a void so full it licked me all over like a cat washing a kitten. For a minute or so I just let it. *Then* I panicked. I turned and ran. All the devils of hell followed after, clutching at my back. I crashed into a wall, turned, ran again, stopped, holding onto the wall and gasping. My own scared breath was loud. The wall beneath my hand held steady.

I would feel my way like a blind boy.

I stilled my breath and set off, feeling my way back in mortal terror every step of the way, till I came to an open doorway, an unseen gaping mouth breathing coldly on me. I couldn't get past. God knows what lurked silently inside. How long did I stand there? Time froze, I froze, the universe froze. How long until I felt my soul leave my body like a ribbon of smoke and float loose and free through the air, thick with a million other lost souls all hoping for a landing. I floated past the door and found myself once more on earth in Jamrach's pitch-black shop in the middle of the night, groping my snail-like way along the wall towards where I knew I must find the right turn into the passage that led to the front.

I found it and hauled myself around it as if reaching the top of a mighty mountain. Something touched my ear, a mere flicker, the breath of a fly or a gnat.

I crossed Sinai, inch by inch, fading in and out of myself, and when there were no more walls to hold onto, launched out across the void. I walked slowly, arms before me. Something caught me in the soft part just under my knee, pain pranged through me, sharp and sickening. I went flying and hit my head on something.

I was lying full stretch against something soft that jingled and jangled softly.

So tired.

I cried. Not a trace of light from the shutters. There was no point in getting up again. When I put up my hand to feel, there was a large lump swelling hot on my forehead. The rest of me was icy. I cried, drew up my knees and hugged myself. My brain swirled with all the colours of all the things from every part of the world, all brought here by the sailors and the captains, come to rest at last. As I began the slide down to sleep, there arose before my eyes the tall ship upon the wall, the last thing I'd seen before the light went out.

Did I sleep? It was more of a floating in and out of the real; a pitching, drifting, endlessly renewing progress through a night with no limits and no friendly striking hours. And at some point, some sudden peak of wakefulness, my mind cleared miraculously and stood watching and waiting at full attention. Then something lay down next to me and put its arms round me from behind. True and solid, it cleaved to the length of me and hugged hard.

It was as real as anything I ever felt, but then again, since that night I know that I have taken for true things that were not.

Of course, it could not have been human, because it would have had to put its arm through the floor in order to hold me.

39

The feeling I had was beyond fear. It was a giving in, a swift plummet, a death.

I don't remember anything else.

The morning assistant woke me up, the turn of his key in the lock. The light found me lying by a sack of shells that jingle-jangled as I sat up, squinting at the glare.

'What the devil are you doing here?' the man said rudely. 'You the new boy? You been here all night?'

I tried to tell him what had happened, but he couldn't be bothered to listen and shooed me out. The sun was above the house tops and I was late for work. I'd missed Spoony's. I ran straight to the yard. Cobbe was hauling hay. 'Gor, what you done to your noddle?' he said. Tim was on the ramp, but he jumped off the side and ran straight up to me.

'Sorry, Jaf,' he said, smiling as if it was nothing. 'Couldn't help it, could I?'

'I've lost my job!'

My skin crawled with weariness.

'Well, it wasn't your fault, was it? They can't sack you for something that wasn't your fault, can they?'

'How do you know? You did it on purpose.'

My eyes burned. I ached all over. I hit him in the chest.

'Oy!' he cried, backing off with a hurt look in his eyes. 'What's up with *you*? Wasn't my fault.'

'You locked me in!'

'I know. Only twigged when I seen you come in the gate just now. And there were the keys in my pocket.'

'You knew!'

'I didn't. I met a couple of friends, you know what it's like. I thought you'd finish up and go home. What you done to your head?' He reached out but I jerked away.

40

'I fell over,' I said. My voice caught and my eyes overflowed. 'The lamp went out.'

'Baby,' he said, smiling, 'don't cry.'

My nose ran.

He had the cheek to try and sling an arm round me. I hit him again and we scuffled futilely, falling under the ramp. Cobbe barked a warning from the end of the yard.

'I hate you!' I screamed.

Tim held my wrists and I kicked out at his knees.

'Look, Jaf,' he said in an infuriating, reasonable voice, 'you won't tell Jamrach, will you?'

'I will! I'll tell him!'

I looked around for the big German but there was no sign of him. 'Fucking hate you, Tim Linver,' I said, and kicked and pulled free and ran towards the door to see if Jamrach was in the office.

'No!' Tim ran after and grabbed my shoulder. He was pleading suddenly, really scared. 'Don't tell him, Jaffy. If you tell him he'll get rid of me.'

'Serve you right.'

But Jamrach wasn't in yet. Only Bulter, his feet on the desk, picking his teeth with a long fingernail.

'Here, you two, out of here,' he said.

Tim dragged me out into the lobby. He had tears in his eyes. Good. We ran through the silent bird room. 'It was a joke,' he said desperately. We were out in the yard again. I picked up my broom and ran at him like a jouster, chased him right up against the alligator pen.

'You're mad!' he yelled.

I bashed him with it, hard as I could, over and over.

'Stoppit! Ow!'

'Pack it in, you two,' growled Cobbe, 'he's here, I heard the carriage.'

I dropped the broom and ran for the door. Tim ran after, grabbing my arm. 'Jaffy!' His face was white. 'Please,' he said, 'don't tell. I'll give you my telescope. I promise, I'll give you my telescope if you don't tell him.'

And there was the front door and the voice of Mr Jamrach cheerfully greeting Bulter.

'Please!'

I wanted that telescope. Dan Rymer's telescope had been all around the world twice and he had given it to Tim. Dan Rymer had first seen the great Patagonian condor soaring high above the blue sierras through that telescope, Tim said. Once, once only, I had been allowed to look through it, and only for a few seconds. I saw the world anew. I saw the querulous shadow in the eye of a starling.

'Please!' said Tim.

I worked till about ten, then I fainted. Or something. Just fell over.

We'd had in three small elephants. I suppose they were very young, one of them was no taller than the big mastiff that used to guard the tannery in Bermondsey. They were not happy. Each had a chain round its foot. Side to side, side to side, trunks curling and unfurling in time, great feet lifting and listlessly kicking, turn by turn they swayed together with no space to turn about, an endless dance. So hypnotic was their movement, so steady and slow, that it got in my head and made me dizzy, and the rake fell from my hands and I fell over. Next thing I knew I was in the office, lying down upon a scratchy coat, and Mr Jamrach was pouring water in my mouth from a jug. Bulter and Cobbe were there, and Tim's gawky neck was sticking up, an anxious face peering over Jamrach's shoulder.

'What's this? What's this?' Jamrach said. 'Are you ill?'

'I'm tired,' I said, 'and I haven't had my breakfast.'

'No breakfast! Why not?'

And then it all came out that I'd been up all night in the shop and missed my shift at Spoony's.

'Tim locked me in,' I said.

'I was going to go back but I forgot!'

I hated Tim at that moment. 'He did it on purpose,' I said.

His face went red. 'I didn't.'

'He did.'

He started to cry.

'Tim,' said Jamrach sternly.

'Please don't sack me, Mr Jamrach,' Tim said wretchedly. 'I didn't mean anything by it.'

'Are you telling me,' said Jamrach, 'that you locked this boy overnight in the shop?'

'It was a joke,' said Tim.

And that was the only time I ever saw Jamrach lose his temper.

His thin lips went hard and quivered. He roared. He cried that Tim was a wicked boy, a vile, cruel boy who'd end up on the gallows and serve him right! He could get out now! And never come back! 'Always have to be top dog, don't you, Tim?' he said. 'Well, I'm finished with you!' and lifted me up onto his knee.

And now I was sorry for Tim. He begged. He sobbed. His face was a wreck. He said he was sorry, he didn't realise, he'd never ever do such a terrible thing again, never, never.

'Go away, Tim.' Jamrach touched the great lump on my forehead. 'Where did this come from?'

'I fell over in the dark,' I said.

Tim stood by the door, hands hanging helpless, tears pouring down his face. 'I'll give you my telescope,' he said in a watery way.

'Don't sack him, sir,' I said.

Jamrach heaved a great sigh. 'Why?' he asked. 'Why should I keep him after this?'

'I don't know,' I said.

The soft snuffling of Tim crying was the only sound for a moment. Jamrach's eyes were sad.

Bulter put his head round the door. 'Mr Fledge's man's here,' he said.

They come from all over. Russia, Vienna, Paris. Clever men. Jamrach cursed in German. 'What's he want this time?' he said. 'A unicorn? A hippogriff?'

Bulter sniggered.

'Where is he?'

'In the yard. Looking at the elephants.'

'Tell him to wait,' said Jamrach, and sighed again.

When Bulter had gone, Mr Jamrach put me down and stood up. He brushed his knees. 'Tim,' he said, 'wipe your nose and stop whining. Make yourself presentable and go straight over to the Spoony Sailor and tell them there exactly what you did, tell them Master Jaffy is in no way to blame, and he will be back at work this evening. Tell them I sent you and that I vouch for Jaffy. Then you can get yourself back here as quickly as possible and get back to work.'

Tim ran.

Jamrach took me by the hand and led me out through the yard. 'A moment!' he called to a tall thin man standing by the elephants. There was a door at the side which he unlocked, and through this we passed into a narrow alleyway with high brick walls and weeds growing out of the cobbles. I had never walked like this, hand in hand with a man as I had seen others walk with fathers, and it made me feel peculiar. My own father's name I didn't know for sure. Sometimes Andre, sometimes Theo, you never could tell with Ma. A dark sailor with a glass to his eye. At the turn of the

44

alley was a little house with an open brown door moulting paint. Jamrach rapped with his knuckles.

'Mrs Linver!' he called. 'Patient for you!'

There appeared, wiping her steamed-up eye glasses on her apron, the wild-faced woman who had stood at the front of the crowd when Jamrach rescued me from the tiger. Her bulbous, unseeing eyes wavered over me with a look of startled and over-done emotion, then she put her glasses back on and focused. 'The little tiger boy!' she exclaimed, dropping to one knee in front of me and taking me by the shoulders. Mr Jamrach told her all that had happened and said she should give me a good feed and send me home to bed.

'I'll skin that boy!' she cried when she heard of Tim's crimes.

Mr Jamrach took himself briskly away down the forlorn alley, and she took me by the hand and led me into a room full of drying laundry that was draped all over everything, chair backs, a table, a massive rack which hung from the ceiling above a blazing fire. A round, pale, hairless man sat in a saggy armchair by the fire, smiling vaguely and whittling away at a stick of wood, and the little girl who'd smiled at me from the crowd was there, standing by the range, turning with a dripping spoon in one hand. She smiled again.

It was not love at first sight, but love at second sight. Her hair was straight and fair, her face bright and innocent, her apron filthy. She had dimples.

'Ishbel,' her mother ordered, 'get him some porridge. Your brother's a nasty horrible boy,' scrubbing my face and hands and knees with a hot cloth as she talked, her voice thin and quavery. 'Well, you can see why the old man's taken a shine to this one,' she said, rinsing out the cloth, 'just like poor Anton, he is. Bless!'

I saw the gnawed-down nails and bleeding fingers of the fair-haired girl as she cleared a space at the table for me. She pushed

45

a bowl of porridge under my nose. Her skirt was dark red. I thanked her and she dipped a sarcastic curtsy. 'Welcome,' she said, twirling away and sitting down by the man's feet. He had a look of Tim and of the girl, how it might be if you shaved them and puffed them up like balloons and took away their wits.

'Don't make yourself too comfortable, young lady,' her mother said, but Ishbel leaned back against his legs, put her arms round her knees and her head on one side and stared at me with open curiosity.

Tim appeared in the open doorway. His mother ran over and screamed in his face. 'He'll give you the boot! You hateful boy! You! You! He'll give you the boot and no doubt! You'll ruin everything!'

He blinked hard, walked over to where I was scooping porridge into my mouth and put out his hand.

'I'm very sorry, Jaffy,' he said, steadily holding my eyes. 'I really am. Truly. It was a mean thing I did. You've still got your job. I've been to Spoony's and I've told them.'

I stood up and we shook solemnly.

''S'all right,' I said.

Midday. Ma was asleep when I got home. Mari-Lou and Silky slept too, long dreamy sighs behind the curtain. I got into bed next to Ma, hugging my telescope. Dan Rymer's telescope that had travelled the whole world round. She did not wake, but gathered me into the crook of her arm, and a tall ship bore me away through painted waves into a long sweet sleep.

46

3

Mr Jamrach liked children. Tim and Ishbel had been running in and out of his yard to see the animals since they were little. They were twins and made him laugh, and he gave them pennies for odd jobs. When Tim came to work he'd made him go to school two days a week, and now he did the same with me. By the time I was eleven I could read and write. Mr Jamrach said he needed his boys to be able to write things down and read off lists. I was quick. Ma was impressed. 'You clever boy, Jaf,' she said when I read the posters plastered outside the seamen's bethel.

'*Grand Fair, Thames Tunnel,*' I read smugly, '*Madame Zan-Zan Fortune-teller. Crinelli's Puppets. The Marvellous Marioletti Brothers. Snake-Charming. Fire-Walking. Swingboats. Entrance 1d.*'

He let us finish early the day of the fair and slipped me and Tim a coin or two each as we pulled off our working boots outside the shed. We spruced up at the pump and changed our clothes, pushing each other about and shaking water from our hair, poking our ears as we strode down the alley. Ishbel had worked the afternoon at the Malt Shovel and drunk some gin. Maybe that's why she was so sharp. At any rate she started screaming at Tim as soon as we walked in, which wasn't unusual.

'You were supposed to fetch the coals before you went out!' She was ladling soup and had a face full of steam. 'You lazy pig!'

'Shut your trap, woman,' Tim said loftily. 'Who are you calling a lazy pig? I've been shovelling shit since five o'clock.'

There was a slightly deranged look about Mrs Linver. Her eyes bulged and her hair was dripping wet against her forehead. 'Shut up!' she screamed, tucking a bib into her fat husband's collar. 'I'm sick to death with the pair of you! Sick to death!' She plucked a half-finished mermaid from Mr Linver's pudgy hand and dropped it into a basket on top of a dozen finished ones. Apart from when he was eating, that's what Mr Linver did all day with uncanny consistency, as if he'd been wound up: turned out wooden mermaids for his wife to flog in the streets, blobby-faced women with huge, bulby breasts and curled fishtails upon which they could sit. He'd been a sailor, and a handsome one too, though you'd hardly believe it. Ishbel remembered him running up and down the alley with Tim on his shoulders and everybody laughing. But he'd come home witless when the twins were six, having taken a knock from a spar somewhere in the vicinity of Cape Verde. No one took any notice of him. He was like the chair he sat on. No one took any notice of me either, so I took my accustomed place at the table and waited to be served. Ishbel flounced two bowls of soup to the table and thumped them down so hard that some of the thin brown liquid slopped up and onto the oilcloth. She was twelve now, a great sulker.

'It's not fair,' she said, 'you come home all washed and ready to go and I've not even had a chance to comb my hair.' She pulled the greasy handkerchief from her forehead and shook her head.

'Oh, you're all right,' her ma said, 'it won't take you a minute.'

Ishbel pulled a hideous face at her mother's back, drawing all the muscles in her neck and jaw so tight that they quivered. 'Who do you think got the bloody coal in?' she demanded of Tim. 'Me. Me me me me me again. I'm sick of you, I hate you, you do this all the time.'

Tim, hair still wet from a dousing under the pump in Jamrach's yard, sat down to his soup with a lopsided grin intended to irritate. Mr Linver leaned forward and gobbed on the fire.

'That's foul,' said Tim.

His father turned an expression of almost hatred on him, fleeting but unmistakeable.

'And I've got to work again tonight,' she said, 'and I'm not going to, it's not fair, so there.' She grabbed a canikin, dipped it in the soup pot and swept away into the other room.

'Oh yes, you are, young madam!' her mother yelled after her.

The room next door was full of thuds and bangs and theatrical sighs while we ate our soup. When we'd finished Tim and I went outside and sat in the warm sun in the moss-lined alley, passing a pipe between us. We didn't speak. At last Ishbel came out, wiping her mouth.

'I'm not going with you two,' she said.

Her mother's voice flapped after her through the open door. 'Oh yes, you are, young madam!'

'I'll go with Jaffy,' she said, ignoring me and looking at Tim, 'but not you.'

This was momentous to me. We three had been mucking about the shore together for three years now, me always tag-along, stumbling and running every now and then to keep up with them, and they always shoulder to shoulder ahead, fair heads bobbing side by side.

But, 'The devil you will,' said Tim, untroubled, sticking his hands in his pockets and hunching his shoulders, and off they went in front as usual. Ishbel's hair was matted on the back of her head and plaited underneath, but her plait was coming loose.

It was a public holiday, thronging. We walked down to the river and paid our pennies and passed under the arch to the cool under tunnel where the fair went thrillingly on and on along the pavement, one thing after another as far as the eye could see: fortune-tellers, donkey rides, pinch-faced little monkeys wearing blue jackets. The barrows of the clothes sellers were decked out with brightly coloured ladies' dresses, high above us like lines of airborne dancing girls. I smelled lavender, sugar, sarsaparilla.

Ishbel walked in a swinging about kind of way with her hands clasped behind her back. She and Tim had scarcely said a word to one another since we'd left their house. We wandered about for a bit and ended up watching all the fools falling off the slip-pery pole.

'You go on it, Jaf,' said Tim.

'No fear,' said I.

'Coward,' he said.

'*You* go on it.'

'What's the point of me going on it? I've done it millions of times.'

'Ha!' said Ishbel.

He smiled. Small baboon wrinkles appeared at the sides of his nose.

'You go on the bloody thing, Tim,' she said, 'you're so clever. You leave him alone.'

'He needs it,' he said. 'Needs pushing a bit. Don't you, eh?' Pushing me a bit, not much, just enough so he could still say it was all in fun if I complained. 'Don't you?'

'He don't need you pushing him,' she snapped. 'Who'd want you pushing him?'

'He does. Don't you? See, see? Go on, Jaffy, go on, you can do it. It's always the little ones do it best, it's a known fact. You give

50

it a go, boy. You've only got to stay on for a minute and you get a guinea. That's good.'

No sir, not me. No fool, me.

Still, somehow I found myself up there on the wooden steps that went up to the tail end of the greasy pole. The pole was long and dappled and round, like a stretched horse with a wispy tail and a painted head. I looked at the horse's arse, the few sad wisps of fibre sprouting there. I saw a sea of faces, all delightedly waiting for me to make a horse's arse of myself. I saw Tim grinning off to the side, and the hem of Ishbel's skirt. I spread my legs and, knowing I was doomed for the drop, launched myself up and over the horse's arse and onto the slippery pole. It was like climbing onboard a slug. I put my hands before me, gripped slime, shunted forwards and for one strong moment sat with head held high before the pole rolled me round. With my hair hanging down backwards from my head, I clung on, ridiculously, like a drop on the lip of a tap, destined to fall. Then I fell on my back in the sawdust, floundering like a fool, and the people roared.

Red-eared, I stomped through the indifferent crowd, past his grin and her brown eyes. Away. He ran after me and grabbed my elbow. 'Don't be stupid, Jaffy,' he said, seeing my face.

I cursed him to hell.

'Don't be a baby, it's only fun! I done it. *She* done it. Showed all her bloomers and all, didn't you, Ish? What's your beef, Jaffy?'

It was nothing. Everyone fell off the slippery pole, that's what it was for. It was just Tim doing what he always did, trying to put me in the way of ridicule. My own fault for doing what he told me. It was fury at myself that made me lash out and punch him right in the middle of his stupid smug face. That and the sudden tipping of a scale by one last grain of rice.

'Oy!' he yelled.

He didn't even bleed. That infuriated me even more. He didn't hit me back either and that was worse, the final insult. I swung at him again and forced him to protect himself, and we scuffled, me near tears, till a woman came out from behind a pie stall and chucked a bucket of cold water over us as if we were dogs. The three of us ran.

We stopped where the swingboats flew up to the great vaulted roof.

'Come on, Jaffy,' Ishbel said, brushing down my drooping shoulders, 'me and you'll go on these.'

'What d'you mean?' Tim cried. 'We only got two bob. Who's paying for him, then?'

'I am. Bugger you,' she said.

'That means *I* can't go on!'

'Boo hoo hoo!' She shoved her face in his. 'You're a cruel, mean, nasty, horrible pig, you are, Timmy Linver! Yes you are.'

And she grabbed me and dragged me onto a red and blue swingboat whose occupants had just now been brought to earth and disgorged.

I had never been on a swingboat before. Me and Ishbel faced one another, grinning wildly, the world lurching up and down, up and down, the boat like a painted crescent moon in the sky. The babble of the crowd waxed and waned. There was laughter, mine and hers. A smear of rouge remained on her cheek from her afternoon at the Malt Shovel, where she danced in brass-heeled shoes the colour of blood, and the men clapped time. When we came down Tim was nowhere to be seen. For a moment we stood taking this in, not speaking. I had never been alone with her before.

She shrugged, slung an arm round my neck and hoicked me away from the fair and through the streets as if I was her little brother. She'd grown up so much faster than me. That's girls for you.

We wandered vaguely in the direction of home, wordless. A fat man with terrible burns, old and much puckered, had set up a Happy Family cage by the corner of Old Gravel Lane. He had dormice in with a cat and a rat and an owl, and they were all just living there and not bothering each other. Ishbel said it was like the lion lying down with the lamb, but I knew how it was done. They put stuff in their feed to make them sleepy. I didn't tell her though. Outside the seamen's bethel she bought me a ginger beer and told me to wait while she went inside and lit candles for the boys. The boys were two brothers lost at sea not long before she was born. The spotless saints, Tim called them in a faintly derisory way. Nothing was left of them about the house, but their spirits hovered invisibly there like benevolent angels, and every now and again at night when the chores were done and she was sitting by the fire, Mrs Linver would take off her spectacles and polish them sadly, weep a few tears and curse the sea on their behalf. You couldn't blame her. Two sons gone and a whittling blob of a man sitting across from her. And still, Tim said he was going to sea. Couldn't wait. That's where real life was, he said. Soon as the man would take him, he'd be up and off with Dan Rymer. 'Died at sea.' That's what it said after the names in the big book in the seamen's bethel, died at sea like my father. I asked Ma once if his name was in there, but she said no. The ginger beer was good and sharp. I smelled fish, and lavender. A sugar wagon rolled by groaning, a knock-kneed brown horse between the shafts. The sound of hammering and singing was carried on the breeze, and the sun was warm. I closed my eyes and thought of her turning on her heel, flouncing her skirts as she flashed an ankle, the sailors in their threadbare duds throwing pennies. When she was doing laundry or hauling water from the pump or jumping around on rotting wooden piers with me and Tim, she was a matt-haired hoyden, but at work she was a small painted woman with leaves in her hair, dancing on a stage and blowing kisses at sailors.

53

I'm not sitting out here like a pile of washing, I thought, and followed her in. I'd never been inside before. There were a lot of people sitting about in the pews and a woman lighting a candle. Ishbel was looking at the pictures: Jephtha and his daughter, Jonah spitted up on shore, Job and his flaming boils. An arch of words above read: *I am a brother to dragons and a companion of owls.*

She came over and gripped my arm. 'Come on,' she whispered, 'I've got strawberries.'

'You were ages,' I said.

'Poor Jaffy.' She ruffled the top of my head. 'Were you getting bored?'

Often she treated me like a dog. Usually when you hear someone say they were treated like a dog, it means getting kicked about and locked out and told to get under, but not in this case. Ishbel liked dogs. In time she took to cooing a little whenever she saw me and tickling me behind the ears, a thing she'd also do to any old mutt encountered on the street, and I didn't mind at all.

'Let's go to the boat,' she said.

No longer trailing behind, I walked along beside her like Tim. A wreck called *Drago* lay aslant on the foreshore in a muddy creek long silted up with effluent, reached only by a sideways climb along a slimy black wall. There were hooks here and there, and if you took your shoes off and slung them round your neck and didn't breathe in too deeply, it was easy.

The *Drago* had once been a proud little fishing craft, big enough for three or four men at most, with a canvas roof flung over the half of it, and a box at one end where they'd stowed the fish. We put the beer there now. The benches were gone, but if it wasn't too wet you could sit on the floor and crumble the old wreck's wood between your fingers and watch the quick black beetles emerge from its soft depths. We used to play games here when we were younger. He father, she mother, me kid. He captain, she

54

first mate, me cabin boy. And the best one: me robber, she posh lady, he policeman. These games had given way to flights of fancy, stories we conjured between us of monsters and beasts stranger than any we ever saw at Jamrach's. We scratched pictures of them on the insides of the boat, and gave them names like *mandibat* and *camalung* and *koriole*, and we knew all their habits and natures and peculiarities. Great humped beasts came up from the mouth of the Thames, slow, hot, darting forked tongues. We shared a mind's eye that saw these things from the bow of the *Drago*, facing out across the river.

But we hadn't been for ages.

She had four strawberries wrapped in a bit of wet cloth. 'Get the beer, Jaf,' she said.

We sat in the bow and shared the spoils. I don't know where the strawberries came from. She didn't have them when she went into the seamen's bethel but she did when she came out, so perhaps she'd stolen them from someone in there.

Two each, ripe and squashy, gone in a flash.

'Wonder where Tim went,' I said.

She shrugged, passing the beer. 'Do you think we've upset him?' she asked.

'Probably.'

'He'll get over it.' She licked her strawberry lips.

'Anyway,' I said, 'he doesn't care when he upsets other people.'

She smiled and said, 'He doesn't mean to be a pig.'

'I know. He just is.'

We laughed.

'He's always been a jealous boy,' she said simply.

The bottle was wet from her mouth. I took a good long swig.

'I'm not going to work tonight,' she said. 'Don't feel like it. She can't make me, can she?'

'You'll catch it.'

'So?'

'She'll wallop you,' I said.

She did this sometimes, just couldn't be bothered with all the palaver of dressing up. Much spoilt and fussed over, she was also much slapped and pushed. Once she said she'd only get ready if her mother brought her a cake, and when she got it she smeared it on the pretty dress hanging over the back of the chair, waiting to be slipped over her head ready for a good night's work.

'You evil little bitch!' her mother had shrieked. 'Do you know how long I worked on that?' and thwacked her hard on the side of her head and made her cry.

Tim never got hit though.

'I don't care if she does wallop me,' said Ishbel, reaching for the bottle.

'Yes, you do.'

'Well,' she said, 'it doesn't make any difference; I'm not going. I'll stay here till it's dark.'

'You can't do the wall in the dark,' I said. 'If you stay here till dark, you'll have to stay all night.'

'I will!' she cried, jumping up with a grin. 'All night!'

'Me too!' I stood up.

She gave me the bottle and did a funny dance, all flailing arms and tapping feet. I was afraid the rotten boards would collapse underneath her and we'd both go plunging through to the filthy, freezing water.

'Stop it,' I said. 'If you want to dance you might as well go to work.'

She stopped. Her shoulders heaved. 'We can't,' she said, 'it's too cold.'

'What?'

'Can't stay all night. We'd freeze.'

That was true.

'I know,' she said, 'we'll just walk around all night till it's really late.'

She was assuming my company.

'Let's go west,' I said, 'past the Tower. Let's just keep walking that way along the river all night and see where we end up.'

'We can sleep under hedges,' she added, 'and beg. You can be a gyppo and tell fortunes. I know a girl at the Siamese Cat that tells fortunes, it's dead easy. You look like a gyppo anyway.'

Tim came whistling along the wall. He was a good whistler. First we heard him, then his dirty bare feet appeared over the canopy and he dropped down beside us, frog-fashion, pulling his boots from round his neck and tossing them up the boat. 'What's the fun?' he asked.

'We had strawberries,' I said. 'You missed them, but there's some beer left.'

Ishbel tossed the bottle and he caught it and took a swig. The sky had that look it has, as if it's about to settle down for the night.

'I'm not going to work,' Ishbel said.

'Don't say.' He smacked his lips and swigged again, wiping the bottle top considerately with a big, grimy palm before handing it on to me. It was as if nothing bad had happened between us. A great flapping of birds' wings crossed the river.

'I'm hungry,' I said, 'I could eat a horse.'

'That's a thought,' said Ishbel.

'Any boodle?' asked Tim.

She shook her head. 'Spent it.'

'Ah well,' he said and took a pipe out of his pocket. We sprawled in the bow, smoking as the evening cooled and dimmed. Ishbel lay on her back with her feet resting on Tim's knees.

'I don't know what to do,' she said. 'Should I go?'

'Up to you.' He watched coils of smoke stalk and twine in the still air and sang 'Tobacco's but an Indian weed', a song Dan Rymer taught us once when we were roaming about and met him on the Wapping Steps.

> Grows green in the morn, cut down at eve . . .

Ishbel kicked him. 'Miserable,' she said.

He laughed and continued and I joined in. We'd sat on the Wapping Steps with Dan. Dan smoked a long white pipe, it stayed in the corner of his mouth while he sang:

> The pipe that is so lily white,
> Wherein so many take delight;
> It's broken with a touch,
> Man's life is such . . .

And we'd all joined in the chorus:

> Think of this when you smoke tobacco.

We sang it round the yard sometimes with Cobbe, and laughed. But we could never remember all the words, nor could we now, so we gave it up and lay for a long time in comfortable silence, till Ishbel said in a small, sad voice, 'I'll have to go back now, I suppose.'

Tim opened his eyes and stroked her foot. They were not identical, but not far off. His chin was longer, her hair a shade darker. She had dimples on both sides, large, flickering, nervous things that flashed on and off. He had none. It must be funny to look at another face and know it's just like your own. Like looking in a mirror. Sometimes they stared into one another's faces as if fascinated, and once I'd seen them close their eyes and explore each other's features with their fingers, hers bloody from biting, his long and graceful, like blind people do. It made them laugh.

We sighed, tossed the empty bottle overboard, slung our shoes round our necks and went in turn along the wall.

Mrs Linver made us have a wash, then gave us some broth, thin and delicious. The old man whittled, the fire crackled. There we were, the three of us sitting at the table messing about and niggling at one another, when their mother came bustling over and offered Ishbel a nip of gin. 'A drop, lovey,' she said, 'takes the edge off.'

'I'm not going,' said Ishbel, not looking at her but taking the gin anyway.

'Now, don't play stupid.' Mrs Linver scowled at the rat's tail hair straggling over Ishbel's shoulders. 'Have you taken a comb to this all day?'

'No.'

'I can see that. You'd better start getting ready.'

'Can't make me. No one can make me.' Ishbel glanced at me with mischief in her eye and suddenly smiled. *You* understand, her look said.

Her mother had turned away but swung round. 'I haven't got time,' she snapped. 'Up. Now.'

'I'm not going.' Ishbel knocked back the gin in one and slapped her lips.

'Don't be soft,' said Tim. 'It's only work. We all got to work.'

'I'll work when I want to,' she said.

'If you don't go down there tonight, they'll not have you back.' Her mother took hold of her arm and tried to yank her off the chair, but she just laughed and held onto the table. Only when it began to tilt and wobble, me and Tim hanging onto it, everything falling over and splattering about, only then did she let go and allow her mother to drag her to her feet.

'I'm not going, you stupid woman!' she shouted right in her mother's ear.

59

Mrs Linver winced and rubbed the side of her head.

'I'm tired!' Ishbel screamed. 'I don't feel like dancing, can't you get that into your stupid head?'

'That's dangerous!' her mother screamed back. 'You can make somebody go deaf doing that!'

'I don't care!'

That's when her mother slapped her. I'd seen scores of these scenes, but this one was different. This time Ishbel slapped back. It was quick – a second – and there were her mother's glasses askew, and her mother's eyes exposed. We all gasped. Ishbel began to cry and fell on the floor by the old man's knees. He shifted his benign glance towards the top of her head vaguely, scraping gently away at the scales on the tail of his latest mermaid.

Mrs Linver took off her spectacles. Her mouth was trembling, her eyes pouched and meekly narrowed. She wiped the glasses on her apron with shaky hands, glancing up at us, mournfully blind.

'Oh, Ma!' cried Tim, jumping up and running over to give her a hug.

'You'll find out one day, you selfish girl,' Mrs Linver quavered.

Ishbel jumped up, face streaked with tears. 'I know, I know, I know,' she said harshly.

'It's all right, Ma,' Tim said. 'Don't upset her any more, Ish. It's all right now, Ma.'

'Yes yes yes, of course of course of course.' Ish smiled extravagantly and leapt to her feet. 'Time for work! Time for bloody work.' And off she flounced into the inner room.

She was sullen as we walked her to work twenty minutes later. She'd put on too much powder to hide the slap mark on her cheek, and her lips were too red. 'You never stick up for me,' she said to Tim.

'That's not true.'

'You always take her side.'

'What am I supposed to do? *I* have to go to work. I'm up four in the morning sometimes. So's Jaf. Everyone has to work.'

'I'm sick of it,' she said and kicked a stone. When she looked up again her eyes were shiny.

I put my arms round her. 'I'll wait for you and take you home when you've finished,' I said.

'No need for that.' Tim pushed against us.

She gave me a hug. 'Thank you, Jaffy.' The white grains of her powder got up my nose and made me want to sneeze. She looked like a doll. 'You're very noble.'

'Noble?' snorted Tim.

I wanted to hold onto her. But I let her go.

He came round her other side and placed himself in front of her, saying nothing. For a long time he just looked into her eyes, his own rough and tender. Something was passing between them, some brother–sister thing I could have no part in. His shoulders were hunched, his lower lip pendant. There was something old in his face. Where it was coming from I couldn't tell. She softened visibly.

We walked on, the three of us separate. At the Malt Shovel door, she turned to me and said, 'You might as well run along home now, Jaffy. Thanks ever so.'

'She's got to get ready now,' Tim said.

Ma was out when I got home. I remember I took down Dan Rymer's telescope and poked it out of the window and looked over Watney Street, closing in on odd details here and there in the thickening dusk: a face, a cat, an artichoke, a shining puddle under the pump.

A long time ago it went to the bottom of the sea. Wish I still had it. It was a lovely thing – the patterns in the high-polished mahogany, the lacquering on the brass. On the sunshade, silver engraved with a feather pattern. The telescope I have now is stout and plain, but you can't fault its clarity. I look at birds, and on certain nights I look at the stars through the mesh over the garden. I got to know the stars well at sea. You can't rely on the sun and moon – they do funny things sometimes – but you *can* rely on the stars. When you look at them through a telescope, they start to flutter like little white wings burning in a silver fire. Then, if you focus your lens here below on a bird's eye, you can see the shine in it, the life. And sometimes a thing comes so close it makes you jump.

It's the same when you look at the past. Far away the white wings twinkle, nothing can be known. Further in, details: the riggings of great ships that web the darkening sky; rooftops, clear on the inner eye, magnified; and sometimes a pang, up close. Tonight is a late spring night. The carving on a piece of scrimshaw, rough beneath my fingers, reminds me of the feathers engraved on the old telescope I had when I was a boy, and I remember a long-ago night: a wonderful day gone, my heart thrumming softly, coming home and crying, and not knowing why, swooping here and there with my all-seeing eye over rooftops, thinking about Ishbel. She'd be on the stage, grinning wildly, catching coppers in her small, bloody, stubby-fingered hands. She'd sing 'Little Brown Jug', 'The Blind Boy At Play' and 'The Heart That Can Feel for Another', and the drunken sailors would laugh and weep.

PART TWO

4

So much for Jaffy the child. He didn't last long, did he? What was he? A butterfly thing. A great wave came and took him away. A tiger ate him. Only his head remains, lying on the stones. Let it speak. Let it roll around old Ratcliffe Highway, a hungry ghost, roaring its tale for all who will hear. I know why the sailors sing so beautifully on their boats out in the river, why my raw senses wept when I listened in my Bermondsey cot. I found out when I was fifteen.

Tim was a bigwig now. When Bulter got married and moved away, Jamrach had said he was too clever for the yard and too dreamy to work with animals, so me and Cobbe and a new boy now did all the dirty stuff, and Tim was an office boy and got more money. He wore a collar to work. His mother starched it for him every night. By this time, we were close. He could still be a swine, but he was just one of those the world forgives. Some are. I didn't speak to him for three weeks once and he couldn't stand it, came over all noble and upright and faced me like a man, said I was the best friend he'd ever had, the only real one. Life's short. What can you do?

The day we heard about the dragon, he was in the yard with

us, bouncing from foot to foot in the cold. Mr Fledge's man and Dan Rymer had been in the office all morning, hard in talks about something momentous. They'd sent him out so they could be private.

'Something's afoot,' he kept saying importantly, affecting to know more than he did. There were kiss curls on his forehead, and his eyes were bright. His breath hung on the air. They called him in when Fledge's man left, and ten minutes later he came running back out.

'I'm going to sea! With Dan! We're going to catch a dragon! And we'll be rich!'

'There are no dragons,' Cobbe said.

But Tim babbled on about how Dan knew a man who knew a man, who saw one walking out of a forest on an island east of the Java Sea. How Mr Fledge, who always wanted what no one else had, what no one else had ever had, was now determined to be the first person in the civilised world ever to own a dragon. A ship was leaving in three weeks' time and Tim would be on it, right-hand man to the big hunter, sailing east and still further east till they'd rounded the globe.

'He's gone off his rocker,' Cobbe said, pointing to the side of his head. 'That's what it is.'

I pictured a big flying monster that flaps its wings slowly like a heron, breathes out fire, fights heroes, sits on a hoard of treasure or eats a girl. Very big nostrils, round, the sort you could crawl up like a Bermondsey sewer.

I was the one who was good with animals, everyone knew that. Why wasn't I going?

'I don't think much of your chances,' I said, 'not with the fire.'

'What fire?'

'They breathe fire.'

'Don't be stupid. That's only in storybooks. Don't believe me, do you? Come on.' He was mad, beaming with delight, pulling me along into the office where Dan Rymer and Mr Jamrach were drinking brandy in a thick smog of smoke.

'It's true, isn't it?' Tim said. 'Tell him.'

He went behind his desk and leaned back horizontally in his chair with his long legs stretched out across the desk and his fingers knotted behind his head.

'It's true,' Jamrach said. 'Fortunately Mr Fledge has more money than sense.' He and Dan burst out laughing.

'A dragon?'

'A dragon of sorts.' Dan doodled on a scrap of paper. 'If it exists. Certainly the natives believe it does. The Ora. There have always been rumours. I talked to a man on Sumba once who said his grandfather had been eaten by one. And there was a whaleman once, an islander. He had a tale. There are lots of tales.' He showed me what he'd drawn. It looked like a crocodile with long legs.

'It's not a dragon if it hasn't got wings,' I said, 'not a real dragon.'

Dan shrugged.

'We'll be gone three years,' said Tim rapturously.

'Two or three,' said Dan. 'Depends.'

'On what?' I asked. He shrugged again.

Mr Fledge owned a whale ship called the *Lysander*. It had sailed out of Hull and was this moment loading at the old Greenland Dock. They'd join the whaling crew on the voyage and take care of wildlife – should there be any – on the way home. 'Bring back a dragon,' Fledge's man said, 'and you'll never have to work again.'

I let Tim crow for a few days then went down to the Greenland Dock. The *Lysander* was a very old vessel, one of the last of its kind, I should say, and it was looking for crew. I signed. Mr Jamrach knew well he could get another boy for the yard.

'You need me for the animals,' I said when I told Dan I was going. 'I'm better than him.'

He leaned his head back and squinted into the white smoke trickling up his face, and said, 'Oh well, I suppose you can keep an eye on Tim.'

Poor Ma, though, she was distraught. 'Oh, I don't want you to go to sea, Jaffy,' she said when I told her. 'I always knew this would happen one day and I always wished it wouldn't. It's a horrible life. Much too hard for a lad like you. You can't turn back when you're out there, you know.'

She was living in Limehouse those days. She'd taken up with a fish man by the name of Charley Grant, a good enough sort. She was preparing herrings on a board when I told her, slitting their bellies and slapping them down, whacking their spines flat with the blunt of a knife.

'I know that, Ma. I won't want to turn back.' It seemed wrong to show my delight considering the state of her, but it was hard not to. She'd gone red and was fighting to keep in the tears. As for me, my feet were lifting from the ground.

'Hark at him,' she said, 'he doesn't know what he's talking about.'

Poor old Ma. You'd never take her for a child now. She'd thickened and grown weatherbeaten, and her hair was going grey at the sides. Still walked like a sailor though.

'I always knew it would come to this,' she said, with her sore-looking eyes and me feeling bad. I loved my ma. To me, she would ever and always be a warm armpit in the night.

'What you want then, Ma?' I said, trying to jolly her along. 'Eh? What shall I bring you back?'

'I don't want anything, you silly sod.'

'Don't worry, Ma! It'll be the making of me. Can't hang about here all my life, can I? There's no money here. How you expect me to look after you in your old age if I hang around here all my life? This is a chance of a lifetime, this is. Think!'

'That's the trouble,' she said, pushing me aside with a fishy hand and taking off her apron, 'I'm thinking all the time. Oh damn. Have you eaten?'

'Had plenty. Look, Ma, just pour me some tea, will you?'

'Well, it all sounds ridiculous to me,' she said, going over to the fire.

I laughed. 'And there's the beauty of it,' I said. 'It is! Be proud! You can tell everyone: my son's gone off to catch a dragon. Like knights of old.'

'You said you wasn't going to be involved in any hunting!' She turned accusingly, the poker in her hand.

'I'm not, I'm not, I'm not, I'm only saying. Of course I'm not.' I laughed again. I felt quite hysterical. 'That's Tim, not me. But I'm part of the enterprise.'

How very important that sounded. How I milked it with the girls at Spoony's and the Malt Shovel. The enterprise! The great enterprise!

'You're only fifteen,' she said, 'and you know you're not a big boy.'

'Don't I just.'

Oh, didn't I just. It had its rewards. They loved me like a babe, those big whores, all wanted to take me into their soft, lemony, lavender bosoms. Many a time for sure I sank my face in there between the creamy swells and drank deep like a babe of mother's milk, and never a penny was I charged for what others paid for. I was a big man now, though. Fare thee well, you London girls. Jaf Brown is off around the world, and when next you see him he'll have a tale to tell.

'Oh, Jaffy, I don't want you to go!' Ma palmed an eye angrily. 'I wish you'd—'

'Please, Ma,' I said, embarrassed and irritated.

Please don't spoil it for me, I wanted to say. I don't want to have to worry about you while I'm out there, do I? Please please, Ma, don't make it hard.

'There's money in it, Ma,' I said. 'A lot of money in it. He's a very rich man.'

'Oh, sit down,' she said, 'have your tea.' She knew there was nothing she could do.

'That's nothing,' Tim said when I saw him. 'You should have heard *my* ma. Funny!' And his long, fluttery fingers flew up around his face. '"Oh, not you! Not you too, Tim! No-o-o! No-o-o-o! Oh, Lord God in Heaven! N-o-o-o-o!"'

We laughed. What's a boy for if not to break his ma's heart?

'Let's go to Meng's,' he said.

Ishbel was in Meng's with Jane from Spoony's. That's what she did. Work all night bringing in the money at Quashies, at the Rose and Crown, at Paddy's Goose, and in the afternoon go to Meng's. *Drago* was long gone, broken up bit by bit over one sweltering June week when the sloppy green weeds smelled like Neptune's armpit. Meng's was our *Drago* now. A Chinaman in a shiny red coat stood at the door. The pictures on the walls were silky and the great mouth of the fireplace glowed yellow. I got next to Ishbel next to the wall, Tim on the other end of the bench sprawling round ginger Jane and chewing on a liquorice twig.

'Oh, here they are,' drawled Ish sarcastically. 'Hail, the mighty explorers. These bum boils are leaving me, Jane.'

'I know,' Jane said, tweaking her tight red curls. 'It's all the talk.'

'Three years! What am I supposed to do all that time stuck here all on me tod?' She put her arm round my neck. Two years since we'd started cuddling, but she never let me kiss her. She was driving me mad.

Meng wanted to know if we were buying. Tim nodded and paid for us both.

'Three years?' said Jane. 'That's a very long time.'

'Maybe less,' I tossed in in the interests of truth.

'Well, you couldn't very well go much further, boys, could you?' Jane said. 'Bob says he don't want to lose you, you know, Jaf.'

'I think it's mad.' Ishbel fussed her hair, still hanging onto me. 'I think Fledge is mad. Must be, the way you never see him, and he wants this and he wants that and he never shows his face, mad bugger, completely insane if you ask me. Probably lives in a castle and never goes out and wears a mask because he's hideously ugly.'

'No doubt.' Tim was leaning down towards Jane's round creamy throat. 'Who cares? He's paying.'

'It's not a real dragon,' I reminded them.

'How do you know?' Tim said. 'No one knows what it is.'

There was a dragon on the broad mantelpiece, along with a selection of pipes and an owl carved out of wax. I thought of this beast, this old story. Deep in a forest I saw it, great sad red eyes and a crimson tongue, forked like a swallow's tail and thin as a grass blade, flicking in and out. Sitting there, waiting to be found.

'Dan Rymer thinks there's something,' Tim said staunchly.

'Oh, and he knows, does he?' Ishbel said. 'He knows everything.'

'He knows a hell of a lot, that's for sure.' Tim put back his head and blew a great blue cloud of smoke up at the ceiling, smiling. His hair glowed gold in the firelight. I don't even know if he really wanted to go. He said he did but you never knew with Tim. 'Even Jamrach doesn't know the half of what Dan knows about wild animals,' he said.

There are dragons and dragons, of course. It was an eastern dragon we were after. The one on the back of the doorman's shiny red coat and the one on the mantelpiece were eastern dragons, fierce sort of winged snakes with many coils, huge whiskered heads and enormous, bulging eyes.

'It's not a real dragon,' I repeated. 'It hasn't got wings.'

'I'm glad you're going, Jaf,' Ishbel said. She put her face right in mine so I could taste her spicy breath. I pulled back a little. It was always a now and then thing, and only when *she* felt like it. That wasn't fair.

'Glad to be rid of me?' I said.

'Don't be silly.' She put her head on my shoulder and it wasn't fair. 'You're the one with sense. You've got to look after him.'

Tim, sinking into the lap of Spoony Jane, snorted at the idea of me looking after him. I placed my arm about Ishbel's waist and she let it stay there. 'It's only a big crocodile,' I said. 'It's just a crocodile hunt, that's all.'

'I know,' she said, smiling, her heavy eyes sleepy, 'and perhaps it's not even there.'

Tim slept in the round lap of Spoony Jane. White dress, white shoes, Jane herself smiling as she hummed a little tune I knew from Ishbel, who sang it years ago on the balmy corner of Baroda Street by the herb man's stall. The sky raining, dark spatters on the stones, the women beaming at the little thing, blue-jacket sailors, her mother standing by with huge-bosomed mermaids in her basket. Painted Ishbel singing 'The Mermaid', combing her hair with an imaginary comb while admiring herself in an imaginary glass. And when she sang 'Three times round went our gallant ship, three times round went she . . .', about in a circle she would dance three times and finish by falling down in a graceful heap of skirts on the pavement, arms aloft waving like seaweed.

> . . . and she sank to the bottom of the sea,
> the sea, the sea
> and she sank to the bottom of the sea.

*

Their birthdays fell on the first of August, his and hers.

For her tenth I gave her a shell. She graced it with a look.

For her eleventh I gave her a flick book. She laughed once or twice, playing with it under the rain-drummed canvas.

For her twelfth I didn't bother and vowed I wouldn't bother again.

For her thirteenth I gave her an orange.

For her fourteenth I gave her a mouse with particoloured markings. She called it Jester and it ran about in her apron.

For her fifteenth I gave her a gold ring I stole from a drunken sailor in the Spoony.

Jester died.

For her sixteenth I gave her a special and very beautiful rat. She loved that rat. She called him Fauntleroy. When she walked down the street Fauntleroy would peep from her hood. He was snow white with bright pink eyes and he liked music. Fauntleroy was with her when she came to say goodbye.

> Lord Lovell he stands in his chamber door
> Combing his milk white steed
> And by there has come Lady Nancy Belle
> To wish her lover good speed.
> Oh, I'm sailing away, my own true love,
> Strange places for to see . . .

For the life of me I can't remember the next line.

I've seen strange places and they have seen me. They have watched me with a calm appraising eye . . .

Two days before we sailed I was standing in the silent bird room, a place that drew me back again and again, and I got a feeling of being watched.

'Just came to say goodbye, Jaf,' she said.

'Aren't you coming to see us off?'

'Oh, I will,' she said, 'but they'll all be there then, won't they?'

I fell on my knees and kissed her strong stumpy hands and bitten nails and wept and told her I loved her. No, I didn't.

I said, 'Oh,' and that was all.

'I've only got a minute,' she said.

'Work?'

'Ma wants me.'

'Oh.'

'It's going to be funny with you lot gone.'

I laughed. 'Wish you were coming?' I asked.

She pulled a face. 'Whale ships stink.'

We were awkward. This may be the last time, I thought. I put my arms out and gathered her in close. 'I hate you both for going,' she said, suddenly tearful. When I kissed her on the mouth she kissed me back. Long sweet minutes till she pulled back and said she had to go, and took my hand and dragged me outside with my head reeling. I walked her to the back gate. Cobbe was mucking about in the yard. The lioness was gnawing peacefully on a lump of beef, holding onto it with her paws, licking amorously, eating with closed eyes.

'You'll look after him, won't you?' Ishbel said. 'He's not as brave as he makes out, you know.'

'Neither am I.'

'Pa won't shake his hand,' she said. 'He cried. Don't tell him I told you.'

''Course not.'

We stood smiling in a slightly demented way.

'He's a big baby really,' she said.

'So am I,' I said.

'How's your ma?' she asked.

It might never have happened.

74

'She'll do. She asked Charley to have a word with me about staying and getting into the fish business. "You serious?" I said. "Work on a fish stall or go around the world?"'

She laughed. 'Oh well,' tidying her hair, 'better be on my way,' and was gone.

Three years and come back a man, come back changed. See the strange places I itch to see. See the sea. Could you ever get sick of the sight of the sea? She said that to me one day when we were standing on the bridge. And she had never even seen it, and I pray she never will.

I went home and looked out of the window at sunset. It was May. The sky was a red eye, the rooftops black. There were islands in the sky. The waves were bobbing. It was the Azores, those beautiful islands. Jaffy Brown is gone. He turned, *was* turned, a ghost on a god-haunted ocean. My eyes and the indigo horizon are one and the same.

Early in the morning, a straggle of dockers and lightermen on the quay, a bunch of old women and a few mothers, not mine. Ma had gone all distant on me. We'd said our goodbyes. She hated all that, she said. If you're going to go, just go, and get yourself back as quick as you can, and don't expect me to like it. Mr Jamrach didn't want me to go either. When I'd taken my leave of him the night before he'd clapped me on the arm and brought his face close to mine, and stared unwaveringly with watery blue eyes, making me uncomfortable. 'You look out for yourself, Jaf,' he said gruffly. 'I'll not see you on the quay.' We'd shaken hands very cordially and smiled awkwardly, till someone came to the door wanting birds, allowing me to slip away fast.

Dan Rymer's wife was standing on the quay, a tall, straight-backed, fair woman with children in her skirts and a baby on her arm. A shipload of Portuguese sailors disembarking for a spree cast eyes on Ishbel, come straight from Paddy's Goose in her red shoes.

She didn't cry or make a fuss. Each of us got a peck on the mouth. She hugged Tim for a long time and me for a little less.

'You'll bring him back safe, Jaf,' she said.

I still see her standing there, waving, shielding her eyes from the sun.

5

When at last I set foot on-board, the terror that churned my guts was all one with a kind of joy. I wanted to look a whale in the eye. The only whale I'd ever seen was on a picture in the seamen's bethel, the one that swallowed Jonah. It had no face. It was just a great block, a monstrosity with a mouth. But a whale did have eyes, I knew, and I wanted to look into them, as I looked into the eyes of all the animals that came in and out of Jamrach's yard. Why did I do this? I don't know. Nothing I ever solved.

We were all of us wild, great thumping fools with thumping hearts running about that first morning, making a pig's ear of whatever we turned our hands to. We knew nothing, nothing at all, and we didn't know each other yet either. Eight of us were green, eight out of a score or more of men – men, I say – fourteen our youngest, Felix Duggan, a mouthy kid from Orpington, sixty our oldest, a scrawny black called Sam. Thank God for Dan looking out for us, with us but not with us. Seven years since I met him, but I never knew him till we sailed together. I do now. I know him better than anyone now.

The *Lysander* was a beauty, ageing, well preserved, small and neat. The captain watched from the quarterdeck as we made fools of ourselves, while the first mate, a florid, thick-featured madman called Mr Rainey, strode about swearing and cursing at us in a deranged manner. Christ Jesus, what have I done? I thought. Am I mad? Oh, Ma. The masts and the yards and the sails, the whole great soaring thing was the web of an insane spider against the sky. Ropes, ropes, a million ropes and every bloody one with its own name, and if you got the wrong one you buggered up the whole thing. How we ever got off I've no idea. It was the efforts of those few who knew what they were doing: the old black called Sam, another black by the name of Gabriel, a tall Oriental called Yan, and our Dan. These four got the ship off with the help of a few lads not much older than me and Tim, who'd sailed maybe once or twice before and therefore considered themselves old seadogs. We greenies stumbled and bumbled around getting in everyone's way. I lost sight of Tim. Lost Dan. At every moment I tried to look as if I was confidently on my way from one important task to the next, wearing a face I hoped gave an impression of eager intelligence. I caught sight of the dockside moving away, the people a blur, heard the sudden sweet hollow chiming of a London clock bidding me a long farewell.

A boy with a round dark head appeared very suddenly in front of me in my confusion. His face was awkward, stoic in its expression, the mouth self-conscious. He looked like I felt, wavering on his feet with no idea of what to do. For a second we locked eyes in dumb mutual understanding. Then he smiled with his mouth still closed and stiff, a peculiarly leisurely smile for the circumstances.

Mr Rainey, a clatter of boots and a horse-like snorting, landed between us from above like a god-thrown thunderbolt. 'What do you think this is?' he demanded. 'A garden party?' clouted the boy on the head and sent him flying. 'Cretins,' he roared, stomping away down the deck, bandy-legged and malevolent. God knows why he didn't hit me. Too zealous in his progress towards the next target, I suppose, some poor boy above in the rigging: 'You fucking imbecile!' he screamed, head back. 'Fuck you, fuck you, fuck you and all your fucking bastard kin! Get down here!'

I got away quick, looked for Tim, but couldn't see him. I stood useless. Someone clipped me on the back of the head and told me to look sharp.

'I don't know what to do!' I appealed, suddenly outraged. How could anyone expect me to know what to do?

The man was a lanky, skinny thing with a long sensitive nose like an anteater's and arched brows that gave him a clownish appearance. 'Here,' he said, and hauled me to the windlass. Oh God, the bloody windlass. A great horizontal wheel on the deck up near our fo'c's'le – oh, to be down there with my sea chest – pushing it round alongside a big hefty blond boy built like an ox. Even he was grunting and straining, swearing doggedly in his own language. I was breaking my fucking back. The long skinny cove jumped in to help us, straight brown hair, thin as everything else about him, dangling in his eyes. Nothing much on his bones, but he was strong. '*Hup*, now,' he said, '*push!*'

Push. Push. Beyond anything you ever thought you could do, push. I was vaguely aware of the others running about, whistles, shouts, laughter, massive creakings and groanings of the ship as we manhandled her, and of a new weightlessness that gave me a falling sensation even though my feet were fixed firmly on the timbers.

The shipload of Portuguese sailors clapped and cheered us on, and there was no more time to look back to the drifting quay, where Ishbel watched with the dozy lightermen and grieving mothers and the wife of Dan Rymer.

We took the watery road out of town. The wharves and taverns drifted by, the sun grew brighter, throwing gold over the warehouses and the tops of the ripples. Sails flapped in the breeze. The captain, a solid, square-chested, square-faced man with a pale freckled face and thin ginger eyebrows, came and walked among us with a shaggy brown dog at his heels, half smiling at no one and speaking only to his first mate. I was glad there was a dog on-board. I hadn't expected that.

Me and Tim stuck with Dan. We had a lot to learn, he said, and set about teaching us the naming of things right away. All we ever knew fell away behind us like arms letting go. The land became green and rose up on both sides, and the marshes swallowed us up. The mournful calling of long-legged birds swooped above the reeds. Seagulls with savage eyes sailed vigorously on the air alongside, keeping us company all the way to North Foreland, where Mr Rainey sent me up to the masthead.

I'm a good climber and I have no fear of heights; it was the best of all times to go aloft, with the full sea swelling before us and the topgallant sails up to take the wind. First time I'd seen the real sea. Too big when you first see it, of course. A shining you could never have imagined, even though you've imagined so much. Up there, full sail on the *Lysander*, I was riding a living thing. Her bowsprit rose and fell like the motion of a horse's neck at full canter. The spray roared, and the whaleboats shuddered in their holdings. I looked down and saw Dan Rymer at his ease, speaking with the captain on the quarterdeck. Scrawny Sam, his face a mass of wrinkles, ran along a spar with the ease of a waterfront cat, smiling as he went. The captain's shaggy brown dog came trotting along the deck and lifted its leg against the mainmast, and I had no notion of time or the future or anything else at all, and was completely and quite terrifyingly happy and knew that I'd done the right thing.

Later, just before the captain gave his speech, me and Tim had a single minute's peace standing at the rail together looking down at the sea. He put his arm round my shoulders. 'This is the life, Jaf,' he said. He'd been like a dog let off the leash all day. It was being outside he'd missed, not the animals. He was trembling faintly, whether it was because he was cold or nervous, I don't know. It's a strange thing when you first go off into the unknown. You want it and you're scared. Tim would never admit he was scared. Never. He was, though, any fool could see that.

'This is the life,' I said.

That was the whole of our conversation, then the captain called us up on the quarterdeck for the choosing of the watches and the whaleboat crews.

We had three whaleboats, not counting the spares. I didn't want to be on Rainey's. We had Captain Proctor's and Rainey's and Comeragh's – the second mate that is – who turned out to be the tall thin one with the big nose who'd clipped me on the back of the head and told me to look sharp. He and Rainey both had a good six inches on Captain Proctor, who, though stout and strong, was not tall. They stood respectfully, two tall, dark vases flanking a pale round pot, Rainey with his hands clasping some papers behind his back and his feet apart, Comeragh seeming to be smiling all the time. But it was just the way his face was.

'I applaud you, gentlemen, on a magnificent performance,' the captain said, his eyes travelling over all of us, his face revealing nothing. We, who didn't know, took our cues from those more experienced hands who laughed, instinctively knowing somehow that this was a good-natured jibe and not rank sarcasm. A hint of a smile appeared upon the captain's face. 'We shall get along,' he said, with his eyes never lighting anywhere, 'if we all remember one thing.' Long pause, roaming eyes. 'A ship is a dangerous place, a whale ship especially so.' Long pause. 'You will obey orders

81

from myself and any of the mates instantly. There will be no exceptions. It's as simple as that.'

He had a clear ringing voice, well spoken, stronger and far more impressive than his face, which was too boyish for a captain's. The dog, lolling with a stupid expression against his leg, did nothing to lessen the impression. He talked enthusiastically for ten minutes about duty and obedience and pulling together, and said that those of us who'd not sailed before would be given minders, and were to do what we were told. 'Some of you will know that this voyage has a secondary purpose,' he said. 'We have on-board Mr Rymer' – a nod towards Dan – 'whose commission is to hunt wildlife. When we reach the Dutch East Indies we will be briefly diverted somewhat from our primary concern, which is, of course, to take as many barrels of oil as we can. But that need not concern any of you now. You are whale catchers and that is a great and dangerous profession. Your job now is to learn everything you possibly can as fast as you can.'

There was a law on ship as tight as any, he said, with clear rules and clear punishments for the breaking of them. It was very simple. These rules could be consulted at any time as a copy of them was permanently on display in both steerage and fo'c's'le. Anyone who could not read could avail himself of the help of a reader.

'Commit them to memory,' he said. 'They are now your Bible. And this!' – as if from nowhere a terrible flail appeared in his hand, produced with the flourish of a conjurer procuring a gasp from the crowd – 'is what the law of the ship demands be used upon any who break those rules. *Any*. No exceptions.'

He held it aloft, an evil hairy leather thing folded back upon itself.

'Take a very good look at it now, because I am going to stow it away and I sincerely hope it will not be seen again for the duration of this voyage.'

The whip passed slowly back and forth before our following eyes.

'Enough of that!' He tossed it to Mr Comeragh, who looked surprised but caught it deftly. 'Mr Rainey,' the captain said, turning politely towards him, 'assign boats.'

Mr Rainey produced a list and read out names. Now that he was not shouting and screaming, it was possible to see him as something more than a gargoyle. Thick-lipped, overbold of features, he was both handsome and ugly and looked as if life displeased him. Linver, Brown, Rymer, all of us were on Mr Comeragh's boat, I'm glad to say, and a great relief it was too. Comeragh was best of the three. And when the watches were called, I was on Comeragh's watch too, but they'd put Tim and Dan on Rainey's. I wondered if that meant they were better than me, but I was glad I wasn't on Rainey's watch.

'This old crock,' said Gabriel, the tall black, the young one muscled like a wrestler. 'What was I thinking? Bet she don't make it as far as the Cape.'

'She'll do,' said Dan. 'She's old, but she's been well cared for.'

'Don't see many like this now.'

'True enough. Soon won't be any.'

That first supper on deck, all of us from fo'c's'le sitting next to the tryworks round a huge lump of salt pork that sat like a rock upon a tub they called the kid. We cut strips from the pork with our knives and put them on our plates. The salt in the meat curdled my tongue.

'Proctor's not in charge,' said Gabriel.

'No. Rainey's the man,' said a brown-haired Yorkshire boy who'd come down with the ship from Hull. 'He's got the upper hand. Rainey's the one you want to watch.'

'You think so?' asked the boy Rainey clouted, jiggling his knees.

He was a year or two older than me. His name was Edward Skipton, but everyone called him Skip.

'Yes I do.' The Yorkshire boy set his cup down. 'I was with him on the *Mariolina* two years gone. He was second mate then. He knows what he's about, he does, does Rainey. Proctor's near green as you.'

'And I'm greener than the rushes,' Skip said quietly.

'Jesus Christ!' Tim was trying to break off a flat piece of hard-tack with his teeth and nearly breaking his jaw.

'Rainey's hard,' said the Yorkshire boy, 'but he's not the worst. This is no bad ship, this is a playground, this is. You're lucky.'

Gabriel agreed. 'Proctor will be glad of Rainey. Proctor's not cut out for a captain.'

'How do you know?' asked Tim.

Gabriel speared a lump of meat with his knife. He was older than us, fully a man. 'I've seen a few,' he said, leaning back and pulling out a plug of baccy.

First watch was larboard watch, and that was me. It was a fine night, big white stars and a moon. Everyone up on deck mooching about, Felix Duggan fooling with his broom, Comeragh playing with the dog. The cook, a huge Caribbean with a face that never smiled, standing in the cookhouse doorway smoking a pipe. At first it was all wonderful, heady stuff, this gently rolling ship life, the sticky black water brightly roiling under the ship's lantern, the tap tap tap of a hammer somewhere, the creaking and the cracking of spars and timbers. Till step by tiny step, a sneaky progress not to be marked or checked till much too late, a dis-ease crept in on me. The peaceful rise and fall of the rail, the stains on the timbers of the deck, the slip-slap-slop of water like the sloshing of the water on the green-slime piles of a Bermondsey wharf. I closed my eyes. In the dark, everything moved, rose and fell and reared and dipped. Life seemed long and strange and difficult. What is it? My forehead, raging hot, burst out in cold sweat. Oh no, not this. I was sick, that's what it was.

I opened my eyes. No one else looked sick. If I could hang on till midnight, end of my watch. Please not me. Not me. Be strong. Up and down, up and down went the dark blue horizon. We were out in the channel, far out at sea it felt to me, though that's a laugh when you think how far we had to go. Shit. It was coming. No help for it. I ran to the side of the ship and threw out liquid. Just liquid. Good. That'll do. But then it came again, bigger, great undigested and undigestible slivers of hardtack that had refused to be chewed, slimy pink worms of pork flesh that stuck between my teeth and made me gag anew.

Skip saw.

'Once it's up and out it's all over,' he said as I wobbled back from the rail.

Well, that was a damned lie.

I learned something hard in those first couple of days. Being sick didn't get you off work.

Comeragh came by. 'Easy,' he said. 'Let it pass. Every captain was a green boy once, don't you know.'

It passed, but not for ever. I remember little, just the decks alive, the sea calm and shifting, the rolling wallow of our passage through the waves and the strange sea light that seemed to sing. Half asleep, I gazed upon the rails rising impossibly, falling impossibly, nothing ever still. I was glad again I was on Comeragh's watch. Sure, he'd clipped me, but not too hard. It passed as all things must, till midnight freed me and I staggered queasily down into the fo'c's'le and into my bunk. I stumbled in the dark and knocked against someone who groaned. My mattress was spiky. The darkness rocked me like a mother. The timbers creaked. The smell, thick, oily, bloody and juicy, a smell of smoke and bodies, salt and tar. I cried for my ma. I slept with both eyes closed and every sense awake. My dreams were full of lost baby creatures that whimpered and sucked upon bottles. Soft-fingered, they lay on their backs, helpless, surrendered, hurt by an enormity of loss beyond their understanding. How did I know this? I did not. Inside my head was a swelling and a writhing. Every now and then I awoke, sinking and rising. Ishbel came. Sang, Come to me my darling, come to me, dear. She stroked my head against her breast and opened her bodice to me, and when morning came, I hung over my bunk and moaned. The moan was answered by another. I looked up and saw a young black boy leaning over the side of his bunk, throwing up into a wooden bucket held by Chinese Yan, who squatted by his side, rumple-haired and near naked. The foul sweetness of vomit thickened the air. The ship lurched. Someone somewhere retched, something splashed, someone groaned. I opened my throat and a hacking sound came out, a sound like a dog choking on a bone. Yan turned his head, muttering softly in his own strange choppy language, and with one swift movement deposited the bucket under my face. I looked down into the lumpy rejects of the black boy's stomach, closed my eyes and pitched up my guts.

Well, would you not just know it? Tim, in all his golden glory, never was sick. No, never, never in any storm, never in any lasting swell. And there was me and seven or eight more that day weeping, drooling, flung inside out and purged like evil from a perfect world.

The open hatchway shed lurid daylight on us from above. Kill me now. I can't get up. Ma, come, put your cool sweet hand on my head and croon and say: Poor little Jaf, stay in bed and try and sleep again. My mattress stank. And there with his grinning clown face was Mr Comeragh, crying, 'Up! Up now, boys! No more of this.'

Yan left me and the black boy sharing the bucket.

'Look sharp, Jaf,' said Comeragh cheerfully. 'Come on, Bill.'

How we got on deck I'll never know, but we did somehow. There was no mercy, none at all: you worked and you threw up in the bilges and you worked, and that was that. Felix Duggan, cabin boy, a whey-faced kid of fourteen with big soft lips, was first to the masthead that terrible morning. His mouth was open, his lower lip hung sickly. Ach, I thought, ach, take me home, take me home and never let me see the sea again. Could you ever get sick of the sight of the sea? she'd said, standing beside me on London Bridge. Oh yes, dear Ishbel. Yes, I could.

'This is stupid.' Felix scowled and kicked his toes against the mainmast, blinking tears from his eyes. 'Why me? Why not you?' he appealed to Henry Cash, a watchful, supercilious sort who'd earned his sea spurs some years ago and made sure everyone knew, though how he did this I'll never know because he hardly ever talked to anyone. '*You're* not sick. *He's* not sick,' pointing at Tim. 'Why me?'

'Search me,' said Henry Cash, cool as mint. 'Go and ask Rainey, I dare you.'

'There's no whales in these seas,' said the Yorkshire boy who'd sailed with Rainey before. John Copper. I was getting their names by now.

'Who says?' said Cash.

'See?' Felix wiped his nose angrily. 'What's the point of looking for whales that aren't there?'

'I suppose the captain will be judge of that,' Cash said, smiling smoothly and walking away.

'Off to lick Rainey's arsehole,' muttered John Copper.

'He better watch his head if I'm sick up there.' Felix spat viciously on the deck, and with laboured movements commenced the climb up the mast for his two hours.

'There's no whales in these seas,' John Copper repeated. 'Who says? Who says? Proctor? He don't know. There's no whales in these seas.'

Nor were there, not that we saw, not till after Cape Verde. And by then I was in love with a sailor's life. There were times some nights when I knew that at last I'd reached that place towards which I'd been drawn from the womb. The fo'c's'le was another womb, and I wouldn't have been anywhere else, not up in steerage where Dan was, even though he got to eat his dinner up near the cook-house. Too close to the captain and the mates, steerage, you'd have to watch yourself. We had the best of it in fo'c's'le. We had Sam's eerie singing, and a Cape Cod boy called Simon Flower who played the fiddle. The talk went round and round, and the smoke would mix in clouds and threads above our heads; and in those clouds and threads I saw blue worlds, misty uplands, an ever-changing landscape, until early one morning fourteen days from home there came the cry of Land Ho from Gabriel on watch aloft, and they appeared on the horizon, real as the timbers beneath my feet.

Great blue mountains, layers and layers of purple and grey and lilac and rose in the sky. I ran for my old telescope, Dan Rymer's telescope. They were beautiful, the Azores. The weather was soft and sweet and warm. We anchored off Horta on Faial Island. I saw white buildings and the steeple of a church and the great cone of a mountain stark against the clear sky, fluffy white clouds massed around its base. I'd never seen a mountain before, and this one was a volcano. Gabriel pointed. 'Pico Alto', he said. He'd been before. But it was not here on this island, it was over the sea, though it looked so close it might have gobbled us all up in its hot belly. I said something about how peculiar it was that people went on living so close to such things, all the time knowing they could suddenly explode and drown them all in ash and fire, and he laughed and nudged me with his elbow. 'And the world goes on,' he said.

A great grey crag rose up behind the town. I have come to

foreign parts, I said to myself. To where the strange tongues begin, the unknown ways, where mountains spew smoke and fire and even the earth underfoot is of a different substance.

We would buy vegetables and hogs for oil, the captain said. First light tomorrow we'd leave. We left Yan and our cook, Wilson Pride, and a couple more on-board and rowed ashore after breakfast in the whaleboats. I'd never rowed in my life before and my shoulders ached like hell by the time we reached the crowded harbour, rolled our barrels up the beach and tapped them, and gathered round to wait for Proctor to sort things out with whoever it was he had to sort things out with.

We waited an hour. People came down, barefoot women with dark eyes and black hair, shouting to one another in loud rasping voices, old men, crones in shawls, high-pitched children mobbing us in shrill sing-song. They brought potatoes and onions, beans and figs and apples, wild-eyed fowl complaining in wooden cages. I could make out nothing of their speech, a hoarse-throated mixture of English and Portuguese, but John Copper had some of the language. '*Não ainda*,' he told them, good-natured, '*logo, logo*', and I made up my mind to listen hard wherever I went and try to pick up all I could of the various tongues. If I was to be a rover, and I was, it would be necessary. They could have been birds for all I understood of them, these foreign people. What good was that? Plain, unremarkable John Copper earned my admiration with his skill.

The people drew back respectfully when the captain came walking down the beach with Rainey and Comeragh and Henry Cash, the dog trotting circles as if rounding them up, running ahead, running back.

'Samson,' Proctor called, 'heel, heel!'

We brought ourselves to attention with the dog and awaited orders.

Captain Proctor said all was in order for trading. Simon Flower was to take charge of the measuring with Martin Hannah. Those who wished could take a run ashore, those who wished could return to the ship. 'I want fair trading,' he announced, his pale, freckled hand tickling the back of the dog's ear, 'and may I take this opportunity', clearing his throat, 'to remind those of you who choose to stay ashore, that you are guests upon this island. Any misdemeanours . . .' he paused '. . . of any kind . . .', panting moistly, soft-eyed, Samson whined, '. . . will be punished with utmost severity.'

He scanned us with his pale questioning blue eyes as if searching for dissent.

'Utmost severity,' he repeated thoughtfully.

Mr Rainey stepped forward from the small line-up of him and Comeragh and Cash. Why Cash? Standing there with his cool half smile, as if he was a mate already.

'If I might comment,' Mr Rainey said.

'Most certainly, Mr Rainey,' replied Captain Proctor pleasantly.

'It occurs to me that Copper might be a wiser choice than Hannah, sir. Copper has a smattering of the native tongue. Hannah, I believe, has none.'

There was an odd moment. Captain Proctor's hand stopped fondling his dog. Cash gave a slight nod, and Comeragh looked away. The captain's eyes flickered, he adjusted his hat. 'Thank you, Mr Rainey,' he said smoothly, 'a good suggestion. Copper, Flower – fair dealing.'

It was a good choice. John Copper knew what he was about. He told me later he'd worked on his aunt's fish stall in Hull since he was about six years old. John measured fairly with quart pot and pint cup, a frown of concentration pleating the skin between his eyes. It was funny to hear him switch between his native Yorkshire and pig Portuguese as he haggled gamely with the noisy women. '*Três, senhora, três so! Bastante! Obrigado, obrigado, depois por favor.*'

The rest of us who'd gone ashore were free to roam around the town, and a sweet little town it was, full of narrow cobbled lanes and donkeys and flowers and small white houses with patterned tiles upon the walls. Some of the buildings were grand, with fine balconies that overhung the road, flowers cascading, but mostly the houses were poor, and the children who peeped out of their doorways were barefoot and raggy, with bright, dark eyes. The men were shabby. The women carried pots on their heads and wore long cloaks with stiff hoods in spite of the warmth of the day. But there was nothing in the shops we wanted, and anyway we had no money. So after a while me and Tim strolled out of town along a narrow climbing lane hedged with great clumps of pink and purple flowers, and we saw a wooden plough drawn by two oxen, and a couple of men digging in the fields. High bamboo hedges divided the land. Here and there were cottages with scabby thatched roofs.

We climbed till the land became woody. Big rocks poured water down into the gulleys at the sides of the track.

'To think there's this,' I said. 'All the time.' It seemed to me for one moment that unhappiness was a nonsense. I thought of my mother gutting fish in Limehouse and Ishbel coming off Quashies' stage.

'I know exactly what you mean,' Tim said.

It was a funny thing with me and Tim. I don't think we ever really had any proper conversations, not what you'd really call a conversation, not like I've had with others. Skip, for example. Now me and Skip, we could rattle on all day and night. Me and Tim now, we never talked. But we did know what the other meant.

We saw a figure dark upon the skyline, sitting on a high flat rock completely still and engrossed in what may have been a book upon his knee. Skip. Something seemed strange about him, and it took me a moment or two to realise it was the stillness. I'd never seen him still before. Skip was a jiggler. When he stood he swayed, when he sat he banged his knees together.

'What you up to, Skip?' yelled Tim.

Skip jerked.

Tim scaled the rock, grinning.

'Fuck you.' Skip said it like he said everything, quiet and controlled. 'Creeping around like that! Why don't you say you're there? Creeping up on a fellow like that.'

'Who's creeping?'

'You's creeping, fuckhead.'

I followed Tim. It was nice on the rock, warm and airy. Cross-legged we sat, braves a-powwow.

'What you doing?'

'Drawing.' Skip pushed the book towards us.

There was the island, looking in towards the volcano, a few grey, feathery lines that somehow made a picture.

'Pretty,' Tim said.

I turned back a page. There was the harbour, with *Lysander* in the bay, every mast and sail and spar of her. I turned the pages back and there we all were, our faces, our hands, our very ways of leaning against the rail or sitting at the kid – Yan's high-planed face, Comeragh's lanky stance, Bill, my sickmate, eating his dinner, the way his hair bushed about his head. Wilson Pride standing in the cookhouse doorway peeling a poatato

'There's Samson!' Tim pointed.

I laughed. 'There's the captain to a T.' Captain Proctor, chubby, eyeless.

'There's you, Jaf!'

Oh me, yes, it was me.

'I never saw you do these,' Tim said.

Skip shrugged.

'Where'd you learn to draw like that?'

'It's a gift.' He swallowed, a loud liquid clicking sound that must surely have pained his Adam's apple. The sound of dogs barking in a yelping frenzy came from far inland, and he turned his head towards it. 'I've always had a lot of gifts,' he said pensively, holding his mouth in that weird stiff way he had as if he was carrying a mouthful of water. A funny thing to say.

'What other gifts have you got, Skip?' I asked him.

He drew his knees up towards his chin, wrapped his arms around them and started rocking backwards and forwards, smiling his awkward nearly smile. He had a funny face. From the front it was chubby and round, but his profile was odd. Straight as a ruler it set off down the bridge of his nose before the line turned all wavy, drawing to an exaggerated nodule at the tip and falling away into a vague chinlessness. His skin was bad, flecked with eruptions and bumps.

Tim looked at me, pointed his finger at his head and made a face to show he thought Skip was loopy.

Skip sniggered. 'Whistling,' he said in his clumsy, swallowing way.

We laughed.

'I can whistle anything,' he added.

It's true, he was a great whistler.

'What else?' I asked. 'That's only two things.'

He looked at me, not speaking for a moment. 'You wouldn't understand,' he said.

'Did you know you were barmy, Skip?' said Tim. 'Really? Did you know you were well and truly roaring raving insane?'

'No, truly.' Skip laughed. 'No joke.'

'What are you drivelling on about, Skip?'

'What wouldn't we understand?' I asked. 'Do you think we're idiots?'

93

'Not idiots.' He licked his lips. 'Just normal. Normal people.'

'So, aren't *you* normal then?'

He smiled. His mouth was small, hardly there.

'You're an irritating prick,' I told him.

'Sorry.' Skip closed his book and slipped it into his pocket. 'It's just that people don't . . . people don't . . .' He concentrated, frowning. 'Normal, no, I'm not normal, that's true.'

'First thing you've said that's made sense.' Tim lay down on his back on the rock and shaded his eyes.

'It's not a great matter,' Skip said, pulling a half shrug to go with the nearly smile. 'I have the second sight.'

'Oh, well, that,' I said, 'if that's all it is.'

Half the people in Ratcliffe Highway had the second sight.

'Can you tell fortunes?'

'It's not that simple.'

'Can you see into the future?' asked Tim.

Skip thought about it. 'Sometimes,' he concluded.

'So what can you do then?'

'Read your mind!' I said. 'Go on, what's Tim thinking?'

'He's thinking I'm mad.'

We laughed.

'They went to church,' Skip said.

'Who did?'

'Mr Rainey. Henry Cash. Sam Proffit.'

'Did they now?' Tim sat up and rubbed his eyes.

'They went to church, but that isn't where the god is.'

A soft breeze, flowery, gentle, rippled its finger ends upon the napes of our necks.

'Where's the god then, Skip?' I asked. Tim and I exchanged a look. Skip just smiled. A tiny lizard skittered across the rock as if called, and we all laughed again.

'A sign!' cried Tim. 'Oh, mighty lizard, bless me!'

'That's what *we're* going after,' I said, 'only it's a million times bigger.'

'A million?' Tim leaned back on his elbows. 'God, I hope not.'

Skip lay down on his back and stretched out, closing his eyes. His eyelids were thick and heavy, china white. 'This creature,' he said, 'this thing. This *thing*. Think you'll find it?'

'If we do we'll be rich.' I lay down too. It was hot.

'No,' Skip said. 'You won't. You won't be rich.'

'How do you know?'

'I know.'

'No, you don't.'

'I do.'

'Huh.' Tim lay down too. There we three lay under a hot sun. When I closed my eyes everything was orange. I don't have to go home, I thought. I can go anywhere. The world's endless. I could live here. I could live anywhere. It doesn't have to be the Highway and the river and Spoony's and Meng's. I could live on a mountain. In a jungle. Where it's all flowers. Miles of distance and nothing sure and nothing the same. I tried to say it, but it came out wrong, so I gave up.

'Just think,' Skip said, and chuckled as if he'd just thought of something very funny, 'next second. Now! The mountain explodes.'

Tim laughed. 'Boom!'

'Funny, isn't it?' said Skip. 'Any minute we could all be dead.'

'Where you from, Skip?' I asked.

He didn't answer for so long I'd forgotten I'd asked, then: 'Rochester,' he said, 'once upon a time.'

All the boats were fully laden and still there was a bit of whale oil left.

'Think that's sense?' Rainey was barking at Simon Flower. 'Giving it away? Hey! Boy! That what you were told?'

'No, sir,' said Simon, a dark-haired serious boy who gave Tim a run for his money when it came to beauty.

'No more, no more. Tell them no more,' yelled Rainey at John Copper, who was trying to drive away a gaggle of old beggar women as if they were geese.

'How much is left, Mr Rainey?' Captain Proctor, coming along behind, speaking mildly.

I don't know about church, but Rainey had certainly had a drink. It came off him in a waft as he turned. 'Not much,' he said, tilting a barrel.

'What do you think, Mr Flower?'

Simon was blushing furiously. 'Dregs, sir,' he said.

Proctor thought for a moment then decided. 'Drain them off. Let 'em have what's left. Damn little anyway.'

The old women rushed forward and mobbed the barrels, pushing each other about and shoving their cups under the taps. It was getting dark. Dan Rymer was sitting on the sea wall. Far out in the bay, the *Lysander* had lit its lanterns, and lights were appearing inland. Dan called me and Tim over. 'This is your first real run ashore,' he said. 'Stick with me. There is no better guide.'

I didn't know how old Dan was. He was wrinkled, but he acted like a younger man, and from time to time a slow boyish kind of smile would illuminate his ruined face: ruined because there was some handsome ghost still hiding in it, rarely seen and all but completely buried in its dried-up, ageing appearance. He'd always just been Mr Jamrach's favourite supplier, a gruff, familiar, now-and-then presence, and since we'd embarked he'd not had that much to do with me because Gabriel seemed to have taken over my training. But that night in Horta was the night I started getting to know him.

The narrow lanes were fragrant with flowers. The walls of the houses were patterned, coloured. To a tavern – or was it a house?

– I'll never know. A golden light spilled through a door. A woman was singing. Her dark voice came out into the night and it sounded like heaven. Blossom billowed down the walls, hung over the narrow street, purple and white. We came to a room full of good will, the walls full of saints, the tables of men who laughed, and women far finer than the whores of Ratcliffe Highway. These women – these dark foreign women. Their black eyebrows, their brown skin, their complicated way of moving. A rich aroma opened the pores beneath my tongue, sweet herbs and meat juices. There was a fire on the ground, a pot cooking on it.

I was at a table, my back against a wall, Tim to one side, Dan across the table in front of me. I drank something strong and dark and red out of a round leather bottle. A handsome friendly woman, who spoke fast foreign all the time, gave us stew and potatoes and I had never tasted anything as delicious. I thought I must come and live here, take my chances with the volcanoes.

'You see,' said Dan, wagging his spoon at me, 'I know the places to go.'

'Damn right,' said Tim. 'Don't know what we'd do without you.'

'Without me,' said Dan grandly, 'you'd be like all the rest. Uncle Dan knows everything.' He had a slight lisp. He poured freely from the leather bottle and we drank. A girl with braids and a red bandanna sat on some wooden steps and played a mandolin, and I fell in love with her on the instant and knew that I would never leave this place, that I had found my true home at last and would now be happy for ever. The voice of the mandolin was a pealing cascade, unbearably sweet, making tears swell in my chest. There was singing, the mellow singing of happy drunken men. A very small kitten clawed its way up onto my knee, a sweet purring thing that nuzzled into my armpit and commenced suck-ling. Dogs big and small roamed the shadows, under the table, in and out the door. Chickens, stalking, under and over, talking with their mad sharp beaks ajar. Tim was gone. I looked around for him, but the room span, lovely, colours, the fire, the red bandanna, the blue cloaks. Dan was still there, peering at me humorously, a U-shaped grinning mouth, small close-together eyes set well back under a low, furrowed brow. Resting on an elbow, he leaned over the table and looked me in the eye. 'Here's something, Jaf,' he said. 'Never forget.'

When Dan Rymer drank he became his true self. His eyes twinkled, his lips puckered, his limbs loosened up.

'What, Dan?' I laughed, made mad and bold by the strong red wine. It had a metallic edge and reminded me of that thin taste blood has when you bite your lip or your teeth bleed. 'On with the words of wisdom!'

'That's it,' he said, 'just that. Never forget.'

'Never forget what?'

He was smoking a long brown cheroot and he waved it elegantly, creating eddies of startlingly bright blue smoke. 'That smoke,' he said seriously, 'never forget the sight of that smoke as long as you live,' and he hummed 'Tobacco's But An Indian Weed'.

They brought us more wine, and some small cakes, very sweet and moist, bright yellow.

'These are good,' he said, tucking in, and we gorged ourselves, 'these are the *ultima thule* of cakes. These cakes are what you were born for.' He grinned. His arm gestured in a loose circular movement. 'Have you seen the Madonna?'

'What do you mean?' I asked stupidly, draining my glass and immediately wanting more, grabbing the bottle and pouring, spilling a few drops. You couldn't see how much was in the bottle, but it was good and heavy. The kitten was dislodged from my armpit and slithered to the floor with a disgruntled mew.

'The Madonna,' Dan repeated, 'come and see, she's over the stairs.' I didn't want to get up, but he'd risen and gestured me over to where the angel with the mandolin still produced heaven from the tips of her brown fingers.

I followed.

'Look,' he said, 'one of the most beautiful things you'll ever see.'

I looked up. The real girl, the mandolin girl, was on my left-hand side. Her music had faded now, she twinged and twanged the instrument in a random, desultory manner. There was a painting at the top of the stairs, painted right on the wall, the Madonna spreading out her cloak, sheltering the world. How they do it, those paintings, some of the ones you see. You can't see her eyes, but you know what they're like, you just know.

'You know,' Dan Rymer said, breathing warm booze breath on me, 'I have a wife.'

'I know,' I said.

'I love my wife.'

That tall fair woman with babies at her skirts, in her arms. Greenland Dock. London. Dear London. Oh, Greenland Dock. Oh, fried fish and grey skies and the smell of the market on Watney Street as a new day dawns.

'She was born in the marshes,' he said, 'out of town.'

'I saw her.'

'Saw her?'

'On the quay.'

'Of course,' he murmured, 'of course you would have done.'

We gazed in a trance at the Madonna. I looked sideways and saw the mandolin player idly regarding me with no interest at all. I needed another drink. Back at our table I filled my glass near to the brim. I might be sick, yes, but it was far away, not yet. I didn't care.

'Oh, when I was your age,' Dan said, sitting down once more opposite me, 'oh when, oh when, oh when . . .' and waved the hand that held his drink, slopping some over his fingers.

A broad-faced woman sat down beside him and kissed the side of his face. A tiny key hung from a blue ribbon about her neck. He put an arm round her waist and began to sing, throwing back his head and closing his eyes.

> Western wind ablow,
> Small rains rain.
> My dear darling in my arms
> And a warm sweet bed again.

God, he had a voice. Not your average voice, but a voice. I got the tears again, my stupid drunk heart. From the corner of my eye, I saw Tim and a girl slip through a door. My heart gave a sigh, a sinking fall. My sweet warm bed was nowhere. The kitten had returned.

'Her name is Alice,' Dan said.

'Alice,' I echoed.

'Alice.'

Alice, oh, Alice. Where is my Alice? In my lap the kitten vibrated.

Dan Rymer's eyes crinkled with laughter and his lips turned down. He poured me more of the strong red drink and hoicked up his collar. The woman beside him closed her eyes and laid her head on his shoulder, and he wore her like a cloak. When he leaned across the table, she came with him like a fox's face on a rich lady's stole. Speaking in a low and confidential tone, he said, 'Did I ever – did I ever – ever tell you about the time I saw an angel?'

I shook my head. God, I was full. The firelight in the hollows of his face made him very old, shockingly old.

'It was in Valparaiso.'

It was almost a whisper, and I leaned forward to hear, the movement causing a lick of nausea to stir faintly in some unspecific place.

'I was lying in the gutter,' said Dan, 'and a small dog had just pissed upon my shoulder.' He took a drink. '"Dear God," I said. "Thank you. Thank you, my God. It could have been my face."'

I spluttered. The kitten stood up and started walking round and round, digging its claws into my knees.

'Truly, truly,' Dan said, and the woman shifted on his shoulder, 'thou art merciful.'

The room began to lurch about. Thin needles of kitten claw shredded my breeches and pricked my knees. Out in the night, voices played counterpoint. Someone somewhere was having a quarrel, but it didn't sound serious.

'The moon was laughing down at me,' said Dan, getting into his stride, 'sniggering from a canyon of swollen cloud.' He squared his shoulders.

I'm going to be sick, I thought. Oh no, not again, no.

'I shouted at the moon,' said Dan. '"*Who you laughing at?*"' Throwing out an arm. '"Fat Face? Come down here and laugh, I'll show you what's funny!"'

Dan jumped up, knocking the table skew-whiff. A bottle rolled. The cat leapt down and the woman slid sideways.

'"Come down, you old Pantaloon!" I cried.'

He stood, long coat gaping, wild head raised, a grim muzzlish look upon him.

'And it was then,' he said, sitting down again and speaking in a low voice, 'that the angel came. Eight feet tall, I don't know, a very tall creature anyway. Barefoot. Silver feet! Can you imagine that? Real feet of silver, alive. And his wings. They touched the walls on either side of the street. And do you want to know what he said to me?'

101

'Very much,' I said.

Dan leaned towards me, lowering his voice and speaking very seriously. 'He said, "Get up out of that, you fool of a man. Get your bleeding arse out of it and shut your stupid bloody mouth before I shut it for you." And then he *kicked* me.' Dan grabbed his own wrist, jutted his lip. 'But I grabbed his silver ankle! It was cold to the touch. And *up* he flew, away, *up* with me still hanging on, and off away back to my ship with me, and the town lights all spinning round below and the wind rushing in my ears, and the ships in the harbour all spinning round.' He sat back, picked up his drink. 'And he put me down on the quarterdeck, gentle as a leaf. "Count yourself in luck," he said. "Next time I'll drop you in the drink." And he turned the size of a gnat and flew away. And that was that.'

I turned sideways and threw up all over the dusty earth floor. A great warm flurry of big dark women flew about me, clucking and soothing and babying. They took me out in the cool night air and held my head. Did I sleep awhile? Did I dream? The scent of roses was strong, I remember, roses or some other flower, something that bloomed at night. The stars were ridiculously bright as if the sky was shouting. I lay like Dan in his gutter, but no little dog came to pee on me. A soft lap cradled me instead, and I turned onto my side and slept. Later there was the room again, and a dance to clapping hands and jangling music, and Dan in there dancing with them, pipe clamped between smiling lips, eyes closed, arms above his head. Later still, a hand led me to a loft, a bed, corn husks in a linen tick that crackled when I moved, the sense of other sleeping bodies warming the low space around me, the dreaming bodies of people and a few cats, from which arose a canopy of somnolence like the faint hum from a wasps' nest in the eaves.

It was dawn and I was fast asleep when Dan shook me by the

arm. We crept below, through the snoring room where we had caroused last night, past the sleeping snout of a black pig asprawl before the quietly ticking fire, past coiled cats and twitching dogs, and hens breast by swelling breast along a stone shelf.

We had hogs on deck. Just walking about. Felix Duggan cursed and shooed them as he tried to sweep up. Silver ribbons ran down the cliffs. I looked back, but already the red roofs were out of sight. Seemed stupid to me, setting off just as it was obvious the weather was on the turn. The clouds were thick and massy, bruised here and there. The waves were noisy, buoyant. Not long after we lost sight of land, the fog came down.

'Do you think we'll ever see a whale?' I asked Gabriel.

'Not in this, son.'

We were standing at the cookhouse door to get the smell of pork. Wilson Pride was feeding scraps to the dog.

'I never saw it like this,' I said. Gabriel laughed. His sea cap was pulled right down over his face. 'This is nothing,' he said.

'I know.'

'Hear you were sick bad last night, son.'

'Yeah.'

'That island stuff. You have to watch it, son. Look at me. Do I have to get drunk all the time? Not me, son. Look at me. You do like I do, son, and you won't go far wrong.'

'Do you think we'll ever see a whale at all? Ever at all, even when the fog goes?'

'Oh, we'll see a whale all right,' he replied confidently. 'You'll get sick to death of whales before this jaunt's done; you'll see a whale and you'll say, "Ha, so what, whale, ha".' He gave an exaggerated shrug.

'How many whales have you killed?'

He shrugged again, this time more normally. 'Hundreds.'

103

'How old are you, Gabriel?'

'Thirty-four. Thirty-five,' he said.

'Have *you* ever killed a whale?' I asked Wilson Pride, who'd gone back to his counter and was pouring water over a block of hardtack so hard it could have cut a diamond.

'Not me,' he replied. Wilson always went barefoot. His feet were very large and flat, the heels startlingly pink, and he was always washing them. You'd see him soaking them on deck in a bowl of seawater.

'Who told you I was sick?' I asked Gabriel.

'Tim,' he said.

Of course.

The sea fooled and niggled.

Tim never got sick. Did I say?

After the Azores we had rough seas. I never saw the flying fish before this time, these swift, shimmering things that skim the waves, rainbows flying from their backs. And birds who never neared land, nobly spanned, fearful of eye, cruel clawed. In their shrill, crack-voiced thousands, they clouded our ship from the Azores to the Cape Verde Islands, faithful in the rain. As for whales, not a puff to be seen. The winds tried their lungs. Proctor sent Gabriel, our best helmsman, to the wheel. We stowed away the studding sails and top gallants in a torrent, and ran before the wind to the Cape Verdes.

They were nothing like the Azores. We anchored somewhere all drenched and bleached out, with great mountains of salt rising up against a sky the colour of dishwater. South from there the wind died down, but the rain was endless and we couldn't get our sails dry. And when the rain stopped, we sailed into a calm that kept us crawling for days, a sleepy ship of sleepy men, a month or more out of London and all of us greenhorns believing ourselves by now to be weathered old hands. We were nearing the Equator and still hadn't seen a whale, but no one seemed to be worried about that. We met another ship, the *Gallopan* out of New Bedford, and so embarked upon a gam – a meeting of ships, a bit of fun – and that was my first and best gam, and went on for three or four days till I began to think that we were out here on this ocean for no other reason than to drink rum, eat Wilson Pride's salty pork dumplings and play cards of an evening.

At last the calm ended and we were able to go our ways. On the night before we parted company we dined on salt beef and carrots on the *Gallopan*'s deck, each of us with a thin slice of fresh bread instead of hardtack, just as the captains and mates got all the time. And after a good rich duff of plums and damson jam, Simon got out his fiddle, and one of the *Gallopan*'s men went down below and came up with a squeeze box that looked as if it had sailed the seven seas at least seven times. Everyone joined in singing all the old songs, Sam Proffit's glassy voice ringing above all the rest, a thin silver ribbon like the silver ribbons running down the cliffs when we left Faial. It could have been a woman's voice or an angel's, and it drove Felix mad. 'Grates on my bones,' he used to say when the old man started on his Sunday hymns. Very devout, Sam was. I loved his voice. On first hearing, it was piercing and unpleasant, but it grew on you the way a bird with an irritating call does, becoming sweeter with familiarity.

There was a big moon that night. Over on the *Lysander* a bright light burned in the officers' quarters. There lay our ship, all at peace, the captain's dog scratching itself happily on the deck. 'Blood Red Roses' they were singing. 'Go down you blood red roses, go down.' The high strange sound coming out of Sam's worn black face was a ghostly descant to the rough voices of the others. 'Go down you blood red roses, go down.' John Copper had tears in his eyes. One of the *Gallopan* crew was singing the thread: 'Growl you may but go you must, for if you don't your

105

head they'll bust', and we were all joining in on the chorus: 'Go down you blood red roses, go down. Oh' – this a great tipsy roar – 'you pinks and posies – go down you blood red roses, go down.'

No one but me, for I was sitting next to him, noticed when Skip slammed down his tin cup, put his arms round himself and started rocking from side to side.

'What's up?'

Ignoring me, he got up, walked to the rail and stood gazing across at our ship. Something peculiar in him made me follow. 'What's up, Skip?' I said. His eyes were wide. That was strange. Skip didn't have wide eyes. He was staring up at her sails. 'What?' I looked up too and saw nothing.

Then he looked at the black waves washing against *Lysander*'s side, and his throat clenched loudly.

'You not well, Skip?'

His lips were drawn back like a dog's. 'Can you see them?' he said.

'See what?'

'Snakes.' He was shivering.

I stared at the sea, the ordinary sea, and our ship, just as she ever was. 'I don't know what you're talking about.' I wondered if I should go and tell someone.

'Of course, you don't know what I'm talking about.' He sighed, wearily impatient. His hands were shaking on the rail. It was a beautiful night. The singing was growing melancholy and the lights swung out on the water.

'Don't go mad on us, Skip,' I said, 'for God's sake.'

He smiled. 'It's all right,' shaking his head. 'It doesn't matter. It's just something.'

'What are you talking about?'

'Nothing.' He laughed, turning his head to look at me. His eyes were still too big.

'Skip,' I said, 'are you really seeing things down there?'

He nodded sadly, returning his gaze to the sea, once more drawing back his lips from his gums in that peculiar dog-like way.

'*I* can't see anything,' I told him pointlessly, and we stood for a while, both of us gazing down as if hypnotised.

'Don't worry. Look at your hands.' I tried to prise one off the rail. 'It's just the sea playing tricks. It's worse when the moon's out. Does funny things with your eyes.'

'Snakes from out of the sea,' he said, but his hands loosened and fell down by his sides.

'Listen, if you're scared witless by a bit of moon on water,' I said, 'what'll you do when we get to dragon land?'

'That's different.'

'How?'

'Because that's real. I'm not scared of what's real.'

He turned from the rail and I saw that his eyes were narrow again. 'They've gone,' he said. 'Gone back down into the sea.'

Normal, or as normal as he could ever be.

'But they're not real,' I reminded him. 'You said it yourself.'

'So?' And he just walked away as if nothing had happened.

I told Gabriel about this and he said, 'There's a word for it, Jaf. Mad. You meet a lot of mad people at sea, particularly on a whale ship. Long as he can do his job.'

'True, but what if it happens while he's out in a whaleboat? What if he's supposed to be pulling along with everyone else and he sees something that isn't there and starts watching that instead? I wouldn't want to be in a boat with him. Do you think he's all right?'

'Look,' he said, 'if they laid off all the mad sailors there'd be no one left to man the ships.'

But later he gave me a nudge and said, 'Keep an eye on him though.'

107

I told Dan about it too, and he said much the same.

So, there we were keeping an eye on Skip as we crossed the Equator. I was thinking of Ishbel. I was thinking of Ma. I was thinking how when I got home, I'd never be able to tell them, never be able to describe all this, the way it felt, the miles and miles of empty sea and never a sail and never a sight of a whale or anything, and all of us rubbing along together like we did, with the timbers groaning and the smells of oak and pine and the murkier smell of men. How to explain how safe and good the fo'c's'le? Home with the hatch down. That's how peaceful it was when at last, six weeks after leaving home, we encountered our first whales.

It was Tim sighted them. God caused the great glory of the deep to appear for Tim – who else? – and Tim seized his moment joyfully.

'*There she blo-o-ows!*'

Loud and clear. His voice broke a little, but what matter? We were so thoroughly prepared, we all knew exactly what to do, yet for a moment or two we greenies froze.

'Where away?' Rainey cried, and Comeragh called all hands.

'Right ahead – a school of sperms.'

'Haul up the mainsail and spankers – helm down – back – clear away boats – lower away!'

Sam and Gabriel and Dan and Yan set about the boats calmly. Captain Proctor came up and stood on the quarterdeck with his telescope to his eye, and the dog sat at his side, wagging its tail.

'Flukes!' yelled Tim.

We ran to the rail. I saw nothing, only the sea and the endless horizon. Bill, my friend of the sick bucket, was on one side of me and on the other was Dag Aarnasson, a big strong boy with white-yellow hair. He must have had better eyes than me. 'I see it!' he cried.

Then Bill started jumping up and down and pointing. 'There! There!'

I couldn't see anything.

A cheer went up.

'Keep it down, you fools!' Proctor roared in a voice we'd never heard before, a real captain's voice full of command that must have been kept in reserve all this time for just such an occasion as this. We jumped to. Ours was the waist boat. The line was already in and Simon stood sharpening his harpoon. Far above, Tim leaned out over empty air.

'She breaches!'

'A shoal of sperm,' Captain Proctor called out sharply, 'twenty at least.'

We ploughed on. Rainey walked about the deck sticking his big nose in everywhere and swearing all the time as if there were no other words would do it. Henry Cash always seemed to be striding about everywhere too, always looking as if he was in control of some very important situation.

'White water!' cried Tim.

A mile from the shoal we hove to. A ghostly feather appeared, far, far out on the sea, just for a second, and my heart was beating very very fast. Tim, down from his eyrie, ran over to me, out of breath. 'This is it.' He could hardly get it out. 'This is it, this is it, Jaf,' he said and gripped my hand hard. My mouth had gone dry.

Dan pushed in between. 'Let's go and catch a big fish,' he said.

We set the whaleboat down as gently as a baby on the waves, with Comeragh in the stern and Simon in the bow, then we slid down the falls each to his place, me and Tim and Dan and Sam. The boat bobbed lightly like a feather. I looked up and saw the ship keepers, Wilson Pride's wide, black face impassive, sulky Joe Harper, Abel Roper slouching to the helm as if a burden was on his wiry shoulders. Joe and Abel were jealous. They'd have loved to have been going out with us. I'd not have swapped with either, but at that moment there was a great longing for the solid deck beneath my feet and a safe height from which to look down. The boat was nothing, an old matchbox waiting to be capsized by a black island of whale flesh, turned to matchwood floating on the water by the careless flick of a massive tail. Show fear? Not a bit. I looked over my shoulder at Simon sitting in the bow. If *I* was scared, he must be terrified. It was his first time with the harpoon. He'd been practising. Take aim. Throw. Take aim. Throw. If he arsed it up and made the creature angry – ha, well. He didn't look scared though. He was inspecting the tip of his harpoon with a frown, his cheeks very flushed.

The captain's and Rainey's crews floated nearby. There were voices, laughter. Comeragh was the only one of us in our boat could see where we were going. I was next to him, facing him. He smiled at me. 'We're going to pull like fucking hell, lads,' he said, and his long fingers closed round the steering oar. 'We'll beat those bastards.'

And the race began. Because that's what it was, a race to win. We pulled, we pulled like fucking hell towards an unseen quarry. Comeragh stared over our heads with flaring nostrils, never blinking, calling which way to pull. We flew. I saw another boat from the corner of my eye, the captain's bulky form astern, the blond head of Dag like a beacon, the crew bent-backed, straining. A mile or more and my shoulders burned. Jesus. Comeragh laughed. 'Get ready,' he said, and made a sign for silence. I looked up. His eyes were fixed on something beyond. He had a way of calling a whisper, loud enough for us all to hear, but not loud enough to gally the whales. He leaned forward at the steering oar and called us to pull two, pull three in his whisper command, eyes still fixed on what we could not see. My back and shoulders were on fire. When at last he called 'avast' and we rested, I was drenched and all a-tremble and my palms were scorched.

I blinked sweat from my eyes. My nose streamed. *Lysander*, three great masts and white sails, my home, was far away.

'Simon,' said Comeragh.

And then I looked.

A whale. Black, gleaming in the sun. Block-shaped head out of the water, high as a cliff. Too close.

'There she is, a beauty,' Comeragh said.

I sensed the other boats, other whales further away, the sea churning and living, but all I saw was our whale. Her ridged tail, a lovely shimmering thing like a moth, flourished, slapped down and went under. She was gone. The sea heaved, the wash lifted us high.

Simon stood up with his harpoon. One leg was bent and his knee was shaking.

'Any minute, any second,' Comeragh murmured, 'she'll be up and – here, here, here, where are you, my love? Up you come now for Daddy – get steady, Simon, she'll take you by surprise, she will, she's a little teaser she is, she's a little – where are you, darling? It's a lovely day, come up and talk to me, don't be shy, come up and—'

She exploded through the surface in a cascade of silver, further away, thank God. She was the length of two of our boats.

Simon relaxed slightly. 'Pull two,' said Comeragh, and we slid along the water, creeping like a beetle towards an elephant. Down she went again, sudden as before. We crept. She resurfaced, further away. This seemed to please Comeragh, whose eyes had been worried, but who now smiled. 'I have you, madam,' he said, and we followed.

I lost sense of time. We went far from the boats, but there were other whales, playing like kittens about us. We ran with them, rainbows of spray on the air, always following the same whale, which sounded and breached, sounded and breached, drawing us on for miles. God knows how Comeragh always knew just where she'd breach. Our aching backs had turned to water and no longer mattered by the time we closed on her. She was tired too, sitting on the water, a small sad shining eye watching us, interested. What a peculiar place for an eye, I thought, right down on the side like that. What kind of a face is that? Like an elephant's eye, the elephants in Jamrach's yard. Good old elephants! Her white mouth opened on sharp little teeth all along the lower jaw.

Simon stood with harpoon poised, leg braced against the cleat, broad shoulders knotted. She spouted a thick mist-cloud of stench that covered my face, stinging my eyes. I closed them.

'Now!' said Comeragh.

Opened them.

Simon froze, a ridiculous small thing trembling before the blunt black head. The harpoon shivered and flew and fell short. Sam pulled it in immediately, the veins thick and knotted on the backs of his hands, and Comeragh cursed. 'Take the oar, baby,' he said to Simon, moving forward with an agility that scarcely moved the boat, 'get back there.'

Simon passed me with tears streaming down his face and took the steering oar, wiping his sleeve roughly across his eyes.

A whale sees nothing before or behind. It sees two worlds, either side. I don't know what the whale saw. To me it seemed she was looking at me all the time, that's what it was like. As if she was curious. I dare say there were wiser whales. Comeragh darted and she was struck. She pitched, turned the front of her head at us in a soundless scream, thrashing her tail three or four times and causing the sea to boil, then fled along the slippery surface of the sea with the harpoon quivering in her side, dragging us after. We jumped and bounced, teeth clashing, bones rattling. No fighting it. When she sounded, I thought we'd go under for sure, but we flew on, the elements screaming in our ears and the whale line singing and vibrating, till she surfaced in front of us, making the sea pitch us high.

She rolled, open-jawed. Salt stung my eyes. Comeragh rose steady in the bow with the lance. 'Pull in, pull in', a voice said, and we hauled hand over hand nearer and nearer to her, Sam leading. Her eye was still bright. It blinked slowly, once. Then the stabbing began. The lance was twice the length of Comeragh but he handled it with such skill that all my fear evaporated. She rolled over, snapping her jaws. She twisted. The sea turned red. He stabbed her again and again, seven, eight, nine times, probing determinedly for the heart which, when found, caused her to spout a dark spume from the blowhole, a fountain of blood that burst up and rained down from on high all over us.

'Back! Back!' cried Comeragh and Sam, and we took oars and got away and watched her die.

It was then I truly realised the whale is no more a fish than I am. So much blood. This was not like the fish on the quay, fresh caught, lying flipping and flopping, death on a simmer. This was a fierce, boiling death. She died thrashing blindly in a slick of gore, full of pain and fury, gnashing her jaws, beating her tail, spewing lumps of slime and half-digested fish that fell stinking about us. It was vile. So much strength dies slowly. We watched in awe, wordless. Ten minutes, fifteen, more. As she thrashed, she swam around in an ever dwindling gyre, and I begged her to die.

How long till she listed? No more than twenty minutes. She heeled at last and lay still, one fin pointing at the sky. So passed Leviathan.

We pulled in the line, Sam leading. Stronger than he looked, Sam. We were rowing in blood. A foul flotsam, the contents of the whale's stomach, bobbed around us. My part was to keep the line from tangling, see it safely back into its tub. Tim turned and looked at me. We were the two greenhorns on our boat. We had no way of knowing what we were feeling. We just looked at each other.

It was getting dark as we towed the whale back to the ship. We were shaky and dumb, but a growing euphoria coloured the horror. First whale of the season, she was ours. *We* were the boys.

Not the captain's boat, not Mr Rainey's. Ours, Second Mate Comeragh's. It was bad for Simon though. Back on deck everyone started congratulating him, thinking that as boat steerer he must have been the one to have taken the whale. And he had to tell them how he hadn't been up to it and Mr Comeragh had had to take over. Me and Tim though, we were laughing now. Dan came and clapped us on the shoulder, very serious. 'That was good,' he said. 'Good. Kept your heads.' We'd kept our heads. We'd come through. They tied her to starboard with her head facing the stern.

Knowing I was safe, a certain wildness came over me now. Here I was back on the dear old *Lysander* with my good fellows, alive. It was getting dark and the fires had already been lit under the try pots. Rainey and Comeragh stood on the cutting stage and set about hooking her near the fin. The windlass was set to and she was peeled like an apple, slowly, turning and turning like a pig on a spit, till the blanket strip, wide as a double bed and long as to the top of a house, hung dripping blood from the rigging. Yan and Gabriel swarmed up and hacked it off, and we dropped it down to Henry Cash and Martin Hannah waiting in the blubber room below. And when another and another and another strip had left her and gone below, she was a monstrosity, a creamy gleaming grub of a thing clinging to the side of our ship in the dark, with her great head still intact, smiling. But they

114

cut it off at last, and we hauled it up with the block and tackle and there it lay on our deck, a terrible thing two men long.

Dag Aarnasson, who had done all this before, went up on top with a knife and cut a hole in the top big enough for us to dip our buckets in. There was a single moment when everything lurched and a cloud came over my eyes, but I hung onto a rope and gritted my teeth and held on tight till things cleared, and then I made a vow that I would get through this without disgrace, and took up my bucket. If you have never scooped the oil from a sperm whale's head with a bucket, you will not appreciate the strength it takes. There are hundreds and hundreds of gallons of oil in a sperm whale's head. It is thick and white and the more you scoop, the gloopier and heavier and more spunk-like it gets. It's like trying to empty a bottomless well, and it breaks your poor fucking back, which by this time has gone beyond simple pain. And when at last it's nearly empty, someone has to go down inside the head and get the dregs. Skip did this, impassive, whistling as he worked, while the rest of us set to chopping. Wraiths, we lurched upon the slippery deck. Felix Duggan got sick, ran aside and vomited, stood groaning with his hands on his knees, water drooling from his big pink lower lip. The mates upon the cutting stage worried away at the wormy innards, looking for ambergris, which ladies wear upon their wrists and in the valleys between their breasts. Piled about the deck were great heaps of hacked flesh that bled and shone and gave off a sweet stink that made my guts clench with a kind of perverted hunger. The try pots boiled and heaved and were skimmed constantly of an evil scum, which rose to the surface and was thrown into the fires beneath to spit and crackle and belch forth a thick black smoke with a charnel house stink. Firelight shone on the boards, awash with oil and blood.

We chopped and chopped. Again and again our knives grew

115

blunt and we honed them and set to again, wiping sweat from our dripping brows. Blubber's tough. We cut and heaved, passed our hunks to Sam and Yan and Dan and Gabriel, who, singing and smiling like women in a kitchen, sliced again like skilful butchers till the strips they called bible leaves appeared, like pages in the flick book I had made for Ishbel five years ago. All were swallowed in the try pots.

My clothes stuck to me. Oil. Oil to make putty and paint and soap, oil to grease and varnish, oil to burn in millions of lamps. I was soaked in a sticky gum of filth and gore, grease, sweat, bile, the puky juices of God's greatest creature. My hair stuck close to my head, fast glued. Still – who better than me for this? Had I not scoured the Thames sewers for pennies?

'Sleep in your clothes, Jaf,' Dan said when my watch ended.

I thought he was mad.

'If you change for every watch, you'll be out of gear before we're a quarter through,' he explained.

So I slept in the reek of myself and the whale, and it wallowed through my sleep and gave me dreams of slaughter in a wild jungle place. When I arose for the next watch, the try pots still bubbled and the decks were still slippy. My clothes had dried upon me and become a second skin, and the bones and organs of the whale floated alongside the ship in a great snapping of sharks and a feasting of seabirds. I stood with Gabriel looking down. Morning had come.

'Take it all in, son,' he said. 'Doubt you'll get the chance again.'

'Why so?'

'The whaling's done for,' he said, and grinned.

'Why?'

'No call for the oil no more. It's all this new stuff now. They'll always need the bone for the ladies' stays, but they won't be wanting all this oil no more.'

'What new stuff?'

'Oil under the ground,' he said.

It was three days till we were done. Stores sound, hatches down, decks all scoured and pure.

Onward. Different.

6

We turned east. It was rough round seas after that, the ocean breathing in and out, in and out, range after range of rolling hills, up and down whose howling slopes we climbed and rolled as the winds wailed and the dark water swelled and heaved. These bloated seas were full of ships. We passed them, distant toy things sighted through a whistling grey madness, bird blackened (as were we), clouded by crying hordes. Sometimes we drew nigh and saw dark, tattooed faces on their decks. Sometimes we met, and the faces, white-eyed and sea stained, became real and took on names. The days mingled. My sea eyes changed, becoming water wise. In two months we took five hundred barrels of oil, and were down a boat and a man. A fellow called George deserted at the Cape. The boat was smashed to splinters in an angry sea while being hoisted up *Lysander*'s side.

We met a ship which gave us our letters and the newspapers from home. Not all of us got a letter. Bill didn't, nor did Yan or Felix or Skip, and there was nothing for me either. Tim had one from Ishbel.

I watched him read. First he smiled, but after a moment or two this faded and his eyes scanned backwards and forwards seriously. On the back of the paper I could see the careful horizontal lines of her writing, with the long deep loops and the slight forward slant, and the long vertical lines with which she'd filled the margins. At the foot of the page was her name, writ larger than the rest, the I of Ishbel a flourish.

Tim turned the page and read the other side. Lines, all indecipherable. But there near the top I saw my name along with his: 'Dear Tim and Jaffy'.

'Hmm.' He gave a small down-the-nose laugh, shaking his head, glancing up at me and looking down again. 'Sends you her fond regards, Jaf,' he said brightly, turning it again and rereading the beginning.

'Has she seen my ma?'

He didn't reply.

I crowded him. 'Let's see.'

'Oy!' He flinched the letter away from me.

'It's for me too,' I said.

'No, it isn't. It's a private letter. Look.' He showed me the envelope. '*My* name. It's mine.'

'That's not fair,' I said, 'the letter's got *my* name on it too.'

'It has not! What are you talking about? You didn't even see it.'

'Didn't get a chance, did I?'

'It has not got your name on it, Jaf,' he said, as if to an imbecile. 'It's mine,' and folded it up very small and tucked it away in his clothes. It was like old times, all his little spites. I hated him again, even as the doubts came in. Had I really seen my name? Yes, then again no, then again maybe. I could have killed him there and then, throttled him with my bare hands.

'You're a rotten friend, Tim. Did you know that?' I said. 'What a rotten friend you are.' With horror I felt tears rising.

He smiled in a strange bland way. 'The old man's gone,' he said.

'What?'

'The old man. Pa. He's dead.'

I didn't know what to say. For all the notice Tim had ever taken of his dad, he might as well have been the coal scuttle.

'Oh,' I said coldly, clamping my teeth with the urge to stick my thumbs in his throat. 'What did he die of?'

'Death,' he said lightly, 'that's what he died of, death, Jaffy, old boy.'

'My name was on it,' I said, 'at the top. She wrote for both of us.'

'No, Jaf.' He looked at me sadly. 'She didn't. I'm sorry, you really are mistaken. She sends her fond regards. At the end, she sends you her fond regards. I told you.'

I wished Ma could write. I missed Ma. I missed Ishbel. Suddenly I had to turn away because of tears in my eyes. Bastard. I'd kick him overboard.

'No more bloody mermaids,' Tim murmured.

'I saw my name,' I said.

Tim turned his head on one side and raised his shoulders, frowning indulgently. Would I lie to you? the look said. Perplexed that I could doubt him.

I walked away and stood at the rail. My chest hurt. Who cares? And anyway why couldn't she write me my own letter? I ironed out the pain till nothing existed but the foam-flecked decks and the dim dappled fo'c's'le that creaked and groaned through the days and nights. Why was I here in this cramped mad moving world? There was no time alone any more. No time, no space, no dreaming place but sleep. George did the right thing jumping ship at the Cape. I missed the sound of the market and the smell of Meng's and the ring of the bell on Jamrach's door, and the smell of straw and dung in the yard and the ring of cobbles beneath my feet. I had a place there. Here I was a dogsbody.

Foam flew in my face. The world was too big. I turned and saw Dag standing as still as he could as the world rose and fell around him, his creamy-yellow hair plastered flat to his large head. He was trying not to gally a huge white bird that had alighted on the rail and clung mad-faced there, opening and closing its curved beak and spreading out its wings. Why so angry?

Foam fell like snow. A wave exploded upon our bow, shattering like glass, soaking us up as far as the cookhouse, and when I could see again the bird had gone.

'What is this thing then?' Skip said.

'What thing?'

'This thing. This dragon thing.'

'No one knows.'

Supper was over and we were having a smoke on deck. Skip was doodling idly in his drawing book. 'This thing,' he repeated, 'this dragon thing, what is it?'

'The Ora,' I told him, because that's what Dan Rymer some-times called it. I called Dan over. 'He wants to know about the Ora,' I said.

'I don't know anything about it,' said Dan, lounging against the mast. 'I met a man who met a man who met a man who met a man who . . . That's the kind of a thing it is. There are stories. It's a big, fierce thing, of course. And there are islands the natives stay away from.' He'd been speaking very seriously, but here broke into a grin. His teeth were yellowing at the tops, his forehead scored by three or four very deep lines. 'Listen to me, me boys, and I'll tell ye tales to curdle your blood,' he crowed, rubbing his hands together and licking his lips.

'Can I come with you when you go after it?' Skip asked.

'No.'

'Why not?'

'Because I said so.'

God knows why he was taking Tim. I would have been better. Any day. 'What if it's really a dragon?' Tim said one night as we lay smoking in our bunks. 'A real dragon, you know. Breathing fire. Wings. All that? Jesus!' He said it so everyone could hear.

'What d'you want to come for anyway?' Dan asked Skip. 'Eager to die?'

Skip shrugged amiably. 'I don't mind,' he said.

Dan sat down with us and lit his pipe. 'Of course you don't,' he said.

'If I can go after a whale,' Skip said, shading away steadily with his pencil, 'I can go after anything.'

'Not so.'

'Yes so. It's not fishing, you know. I know all about fish.'

'No,' said Dan.

'Isn't it funny,' Skip said, turning to me, 'the way a thing can be two different things at the same time?'

'What do you mean?'

'Like wanting to do something and not wanting to do it at the same time,' he said, 'like when my brother Barnaby drowned and I went and looked at him on the kitchen table and it was happy and sad all at the same time. Or like when you're killing a whale and you feel like you *are* the whale.'

He showed me his sketch. It was his idea of a dragon, a tragic and majestic old thing.

I could understand why Dan wouldn't take Skip along. Too unpredictable. *I* wasn't though. I was good with animals, everyone said so. I had a feel for them and no real fear, only a respect for their powers that gave me a healthy caution. Why should Tim be hunter's mate and me only a dogsbody? I got Dan on his own later and asked him outright: why him and not me?

123

He blew smoke thoughtfully out of the corner of his mouth and said, 'One. Because I promised him. Two. Because he's the best man for the job.'

'*Tim?*'

'Him for the hunt,' he said, 'you to take care of the creature once it's caught.'

Seas have natures, like people. Since we left the Crozets behind, the change had seeped its way into everything. We were blown still, but the wind was less chilling, batting us along like a cat with a ball of wool. First there were islands here and there, reassuring blots of land upon the vastness of the ocean. Then there were none. The change was a somnolence thrown over us after the islands vanished. Now I saw the earth curve and felt as dizzy as a poor gnat on the brim of a drain. The sea changed colour, became a thirsty blue. But I sensed something more, something I had no words for, something that scared me witless. An enormity. As if something was hidden here, something under the sea, something under everything.

I tried to tell Tim.

'Just my luck', he said, 'to get stuck out here with a lot of lunatics. Christ help us come full moon.'

Now that we were drawing nearer to its homelands, the idea of the dragon was beginning to sink in. Joe Harper and Sam Proffit were working on the cage for it on the deck. Comeragh stood watching. 'Make damn sure it's strong,' he said, shaking out his handkerchief and laughing at the idea of the thing getting out and taking a stroll along the deck. 'Down into the fo'c's'le!' he cried with nasal delight, blowing his nose loudly.

'Aft in the captain's cabin,' smiled Sam.

Joe thumped the sturdy timber with his fist. 'You could put an elephant in that,' he said confidently.

124

'Or a tiger.' That was me. The cage was much like the one my tiger had escaped from.

Tim piped up. 'Jaf was taken by a tiger once,' and everyone looked at me. 'Tell 'em, Jaf,' he said. 'Go on, tell 'em about the tiger.'

So I had to tell the story again about how I met Jamrach. Or rather Tim told it.

'Great big Bengal tiger! Head this big! And this little squirt here two foot tall walks straight up to it like it's a little pussy cat and gives it a pat on the nose—'

'Not a pat,' I said, 'a stroke. It was a stroke. I wanted to see what it felt like.'

The three of them were looking at me, Sam and Joe and Comeragh, impressed. Mr Jamrach came out of that story very well, but it was me that was the hero, I knew that by now. Jamrach had bravely wrenched apart the beast's jaws, that was true – though as I remember it being spoken of at the time, it was more like he got behind it and grabbed its throat and that made it open its mouth and cough me out. How should I know? I saw none of it. I remember being in the tiger's mouth though, oh yes, I still remember. That's why I was the hero. Not many had been in a tiger's mouth. Not a one of them that didn't in some way envy me that.

'Now there's a story to tell your grandchildren,' Mr Comeragh said, smiling. He had a terrible cold and his top lip was red and peeling.

Of course, the story was all over the place an hour later, and I had to tell it again and again so many times over the next couple of days that it recurred in me like a great wave, the very deep memory of it in my flesh and bones. I was cock of the fo'c's'le for a while, which made a welcome change. It didn't last, of course, but for a sweet day or two mine was the story circulating in the smoke as we lay on our backs on our bunks and in our hammocks, the smell of mildew, smoke rising under the low, oak ceiling, a cloudy room, dim by half lantern.

The head of Skip's bunk lay up against the head of mine. 'What was it like really?' he wanted to know. 'Can you remember? You know, can you *really* remember? When you were in its mouth.'

'Oh, I remember.'

It comes back in my dreams again and again. In different ways. Now I'm a sensible lad, wouldn't go anywhere near a tiger's mouth, but then it was just a great glory. I *could* never and *would* never be there again.

'I can't describe it,' I said.

He was quiet for a while, then said ruminatively, 'I wonder if it was like that for my dog, Poll.'

'If *what* was like that for your dog, Poll?'

'When she was killed,' he said. 'She was killed by a bloody great mad bloodhound down on the foreshore down by the reach. It was after someone and she got in the way and it grabbed her by the head, whole head in its mouth, huge great mouth it had, all slobbery, and it grabbed her by the whole head like that and threw her over its shoulder and – crack! – neck broken. Gone.'

'I doubt it,' I said. 'That sounds much worse than what happened to me.'

I relit my pipe, took a smoke and passed it back over my head to him. 'Still,' I said, 'I don't suppose she'd have suffered much. Well, not for long anyway.'

I heard him popping his lips as he tried to blow smoke rings. 'I used to say: here, Polly-dog! Here!' he said, holding smoke in his throat.

This got us onto the subject of Jamrach's and how I worked there in the yard, and all the beasts that came and went over the years. It was the mention of the silent bird room that got him. I

126

told him how they sat there unmoving in those tiny boxes, song-birds with locked throats, and he said that was all wrong. He said he hated to see a bird in a cage. 'It's something to do with the wings,' he said, 'it's when they can't open them up.'

We smoked silently and I thought about how that room had saddened me as a child, but I had grown used to it over the years as it became an everyday thing. It was just how the world was.

'They're not kept like that for ever,' I said. 'They're sold on.'

Skip said he remembered a fish that his grandmother had. He said he was terrified of his grandmother; she was very old and ugly and she had horrible brown leather skin in big wrinkles and wore thick round eyeglasses with a patch over one lens and the other so thick it made her eye look as big and swimmy as a fat fish, and it stared at you in a peculiar way that made you think she was a witch. And she had this poor fish, a big goldfish with a swishy tail that she kept in a little glass globe like the kind they cupped on your skin for a boil. It lived in this in a few inches of water, just enough so it could turn its body round and round in one continuous loop forever. And that's what it did. He said it was horrible. Something in the glass magnified the fish, just as the eyeglass magnified his grandmother's eye, and when you went in her nasty poky little room you'd see the swirling goldfish thing like a shiny eye, and *her* eye too, and it was as if both of them were her eyes watching you.

Next day Skip turned strange again. We'd taken a whale, and it was while we were in the middle of it all, when the try pots were blowing out smoke and the firelight making demons of us and leaping and dancing on the blood that dripped down onto the deck from the stripped blubber. Skip was by me on the wind-lass and he suddenly let go so that it juddered and jerked and knocked me back. Just let it go and walked away as if someone had called him.

127

'What the fuck do you think you are doing, Mr Skipton!' Rainey roared.

Skip seemed not to hear.

Rainey took a step as if it was a deep breath, threw back his head and marched after Skip with his nostrils flaring like sails. Martin Hannah jumped in beside me and took Skip's place and we pushed like hell, heads up, watching. Skip walked up the steps and onto the quarterdeck, looking straight ahead of him, stepping firmly, running the last couple of paces. He stood dead still looking up at the evening sky for a moment before laying himself down delicately upon the deck, curling up his knees and hugging himself with his arms, tucking his head in and giving a little judder of the shoulders as if of pleasure at turning into a cosy bed for the night.

Rainey stood over him kicking and kicking him in a spoilt and furious way. 'Get up! Get up, you bastard!' he screamed. 'There's not a thing wrong with you. How dare you leave your post!'

Gabriel ran up with Abel Roper. Proctor appeared.

Skip rolled onto his back. Something about the look of him disturbed them.

'For Christ's sake,' said Proctor, 'give him room.'

'There's nothing wrong with him,' shouted Rainey, 'he's just trying to get out of work.'

'I don't think he's pretending, sir,' said Abel. 'Felix, go and ask Wilson for the salts.'

When the salts were applied under his nostrils, Skip sneezed violently and sat up, only to sink back down again immediately.

'What's wrong with him?' Proctor asked.

'It's just a funny turn,' replied Abel.

'Ha!' Mr Rainey barked. 'Ha!'

'Put him down below,' Captain Proctor said. 'Let him sleep it off, whatever it is. No good him staggering about the deck in this condition. What are you all standing around here for? Doctors, are you? Back to work!'

Skip's eyes were looking off in two directions as they hauled him across the deck, one arm on the shoulder of Abel, the other on Gabriel. He started to laugh. 'Take me on the ferry!' he shouted. 'Take me on the ferry!' Then he threw up.

He was fine in a couple of hours.

It was nothing, he insisted, he just passed out. It wasn't true, of course. Later that night when just a few of us lay in the fo'c's'le, he told the truth. 'There was something following the ship,' he said. 'I went to look at it.'

We all leaned forward to hear.

'A bird,' I said. 'A cloud. A goney or a cormorant.'

He said it was an eye with wings. An eye with wings, in the sky, following the ship. 'Here,' he said, pulled out his pad and pencil and drew it for us.

No one spoke for a few seconds, then Tim laughed. 'What colour was it?' he asked.

'I don't know,' Skip replied seriously.

'Blue? Brown? A lovely green eye?'

'Horus,' said Gabriel thoughtfully.

'Did it have an eyelid? Could it blink? Did it wink at you?'

'Nothing like that.'

'Horus,' repeated Gabriel. 'I believe Horus is an eye.'

'What's Horus?' asked Skip.

'A god.' Gabriel frowned, considering. 'A god of the pharoahs.'

'How d'*you* know about pharoahs and gods?' I asked him.

'I've been around,' he replied.

'Maybe it was my brother, Barnaby,' Skip said.

Tim settled back with his arms behind his head. 'More like this pharoah thing, if you ask me,' he said. 'Sounds more likely somehow.'

'But what is Horus doing following you about, son?' Gabriel asked.

Skip said it didn't surprise him. He'd been visited by gods before.

'A*ha*,' was Gabriel's response, and not much more was said. We watched Skip more than ever after that though, all of us, and the voyage continued tranquil as we sailed on through a thick green sea, in which, at last, islands once more appeared. Long white strands. Palm trees that beckoned like graceful women. Shapes like giants loomed from the mist. Highlands rose above the sea. Cliffs of pink and sage green. The smell of the islands was earthy and spicy, and the sea was clear. You could look down and see bright fish swimming below, fronds of barbarous plants moving like slow music, long ridges of fantastic shapes and colours that thrust and pointed up to the ceiling of their sky, which was the surface of our sea.

We anchored in a harbour somewhere and the white man of those islands came down and spoke with Captain Proctor and Mr Rainey on the beach. Mr Comeragh was fluey and didn't go ashore. A hundred dark slave faces watched us from the forest fringes at the top of the beach. When Captain Proctor returned, he said there was sickness on the island and we would not be going ashore. Abel Roper, Martin Hannah and Joe Harper went down and loaded fresh water and coconuts, and we went on our way.

A day passed, two, three. Those seas turned me in and deeper in on myself, so little speech any of us seemed to have at that time. Islands came, islands went, suns rose and set, the ocean flowed on, and the sense of immensity returned in me, uncomfortable, an apprehension of something far beneath, beyond my grasp.

We reached a long shadow on the horizon, very far. Low-lying cloud, soft grey. Doves and ladies gloves and goose breasts.

'Land,' said Gabriel, leaning sharp sideways from the helm.

It came up like a soft roll of dustball, kitten fur. Cloud wall.

Land.

Long land. Miles and miles and miles of land, this way and that, long long miles of green jungle and a scattering of islands.

Proctor called us all once more upon the quarterdeck and said there were Malay pirates with spears in these seas, murderers, savages. 'Now,' he said in the big captain voice he kept for these occasions, 'we are truly far from our homes. These are dangerous seas.' He glared at us as if it was somehow our fault. 'Dangerous seas.'

'I'm scared,' whispered Tim in my ear.

Proctor said our normal course from here would take us straight up through the China seas. Good whale seas, the China seas. Good whaling, good sailing, all the way to the Japanese grounds. 'However,' he continued, 'as was explained to you all when you made your marks, we are also bound to fulfil a certain commitment to our ship's owner, Mr Malachi Fledge of Bristol.'

I was amazed. I'd never heard Fledge called anything but Fledge before.

'Mr Rymer. Would you say a word?'

Dan shambled forward. 'You all know,' he said gruffly, 'I'm charged with finding and taking alive an animal that may or may not live on some of the islands to the east of here. You know all about this.' He paused. 'I never knew anyone who saw this creature but I met a man in Surabaya, who told me he'd spoken to a Lamalera whale man, who'd seen something come out of a forest on an island out from Borneo.'

A showman at heart, Dan looked down and fiddled with his pipe.

'And there were remains,' he said softly. 'Two fishermen. Killed by something, and eaten.' He looked up. 'In any case, Mr Fledge has heard these things too.'

'These remains,' Mr Comeragh said in a thick voice, 'where

131

were they found?' His nose was so big you couldn't help but imagine he must have twice as much snot as normal people because of the size of that conk.

'On Rinca Island, Mr Comeragh,' Dan said, looking at him. 'On a beach. Rinca Island is not far from here, as you know.'

Comeragh raised his eyebrows and nodded.

'So that's where we go?' Mr Rainey asked.

'Not necessarily, Mr Rainey. Pulau Lomblen is where the man who saw it lived. We start there. To sniff the air. Then to – wherever seems wise.'

'We can get a boat at Pulau Lomblen,' the Captain remarked.

'You signed up as whale men,' Dan went on, 'not dragon hunters. Apart from me and my two boys, none of you will have anything to do with the animal. If the creature exists Tim and I will find it and drive it down to the shore, where the cage will be waiting.' He looked at me. 'Jaffy will make sure the creature goes in the cage and see that the door's made firm as soon as it's in.'

This was the first I'd heard of it.

'That sounds easy,' whispered Tim down my neck.

A big smile broke out on my face.

'None of you will approach the creature,' Dan continued, very serious. A terrible urge to laugh was stealing over me. 'You will be equipped with drums.'

'Drums?' whispered Tim. I snorted.

'And torches,' said Dan. 'You form lines and as soon as the creature appears you scream and shout and jump up and down, and bang whatever you can and wave your torches on all sides and drive the creature towards the cage. Tim and I will be right behind, driving it down the beach. You will close in on either side till it has nowhere to go but the cage, and if at any moment there appears to be any serious danger to any man, I shoot and kill. Understood?'

There was a solemn nodding and a murmur.

'I will not risk a man,' Dan said.

Captain Proctor stepped forward, smiling. 'I think we will need some training for this,' he said gamely.

'Of course.' Dan grinned. 'Though you're whale men, remember. If you can hunt a whale you can hunt anything.'

'Huh,' said Skip.

'What if it breathes fire?' a voice piped up.

It was Felix Duggan, his wide eyes looking truly scared. Everyone laughed.

'I don't think it will breathe fire,' Dan said, 'I truly don't. But if it does, I tell you what we do.' He looked very serious then burst out laughing. 'We run like hell!'

Everyone else laughed too.

'Don't worry,' Dan said, 'you'll hear us coming, pants on fire. In the boats and back to ship.'

'What if it flies?'

That was John Copper.

We all saw it, the mighty flying dragon, vast scaly wings, streams of fire blasting all to waste before it, scorching the earth. Flying after our ship. An eye in the sky.

'There are no credible reports that it flies,' said Dan.

It.

Dan said: 'We give it two weeks. Then on with the whaling with or without the beast. No one is obliged to take part in this. Anyone who really wishes to can stay with the ship.'

'Fairly spoken, Mr Rymer,' said the Captain. 'I for one look forward to the experience. If we do succeed it will be a great thing, a great thing indeed.'

'Chances are we won't find anything,' said Dan wryly. 'Chances are we'll poke about on a few islands and come back with nothing but a poll parrot.'

Captain Proctor chuckled. 'Now,' he said, 'to business.'

Business meant the Straits. We sailed on among the islands, and passed many small boats, any one of which could have been a pirate craft for all I knew. None were. How could you ever tell? The others, Gabriel and Sam and Yan and even John Copper just seemed to know. 'That,' they'd say, 'that's just a sampan.' As if it was obvious. As far as I was concerned, those faces looking up, they could have all been Yan's dad. I wouldn't know the difference between a pirate and Yan's dad. Then a great ship of the line loomed on the horizon, and a high mountain appeared on our larboard side. The ship passed us at a great distance, heading for the open ocean. Land closed in. The sea was fast and there were sandbanks, but we made no poor moves, and by late afternoon had passed the narrowest part of the passage and taken the eastern channel where an island divided the opening sea.

We emerged into an inner sea of islands, some no more than just rocks. The sun was setting. A thick forest of cloud lay motionless on the horizon, here and there throwing up foamy explosions of wild cumulus. Long ripples moved over the sea, and the orange rays of the sun radiated behind the clouds in the likeness of a flower spreading its petals. Then it sank, and all was red, dark blood red, and the sea black.

We awoke to a long blue coastline. For a long time we had only good sailing, and a kind of peace settled over the ship. I felt we had reached those storied places, the siren realms where mermaids sing and lotus-eaters gorge, where Sinbad the Sailor paces the deck and dreams of crystal streams and rubied caverns. I thought of islands that come and go, are found and not found again. Days and days went by, and I fell into a long delight. We took a whale now and then. For a while burnt flesh and boiling oil was thick about us, but we sailed on, out of the stench and into the wine-sweet air, a good draught of which was like apples and spices and flowers. A pod of dolphins joined us off an island of white sand and coconut palms, rode our bow wave joyfully for a mile or two, shiny backs breaching the air. They left us and took with them the time of stillness. After them the breezes got up in a jolly, whistling kind of way, and the waves began to rise against a mountainous region to starboard, breaking hugely over miles of shimmering strand that edged a dense green jungle, whence came, faintly but definitely carried on the occasional stillnesses between gusts, the sound of drumming. Slow, thoughtful in tone, like a single voice exploring its range, the drumming was all of a one with everything else. I was afraid of the drumming – the voice of a jungle through a growing thinness in the air, announcing mist.

The dolphins called the breeze called the drumming called the mist. That's how it felt.

That is how it has felt so many times. As if one thing led to another like notes in a tune.

The wind dropped completely and rain came down in a torrent, sudden as an upturned bucket. Thunder grumbled on the edge of the sky, an old dog growling in its sleep. I came down from the mast. Sheet lightning flashed over the jungle. All the world was grey and heaving, and we battened down and rode it. For three hours or more the rain pounded, but the storm was never overhead. It was on the other side of the long land mass. When the lightning flashed it was beautiful, silver echoes on a world washed out, on mast and spar and binnacle, on the great, thrown-out cloth of the sea.

It was evening by the time the rain had progressed from mad to sane. We hove to far out in the bay of what might have been the same island or another. Wilson Pride had made a nice stew of bacon and beans with dumplings, and we ate below because of the rain. I was on larboard watch and it was still raining when

I went to bed, but when I opened my eyes in the morning the daylight stealing in through chinks in timber was hot and white. On deck all was sun-leached, not a spot of moisture remaining. Captain Proctor was in conversation with his first mate by the aft companionway. Mr Rainey seemed bothered about something. You would have thought from his increasingly florid and extreme facial appearance that they were having words, but Captain Proctor was chuckling in an affable and amused way. He said something, and Rainey turned sharply and walked away.

Gabriel said later it was about a whaleboat. We had no spares and Rainey wanted to put in somewhere and get at least one new one as soon as possible. Rainey wanted to go back to Surabaya for one, but the captain said we'd come too far and would go straight on to Pulau Lomblen, where Dan Rymer hoped to find the Lamalera whale man who'd seen a creature walking out of a forest, the one of whom his Surabayan friend had spoken. Comeragh was for going back too, but Dan Rymer had said we could get a boat in Pulau Lomblen.

We couldn't. There were boats in Pulau Lomblen, but *we* couldn't get one. Still, we didn't know that then, so on we went and were at Pulau Lomblen three days later.

7

*O*h *Lord, please tell Billy Stock to stop frightening the little ones . . .*
In my head on waking, that old black man's voice, Sam.
Sam Proffit. Coming back through time, sudden, real, a
tic of the brain, time flying by, a blink – clear in my mind as if
he stood in the room. Just as he stood in the low fo'c's'le with his
hands together in prayer – then – but then is now – his eyes
closed, a small mischievous grin about his withered lips. A pious
old man, the changing light rippling over him, the walls dappled
and stippled grey. Oh the beauty of it—

It was dark and I was afloat on something, it could have been
the sea or waves of another kind, could have been anything.
Thick black waves of sleep bearing me up. At first I thought it
was *Drago*, our old *Drago*, and that I was lying at rest on the dry
boards and she'd gone sailing off along the Thames making for
the sea.

But she broke up a long time ago, *Drago*. *Here*'s where I live
now. A voice has awoken me again with the sounds of voices
on the street. There's a high singing somewhere near, maybe in
the alley that runs between Ratcliffe Highway and Pennington
Street, as drunkly beautiful as lost angels. Who is she, this singer,

siren of the cliff tops, throwing her silver voice sharp as knives through the thick black? This is where I live now and it does me well. There are smoky rooftops over which I can look, and above them a lovely northern sky that never burns. I love these rooftops dearly, so much so I sometimes find my eyes grow moist. London – how I dreamed of thee in the hot places. Flowers and fruit and wine and trees high, thin brown boys diving for pearls, great waves rushing in, and monkeys in the trees, long-limbed and thin of face, the fierce eyes of the big ones, the soft scared ones of their babies hanging on underneath. The blue light settling on the horizon. The colour of the edge of the world is . . .

. . . indigo.

It scintillates . . .

I am sailing like Sinbad on strange eastern seas and a big star is falling down the dark sky, and somewhere close the sirens are singing and here is Sam Proffit saying:

'Oh Lord, please tell Billy Stock to stop frightening the little ones.'

That raised a snigger because Billy was only my age, and we were nearly the youngest. Only Felix was younger than us. Billy was full of horrible stories about cannibals that sucked people's brains out while they were still alive.

Sam stands in the low fo'c's'le, a dappled man, a great singer of hymns and sayer of prayers. And we need our prayers tonight. Tomorrow we land on this new island. This is the one, we all feel it. It's something to do with the two Malay trackers Dan picked up on Sumba, where we heard the gongs and saw the smoke from a funeral pyre rising over the trees. We went to a village and drank a bitter drink, and there were birds everywhere, bright green flocks that shifted like turning wings against the deep blue sky. I lay back and watched, the brightness hurting my eyes. Birds should be free,

I thought. We waited for Dan to come back from wherever he'd gone off to with his enquiries, and he came back with red teeth and two friendly silent men, one who smiled, one who didn't. The one who smiled had blue symbols tattooed on his forehead. They sleep with us in the fo'c's'le but we share no language. Their demeanour has grown serious since we left the last island, the ninth or tenth, I don't know. The islands are wild. It's what I always wanted, the world, the wild, I'm looking it in the face as hard as I can. I want to walk up the slopes of a volcano and stare down its throat. It would be like staring into animal eyes. A volcano is dragonish. Why should there not also be a dragonish beast in these parts?

Dragonish people? There was a volcano looming like a living giant across the bay as we drew near Pulau Lomblen, and another watched over us when we talked to the whale men on the far side of the island, where the children left their games and ran past the boats lined up along the curving beach, to see the captain and the mates and Dan sitting in a circle with their loin-clothed fathers. And Tim and me too, honoured assistants of the big hunter. Even the captain was practically kowtowing to Dan by then, which was why we were on the beach and not sitting down to a good feed in the island's capital, where there was a Dominican church, and a kind of inn, and you could buy scrimshaw and get drunk and watch the pearl fishers returning in their boats. Sweat ran down my sides. Pretty faces, black eyes, the women, naked-breasted, lingering on the wooden platforms of their little straw-roofed stilt houses. One I will never forget came down and gave us milk out of a big green coconut shell, a girl of about twelve whose breasts were buds, whose hands were a child's with small pink pearls for nails. She stood waiting for the empty shell, holding my eyes for those few moments in calm contemplation. Her hair fell down straight on either side of her face and over her shoulders, thick and wiry to her waist. The wispy brows above her sleepy eyes were delicate smoky plumes, high gabled, upturned. Her nose was large and lovely, her lips overblown. I fell in love with her at once. Yes, yes, I will be a whale man here, I thought, take out the boats and bring back glory. Return to her at night. The world is full of wonder. And smell no more the herb man's bower on Rosemary Lane and see no more the peeling posters plastered on the walls outside Paddy's Goose.

Wonderful that Dan could talk to these people. Only he could, in whatever language it was he used, God knows I heard English and Portuguese, even Latin in that jumble, all mixed in with the native lingo. But they seemed to understand, and flung the talk back and forth and around.

'Oh Lord,' said Sam, 'give us a good day tomorrow.'

We stood with heads bowed, hands together like obedient children.

'Oh Lord, thank you for good weather.'

'Amen,' we mumbled.

Then we had the Lord's Prayer – '. . . deliver us from evil . . .' – hanging our heads and thinking about cannibals and swamps and monsters awaiting us tomorrow. Billy had never shut up since we'd left Pulau Lomblen. You'd never get him on shore round these parts in a million years, he said, and Joe Harper agreed. There were tribes on these islands that thought no more of eating a person than they did of a chicken or a fish, they said, and when Tim said Dan knew his stuff and wouldn't see us wrong, they asked how did *he* know? Did Dan know every single island? Did he? And if there was supposed to be some dragon thing that no one had ever even seen on this particular one, it was going to be a wild island, wasn't it? One no one knew about. You could have anything on an island like that.

To look into the eyes of a cannibal. I turned away from the thought, but a fear crept in and peered over my shoulder.

'Was cannibals once,' Gabriel said, 'but no more, not here-abouts. Not till you get to the Southern Sea.'

'Aha!' said Bill. 'See! If there was once, then there still is. They don't *change*. It's in their nature.'

'Like dogs, you mean,' said John Copper, 'can go on nice and sweet for years then suddenly . . .' baring his teeth.

'That's exactly it,' said Bill,

Gabriel, his long legs hanging naked over the edge of his bunk, the brown skin yellow where he kept scratching his shins. His gaze sliding sideways and his big lower lip hanging loose, pink inside. 'I saw a terrible thing once that made me think,' he said. 'I saw a snake eat a dog. A small dog, though whether it was a pup or not I couldn't say. It swallowed the poor thing whole, but it took a long time and the head was the last to go. And the poor thing was crying out at first, but by the end it had given all that up and it was like someone who cries silently.'

We were all quiet. He looked around, big-eyed.

'You know, when someone is crying but not making any sound. Shaking with it, and its eyes closed tight and its mouth drawn back. That poor dog has stayed with me.'

Another silence.

'Why didn't you stop it?' John Copper sounded angry.

'John,' Gabriel said, 'why do you think? For fear of the snake. It was a monster. And it held the poor dog in its coils to keep it, what could we do?'

'Where was this?' asked Tim.

Gabriel thought for a moment. 'On an island. Not here. Out in the Southern Sea.'

The Southern Sea was beginning to sound to me like a very bad place.

'You could have stopped it,' John persisted, 'you could have done something.'

Gabriel shook his head. 'No. There were three of us, you see, and one was our captain, Lovelace, and he told us not to. You didn't go against Lovelace.'

'If I ever meet Captain Lovelace,' said John, 'I'll kick his face off for him.'

'How long did it take?' I asked.

'Too long.'

'How long?'

'Oh, much too long, little Jaf.'

I hated being patronised.

'Dogs don't cry,' said Billy Stock.

'Yes, they do,' said Skip very quickly.

'Took about five minutes,' said Gabriel.

'And you just stood there and watched it?'

'Yes. Lovelace was very interested to see it. We all had to stay very still and quiet. It was strange. Made us all feel strange. Stayed with me.'

John Copper started to cry. He was furious. Lay down and thumped his mattress. 'I hate it,' he said.

'Hate what, son?'

'I don't know. Just hate it.'

We'd seen so many islands, some no bigger than a rock, others meandering along for miles with mountains rise on rise, and mangroves that seemed to walk on the water's edge with their rooted limbs raised delicately like a lady's tea finger. Coconut palms, blue sky, puffy clouds, pale green rocks, bald heights, lush lows, on we sailed. We went ashore on four or five. We took on bananas and big green fruits. The two Malays and Dan would talk their funny pidgin talk and off we'd go a-hunting, all of us hanging around the beaches while Dan and Tim and the Malays got all the fun, heading off with serious intent up some bird-haunted green slash in the land, with the Malays going before, examining the ground as if it bore gold. Hours later they'd emerge from the forest with maybe a wild pig or two, and once, the still steaming quarters of a buffalo they'd skinned and butchered on the high plain.

But no dragons.

Not a single little tiny dragon even, not a sign, not a footprint on any of those wild sweeps of sand, not a glimpse of a some-thing through the thick clusters of vegetation. No weird, unearthly calling in the night.

We all spoke as if the thing didn't exist. But before I slept, sometimes I'd think about the beast and wonder why it was that I could not get it out of my mind, how it had come to hover over me with scaly wings that grew ever more devilish with every passing day. And suddenly, that night, the night before, I was very afraid. Those Malays, they knew something. They took a boat yesterday morning, and poked about on the shore and in the fringes of the forest for no more than an hour, and when they came back they were changed.

All of us felt it, but no one said it. This was the island. Neither big nor small, rocky green, high mountains of harsh brush jutting the sky above jungle and weeping bays. Its seas were fast and rough, as if it didn't want to be reached, and it terrified me. The gongs of Sumba played in my head as I lay thinking in the night; they'd been playing in my head ever since we'd left that place, their low droning somnolence sending out into the darkness long sound ribbons that scarcely vibrated but changed constantly in some shimmering way, simple as silk. The music was like a snake swallowing its tail, a lullaby that repeats and repeats, softening and sharpening your senses at the same time, like a drug. My mouth was dry with fear and my throat clenched when I swallowed, and I fell into a gloom so profound it was like a sudden nausea.

143

I kept thinking about that poor dog getting eaten by a snake while it was still alive and knew what was happening. I kept seeing its silently crying mouth as it was crushed and ingested, and I thought about the god that could conceive of such an entrance into death, and felt cold and hurt and scared more than I had ever been. And when at last I fell asleep, it was into a terrible nightmare, the kind that wakes you in a pounding-heart sweat and leaves you shaken out and horrified by the contents of your head. There was a big tank full of blood in a dark attic room, parts of bodies moving about in it, swimming around each other like eels; and there, right in the middle of it was a man's face, full of horror – oh, the horror, it's what woke me – a real, whole man desperately trying to swim out but with no chance at all. An arm came up out of the gore and a spread hand, coated in thick clots, pushed his face down under, and I woke in the creaking fo'c's'le and wasn't sure if I'd screamed or not. But no, it seemed I hadn't.

I was hot. This filthy heat going on and on. God, I was shaking. Nothing had scared me this much since I got stuck in the dark in Jamrach's shop when Tim locked me in. There he lay across from me, breathing the sweet sleep of unconcern. Bastard, doing that to me. A two-edged blade, our Tim. You should have seen him since he'd been going off all cocky with Dan and the Malays, coming back with feathers stuck behind his ears and a band round his head. Beautiful, he was. Brown as a native with his eyes bright baby blue and clear, and his hair all goldy-white, stalking back from the jungle like a dirty sweaty Apollo, buffalo blood under his nails, a head taller now than Dan, sage old simian by whose side he walked. Doesn't say much.

Why should he be sleeping so sweetly there and me awake? He needed his sleep of course, with what he had to do.

'Tim,' I whispered.

'What?' he replied at once. He wasn't asleep.

144

'Are you awake?'

'No.'

'I had a horrible dream.'

'Never mind, Jaf,' he said, 'it's only a dream. Only in your head.'

I thought about this for a moment. It gave me an invaded feeling. 'How did something like that get in my head?' I asked, as if it was an earwig that had crawled into my ear.

'Like what?'

We were whispering so as not to wake the others snoring softly around us.

'I don't think I want to talk about it just now,' I replied after a moment. 'In the night and all. Tomorrow maybe.'

'Suit yourself.' He yawned mightily.

'*Some* dreams . . .' I said after another moment.

'I know.'

We drifted separately.

'I'm scared, Tim,' I said.

A pause. He knew I didn't mean just the dream.

'So am I,' he said, and reached out and squeezed my shoulder briefly. 'Silly old Jaf.' He gave me a small push.

'Do you ever think of home?' I asked.

He thought. 'Of course I do.'

'You don't seem to. You never mention it.'

'Well, neither do you.'

'S'pose not.'

A longer pause, then, 'Everyone thinks of home,' he said, 'but it doesn't do to be rambling on about it all the time.'

'Like Dan.'

It was true. Dan in his cups, sentimental, cloudy eyed, toasting Alice, recalling the first smiles of his last born.

'True. But that's Dan.'

'If he's so wild about home and hearth,' I wondered, 'why's he follow a trade like this?'

Tim snorted softly. 'She wouldn't seem as sweet perhaps if he was with her all the time.'

'Remember sarsaparilla?' I said. 'From the herb man?'

'Ah! What would I give for a lovely cold cup of sarsaparilla! Remember the smell.'

So clear, a lattice of herbs above the herb man's stall, rosemary, camomile, milky feverfew.

'Saturday night at Spoony's,' Tim said.

Push through a swing door into clouds of smoke and laughter, cut some hard and smoke it with a bottle of wine till your head gets tipsy and you jaunt down the narrow passage in the dim gaslight, and duck under the chintz into the dancing place all a-thunder with feet. Girls with ruby lips and bouncing bubs, merchant sailors, caps awry. The piper with his wild elbows, steel heels a-flying. A gold watch hangs askew above the mantel.

'Yeah,' said Tim, 'home sweet home. You still scared?'

'Yes.'

'S'all right,' he said. 'Here, give us your hand.'

I held mine out and he took it. 'You know,' he said, 'when I go home I'll be the man of the family.'

After that there was no more talking. I thought about Ishbel and her mother in that house together, and wondered how they were managing. She'd hate it. Her mother drove her mad. I suppose they wouldn't miss the old man so much, those mermaids never brought in much, but they'd be glad when Tim was back. I could see her, sitting by the fire gnawing moodily at her terrible nails. What was she doing? Someone would have her, good-looking girl like that. Out she'd be, with some beau, some sailor. I wouldn't think about it.

Tim's hand slid out of mine when he fell asleep. As for me, I got not a wink till the seventh bell and by that time it was hardly worth it.

We rowed in through house-high rocks covered in barbarous plants like halted green explosions. A river ran down from a high forested ravine, skirting one edge of a sheltered beach, horseshoe-shaped, fringed with creamy-blossomed trees and split about the other edge by a long spur of dark pink rock. Beyond, upland and inland, tier on tier, slender shock-headed palms leaned elegantly one way, as if about to pull themselves up from the earth and set off on some sweeping migration. On either side of the bay, tall crags rose up.

There we were wandering about on the beach like great fools, waiting with sticks against the dragon. The sand was damp and flat and rippled, scattered with rocks here and there, and the sky was grey and cold looking, but I was running with sweat. The heat seemed to come from within as well as without, as if my organs were slowly cooking in the oven of my flesh. Out in the bay were three or four islands, rounded tumps of shaggy green. The cage was placed at the narrowest part of the beach. If ever a place was dragonish, this was. The arms of the bay sprawled out to sea, long reptilian forms lying half submerged, dark grey, black, elongated piglike snouts ready to snap. The scaly muddy-pink spur that Dan said was a lava flow down the beach could have been the long claw of a giant foot. Here and there the rock looked pulpy and squelchy, as if a giant had been playing with clay. Everywhere you looked there were faces in it. And the tracks were plain, over by the river, one single trail of eerie hand-like tracks, clawed. The size of big dinner plates.

A peculiar red-spotted crab scuttled by my foot. Felix was collecting big white curly shells and stacking them up by the boats. Next to the cage, Martin and Abel and Dag were splitting wood, making stakes. Waves, white-tipped, came coursing in. The edges of the beach where it joined the forest were strewn with fallen debris. I wandered about looking at things with my telescope, red and blue birds in the trees, the rocks at sea, the ravine, till I strayed too close to the trees and was suddenly scared, looking into the pale, fluttering green within. The trunks of the trees were silver streaks. The silent echo of something infinitely denser and darker brooded deeper in, a hollow howling like a throat.

I heard voices.

The hunting party had only been gone a couple of hours and here they were coming back already.

Everything about this landing was different from the others. They were excited, there was something in their faces. There were more tracks, they said, on higher ground. Need more stakes, more rope. A lot of rope. The plan was changed. We'd stay here a day or two, set up rough camp on the beach. 'We four,' Dan said, 'we'll trap it on the high ground and bring it down. But we need more manpower. Three more.' He looked at me and smiled kindly. 'Now's your chance, Jaf, if you still want it.'

'I do,' I said, and that was when the voice that watched in my head piped up: You're mad, you're mad, you don't have to go. You never had to go. Stay here, you fool. Play faro with Billy Stock on deck. No one cares whether you go or not.

'Go on, Jaf,' Tim said, 'it's a great thing being out there. You've got to come.' He touched my arm. 'Come with us, Jaf,' he said, and his eyes were almost pleading with me to go and keep him company.

I laughed. 'You try and stop me,' I said.

'Good.' Dan clapped his hands. 'So – who else is for it?'

'Me,' said John Copper, 'me.'

And Dag Aarnasson.

*

148

A massive millipede rippled across our path, a vile red thing like a nerve. The trees were full of bright birds.

Anything might be poisonous in a place like this. They might drop on you from above, scrabbling down your neck. Scorpions. Spiders with teeth. Who knows what's up there? We walked silently, single file, with the Malays going ahead and Dan in the rear. I was glad of him back there, glad of how unconcerned he seemed, gladder still when we came out above the forest onto a grassy, rocky place with scarcely a tree. But then I began to think about snakes in the long grass, and my fingers kept carressing the handle of the shooter slung against my hip. What good would that be against a snake? You wouldn't see it till it was too late.

Dan called a halt. He said we should go east. He said he was going to rope the dragon. He said there was no longer any doubt that it was there, and we were going to take one alive. It sounded ridiculous. Rope a dragon? John laughed nervously. Dag's face was a weird flat jutty thing with staring blue eyes. 'I don't understand,' he said in that slow heavy way of his.

'Ach,' said Dan, 'don't worry about it. Me and these boys here will see to all that. You just keep back and do as you're told, and we'll all be fine. You come in at the end with the rest of the rope when it's safe, and help us get it on the hurdle.'

'What hurdle?' I asked.

'The one we haven't made yet,' he said. 'One thing at a time. First we find a place to lay the bait.'

'What bait?'

'You, Jaf,' he said, rolling his eyes. 'Why do you think I brought you along?' He laughed and pushed my head. 'We don't have the bait yet either. One thing at a time. First find the place, then kill the bait.'

We walked for the rest of that day up and down rolling swells of savannah, along animal tracks, well used by who knows what.

Dag and I walked side by side. Donkeys, I thought, that's us. Native bearers. All right for him, the size of him like an ox, but it was hell for me. Sweat ran into my eyes. My shoulders burned from the weight of my pack, and the stakes I carried rubbed them raw. Dan and Tim and the Malays were less heavily burdened, them being protectors and great hunters, weapon-bearers, trackers. Tim looked back and laughed at us, me so small and dark and Dag so big and fair. I never really knew Dag before this. He was about twenty, a quiet man with a gentle, watchful air, and as he was easy-going, he made a good travelling companion.

'Is it cold where you come from?' I asked him as the heat cooked me.

He grinned. 'Very cold in winter. Snow to here.' He motioned above his head.

I whistled. 'How do you bear the heat?'

'At first,' he said, adjusting the coil of rope upon his shoulder, 'it was difficult. But I . . .' – he made impatient winding motions with his finger and I saw that his nails were seriously bitten, almost as bad as Ishbel's – 'I . . . I got used to it.'

'Perhaps I should have gone north,' I said, wiping sweat from my brow with my filthy palm. 'To the ice. See polar bears. Eskimos.'

He smiled. 'We want what we don't have. I could not wait to see the palm trees. I saw pictures in my father's books.' His smile was big and completely semi-circular, brightening his large square face. It seemed to me exotic that a father should have books. I got a picture in my head of a gent in a black suit of clothes like a country vicar.

'Your father had books?'

'About the places he's been. *He* was a sailor too. And my brothers. I have three.'

Dan turned and glared at us. He was going on ahead now with the Malays, and John and Tim were bringing up the rear. We shut up and plodded on.

'Do you have Eskimos where you live?' I asked an hour later. I would have said it was late afternoon, but it was hard to tell from the sky, which was still sullen though the rain had not materialised.

'Not where I live,' he replied. 'They live in Greenland. And Canada. And other places. No, we have the Lapps.'

'What are the Lapps like?'

'They are northern people,' he said. 'They keep reindeer.'

It was funny walking along in that hot place talking about the far north. How beautiful those icy regions seemed to me. I imagined the deck of a ship all briny with frost, ice sharp as an arrow, tincture of emerald, tincture of blue. A frozen ocean, magnificently still and serene.

Ahead, the Malay with the tattoo held up his hand and everyone froze.

How long we did not move I don't know. Everything became very clear, every blade of grass. When I swallowed, my throat creaked. Dan motioned us cautiously forward with his hand without even looking back. We crept. And when we were gathered—

Sudden, so my heart jumped up like a man started from sleep by a bell – bolt upright, stab! – then the hammering as of a demented woodpecker . . . a deer, leaping across the path ahead of us. One instant, a graceful prancing arc, and it was gone into the long grass.

We stood staring and waiting. The silence roared. Then we followed the Malays' stalking feet, step by wary step, a distance of no more than a few yards before we stopped again, brought up short by a stink like a blocked privy.

151

The grass sang.

Something huge and dark came out of the scrub twenty yards or so ahead of us, running very fast on four bow legs. It plunged into the high savannah in the direction the deer had gone. Time speeded up. We moved forward at a good pace, and all I knew was the high grasses on either side of me whispering at our passage, and the back of Dan's head, and my shoulders hurting and my breath beginning to scrape a little. A good hour of it till we slowed down and closed ranks again close by the edge of some kind of rocky escarpment. There could be no more talking. We'd come so far now into the island that I'd lost all sense of scale and direction, and had no idea which way the ship was or how far away, no idea whether the rock face to our right was the height of two tall men or as high as a mountain. The quick black shadow had scuttled before my eyes a million times as we walked. How many more of those things were out there, hiding in the heavy brush, watching with hard reptilian eyes? I was never more afraid but never so brightly aware. I felt as if my eyes were wide and over bright, and the others looked the same. Even the Malays, whom I'd considered knowing and unshakeable and well-nigh invulnerable, all but shimmered with an unhinged energy. I'd faced the great whales, but they were known.

And now a dumb show began. Our blood was up. We were in the wild, and the wild has teeth and claws and eyes and a stink like the rotting of a day-old carcass. I saw only a dark living bulk of great size, four bandy legs running. So fast. Dan and the Malays talked with their hands and shoulders and eyes. I wanted to be Dan. I wanted his gift for roaming the world talking to everyone he met. I wanted his ease in outlandish places and the way he never seemed afraid. I wanted the fear that moved in my belly to transmute into serenity. The smaller of the two Malays spotted blood. Something is leaving a trail. He moved his forearm in such a way, how he did it I don't know, he made it look like a deer. Palm towards us, keeping us back, he went forward. For a while he stood absolutely motionless looking through the thinning bush, then beckoned us cautiously on.

We came like ghosts. I saw the deer first, through the high grass. She was far away on the side of a long balding slope, near dead, her blood trail following her faithfully not quite to the shadow of the rock to which she'd dragged herself. She'd collapsed in the dust. A stain of blood widened about her and she was trying, hopelessly but doggedly, to raise her head up sideways. Then I saw the dragon, just above and beyond us, completely still on a low wrinkle of land overlooking the plain, no more than a deck's length from me. A huge, brownish-grey thing with black head and legs, bigger than a tiger, longer and lower but raising its powerful chest and head as high at the front and trailing behind it a mighty weapon of a tail.

It was magnificent. Its feet were like giant hands, splayed and slightly inturned, knobbly and wavy and tipped by long black claws that curved like sickles – a kind of a lizard obviously, but like nothing I'd ever seen. We'd had geckos and chameleons and iguanas at Jamrach's, even a Gila monster once, but they were nothing compared to this. The size of it! That chest, the muscles in those arms, the skin like ancient armour, scaly and notched and scarred like the ears of an old tom cat, yet loose and wrinkled, hanging in baggy swathes under its belly and throat. Its closed mouth was like a crocodile's, a crooked line that meandered along its lower jaw. A slick tongue darted out and in, forked and yellow.

It began to sway its head a little, slowly, snakeish, side to side. How long did we watch? Minutes.

After a while it looked towards us, but not, I think, at us. It had a broad and slab-like face with large nostrils and cold, overhung eyes set very wide on either side of its head. A sour, displeased face. Its jaws opened and I saw crocodile teeth. Then it turned its face away and moved forward, showing none of the speed we had seen before, but walking ponderously as if feeling its weight. Slowly, it slid down the short incline and lumbered on across the broad plane towards the deer, head now low to the ground, snake-like with its darting tongue and questing, forward movement. Its departure caused us to relax, but the Malay tensed every muscle and warned us with one chopped movement to keep still. We watched the dragon amble about in a vague sort of way for several moments. Clearly it was not interested in finishing off the poor deer, not yet. We watched till the creature was no more than a pointed tail disappearing into the scrubland beyond the clearing.

The Malay turned and motioned that we make a slow and silent retreat, and back we went as we had come till we were once more at the great rock face.

'The size of it, Jesus Christ the size of it,' John Copper said.

Dan showed nothing. Just a mysterious smile.

'Why didn't we go after it?' I asked.

'Ill prepared,' said Dan. 'No hurry. Now we know what we're up against.'

He went a small way apart with the Malays for a parley. There was an air of tense celebration, a burst of quick laughter among them.

'Jesus Christ,' said John again. 'Got any blunt on you, Jaf?'

We four – me and Tim, Dag and John – sat down and lit a couple of pipes.

'That's it, all right,' Tim said. 'Fucking monster.'

'It's not a dragon,' I said. 'It's like he always said. A big croc-odile.'

'Big though.'

'Still, not a monster.'

'I never saw anything like it. It's like—'

'Ugly, horrible-looking thing. Did you see those claws?'

'And the teeth?'

'Jesus, how we going to—'

'Slow though. Not nifty.'

'Didn't you see it run? Before? Back on the path. Didn't you see that?'

'It shifted, all right.'

'It's only an animal,' I said.

'What were you expecting? Saint George and some girl tied to a rock? Of course it's only an animal.'

'It's just a wild animal. We can catch it. Dan's caught a tiger, he can catch this.'

'That's what he does, he brings them back alive.'

Dan came tramping over and told us we were camping here for the night, and tomorrow we'd move on a little further and find a place to set the trap. Here? With those things roaming about? Come tomorrow all there'd be left of us would be our packs, lying forlornly among our scattered bones. But Dan said, no, here was fine, we'd light a fire and set a watch, and so we did, and it was in fact quite comfy and sweet the way we all sat round that warm glow of a fire in the midst of the dense black wild all about us. Dan passed around a small flask of brandy and we drank and smoked our pipes, and the Malay with blue tattoos told what sounded like jokes in his own language and made us all laugh even though we didn't understand a word. It was just his face and the way he talked. And in the end I slept well, waking only when the others were already moving around and the sudden morning light was about to break.

We ate a little hardtack, packed up and moved on. I thought we would have made the trap soon, but Dan was in no hurry. That fierce-looking beast and everything that happened last night seemed a dream as we plodded on and on, the sun rising higher and higher and hotter and hotter, the clouds clearing above some high ground ahead. In front of us a baldy crag rose up, and water came down the face of a rock, splitting round a jutting spur of jungly growth much further down. We were walking into a lusher part of the island, at least in these low places. Low, I say. I had forgotten how high we'd climbed from the beach. Up here the air was sharp and ripe like a bursting plum. Why didn't we set the trap? I didn't like this, walking on into a territory of good cover. As well as the long grass in which any low thing might lurk unseen, we now had a growing shrubbery on our left-hand side, a patchy place of scattered bushy clumps, behind any one of which a dragon might lurk, two dragons, three, who knows, there could be a dozen of the things out there. Why not lay the trap now? Wasn't one place pretty much as good as another? But no, not so, says Dan, God knows why. What good if we're all exhausted when we have to face it? So on and on, till we sensed a foulness on the air and came to an edge no one expected and looked over and saw . . .

A mess of them like eels slipping wormily over one another in a muddy tussle over a foul carcass, a red and pink rag trailing festoons, the grinning head of which, half severed and hanging back, revealed it to be one of their own. Another watching, a huge thing, solid and impassive as a rock, huge, trunk-like legs planted before it. Yet one more, smaller, flicking its flat forked tongue as it slowly crawled away, full. Six, seven, eight, nine, ten dragons, I don't know. They were messy feeders, worse than sharks, drooling as they ate, dragging and shaking and ripping, snapping greedily, lifting their great gulping throats to swallow. At some point the big one at the side began swinging its head heavily from side to side, then waded in like a burly bully of a drunk and soon was pigging it with all the rest. Such weary majesty this one had, and so much bigger was it than all the rest, that it very quickly became centre of the scene, with all the others writhing around it respectfully while scarcely touching it. So it was able to eat more or less undisturbed, taking huge bites with wide-open mouth – the size of it, the way its jaws stretched horribly wide, snake-like, the way a shining pink membrane of blood-hued saliva stretched between upper and lower jaw, and more dripped down from between its sharp little razor teeth. It stopped after a while, closed its mouth and raised its head, turning a little sideways in our direction, darting its tongue. We'd taken cover, but I swear it looked at me. Straight at me with a demon bright red grin. Gave me the chills. There are worlds between the animals of Jamrach's and the animals of the wild, worlds between a croc in an enclosure and a dragon free. I'd been nearer to wild animals thousands of times, but here there were no barriers. This was real fierce beasts in the real wild and nothing between me and them. A cold gush of fear pierced through me, starting somewhere deep in my belly like sickness, and invading all of me, right down to the extremities within a second or two. I thought the monster would come leaping up the cliff face to eat me as it was eating the dragon carcass, which was now scarcely more than a few ribs and some savaged hide. But instead it closed its mouth once more and returned to the last leisurely pickings with an air of boredom.

We watched till there was nothing left. They downed the lot, bones and all, and one by one moved heavily away into the scrub, all apart from one that headed off up the straight side of the cliff face opposite, like a gecko up a pane of glass, climbing quickly and gracefully with its huge curved claws outspread.

It gave me a fright to see it climb like that. Imagine climbing, chased, slipping, sweating.

'See that,' Dan said, when we had drawn back from the rocky edge and regrouped. 'It could climb a tree easy, I'd say.'

157

'No need to sound so fucking cheerful about it,' said John Copper. 'I'm shitting myself here.'

'We all are, John,' said Dag, and slung an arm about his neck roughly for a second. 'Aren't we?' he appealed to the rest of us.

I nodded vigorously. Tim said nothing.

Dan became serious. 'Listen,' he said, 'I didn't bring you out here as lizard food. What's the matter with you all? This is a hunt, it's no different from going after a whale. You do as you're told and no one comes to any harm. Look,' he took out his gun and pointed it at the sky, he smiled, 'you're all armed. Any doubt at all and you shoot. No second thoughts. I won't let any one of you be harmed, so stop whining.'

'But there's so many of them!' John wailed.

'So there are,' said Dan. 'That's good.'

'Good,' echoed Dag, and a huge grin spread madly across his face.

'Yes,' repeated Dan, with emphasis. 'That is good. I know what to do now. Now I know what to do.'

Dan killed a boar. We trailed its bloody carcass a mile or more till we came to a place where the trees thickened. Here he set us to making a hide and banging in stakes in a ring, weaving them round with rope lashed fast. The smaller of the Malays, deft as a squirrel, shinned up a tree with another rope in his mouth. At the top he held on with the strength of his legs, tying the rope with his hands before sliding back down to join us, hauling down the sappy branches. They spread like a sheltering fan over the trap. We hacked clear a doorway wide enough for the thing to get in, and Dan set up a rope contraption that went round the doorway and back to the hide. So we watched and waited, taking shifts.

We waited half a day and the sun went down. We moved from the hide and set up a camp not far away, lit a fire again, but there

158

were no jokes tonight. Dan said we had to keep quiet. We were in no danger, he said. If it comes, it smells the bait and goes for that. We'd hear it if the trap was sprung, believe me. Oh, believe me, he said. No fears, lads. I've done this a million times. So we sat around whispering to one another and chewing hardtack and thinking of the others down on the beach gorging on meat, and wondered if they were wondering about us, where we were and if anything terrible had befallen us. My belly was getting sore. When it was my turn to lie down I didn't sleep, just drifted into a peculiar place in which the island had become a vast ship sailing on through hot darkness, and I twitched and murmured till it was growing light again.

In the fading dawn, the island birds whistled and chattered and carked in the forest beneath us. Blue Tattoo had gone scouting. The smaller Malay sat cross-legged, picking sleep out of the corners of his eyes with patient zeal. I went out for a pee and saw how dark the sea was on the horizon. Indigo. You could see islands from here. And how still it all was, just for a moment, till I was joined by Tim.

'Shouldn't come out on your own,' he said, peeing beside me.

So the morning rolled on as the day before, waiting, watching, seeing centipedes the size of worms come out of the rough thatch of the hide, thinking of the crawly bodies in the mud like a bunch of maggots at a bit of liver. Nasty things. Muddy things. The dragons of stories were beautiful, flying the sky wonderfully winged, deadly but magnificent. But these – these were massively ugly, with a brutal, careless power more nightmare than fairy tale. Their eyes lacked anything a human could comprehend. More so than a whale, more so than a snake, more so than a frog. That one had looked at me. I was sure it had. It looked at me and it was like being seen by a demon.

Blue Tattoo, our silent scout, came silently beckoning, two hours after sunrise. 'Dragon,' he said, the first English word I'd heard him speak. Dan, pulling up his breeches as he emerged from the bushes, nodded once sharply. You'd have thought he was just strolling back from the privy. The rest of us went in twos, having a horror of being disturbed in the middle of a shit by a big scaly head with evil teeth emerging from the undergrowth. It was hard to go, even with Dag keeping watch and saying 'sure, no dragons' in a hearty whisper every twenty seconds. Dan was mad though. Maybe you had to be mad to prosper in his line of work. Mad or stupid or in possession of a sixth sense; all three perhaps.

'So, lads,' he said, calm as can be, 'this may be the one', and set off with a worried-looking Tim in tow. I knew Tim was worried not because he showed it but because he'd gone very quiet and was keeping away from everyone as much as possible, apart from Dan, with whom I was vaguely aware he'd been going off into little huddled conferences all night long.

Stealthy as cats, licking our lips and squaring up bravely, the rest of us followed.

The hide was cool and green, out of the sun, tamped down flat from the watches. Through the overhanging leaves we saw the dragon edging along the fringe of grassland, then striking across open scrub towards the trees. It was a big beast, mightily draped in skin, a syrupy drool dripping from its closed jaws. It had seen the boar, or at least smelled it. I could hear the buzzing of lively early morning flies from here. The dragon approached steadily, with purpose. There was something of the elephant in the stolid girth of its legs. A few feet away from the trap it stopped, one foot slightly in front of the other. So close. So big. The brows hung over, the small still eyes not dead, but full of a sharp alien consciousness. It looked straight at the hide and us.

And so, a frozen moment that went on and on, long enough for a million itches to come and go and for the long red crawlers to wrap themselves unimpeded round your cringing shanks like the worms of Thames mud. Long enough for us to note the curved cruelty of the creature's claws, the slippery roundedness of the snaky tongue, the sheer mass and bulk and power of the thing. It would be like tackling a rhinoceros.

Half an hour it stood, ineffable. Then everything happened very fast.

It turned once more to the buzzing meat and nodded slowly once or twice, raising itself high, then charged. Dan let go the trigger, the tree sprang up, the rope pulled tight round the dragon's belly and it went mad. It was supposed to go all the way in the trap but it had got caught half in and half out of the doorway, and it kicked and bucked and twisted there like a salted slug, snapping dementedly and hammering the earth. A thick purplish-brown clag of half-digested slime spewed from its jaws. They were out the side of the hide, Dan and Tim and the two Malays, but they couldn't get near. The stakes were cracked and bending, the dragon sliding in its vomit, rolling in it, the four of them stalking it round, keeping back. The tail beat like the flukes of a whale and made thunder, the long sharp claws clenched wildly at anything within reach. It was a killer, and it was furious and terrified.

It broke free, the rope round its middle trailing a long sliver of wood the size of a broom.

Dan had been right to choose Tim for the hunt. He was just where he needed to be and he was calm, or at least he *seemed* calm. Is that bravery? I don't know if he was brave or just in a trance. He got scared, I knew. Maybe he was now, but if so, he'd put the fear away in some other part of himself that didn't show. Not to anyone else anyway, but to me because I'd known him so long. Those veiled yet humorous eyes, self-conscious. That set mouth. He had the fear certainly, but he wasn't going to break.

Me, I might have run. I might have jumped the wrong way at the wrong moment. So might he, but it wouldn't be because his nerve failed. I was proud. Our Tim, Ratcliffe Highway Tim, a golden brave in a hunt. He was all sure movement, manlike. They all were, the Malays lithe and nearly naked, Dan, who was not elegant, but a hard hunched little knot of a man, suddenly graceful and skilled as a dancer, stepping forward with the rope made into a noose and throwing it resolutely at the creature's head.

It missed and he dragged it back and had it recoiled and rethrown in a second. It missed again, and again. The dragon frothed, convulsing, voiding itself from both ends and soaking the ground with sudden spurting shoots of piss. He got it with the fifth throw. The rope dropped magically over its head during an upward thrust, pure luck or genius I'll never know. Dan was sweating and red in the face. He stepped back, throwing the end of the rope to Tim and immediately swinging another coil down from his shoulder and getting ready to throw again. Tim hauled off and tied his end to a tree, his lips moving as if he was singing or praying and his eyes glazed.

The whole thing took only a few minutes, I suppose. We came from the hide when Dan called us, when the monster, still furiously kicking and heaving, was secured to the trees by three strong ropes, one at each end and one in the middle. Nine or ten foot long, that thing was, and stinking to high heaven. I sometimes think my life has been overfull of stench. The creature was caked in its own shit and piss and vomit, and the carcass of the boar was beginning to stink too. The air of this place was now thick and hot with a smell that made me think of Bermondsey pure sellers, their hallways full of buckets of compacting dog shit for the tanner's gate. It was the kind of smell that makes walls cringe and plants curl and die.

They cut the stake away. All of us helped now. My heart was hammering like mad, my cheeks were burning and I felt funny, as if I was coming down with a fever. Our faces were wild and tight and surprised, and we laughed at one another amazedly. Dan quieted us. The Malays were laughing too, and a sense of suppressed carnival seized us. Dag, the strong one, hacked down a young tree to which we tied the creature – I could not call it a dragon seeing it like this, not a dragon, it never was – swaddling it very securely like a terrible mad baby so it couldn't struggle too much and damage itself. All of us got covered in its filth. It was a giant reptile with a dreadful head all coated with its own slime. It struggled all the time, a frantic pounding panic it could do nothing to control. It was possessed. If it got loose it would rip us all limb from limb.

It took all of us to carry it. We'd been out for two days, but for part of that time we'd backtracked. It took us a day to reach the ship, going downhill all the way. The animal struggled nearly all the way, only falling quiet from exhaustion from time to time just long enough to get the strength back to kick a leg, twitch a few muscles, clatter its jaws, jerk like a landed fish, flop and gape and shudder.

Dan walked alongside me and told me how me and him were going to put the dragon in the cage. We had to go in quick while it was in a daze, he said, and take the ropes off the head and tail. The one round its middle would stay for the time being.

'Here's what I think, Jaf,' he said. 'I think we put him in head first, then I go in and take his head while you get the tail. Think you can do that?'

'Have a go,' I said.

'Listen,' he said, 'the tail's no less dangerous than the head, fact it's probably worse, it's got a life of its own and no intelligence. Think of it like a big pulse that might throb at any second.

All the power's in the tail. Get in and out fast and be ready for anything. Don't take chances.'

'Sure,' I said.

That tail in an enclosed space, I was thinking. But Dan would be in there first holding its head (the teeth, the jaws that snap) and everyone would be standing by. And I was the one who was good with animals. I felt like laughing. Dan said we weren't too far from the shore now, though God knows how he knew. The dragon was giving up, just hanging there with no more than the odd kick now and then. It was starting to get dark, but there was a big moon, thank God; and thank God no other beasts came near, no scorpions ran, no snakes hissed and bit unseen in the grass. It was dark when we arrived. The Malays went ahead with flares and we followed them out from the tree line and saw a moonlit bay, faces in the flickering light madly grinning and staring, everyone running to greet us, all lit up orange against the black. A big fire burned down by the sea.

Captain Proctor came running, his face fat and pink and eager.

'My God!' he was crying over and over. 'My God!'

Samson ran after him, but stopped short and put his head down when he saw the dragon and began to bark. Proctor grabbed his collar, muzzling him with one hand. 'I'll tie this one,' he said breathlessly, hauling him away.

Getting the dragon in the cage was easy. It was exhausted. Gabriel, open-mouthed, wide-eyed and very serious, lifted the bars high and we pushed the thing in. It was my turn now. Me and Dan. We went in to remove the ropes. Dan took the head, I the tail. I didn't think. I seized it, loosed the knot and slid the rope smoothly, pulled it away and was out of the cage, Dan after me a second later. Gabriel dropped the bars, Yan and Simon shot the bolts.

A deep, roaring cheer went up. The dragon shot all of its limbs out at once as if stabbed, raised its head blindly and went wild again, a renewed frenzy so punishing and despairing that it struck us all dumb. If you could have seen that monster flickering in the firelight, beating itself senseless against the sides of its cage. I prayed to God Joe Harper's work held good. But the cage was solid, timber and steel, and the dragon was weaker by now of course. Even so, it continued a good half an hour with its writhing and lashing and hissing, till at last it fell into an agonised drooling stasis, slit-eyed, flat on its belly with four fat stumpy legs and long tail spreadeagled. Twenty cruel talons flexed and clenched with a rapid unconscious innocence, like the hands of a baby screaming with colic.

8

It was *my* time now. Tim's part was done. I was the boy who was good with animals. I was to accompany the dragon at all times now. It was me stayed with it rowing back in the boat, me stayed with it when they hauled it over the side, me loosed it from the cage into its pen under the fo'c's'le head. It was me and Dan hosed it clean as we could, gentle as we could. The hogs started going mad at the smell of it, and Wilson and Gabriel had to shift them away aft. And when we'd cleaned the poor dragon we hosed ourselves clean, and threw our filthy clothes over the side as a bad lot and got fresh ones. To be clean and dry and safe on-board *Lysander*. To sleep tonight in my bunk. The smoky old fo'c's'le my home. I was dreaming on my feet, awake and talking as you do when really you know you are asleep. You begin to think you're in one of those dreams where you think you're awake, and then you're not sure, and then it all starts to go funny and you know you must be dreaming, but you're dreaming in a dream, and suddenly it's all layers going in and in and in, like the rings round an old tree stump or striations in an elaborate rock, and you get scared. Then you wake up. But sometimes I wonder whether I ever really did wake up again. These dreams are so real and true, I don't suppose it much matters one way or the other. You could say I got lost in the rock striations.

The pen was the size of a small room and had a pool about six foot square in one corner, drainable from the deck, and a trap-door to put food through. It was sheltered from the weather, with straw and greens and sand, and even a rock or two to make the creature feel at home. No one should go near it but me and him till it was settled, Dan said, shooing everyone away.

'Give it peace,' he said. 'Pity the poor thing.'

Wilson made a great feast of best salt beef and sweet potatoes, and we ate and drank till stuffed and told our tale a hundred times. However we told it, something was missing. How say? The awe, as if I'd come to the edge of a big hole in the earth and peered in and seen something wild and unspeakable looking back. Tim wore a constant diffident smile and joked about the whole thing, and the laughter of relief, slightly mad, billowed in gales about the deck. They must have heard us on the island, all those strange creatures, and the lonely beast must have heard us in his pen. I thought of him in his misery. I would restore him to life and health if I could, and bring home to England a thing of wild splendour that would do me proud.

That night I slept dreamlessly, waking bright and sparkling from a crystal spring, renewed.

It was with some cockiness that I performed my ministrations to the wretched thing that first morning under the gaze of dozens of eyes. No more slaving for me. No more swabbing and scrub-bing, hard sand in my cuts. My new responsibilities gave me a leg up the pecking order. Already I was the one they were consulting on questions of dragonology. As if *I* knew. They were mad to see it, but I'd only let them near one at a time and not too close, not wanting to upset it again now it had quieted down. It had gone into a corner of the pen and was lying flat with its eyes closed, breathing hardly at all. When Dan went in it didn't move. We had sticks but we didn't need them. I thought it was dying. Actually it was gathering strength.

The last thing I remember of that island is the sound of things crying in the trees as we sailed away.

We paid off the two Malays and said goodbye to them on Flores, where women pounded roots and children crowded our boats, and a man with a milky eye made bamboo cages for birds, domed on top and gorgeously painted. An hour or two I watched as a palace took shape, three storeys joined by wooden pegs, each one smaller than the one beneath. 'Will you paint it like the others?' I asked, but he couldn't understand me. There's a nice life, I thought. Skill and patience and a beautiful thing coming into being. I'd have watched him all day but there was work to do. We took on fruits and greens then headed north through the Makassar Strait between Celebes and Kalimantan, sailing east across clear coral seas, east of the Philippine Islands, on ever further north towards the East China Sea. The first few days were hot and calm, a light breeze blowing from the south. A most islanded part of the world this is, and very beautiful, and for the first week or so I had no concern but the bright glittering blue world arise and afall around me, the bloodred sunsets, the birds that screamed upon the spars, and the creature in its pen. He wouldn't eat or drink, just lay flat and drooling in his corner. I watched over him like a mother with a sick child. I tempted him with morsels of raw meat and fish, tried him with bread and papaya and cheese and dumpling, offered him a live hog. Nothing. His eyes were open but stony still and empty. The only indication that he was actually still alive was the rapid rhythmic movement of his flattened belly as he breathed. Now and again I let the others have a look, but most lost interest pretty quickly, apart from Mr Comeragh, Skip and the captain. And Dan, of course. Dan was always there. Comeragh and the captain came to look now and then, but Skip couldn't keep away.

'Can I draw him?' he asked, so I let him.

'Is it a boy or a girl?'

'Boy,' I said confidently, though I'd no idea. Such a big ugly thing. Of course, he could have been a delicate maid of a dragon for all I knew.

'Think he'll wake up?'

'He is awake.'

'Doesn't do much, does he?'

'Give him time.'

'What you calling him?'

I laughed. As if he was a pet. 'Dunno.'

'I know,' Skip said, 'call him Bingo.'

'Bingo?'

'Yeah. What's wrong with it? Good name for him. Hey, Bingo! Bingo!'

'He's not a dog,' I said.

'So?'

Bingo was stupid. I resisted it for a long time, but it stuck anyway. There's no dignity in a name like Bingo. I never used it.

'How's Bingo today?' Captain Proctor would hail me jovially.

'Fine, sir.'

'Good, good.'

'Here,' Wilson Pride would say, leaning out the galley door with a bone, 'see if Bingo wants this.'

But Bingo never wanted anything.

'Think he'll last?' I asked Dan.

He drew the corners of his mouth down. 'Hard to tell,' he replied. He'd tied a stick onto a ladle and with this was pouring water from a bucket onto the dragon's snout in hopes of making him drink. The dragon's eyes were closed. 'I've seen worse than

170

this come round,' Dan said. 'They grieve, see. You would, wouldn't you? Far as he knows he's died and gone to hell. *You* could do this, Jaf, look. Just don't get too close.'

I wasn't afraid. The poor beast was too beaten. I approached and Dan handed me the ladle. I dribbled water on the creature's snout. Nothing.

Always nothing. Nothing and nothing and nothing. Every day I went in and talked to him. 'Hello, you stupid old dragon,' I said. 'Aren't you up and about yet? What on earth is the point of you, hey? I know it's bad, but you could at least make an effort.' I loosed his rope and made him comfy. 'You won't want for nothing where you're going,' I told him. 'This Mr Fledge, he's filthy rich. A madman. You'll be his pride and joy, believe me.'

Nothing and nothing and nothing, then suddenly, about six days in, he drank. I was about four foot away from him with my stick and the clumsy ladle thing upended over his nose. His eyes blinked, the long yellow ribbon of his tongue shot out and the great crevasse of his mouth opened, pink. His little sharp white teeth grinned for a second. It made me jump and my sudden movement jerked him in my direction.

I was away, out of the cage and the bolts shot. Safe with the bars between us I gave him encouragement. 'Good boy!' I said. 'That's the way!'

His piggy little eyes watched me suspiciously, and not a movement more I got for the rest of that day. After that came a few more days of stillness, when only his eyes moved, watching me as I watched him, as I forked his hay and cleaned the pool. You're only an animal after all, I thought. All the dread that had somehow gathered about his image was by this time dissipated in me. I'd seen his fellows feed and it was fearsome, but if my years at Jamrach's had taught me anything it was that a fierce and ugly demeanour could sometimes veil a complex soul, and that he was.

Those eyes were no more stupid than a rock is stupid. In the worst throes of its madness those ancient eyes had remained fixed as stars, brightly aware, receiving what befell with the clarity of a sage. All life and death the same, the same pain and feeding and fighting and dying. All of that was in the depths of the creature's eyes. All that and all the wildness of his life. No, he was not stupid.

There came a time when I knew he was going to live. He ate a hog. It was a good time for it to happen, just after supper when everyone was hanging around on deck. I'd given him live ones before but he never took any notice. This time, ten minutes after I put the hog in and it had gone for the trough and was rootling about in the greens, I saw that he had one eye on it, watching intently. Poor old pig never had a chance. Never saw anything quick as that in all my time at Jamrach's. The way that thing was still as a stone then – suddenly six feet away, near the end of his rope – snap! With the pig in his mouth. It was a horrible thing to see. Its scream, pure high terror, brought everyone running. He had it by the neck. Sucked and wolfed its whole head and all of its neck side-ways in, down to the shoulders and the beginning of its kicking front legs, mouth stretching impossibly like a snake's, shaking it all the while from side to side, rolling and banging it about on the ground. Down his throat he hauled it in a series of violent gulps, chomp, chomp. A ragged cheer went up. Four or five convulsive efforts and only the back feet remained sticking out, mercifully still.

Then it was gone; no more hog, and him there champing his lips. His tongue flicked out and in.

'Good boy!' I said.

He rewarded me with a short hiss.

'That's fucking disgusting,' John Copper said.

'No it isn't,' said Gabriel. 'You expect it to eat with a knife and fork?'

Dan laughed. 'Boys,' he said, lifting his shoulders and rubbing his hands together like a street corner magician, 'I believe we've done it. I believe we've made our fortunes.'

It was me. *I* made the dragon live. Catching it was only the beginning; making it live was the thing. It was only then I allowed myself to feel relieved, and to realise how much I wanted to get home. Home. Ratcliffe Highway with money in my pocket, the hero returns. Buy Ma a new dress. A bonnet. And Ishbel, what would she want? Buy her a good night out somewhere swanky, that's what she'd like. Treat her. Dance with her. Drink with her, tell her my tales. What would I take back for her? Fans and beads and feathers.

'He'll do fine now,' said Dan. 'He'll do fine and I may very well retire.'

'*You* won't retire.' Tim slouched on the windlass, grinning. 'Can't see you sitting by the fireside for long, Dan.'

'A-ha-ha,' said Dan, 'that's where you're wrong. There is nothing in this world I long for more than to see this voyage out and turn my face from sea for ever.'

'You, Mr Rymer?' the captain smiled. He was there with Mr Rainey and Henry Cash.

'Me, captain,' Dan replied.

We stared at the dragon and it stared back, motionless apart from an occasional flicking of the tongue.

'Old Bingo,' the captain said. 'Suppose they'll name it Rymer's Dragon? They name things after their discoverer, don't they?'

'Immortal!' cried Dan, who'd drunk a fair amount with his supper and was in warm crinkle-eyed mode. 'I'll drink to that. And to the fat bonus every manjack on this tub's well earned. Felix boy, run get my cup.'

'They should name it after this boy here, if anyone,' Mr Rainey said brusquely, flicking a hand in my direction. '*He* nursed it through.'

Me.

Don't know why that moved me so. Rainey with his big, dark face and troubled eyes was the only one on the ship I was scared of. Not the captain. Just as Gabriel said when we were starting out, the captain was not right for a captain. I've known a few now and they keep themselves apart, the captains do, but not Proctor. Proctor strolled about the deck with a faint smile on his freckled face, hoping to be liked. Sometimes he joked: 'And are you an able roper, I say, Mister Roper? Ha ha! Are you an able fellow?'

Ha ha ha. Rainey though, Rainey could strike you quiet with one sour look.

And here he praised me up before all.

Rightly too, rightly so.

Fair man, Mr Rainey, I thought. Goes to show you never can tell.

'Quite right,' said Dan, throwing an arm about my shoulders. 'Jaf's the one.'

Felix appeared with his cup of gin and he raised it high. 'To Jaf,' he said, knocking it back.

'Will you really retire?' I asked. We were back on the fo'c's'le deck. Simon had gone down and got his fiddle and was tuning up, bright pluckings of the strings.

'Certainly,' Dan replied, merry, loose in his gestures. 'All things must pass. I shall end my illustrious career on a pinnacle of glory with this magnificent creature.'

The sun had gone down an hour since, and the sea danced with crazy light.

'It'll be kind of like death, won't it?' Skip said.

'What will?'

'Dan giving it all up.'

'Death in life,' said Dan, 'life in death. Oh, my comrades!' He'd gone into funny ham-acting mode again.

'When you think about it,' Skip said, 'all we ever do is die.'

'What are you talking about, madman?' Tim pushed him. 'Why can't you ever talk sense?'

'The big god told me I didn't have to make sense,' Skip said. '*It* doesn't have to make sense. *I* don't have to make sense.'

'Don't worry,' Tim said, 'you never do.'

'How many years since you went to sea?' I asked Dan.

'Forty-three,' he said without hesitation.

I looked at him, wizened of mouth, one eye wandering very slightly, tried to see him as a green boy like us. It wasn't that hard. He was one of those who more or less stay the same from birth to death.

'It's like Bingo,' said Skip. 'Like his old life on the island and his life now . . .' Simon struck up a sleepy tune. '. . . Like me when I was three years old.'

'You talk shit,' said Tim.

'Three years old,' Dan said, sitting down with his back against a barrel and his legs sprawling out in front of him. 'Three years old doesn't last. I want to see my children grow up.'

'All those things are really dead. Me then. It then,' Skip said.

'You're cracked.'

'He means,' said Dan, lighting up his pipe with a serene air, 'that we're like snakes shedding skin after skin.' He sighed extravagantly at the thought of it, took a deep pull on the tobacco, pursed his lips and coaxed out a few smoke rings.

Much later, reeling home to my bunk, I came up with Gabriel and Simon.

'You seen Skip?' said Gabriel

'No.'

'He's sitting with old Bingo.'

'Come see,' said Simon. 'What do you make of this?'

He didn't see the three of us watching. He was sitting cross-legged in front of the dragon's door talking to it.

175

'It's not just the dark, see,' he was saying, 'it's the way it takes your power away. It's a matter of thought really. Very horrible though.'

He stopped and hummed tunelessly for a few seconds before resuming. 'And in you it may be worse,' he said, 'there's more in you than a three-year-old boy, I suppose. I wonder how old you are.'

The dragon's eyes were open but it was completely still, lying flat with its great head resting between its clawed hands.

'Come on, Skip,' said Simon kindly, 'don't go barmy again.'

He turned his head. 'Don't think I didn't know you were there,' he said. 'I know everything.'

We took on supplies at the island of Formosa. There was a bird market, three dozen or so small fat creatures, yellow, green and white, all crammed in one box, worse than at Jamrach's. I wished I'd bought a cage, a bamboo palace. Two or three in there, I thought, spreading wings, rising through the height of it. I'd put in strong twigs instead of straight perches, with leaves maybe. There's a thought. West lay China, Yan's country.

'Which part are you from?' I asked him, me and him on deck one morning patching our clothes, looking towards the coast. 'Are we near your home, Yan?'

He shook his head. 'Far south of here,' he replied, 'Tsamkong.' His black hair was growing long and parted above his brow in two thick waves.

'So we passed it by. Don't you feel like jumping ship and going home?'

He smiled. His face was burned by the sun, the skin very tight and shiny across his bones.

'I go home in three more years,' he said. 'And you? When for you?'

'In two.'

'I go home rich,' he said, 'if the goddess allows.'

That long coast could be seen as a lilac band shimmering far away, but soon we left it behind and followed a string of islands east towards the Japanese whale grounds. The seas were full of fishing boats and Chinese junks laden with salt. In the hottest part of the day the dragon would lie in his pool, but for most of the time he stayed absolutely still, raised up a little on his front legs, stirring only to eat the fish and birds and hogs I thrust through the hatch into his pen. In time he ate anything: our slops and leftovers, anything. I never trusted him. He was sly. It took two of us to muck out his pen, me with broom and shovel, Dan on guard with stick and gun. Even though we always kept him tethered, he was dangerous. He watched. Once he turned his head in my direction, opened his mouth very slowly and widely and gaped at me, a long, dream-like moment. A membrane of slime stretched shining between upper and lower jaw. Then, just as slowly, he closed it. A horrible display.

How was it we became so afraid of the dragon? Not just as anyone would be afraid of a wild animal with claws and teeth, but as if it was something more. We took on bad luck with that creature. Who was it first said that? In time we were all saying it. It began with a sickness. All of us went down with it apart from Abel Roper and Wilson Pride, but not all at the same time, thank God. It's filthy and foul on a ship when everyone's voiding from either end. Then poor Samson died. That was a horrible thing and *that* was because of the dragon. Samson had the run of the ship till the dragon came on-board. Joe Harper had erected a rough barricade to keep him away from it, but he got through on this particular terrible morning and ran by the cage, and the thing must have dashed at him. I was up on watch and all I heard was a horrible yelping and a lot of shouting and running about.

177

First thing I thought was that the dragon was loose and eating people, but things calmed down quickly so I knew it couldn't be that bad. An hour later when I came down I found out the dog was dead. Scared to death, poor thing: expecting nothing, a bit stupid, and suddenly this monster. He ran shrieking, and the captain caught him in his arms and he went into a sort of fit. Whether it was that, or whether he'd caught his head a good whack on the corner of the tryworks as he fled, he died twenty minutes later. He got a sea shroud as good as any and we committed him to the deep, all of us standing round with bowed heads. Captain Proctor said a few words. Samson had been with him for twelve years, he said. He'd found him in the port of Cadiz and carried him in his pocket through the Bay of Biscay in a storm when he was no more than a pup a few weeks old. A true old sea dog, happier on deck than land, it was fitting the sea should be his final resting place. John Copper cried, and when the sea had closed over Samson's earthly remains, the captain disappeared into his quarters and was seen no more for the rest of the day.

'Time's changed,' said Skip. 'Have you noticed?'

This was later, after supper, me and Skip and Tim sitting by the dragon in a row, legs sprawled out in front of us, sharing a pipe.

'How so?' asked Tim.

'It has. How long since we left the dragon island?'

'Two weeks,' said Tim.

'Don't be silly.'

'It's about – I don't know, a few weeks.' I frowned. I lost count. 'More than two.'

'Well, don't ask me,' said Tim. 'I don't even know where we are. It's hot. It's all the same to me. I'm fat-witted.'

'Much more than two.'

'That's what I mean,' said Skip. 'Time's gone funny.'

'Bloody heat,' I said.

'There's a thought.' Skip passed me the pipe. 'How will you keep Bingo warm when we get to colder climes?'

'Oh.' I'd never thought about it, truth to tell. 'Dan'll know.'

'Is he asleep, you think?' asked Tim

'Hard to say. He's sly.'

'He's not asleep,' said Skip.

'Oh, of course. You know things.'

Skip ignored him. 'It's since we left the island,' he said. 'We've gone into dragon time.'

I closed my eyes, very sleepy.

'I mean the time before the dragon and the time after are not the same.'

The funny thing is I knew exactly what he meant. It was true, something *had* changed, as if we'd sailed into a different air. I'd been groping at it in my mind, thinking it was something only happening in me. His saying it made it real, and that scared me.

That night I dreamed of home. Ishbel and Ma were there, and some of the lads and girls from Spoony's, ginger Jane and that lot, and we were all going down to the river, and all of it tumbled in with the kind of violent sunset you never saw on the banks of the Thames, a dragon-time sunset of crimson and violet. I was woken by shouting on deck. The sea was rolling. Not time, I thought, and slept again and found out later it was old Skip up to his tricks again. Rainey had found him fast asleep by the dragon's cage and called him a whoreson and a bastard and kicked him down the fo'c's'le shaft.

Next morning we were out for open ocean when the weather turned. The air was still heavy and hot and thunder rolled from the west. You could see the squall coming. It's one of the things

179

I love about the sea, the way you can see weather afar. It's like looking at the future. Captain Proctor called out, 'Shorten sails!' and we jumped to and set about turning her round and about direct. I ran and shielded the dragon's pen with a hanging. Gabriel was at the helm but the order was tardy and even he couldn't get us around in time, so we were caught sideways on by the wind and suddenly all was madness and nonsense, the birds and the wind shrieking their devil souls out, and the rigging torn, the sails cracking, the timbers groaning and the huge masts crying mercy. My guts flew into my throat. The deck tilted, we dropped and I rolled, grabbed onto something. Mr Rainey's voice roared over the screaming as the sea rolled over the leeward rail, icy. We'd gone over fast. We're sinking, we're sinking, I thought, this is too low, too low, we'll never come up again, oh, dear Jesus, God, please – the lee side touched the sea, the weather touched cloudy, fat-cheeked heaven.

I ran about, we ran about, I had no idea what I was doing. I saw Martin Hannah hauling on a rope and thought he looked as if he needed help, so hauled alongside.

Somehow we finally got her up and around. She flew before the storm.

'Good man yourself, Jaf,' Martin Hannah said, breathing hard. He was a tall quiet lad I hardly knew, inclined to stoutness, with a faintly threatening air and a slow smile.

'Good man yourself,' I replied.

Then the cry: 'She blows!'

It was ridiculous. Even in this, Proctor's standing on the quarterdeck shouting his head off: 'Down from aloft! Haul up the mainsail – Gabriel! Helm down – set topgallants – clear away boats . . .'

We had to get the spare from over the stern. It was starting to spit rain and the sea was high. But you don't think, you just do.

Soon came the falling rattle of the tackle, the splash of a boat hitting the sea. The flashing of long oars. We plunged and bucked over the sea with aching ears and flayed faces, blind with spray. Tears were blown backwards from our eyes. And we never caught a whale that day, we just lost another boat. So there we were, two down, and the weather frowning like a dragon. While the real dragon pressed flat and mad to the deck with eyes glazed over full of knowledge, drooling a slow spool of greenish slime as hell heaved sick about him.

I knocked shoulders with John Copper.

'Jesus,' he said, a wild look in his eyes. 'Sweet, sweet Jesus, I wish I was back in dear old Hull.'

If I could write I'd make a song. 'Oh, I wish I was back in . . .' Many a sailor song starts that way. 'Oh, I wish I was back in Ratcliffe Highway, Ratcliffe Highway across the sea . . .' I don't know how I'd say it. My own heart song. There are good old Ratcliffe Highway songs aplenty, but none are mine. So as the wild torrent howled and raged and pined for days and we tied ourselves in our bunks of nights, I tried the song, but it would never come whole.

> Oh, I wish I was back in Ratcliffe Highway,
> Ratcliffe Highway across the sea,
> Where a dancing girl with dada dada
> Waits or waits not for me.

I like that: waits or waits not for me.

Time passed, and we were all blind and deaf and dumb. The storm – sick. Rolling. Wedged ourselves in our bunks with bundles on either side. Smell of bilge water came steaming up from the hold. The bulkheads creaking. Close, stinky air. Heavy rolling sea breaking across the waist. Buckets, pieces of wood, other things rolling around the deck. Dangerous. Sea too high for whaling. Till, shocking and sudden, a bright, sweet, clear morning dawned, promising good sailing. It turned into a long day of rainbows and a gentle night of soft drumming rain. After that, three long cloudless days of burning brightness saw us to the Japanese ground, but there was nothing for us there. A week, two weeks. The lookouts were silent, though we spoke to other ships that had taken plenty. So we headed out southeast into the Pacific, towards the Equator and the far Offshore Ground.

Somewhere a few days in, darkness fell.

Seven days of darkness, like a biblical plague. In all that time the sun refused to appear, and the sky glowered close above by daytime, a low, pressing ceiling of dismal black cloud that occasionally gave off a kind of thin droning thunder from beyond the stars. The sea was high. There was no rain and the heat was intense. Day drears gave way to thick nights. On we hauled for better weather, for the sun, for the next change of the times. The captain and his officers walked about the decks, we spun yarn and sewed old clothes and patched sails and cleaned up, and things were not right. The ocean spoke with a softly threatening voice, there was no horizon and nothing to be seen in any direction but a groaning haze. And every time he could, Skip lay down in front of the dragon and stared at it, and talked with it, and listened to it. Listened to it, that's what he said.

He was a mad idiot. I now think they should have thrown him in the fo'c's'le with a kick along the way every time they found him sleeping before the dragon's cage. It was a soft ship, that was our trouble. A shipmate should not be allowed to sleep on deck as he pleases. What captain would allow it? *Ours* would. Proctor was grieving for his old Samson, a soft pup in his pocket in the Bay of Biscay twelve years ago. We hardly saw him. Rainey gave Skip a kicking once in a while in a half-hearted way, but nothing disturbed the haze. Once the captain came up in his nightshirt, disturbed by the shouting. 'I'll be glad when that damned animal's off my ship,' he said, and Dan Rymer, with the grey of the sky on his face and his eyes cold, said he was making a new rule that no one could go near the dragon but me and him, just like it used to be. It seemed so long ago when that was the rule. I couldn't remember when it had changed, how we'd drifted here, it was like Skip said: time changed. Time simply did not play properly any more. It was like an earthquake in the landscape in my head, and I no longer knew what I could count on. All voices were muffled and far.

Skip could no longer see the dragon, but it didn't make any difference; he was still talking to it. He said no words could tell how he and the dragon talked but talk they did, sometimes all night long. He never shut up, going on in this steady voice. He said the wheel was in spin because the dragon had gone insane. It had gone insane because of the cage. It couldn't bear the cage, like his grandma's fish couldn't bear its bowl, and so had gone mad. It wanted to go home. 'That's why there's no whales,' he said, sitting drawing bars and cages. 'They know it's on the ship and they won't come near.'

You know, we'd had a lot of Skip. He must have said a million mad things since we left the Greenland Dock. Why listen to him now? First he got Bill and Felix all fired up, whether he meant to or not.

'It's like this,' said Felix, 'a ship kind of knows things. It's like it's alive, like it knows when it's got bad luck on board. Like, say, a murderer.'

'Or a demon or a—'

'Yeah, a demon.' Skip set about drawing a demon.

'S'like when the sails blow out like cheeks.'

'And it screams.'

And on and on in that dream – seven dark days and nights that had begun to feel eternal. The superstition of sailors is no more than the lone howling of millions of miles between you and dry land and home, making you know you are a thing that can die. Superstition, dark, spiky, high-stepping, stalked with cloven foot upon our decks. And when superstition high-steps on a lone sea deck, far and far from every strand, as the old songs say – then, oh then . . .

Not just when sleeping, not just half asleep on my feet at the masthead, not just tipsy-drifting with a head full of gummy warmth, but always, every conscious second I was beautifully, startlingly afraid, with a fear crisp and invisible as the honed edge of a fine blade.

'Those horrible eyes,' said Gabriel, at the table in the fo'c's'le, lamplight on his face.

The dragon had been shedding skin round its eyes, which gave it a particularly horrific appearance.

'Like a statue,' Simon Flower fiddling with a string of twine. 'Not like a living thing at all.'

'An abomination.' That was Joe Harper.

'I don't like it,' Yan said. 'I don't like it there with its horrible eyes.'

'The ship knows,' Bill Stock said. 'There you have it: the ship knows.'

But now it was no longer just Skip and Bill Stock and Felix Duggan, it was the whole bloody lot of them.

'Evil, fucking horrible thing.'

'Should fucking boil the fucking thing and eat it.'

And Skip, with his thin knowing smile, saying, 'He wants to go home. He can't help it. He was living on his island like he's always done, and then the sky falls down and now he's being sick in a cage and he's gone mad and you want to eat him too. You probably should. He's better off dead. Kinder. Crueller than what we do to the whales, this is.'

'Probably taste revolting,' Tim said. '*I* wouldn't touch it.'

'Might be poisonous,' said Bill Stock. 'You get poisonous toads, don't you? Snakes? I mean, look at its tongue. Nasty thing.'

The dragon was bad luck. Some of us believed it as truth, some as a dream nudge, a kick in the brain. Dread joined the darkness and it had those dark beady eyes surrounded by white circles. I think of Skip now and I'm not sure how true my memories are. It was a long time ago. I remember him as a power in the boat, a round smiling face with a dark cap of hair, scrawnily meek and narrow eyed, never at full ease, always watchful. But now I think perhaps to others he was nothing, hardly noticed. But he it was that set it off, him and his nasty little pictures of cloven-footed demons, I'm sure: this little tinder of fear, which didn't fade even when the darkness lifted, and we sailed on and on with never a sight of a whale and the days running into one another. Certain things I remember. The fo'c's'le, Gabriel saying: 'There's an evil spot out there, they do say.'

Sam smiling. 'Don't frighten the little ones,' he said.

'Everybody knows about it.'

'I don't,' I said.

Gabriel looked at me. 'No? The place where things happen. Where the *Essex* was lost, and more since. A cursed spot upon the ocean.'

Everyone knows about the *Essex*, and all the others. It's legend on the whale ships. It's something of a joke.

Dan began to sing:

> There were three men of Bristol City
> Who took a boat and went to sea
> And first with beef and captains' biscuits
> And pickled pork they loaded she . . .

'I knew a man knew Owen Coffin as a lad,' said Gabriel. 'Sailed

185

with his father, he did. Said Owen was a nice boy, and a good sailor like his dad.'

> There was gorging Jack and guzzling Jimmy,
> And the youngest he was Little Billee.

Poor Owen Coffin drew the short straw and got eaten. He wasn't as clever as Little Billee. Some four or five voices joined in, but we were all sleepy and that silly song came out like a lullaby.

> Says gorging Jack to guzzling Jimmy,
> I am extremely hungaree.
> To gorging Jack says guzzling Jimmy,
> We've nothing left, us must eat we.

'We pass close by that spot,' said Gabriel.

You couldn't help but lie awake at night and remember that poor doomed ship so long ago and all the poor sailors who shipped on-board unknowing. And the other sailors and ships all coming their different ways to the same thing since the first boat ever put out to sea.

I remember a long night of shooting stars, and lying in my hammock, trying out words: 'Where a dancing girl with eyes of blue . . .' No good, no good . . .

> I wish I was back in Ratcliffe Highway,
> Ratcliffe Highway across the sea,
> Where a dancing girl with . . .

Wait.

> Where a *something* girl with dancing shoes
> Waits or waits not for me.
> With bloodred shoes and bloodred nails
> Where a dancing girl with golden curls
> Waits or waits not for me.

186

9

I t was coming to the end of that timeless time after we took on the dragon. A sleepless sleep and a dreamless dream. They'd all been drinking long on deck under the stars. Simon was playing something sweet and sad. I remember a fellow I once heard who played on a little harp on the quay beside the tobacco dock. The music had flowed on and on, always changing like moods. Sometimes it was like walking up and down stairs. Sometimes it pealed with joy. Sometimes it turned your heart to mush. I was drunk on the masthead and was concentrating hard on staying in this bright drunk state before tipping over the edge into sleepy stupidity, unable to make much sense, but keeping my mind sharp by thinking: if each one of those lads down there was a bit of music, what would they be? Making tunes in my head for each one. Some were easy, some were hard. I could get tunes for all but Skip, and with him I couldn't decide between a whimsy and a lament. Nowhere clearer than the ocean for a good bright state of being, of falling with constant clarity into the vortex inside, of sleeping with eyes wide open and waking on a sudden thump of the heart – I jerked awake to the sound of singing down below. Sometimes it felt as if the stars out there, far from all land, were screaming. Hundreds of miles blaring at your head. So beautiful, that night, waking in the sky with the screaming stars all round my head. I shivered. The others below seemed millions of miles away and I feared that I might fall. I'd never felt like this before and wondered if I was getting sick again, but after a moment my head cleared, and fifteen minutes later the bell rang and I went down.

First thing I saw was John coming to take my place. Second thing I saw was the dragon come striding, fast and hungry, humping high shouldered along the deck behind him with its monstrous muscled forelegs lifted high and its claws splayed. Its long stony face was smiling, and the white circles round its eyes made it look quite foul, as if it was staring madly. A pale tongue like a snake darted in and out, a foot or more. At that moment I was back in Ratcliffe Highway, eight years old, and the tiger walking towards me. The same impossibility. Only this time I was scared.

Clack-a-clack went the dragon's claws. I yelled at John: 'For God's sake, the dragon!' and he looked back and gave an almighty yell, and after that it was all madness.

We ran down larboard. Clack-clack it came after, scrabbling for hold on the boards. Everyone was lounging around, a more peaceful scene there could not have been till we burst through with the beast after us, and all hell broke loose. It ran wild about the deck, and so did we. The ship became a stage full of bobbing marionettes, running and shouting, the starry black sky still roaring. Tim jumped up on the tryworks. Joe and Bill were on the windlass. Four or five vanished sharp down the fo'c'sle companionway, and the rest of us rushed this way and that in utter confusion. Simon's fiddle got kicked along the deck. Everyone was drunk, the dragon on freedom. Its claws skidded on the boards and it plunged into the side of the ship, snapped like a turtle, twitched round in a circle and charged furiously into a little knot of men that jumped in all directions. John Copper, Felix, Henry Cash, Yan. Yan shouted in a deep throaty fear-voice. Mr Rainey bellowed somewhere like the wind. Skip appeared from behind the windlass, wild-eyed. Mr Comeragh grabbed my shoulder. 'Up, boy, Jaf,' he said. 'Drive it with me, come.'

Dan Rymer, drunk to hell, grinning like old Father Christmas, stood on a barrel with his arms outspread as if conducting a band, his cap awry and his dirty curls wet, shouting: 'To me! To me! This way!'

I stuck by Comeragh. Comeragh was a good sane man.

'That way, Jaf!' cried Comeragh.

I had no idea what I was doing. Comeragh's long legs flashed along the opposite deck.

The dragon came fast my way and I nearly brained myself banging into Billy Stock, both of us trying to flee. I heard Tim's voice calling plaintively, 'Jaf! Jaf!' and Skip sobbing. I have no idea what really happened, we were all just running about shouting, and the clack-clack of sliding claws was everywhere. Next thing I knew I was running after Comeragh and there was the cage with the door wide open, and Skip's sketchbook lying splayed, some of the pages bent. Comeragh said, 'You stay here, Jaf, get on top ready to close the door when we get him in,' and I jumped on top of the cage. Everything suddenly came clear into focus. I couldn't see past the windlass, I didn't know what was going on, all the shouting and yelling and crashing. I was all a-shiver with my teeth rattling and there was a serious small voice in my head saying, This is bad, this is all very, very bad and you're not ready. And I was alone, miraculously. Then suddenly the dragon appeared in front of me, its muddy head raised up, dark-holed with flat nostrils and ear holes and those beady black eyes full of guile, pink-ringed. There was something about them that brought my guts up to my throat. Its tongue flicked, then it opened its cavernous mouth and closed it again, got up on its hind legs and put its great clawed hands on top of the cage. It could reach me. Its arms were like thick old trees that had been growing for ever. Long yellow flick of a tongue, and an immensely wrinkled throat as wide as a washboard. It looked deep into my eyes and it was not like meeting the eyes of a dog or a cat, or even a tiger. There was nothing there that I could fathom, no mercy, no malice. It was a cold soul I looked into. It would kill me, tear me with teeth. None of it would matter. *I* would matter no more than a green shoot that pushes through the earth and is cropped by a passing sheep.

Comeragh appeared, harpoon poised. The dragon was fast. It flicked round like a fish, the harpoon flew wide and clattered off the edge of the open door – then all so fast I don't know how, Comeragh was down on the deck and it was running, snapping and slavering, he was pushing himself back, heels sliding, kicking at it, but all to no avail, for it opened its long, crocodile mouth wide and sank its teeth into his leg just below the knee and he let out one almighty scream that brought everyone running. It gave a shake of its head that snapped Mr Comeragh's head back on its stem, let go and charged through the yelling mob, which spun about as if stirred in a pot and gave chase. I jumped down, saw Abel Roper fall on one knee next to Comeragh, heard Comeragh cursing heartily and steadily through his teeth. I ran with the others. There was the horrible thing with its fat legs pumping and scrambling back along the larboard deck. And then the end came suddenly, as ends do, a flood of hatred, a bursting tide of it that drove the creature overboard. They poured from the hatches and down from their safe perches, a screaming yelling tide which I joined in triumph. We were legion. We came from both sides and it had no chance. Someone loosed the bolts and opened up the ship so we could drive him over, and down he went, sprawl legged and ridiculous, a splayed fool walking on nothing, kicking at the void, then – an explosion, a hole in the black ocean receiving one more offering.

Gone.

A cheer went up. We gripped the rail, leaning forward and looking over. He must have sunk a fair way down because it took as long as a few breaths in and out for the great block of his head to punch through. Another cheer. He dived once more, deliberately; then up, the shake of a great humped back, a circle-turn of movement, purely graceful. And away he swam, front legs paddling the wave before him, due northwest on a steady course, away into darkness never more to be seen.

Tim was beside me at the rail. Dan Rymer stood behind, put an arm round each of our shoulders, breathing ale. 'There goes our fortune, lads,' he said softly. 'There goes our fortune swimming away.'

'How did it get out?' the captain roared.

'Skipton!' Rainey grabbed Skip's shoulders. 'It was you, wasn't it?'

'It was you, wasn't it?' Skip said, with a simpleton smile on his face.

'You were there, I saw you. You let it out, didn't you?'

'You let it out, didn't you?' Skip repeated.

Rainey struck him hard across the face and he went down.

'Mr Comeragh's got a nasty bite,' Sam Proffit said, appearing at the captain's side. 'Bloody.'

'Fool!' Rainey's boot slammed into Skip's side. 'That thing could have killed someone. Get up! Get up, you son of a whore!'

Still vacuously smiling, Skip shakily rose, one hand vaguely hovering before his brow.

The captain's face wore a look of exaggerated calm, but he

191

was tight with fury. 'Mr Skipton,' he said, 'you have endangered the entire ship.'

Skip laughed, a harsh loud hack that burst from his throat. Blood burst out of his nose at the same moment and dripped down his front and onto the floor.

'Are you mad? Are you mad, Mr Skipton?' the captain shouted. 'What have you done? Do you know what you have done? You could have killed someone!'

Skip shoved his hands under his nose to catch the flow.

'Speak,' the captain said. 'What the devil got into you?'

'Nothing,' said Skip.

'Nothing! Nothing! You are insane. We should have put you ashore at Cape Town.'

'It was . . .' Skip said.

Mr Comeragh came walking lopsided, leaning on Abel Roper. He didn't look too bad, but there was a lot of blood on his breeches.

'Mr Comeragh,' the captain said, 'this fool let it out.'

'Why?' asked Comeragh, looking at Skip.

'It told me to,' Skip said.

Rainey hit him across the face again.

'Do you realise the value of that creature?' the captain said.

'Value? Value?' Skip shouted right into his face.

Proctor blinked sharp and his voice went up a notch. 'We have had enough of you, you, Mr Skipton, you have ruined this endeavour. We had succeeded! We were bringing back a great new wonder of the world. Mr Rainey! Put him in irons!'

'By all means, sir,' said Rainey.

Funny how things change in a second. Skip burst into tears, no longer a mysterious and irritatingly knowing boy, just a kid snivelling for his ma. His nose ran and his breath piled up in sobs in his throat.

'This is bad,' said Abel, meaning Comeragh's leg.

'How bad?' snapped Rainey.

'Very, *very* bad.'

'Oh, God in damnation!' Rainey's eyes looked hollow. 'Kill the fool.'

'What happened?' asked Dan, his calm voice in the middle of it all. 'What happened, Skip?'

Mr Comeragh sat down on the deck suddenly, and Abel peeled back the bloody cloth. 'It's the swelling, sir,' he said, looking over his shoulder at the captain. 'That's what's got me a bit worried.'

Mr Comeragh's leg had blown up like a fat sausage.

'I might want to be lancing that, I might. Looks like a snake bite sort of thing, that's poison in there, that is.'

'Hurts like fucking mad,' said Comeragh tightly.

'Nothing to worry about, sir,' Abel said brightly. 'We'll just get you below deck and cut this boot off and you'll be up and about quite soon. Sam, give us a hand.'

'I thought I gave orders,' Dan said. 'No one goes near the beast but myself and Jaf Brown. Why was this boy allowed anywhere near?'

Not a word. It was me, I let him go there to draw.

'Allowed?' Proctor turned with a look of outrage. 'He was not allowed! Surely, Mr Rymer, it was your duty to set a watch upon such a valuable animal.'

'Certainly, if there was a man to spare twenty-four hours a day, but there isn't,' said Dan. 'An order's an order and should be obeyed.'

Proctor turned on his heel and walked round in a small circle that brought him back to face Dan. 'Mr Rymer,' he said, 'you and your boys were responsible for the animal's welfare. The animal has gone. You are the one who must explain this to Mr

Fledge. For myself, I thank God the damned thing is off my ship. Damn you, Skipton. Put him below!'

Henry Cash and Gabriel led Skip to the hatch, him blubbing and wiping his nose on his sleeve. The captain stomped away up onto the quarterdeck, where his plump figure could be seen motionless in morose contemplation of the eastern sea for more than an hour.

Early morning. A vast canopy of cloud covered the sky in the west, black and slate grey and white. Rough sea, dark grey. Upon the quarterdeck the captain and Mr Rainey. Billy Stock aloft. Wilson Pride in the cookhouse soaking hardtack, Joe Harper carefully mending Simon's fiddle, Felix Duggan yawning, Yan straddling a spar, a knife in his mouth and a rope in his hand.

First thing Dan told us Mr Comeragh was still poorly from the bite. Bled a lot, he said. It had stopped now, and Abel had lanced the swelling, but he'd got a nasty fever. Sam was keeping an eye on him.

'Will he be all right?' I asked.

'I'd say so.' Dan looked tired. 'I have to write a report. Know what he told me? Skip?'

'What?'

'Said he was taking it for a walk around the deck.'

'Jesus.'

'Here, Polly-dog,' said Tim, and laughed.

'Boys,' Dan said, 'don't worry, you'll still do well out of this. We never thought we'd find the thing in the first place, did we? You both did well. I shall make that clear.'

Then he sent us off to muck out the cage. Its open-doored emptiness made me sad. There was the imprint of a long thick body in the straw, the shedded debris of black scales. He was a messy dragon. Didn't care where he shat.

194

'No one will ever believe it,' said Tim, and laughed. 'That we really caught it. No one will ever believe.'

'Jamrach will,' I said, stooping to pick up Skip's sketchbook. 'So will Fledge. He'll send another expedition.'

'Think so?' Tim leaned on his broom. 'Will *you* go?'

'I've been thinking about that,' I said, flicking through the pages. Dragons, demons, bars. 'Depends. Depends what it's like back home.'

'Back home,' he repeated dreamily. 'Feels like a mirage.'

> Oh I wish I was back in Ratcliffe Highway,
> Ratcliffe Highway across the sea . . .

'Suppose we'll never be rich, me and you,' I said, sliding the book into my pocket. It was an easy fit.

Tim laughed. 'I don't care about the money.' He resumed his sweeping. 'I was sure I was going to die. I thought, Blow this, if I ever get off this damn island and get home, I'll never ask for anything more – Jesus Christ, this stinks! – and I wouldn't. I'll not be going to sea again, Jaf, but *you* will, I'm sure. It's not for me. I'm the man of the family now. I'll go home and work for Jamrach and keep my dear old ma happy.'

'Still,' I said, 'you'll have some great stories.'

He snorted. 'And no one will believe—'

'That we saw dragons feeding on one of their own on an island,' I said.

'You got a way with words, Jaf.'

'How far could it swim?' I wondered.

'Pretty far maybe,' Tim replied. 'Not that I know,' and then he sighed. 'Poor old Skip. Stuck down there. He can't help being mad.'

I thought of the dragon in the sea, swimming valiantly back west towards its home. I saw its tough bowed legs walking in the water. How far? Hundreds of miles. It was probably dead by now. All that ancient wildness and power gone. It was just a thing that can die. I saw things die at Jamrach's. It's always the same: a light dimming, going out. The only human I knew who'd died was Tim's dad, and that was just as if an old chair that had stood in the same place for years had suddenly been thrown out.

'Think it's dead?' I said.

'Maybe.' He drove dirty water out onto the deck. 'I have no idea.'

I liked to think of it swimming on for days and days, ever westward, landing on a scrap of land here and there and taking nourishment, eating fish, swimming on and on and on, till it finally hauled itself up onto the shore of its own island. Home.

'We shall never see a whale again,' Dag Aarnasson said.

Nine bells, the air still and hot. The ocean had a troubled look.

'Why do you say so, Dag?'

He grinned. 'Curse of the dragon. So they say.'

'I could believe anything out here,' I said. 'Anyway, it's gone now.'

'True enough.' John Copper, soaked in sweat. 'So, what say we never mention the damn thing again?'

Billy, aloft, called out. The captain shouted: 'All hands ahoy!' I heard the sound of running feet.

Tim, staring past my shoulder, suddenly had a look of wonder on his face. 'Oh God, what now?' he said softly.

I turned.

In the west the dark cloud ceiling had a bloated, boiling look, but was luridly bright in one place. From here, a long, white serpent, swaying gracefully, reached down to the surface of the ocean.

'What is it?'

'Waterspout,' said Dag.

'Tumble aft!' Rainey yelled. 'Every one of you! Gabriel to helm.'

A forked gash of lightning flickered deep inside the cloud.

'Jump to, jump to.' Rainey swept us aft. 'Billy, get down!'

It was coming nearer, a lovely whirling dreamy thing dancing across the water with furious speed.

'Clew him up, clew him up!' the captain cried.

Strange to have to jump and haul when all you wanted to do was be silent and watch. I'd seen many a wonder since I left home but nothing to match this. It seemed as if it ran at us but stopped a mile or so away to observe. It looked as if the cloud was sucking up the sea through a spinning column of luminous mist.

'Main tack and -sheet let go!' shouted Captain Proctor.

A huge brightness was like fire in the sky behind it.

'Don't stand gaping, Mr Linver, jump to!'

We got her round. It was on our lee. I had a moment to look: there was a massive commotion at the foot of the spout, a brightening, as if a spectral ship sailed there. Then again, the whole thing was like a silver column resting on a silver plinth. It climbed and climbed through the sky like the beanstalk in the old story, like the world tree joining earth to heaven. How big was it? I don't know. Monstrous. Everything here was monstrous.

'Topsail halyards let go!'

Then another came, also from the west, a beautiful oyster-pearl column with what seemed like a pale cloud rising within, and then a third, wider at the top like the funnel of a trumpet and tapering down to a place on the water with the appearance of grey fire. These two joined the first. The three stood swaying, sinuous, spinning gloriously on our lee. So beautiful. I never saw anything so beautiful in my life. I could almost say it was worth it all to see a sight like that. First they danced a stately court dance, three willowy girls weaving in and out of one another, advancing, retreating, bowing and bending, coming together to part and circle, deft and elegant in every move as nymphs and fairies but stronger than Hercules. And all the while we ran about settling down the topgallants and tops while the mains snapped and cracked in the growing gale.

'It's revenge,' said Billy, 'that's what it is.'

'Right enough,' agreed Felix sagely.

'Don't talk shite,' Tim said. 'It's weather.'

We tacked round cautiously. The western sky was bunched and black, full of inner movement. A distant sound of shrill singing came from afar. Captain Proctor's face was worried, and that worried me. Lightning shuddered in the clouds. Mr Rainey strode about shouting orders, and we nipped about like wraiths, the sky flashing silently every few seconds and lighting our faces, all of us a-shake and agog in the eerie light.

We were making good progress away when the dance played itself out. The three columns stood for a moment, vibrating finely as if collecting themselves, then, one after the other in perfect harmony, traversed a smooth wide arc and regrouped once more on our leeward side, where with no more ado the youngest – and as it were, the most slenderly girlish – peeled away and ran at us. She came with the roaring of the deluge and unimaginable speed, passing no more than a hundred feet before our stern and raising a wave that rocked us violently and soaked our decks. The wind yanked us round. The sails thundered. A great jag of lightning pierced the west. We struggled with the ship, and as we struggled the second one came, passing after her sister and spinning us round in circles. The decks tilted. The sound of a mountain falling was the second spout, and the sound of sea chests and boxes hurtling around below, the crashing of crocks and pots in the cookhouse, the howling in the rigging. And a great falling about among us lads.

But it was the third that did for us. While we'd held our own against those two outriders, she'd been gathering, drawing the angry sky into a thick funnel like a gigantic bruised lily flower. The first two ran far away, taking the gale with them. They left us suddenly still, breathless and dumb. Then the sky flashed and she was there, with a density to her, an awesome gravity that stopped the blood.

The top was like a trumpet or a chanterelle, a horn of plenty from which the massed clouds of the canopy had burst forth like foam. The stem was a mighty trunk, grey, shot through with quivers of lightning, and she stood upon a shimmering darkness on the sea.

'Let go all halyards,' came the cry, but there was no time.

She charged. The wind came before, screaming. We should have got away. We changed course, tacked about like a flying bat, but she mimicked us, played Simon Says, turning as we turned, changing as we changed. You'd have sworn there was a brain in that thing. But they do that. I know it now. I've spoken with many a sailor's seen the same or near enough. They chase, don't ask me how, but they do. I didn't know that then though, and its dogged stalking pursuit horrified me in more than a merely physical way. I was filled with supernatural dread, as if what came truly was a living monster.

As of course she was.

She chased us no more than a mile full-out flying before we were hopelessly outrun and she hit. I flew out of myself. All was unaccountably silent for a second. I was a thoughtless fear unbodied and unbrained, a fleck of foam on my sleeve, a plummeting spar, a fiery salamander tipping a wave of the sea. I was all these things, but I was not me. Me was gone out somewhere, dreaming it all and watching afar. Yet I felt it all – the shock of cold wet air knifing down my throat and singeing my lungs, the sharp throb of a panicked heart in my chest, the warm sea a huge shining coil, dragon green, a tongue licking over the rail. Sound crashed in with the sea. A horrible cry of pain, outraged and childish. Whose? A fiendish roaring, shouting, things falling spear-like around me on the deck.

The world rolled round and I rolled with it, banged and winded and beaten by the timbers of the deck and the hard outcrop of the tryworks that cracked my knee and sent a fire screaming up into my chest. I fell from there as the world swung all around my head, lurched again, grabbed and hung onto the weather rail.

We were on our beam ends, right over on our side with the waist of the ship awash. I saw Gabriel fly over the helm, and Mr Rainey running backwards on his heels with his arms whirling. His face was stiff, features set in rock, though pure horror stared out of his eyes. I saw Wilson Pride swim out of the cookhouse door, and a tide of rats washed past me on a shivering black stream. Still screaming, whoever it was, a shocking scream, a stabbing scream, a bad-hurt scream. Who? I took a mouthful of sea, it went up my nose and burned me. Abel came sliding along the upper deck, shouting: 'The boats! The boats!' and I heard the captain's voice come deep and loud as a foghorn through a mist of spray. A hand grabbed my collar and hauled me away.

'Jump to, Jaf!' Dan said brightly. 'There's work to be done,' and he shoved me along before him. I saw one of our whaleboats carried away and another stove in, smashed to match wood against the gunwale. We lurched along the side of the cookhouse. A great commotion was taking place beneath our feet.

The mainmast broke with a great crack, toppling like a tree, lifted and blown away like a twig by the wind. Up on the listing quarterdeck they were hanging onto the last two whaleboats. That's not enough, I thought. Dag was there with Tim, grappling with rope, Rainey with blood running down his head, the captain with his face sagging and his eyes bleak, shouting: 'Aft! Aft!' into

200

the wind. Simon was cutting the lashing off the other boat. There was a water cask and a musket and a quadrant in theirs, a bundle of hardtack and a tub of boat nails in ours. Henry Cash in soaking shirt and breeches emerged from the aft companionway, as if from a flooded underground cave, pushing Joe Harper's toolbox up in front of him, shaking water from his eyes. Gabriel jumped down from the rail and grabbed his arms to haul him out, but Henry was for going back down. You could see him drawing in the air to last another minute or so, pushing back the flat dark hair from his forehead and blinking hard. He looked very young suddenly.

Someone still screamed. Who?

'Mr Cash!' Rainey bellowed through the din. 'Come aft now, that's enough!' and the Captain still calling:

'Aft! All hands aft!'

'Where's Sam?' Rainey jumped down into the water. 'Is Skipton up?'

'Aye, sir,' said Gabriel.

'Sam!' yelled Rainey. 'Sam Proffit!'

Yan, wild-eyed, came running with the compasses from the binnacle and flung them in our boat.

'Cash!' roared the mate and captain together.

I saw the boys falling and stumbling aft along the tilted line of the larboard deck: Skip, freed from the irons, thank God, to take his chances with the rest of us; Abel Roper and Martin Hannah; Felix and Billy; Joe Harper still with Simon's fiddle in his hand. John Copper waded in the flotsam of cookhouse debris and dead rats that nudged the quarterdeck like a school of curious fish. Who was it, screaming still? Who was it? The cookhouse wall burst. Barrels rolled out on the surge and went floating joyfully away to freedom or bowling down the deck to send everyone a-scatter and knock Joe's legs from under him, so that the poor fiddle went flying once more and Joe turned a watery somersault over the barrel and landed crash on his face on top of the water. Henry said something to Gabriel and went under once more.

'Cash!' Mr Rainey bawled into the wildness. A mad, staring, bloodied man.

'Keep by the boat, boys,' Dan told us.

With a crack like nothing more than a broken stick, the mizzen-mast snapped near the bottom and fell across the drowned hatch. Gabriel, barefoot, fell upon the mast and began hauling and straining at it. First he tried to lift it, then he tried to roll it, but it wouldn't budge. Big Martin Hannah, vaguely smiling still, threw in all his weight, and Skip jumped in to help him, but nothing was moving that mast and Henry was never coming up again. The sea lapped over the transom, poured up the deck and swirled about the submerged companionways, and a collossal shift took place in the heart of the ship as three or four hundred barrels of oil moved as one with a sound like the end of all days. Sound: the sea, the wild wind, the voices of our crew as the brittle wooden speck we lived on rolled over like the slippery pole at the fair, and the sky flew up as the swingboat soared.

But it never came down again.

The spars cut water. The boats bounded eagerly. 'We're going down!' John Copper screamed from below, kicking out, swimming. Tim grabbed me, his arms round my shoulders. Wilson Pride fished an axe from the floating soup and hacked at spars, expressionless. Gabriel waded for the fiddle. Dan pushed us about. The whole world broke open.

Parts of the ship went dancing away. Henry Cash was under the water. Henry Cash was dead. Gabriel crying, wading for Simon's fiddle.

Tim held onto me, his eyes shining with a horrified, slightly gleeful excitement. Mr Rainey clouted me on the back of the head. 'In the boat,' he said. I seemed to move slowly as if I was in a dream. There I was going out again, dimming down like a trimmed lamp. Not here, here but absent. Turn away, Jaf. Turn aside and watch. Save me from gut fear. Uncreep my flesh.

There was no more screaming. The fo'c's'le was under. She listed. Impossibly more, she listed. Dan and the captain, as if no more than a whale jaunt was at hand, gave orders, straight, mad in the face of madness as if it was normal, this groaning of the quarterdeck, this drenched mob of us. And Henry Cash under the deck, under the water. We lowered away and took our places. Steerage was under. Two boats we had left, not enough. We had Rainey and Dan and Gabriel. Yan was holding a hog. Our boat listed as we drifted out, and the sea threw us up and down, and the wind shrilled at us. Me and Tim were together in the middle of the whaleboat, and we pulled because Dan told us to, pulled like hell with some mad strength come into our arms.

We got away and rested on our oars, watching as the *Lysander* fell over completely and lay on her side with a great slosh and a groan, the tip of the foremast under.

Our two boats came together.

The ship had settled, an upright pointed crag upon the ocean, surrounded by its widening circle of flotsam. Those three great whirling waters were far away now, and the wind had dropped like a fall into unconsciousness. A silence made of sea-soughing filled the world. No one spoke. My eyes were full of seawater and I blinked them clear and looked around. Dan had us both, me and Tim, one arm round each of us. 'Oh boys oh boys oh boys oh boys,' he whispered. I saw Yan's face, a wild thing with glittering eyes and lips drawn back from the teeth, Gabriel's, blank, flat, tear-streaked. Gabriel still somehow had Simon's fiddle, cradled against his wide ragged chest. Alongside us in the other boat I saw the captain gripping the gunwale, the fierce jut of his jaw, and Wilson Pride, Dag Aarnasson, John Copper, Simon Flower, Skip, all alike turned stupid against the vast impossibility of it all.

Where were the others?

No one appeared on the high crag of quarterdeck. No one at all. I saw a head swimming, but it was only one of our hogs striking out bravely for salvation, trotters paddling furiously.

'Simon!' said Gabriel. 'I got your fiddle.'

'Thanks.'

'Here you are.'

Passing it over, hand to hand.

'Billy!' shouted Dag, rising, pointing. 'Billy! Billy Stock!'

Swimming through the spars and floating planks, through bobbing casks and sodden sheets, Billy Stock beating back the water with his sturdy brown arms, coming strong towards us. His head kept going under. All of us grabbed oars and rowed and drew near, shouting to him, stretching out our arms to pull him in. His face was intent, going under, coming up, intent on some invisible thing an inch or so in front of his eyes. He just kept going. Dan got him and hauled him over, he and Rainey laid him in the bottom of the boat on his face and set about getting the water out of him, thumping him on the back.

'That's it, get it up,' said Dan.

Billy coughed and choked.

'That's the way,' Rainey said.

He'd been swimming so strongly. It was as if he'd used himself all up in the water and now he was in the boat there was nothing left. He coughed and choked and sneezed blood out of his nose, then pitched forward out of Dan's grip onto his face in a spew of thin green vomit. Rainey picked him up and looked into his eyes, taking him by the shoulders. Billy's eyes had gone funny: dull and troubled, still and intent. His skin shone.

'Mr Stock,' Rainey said, 'this will not do, you must be a man, Mr Stock, and fight back.'

But Billy's eyes turned white and rolled up and back in his head, and his head lolled back upon the thin stalk of his neck. Mr Rainey got down in the boat and Billy's head rested against his arm.

'Come, come, we can't do without our Billy Stock,' said Rainey.

But Billy just stayed that way, with his eyes gone like white slits in his brown face.

'Oh, Billy,' said Rainey sadly. 'Oh, child.'

'Is he dead?' cried a shrill voice. Skip.

'Dead,' said Dan.

'Oh Christ,' said Rainey, laying Billy down in the bottom of the boat and, thank God, closing his eyes. Now it looked just as if he was sleeping.

'Mr Rainey,' came Captain Proctor's voice, clear and sharp, 'bring your boat round, you're drifting.'

'Is he dead?' cried Skip again, high as a girl. 'Is it my fault? Oh, my God, my God, is he dead and is it my fault?'

If there is anything to be learned from my story perhaps it is this: never go to sea with a madman. Then again, as Gabriel once warned me, I have found that the seas positively seethe with them. Skip was one certainly. Was that why it came to seem that it *was* indeed his fault? Because it did, even though we all knew that his freeing of the dragon had nothing to do with anything that followed.

'It is not your fault, Mr Skipton,' the captain said, 'contrary to what you might believe, you do not control the weather. For God's sake, keep your mouth shut if you want to stay alive. Mr Rainey, we must look for survivors and salvage whatever we can.

We've a long journey ahead of us but it's nothing that can't be done.'

Over on the horizon the sky was dark. It started blowing again, and the rain came down and turned into hail.

10

Miraculous that one poor head can carry so much.

I see my old shipmates so clear, a strange mustering, like old times, old times only yesterday. We stand together on the tilted deck, wide-eyed as children, waiting to be told what to do. The hail pings off the deck and hits our eyes.

Henry was under the deck, Billy was in our boat. Dag said the foremast fell on Sam and the water went over him. Simon said he and Abel Roper brought Mr Comeragh up and put him in the waist boat, but then the big one hit and the boat was taken. Tossed but sound, carried far away, and in it Mr Comeragh with his big-nosed smiling face and dark eyes. How did he feel? Best to lie in the bottom and let the sea have its way and pray, then maybe or not you'd discover yourself alive in the following calm.

There were no more.

Mr Rainey's face was bloody as hell. Captain Proctor took control. 'This is a disaster,' he rasped, eyes narrowed and blinking at the hail. 'Not the first and not the last.' A coughing fit took him and it was a moment before he could continue. 'We will bring these boats safe to shore with all hands. There is no doubt – no doubt at all – that this is well within our reach.'

Hail, blinding.

'Some of our friends have died.' He opened his mouth again but nothing came out, then he sighed, closed his eyes for a second, opened them again and licked his lips. 'We will give decent burials to all we can find.' His eyes were firm and steady, but pulled down at the corners and weepy. He'd managed to keep his glasses on, God knows how. 'Now,' he said, 'we have work to do.'

We had Joe's toolbox, hatchets, needle and twine, a quadrant, two compasses, lanterns, two pistols and a musket, some powder, two terrified hogs. The captain put me, Tim and John to making new sails from what we could save of the old. Wilson Pride went among the rigging, chopping at spars, while Simon and Dan and Captain Proctor himself, cack-handed, set about the making of masts. We needed Joe. Yan was on lookout. Gabriel fished for barrels of water. Rainey got Skip hacking holes in the deck, and he went down himself with Dag and started bringing up boxes of hardtack. We did not mention what had happened. Hey ho, it was just another day and we were doing what we were told. All our tobacco was gone. I would have killed for a pipe, sitting there pricking my fingers bloody, wielding my needle. I could have cried, thinking of sweet smoke, the loveliest thing in the world. The sky too was the colour of smoke, with blue inside the blackness, shining. I was in a state of dreamy infancy. John Copper was joining the sides of a small sea shroud for Billy. The hail had eased to soft rain and I was in bits: one of me on a great adventure, one of me shivering on the sea like sunlight, one of me working on a gloomy afternoon in Jamrach's yard with dear old Crabbe and Bulter . . .

My God, Crabbe and Bulter! My eyes filled with tears at the sudden thought of them.

'Hey Tim,' I said, 'do you remember Crabbe and Bulter?'

Tim turned his head and smiled. ''Course I do. Crabbe and Bulter.'

'Those were the days,' I said.

'Indeed they were.'

One of me still on the ship last night before I came down from the mast, one of me brooding over the waters. My invisible fellows walked and talked as ever in my brain as if nothing had happened.

'Who's Crabbe and Bulter?' John Copper asked.

'Used to work with us,' Tim said.

Skip appeared.

'Hey Skip,' I said, 'I've got your book.'

Dragons, demons, winged eyes, faces in extremity.

'Thanks,' he said.

I gave it to him.

'No pencil though,' he said and smiled.

So on and on floated the day. We built up the sides of the boats, a foot or so, more fore and aft, and loaded them deep as we dared. The hardtack was stowed well aft away from the spray, wrapped in canvas. Water, a couple of barrels for each boat.

Mr Rainey and Simon put Billy in the shroud. They just did it, a job, Simon holding it open, Rainey putting him in, their faces admitting nothing in or out. Then Mr Rainey gathered Billy up and brought him into our boat and we rowed out a little way with the captain's boat following, and came together as the rain faded away and the first hint of sunset appeared.

The captain said:

'We now commit to the deep, oh Lord, the body of your servant, William Stock, our shipmate. Lord, accept him and have mercy on his soul. Our Father, which art in heaven . . .' and we all joined in mumbling the Lord's Prayer, and I thought: Goodbye, Billy, and remembered his face as he threw up in a bucket, angry, tear-filled eyes. A small silence, then Mr Rainey slid him into the sea and the sea swallowed him.

The last of the ship was like the dying of a whale. She bled thick yellow blood from her every seam, from her dead eyes, from her heart. All the oil we'd taken since we left the Greenland Dock. It spread about us on the sea, and she went down slowly into it, shining.

Gone.

That moment, ocean around, sky above. Too big.

The captain consulted the quadrant. Rainey went into his boat and they had a silent powwow. Seemed not to agree, I thought, but at last Mr Rainey came back with his face hard, sucking his lip. The captain said we'd make southeast a few miles away from this place then hove to for the night and take stock in the morning. At least the rain had stopped.

Fix sails, men.

We were six to a boat. On oars, me and Tim, Dan and Gabriel, Yan and Rainey. On theirs, Skip and Simon and John, Dag and Wilson and the captain. Mr Rainey was by the steering oar. The captain held his musket tight. Our makeshift masts served. I don't know how far we sailed. It was a black night and nothing was real. Somewhere we hove to and I fell into a thirsty sleep. We'd had a little water before we turned in, but the captain said we had to be very careful with it, plan for the worst and hope for the best. I felt sick and couldn't eat the hardtack. We slept hungrily, desperate for oblivion. Long before daylight I came half awake and started going over and over a list in my mind, but I was still exhausted and kept losing track and having to start again so it went on for ever. Who's gone? Sam Proffit. Mr Comeragh. Felix Duggan . . .

It seemed important to me that I should think of these people one by one, enumerate, as it were, the things I knew about each. Sam Proffit: old black man, watery eyes, small. Mr Comeragh: has a young son. Felix. Felix Duggan. What do I know about him? Nothing. Round head, pulls faces. Sam, Felix, done them. Mr

Comeragh. Billy: his white eyes. Henry Cash: sleek wet head, shoulders rising out of the water, pushing before him the toolbox. What would we have done without the toolbox? Our saviour. Know nothing about him, never liked him. Thought he was a smug bastard. Sleek wet head, an otter, going down for more, looking younger than before. Who's next? Joe. Joe Harper. Last I saw of Joe he was splashing face down when the barrel knocked him off his feet. He was holding Simon's fiddle, but it went flying. Where was he? Where was Mr Comeragh? Where were Abel Roper, Felix Duggan, Martin Hannah? Going over each lost man in my mind, over and over like counting sheep, asserting their existence and the impossibility of its end.

A whaleboat is a canny thing, twenty-six feet long, slim and beaked and swift. Ours were chimeric, burdened with masts and sails never meant for them, built up, patchwork prowed, laden well beyond their means. Nothing like a whaleboat for skipping over the waves, but these new craft were cumbersome. We laboured west all day till the sun went down. The moon was in the east.

'Ever see that, boys?' Dan says. 'Moonbow. Rainbow at night.'

The moonbow shone on the western horizon, painted on cloud. Under the bow the sky was paler.

'Let's assume it augurs hope,' said Rainey in a faintly sarcastic tone, 'like Noah's rainbow.' His face was hawkish and red. He'd wiped away the blood, and had a rough plaster above his beady left eye, which dribbled constantly into the bruised skin about it.

'What now, Dan?' I tugged at his sleeve like an infant. My voice came out high and throttled. My chest ached as if I was going to cry, but it wasn't because of the situation I was in. It was something to do with the way Dan put an arm round us both when we got in the boat, me and Tim, and the way he'd been acting all the time, as if this was just part of the day's work, the kind of thing that happens all the time. 'Not to worry, lads,' he'd said, same as ever. 'Seen worse than this, I have, believe me. Don't worry, I'll get you home.' He'd even smiled at us. *Smiled*. As if nothing was wrong. I felt strangely towards him, as if he was Ma or something – reminded me of how she used to say cheerful things in the very old days when we lived in Bermondsey, me and her, when there was shouting and screams coming through the wall. Listen to that lot, Jaffy, she'd say, cocking her head and smiling. Life in all its glory. Come here, shall I sing a song?

Yes, yes, things were bad, but we'd get through. We always did.

'What now?' said Dan. 'Well, as the captain said, Jaf, we stick together. Travel with the wind. Plenty bread, plenty water – if we're careful – a good sixty days. We'll meet with another whale ship long before that, I reckon, hard not to hereabouts. And if the worst comes to the worst, we make South America. No question. Tough little boats, these are.'

Mr Rainey looked at him as if he knew it wasn't so.

'Don't you fool us, Dan,' Tim said. 'We're not stupid.'

'I don't fool, Tim,' Dan said, glaring at him. 'You don't know what you're talking about and I do. Keep your head and do as you're told, and we'll all get home.'

The captain's boat drew alongside and we lit the lanterns. Our portions were doled out. I looked over and imagined being in that boat and was glad I was in this. It was safer. Dan and Gabriel and Yan knew what they were doing. The Captain's boat had Skip, sitting there with his white moon face as blank as a plate.

'You're going to be hungry, boys,' Dan said. 'Get used to it.'

A chunk of hard bread and two swigs of water. The hogs got a swig too; we had to keep them alive. No baccy. No drink. Oh God, give me a smoke and the slow burn of rum. A man of liquor, Rainey was sweating for the lack of both. His hands shook and his eyes lamented. He looked like someone who was feeling sick and trying to ignore it. That's how the whole world felt. Stupid and silent, all of us, till Skip, looking down at the lump of hard-tack in his hands, said in a horrified voice, 'It was all my fault.'

'Idiot,' said John Copper, ''Course it wasn't your fault.'

'It's me,' Skip whimpered. 'I've been horrible.' His nose ran.

'That's as may be,' the captain said sternly, 'it's neither here nor there now. Eat.'

'I've killed Mr Comeragh. I liked Mr Comeragh. I've killed them all!'

'Enough!' barked the captain.

Skip put his head down and nibbled miserably at his tack.

'Billy thought it was,' he said a moment later.

'Thought what?' asked Dag.

'Thought it was my fault.'

'Yeah, well Billy didn't know his arse from his elbow, did he?' said Tim.

'Enough!'

We bobbed on a sparkle of waves, side by side, chewing like cattle. There was a nippy wind. The grinding of my jaws was loud in my head, click-clack of bones. Our hog, sitting roped between Gabriel and Yan with an air of stolid endurance, was a hairy old beast with a rounded belly. I gazed at it and wished I was an animal, to know nothing and never think ahead.

'Mouthy little brat, Bill Stock, wasn't he?' said Tim to no one in particular.

'Yeah,' I said after a while, 'he was, wasn't he?'

Some time in a high-tossed dawn, one by one we arose drenched, yawning and groaning from the belly of the boat. The wind had blown all night, and the hog had shat. We got our hard-tack and a drop of water and sailed on. Thank God these boats did not sail easy, for it kept us on our toes. Better to be occupied than idle. Someone had to man the steering oar. Someone had to fix and hammer and bale. Someone had to keep watch. We were overladen and low in the water, and the sea slopped in all day. We tried to catch fish, but had no means. We had wood from the ship. Gabriel set to whittling a spear.

Thirst and hunger came on sharp. The world can divide, can double like vision. So could I. I was here, wide-eyed, mad-silenced, staring at the sky and the dim grey sea, the bruised and laden smudges of cloud, the waves. The rest of my life was a dream. Things went on still, sane, reasonable. The captain and Mr Rainey kept on at us all the time to keep up appearances, making us shave with the edge of a knife and rub our teeth and comb our hair, and say our prayers night and morning. The prayers were Dan's job. He was good at it too.

'Sweet Jesus Christ who died for us,' a calm but ringing voice that carried between the boats, 'have mercy on us in this troubling time. We are twelve souls afloat on your great ocean asking for help. Send us, Lord, a sail. Amen. We will now say the Lord's Prayer . . .'

Twelve murmuring men, hands together, heads bowed.

Days passed.

Meaningless to speak of a tally. A long time ago Skip said time's gone funny, and it had. It was a dream in the blink of an eye and it was a lifetime. When I think of it now it's as if I lived another whole life a long time ago, was born into it, lived it and died in it.

'Wake up there, Jaf.'

Dan had a shaky hand, missing his booze.

'You were dreaming,' he said. 'What was it? Something chasing you?'

I shook my head. A bag of water in my chest. A dam of tears.

Dreams. The dragon, bigger than before, walking down *Lysander*'s deck on its hind legs like a man. I jerked and blinked the wet from my eyelashes. First thing I saw was Mr Rainey, eyes ablaze, spitting a glob of grey into his hand. His face was yellow-green, rotten. I looked about, couldn't see the captain's boat.

'They've gone!' I cried.

'No no no.' Gabriel, steady at the steering oar. 'They are there.'

The waves rolled in deep valleys. The captain's boat appeared and disappeared, sometimes for long minutes at a time. When we saw them they were baling like us. Never less than three of us at it and still all things in the boat were afloat, including the poor hog. I was sorry for the hog. God knows what he made of life, a peculiar thing it must have seemed to him. The hogs and us were all well salted by now. The salt put a rime about our dry lips and red eyes, made patterns on our dirty clothes, intricate as patterns in rock. Things of water, all of us. Made no difference if it rained on and off, except that it filled the boat quicker and had us all a-baling at once, muscles burning, every man in rhythm. We baled until it was our turn to sleep, slept in the water, woke and baled again. Cried, stupid. In my mind always, a warm bed and a fire. The smell of ale and sweat and ladies' powder. We got our hard-tack, got our water. Tim's face always there, stolid, unreadable, even smiling sometimes, and the seas and skies rising and falling. Every day the same. We blew on and on. Our faces seeing only our other faces, day after day, till no one knew who was who, we were all one: a peculiar striving creature, licking its parched lips, goggling its sore eyes at the horizon.

One day the sky changed and we had clear weather come mid-afternoon. Our boats came together.

'Jesus Christ,' Tim said, 'look at them.'

'We look like that too,' I said.

'How's your bread?' the captain called across. 'Ours is wet.'

'Inevitable,' Mr Rainey replied. 'Ours too, but not all of it.'

'Pretty much all of ours,' the Captain said. 'All bearing up over there?'

215

'Aye aye, Captain, all here in fine form.'

'We must lay out the bread to dry.'

Wilson Pride was already doing this, spreading patiently on top of a bit of old canvas, his face fathomless.

'Still got your hog?'

'Oh, certainly. You have yours?'

'Indeed.'

Their hog had a name by now. Napoleon, shortened to Pole. That was John Copper.

I wasn't hungry. There was a funny feeling in my gut, but I wasn't hungry. My portion had served me well enough, but my mouth and throat were getting raw. The captain said we could all have an extra ration of water tonight, our first night of peace for ages. It was wonderful, that little gift of extra. It was warm and sat on my tongue, a still pond. I held it as long as I could but my mouth absorbed it.

'All right, Skip?' I asked him.

His mouth was set in an awkward sneer. He nodded once sharply.

'We are making excellent speed,' the captain said heartily. There was a big red sore in the middle of his forehead like a third eye. 'We're dead in the middle of the offshore whaling ground. It's only a matter of time now, men. Meanwhile – there's plenty to do.'

We set about fixing our leaks with Joe Harper's tools and we spread things out to dry wherever we could.

The sun fell out of the sky.

I drifted asleep in the dark and woke to salt. Bloody salt. Salt coming out of the bread. Salt tack, burning hot under the sun. Laid out like wares on a stall. Made me think of my home, the market people standing in the cold in their mufflers. Lick my lips, I taste salt. Lick my arm, salt. Everywhere. We frothed a little as

we spoke, working our mouths and throats with gurning patience
to make a little spit. Dolphins came, dancing along with our boats.
Wished I still had my old telescope, but it had gone under with
all the rest. Two or three days they were our companions, cheerful
glimmering things that roiled and boiled and made rainbows, but
we couldn't catch one. Those eyeless faces were laughing, and
after a while we started laughing with them, me and Tim, and
went on for so long that Dan told us to shut our fucking traps or
he'd chuck us overboard, which made us laugh even more. I had
a sore inside my left elbow and another coming up on the back
of my neck, and was trying not to scratch. We laughed so much
that Mr Rainey, who'd been retching all day and looked as if he
was bleeding inside, said, 'Dan, knock their heads together', and
he did, but not very hard, and after that we were quiet, but had
to avoid each other's eyes so we wouldn't start again. We got our
water. It didn't do much good. My tongue was all wiggly, drying
up as soon as I got it a bit wet, tingling at the root and in the
sides of my cheeks like an earache.

'Oh God,' I said. 'Why the hell did I ever come on this journey?'

'You came on this journey,' said Tim, 'to keep up with me.
Because I was going, that's why you came.'

It was true. 'Well, I wasn't going to let you have all the glory,
was I?' I said.

'All the glory!' Tim squawked. 'All the glory! Ha ha ha ha ha
ha ha ha!'

'Why can't we eat the hog?' I asked Dan.

'Because we're saving it.'

'Till when?'

'Till the right time.'

'When's that?'

'When it comes.'

I was silent for a moment, then: 'Which is?'

Gabriel, whittling away with a knife at a piece of wood that was much too short, trying to make a spear, snorted laughter.

'Stow it, Jaf,' Dan said.

The captain called the boats together. Good to see again their dirty salt phizogs: the captain's square face with fallen cheeks; the glaring black eyes of Wilson Pride; Simon Flower, his long brown hair like snakes on his shoulders; Dag, rimed white as a ghost; John Copper with sore eyes and runny nose. And Skip, sitting in the stern with his arms wrapped round himself, rocking like a pendulum. John Copper sat next to him. 'I'm going mad,' John said.

'John's finding life trying.' Captain Proctor smiled blearily.

The surnames had all been dropped; we were all plain Johns and Tims and Simons now, apart from Mr Rainey, and the captain, of course, who was still the captain.

'It's him,' said John, jerking a thumb backwards over his shoulder at Skip. 'Driving me up the wall, he is. Keeps poking me all night saying there's an owl sitting on the gunnel, and there bloody isn't.'

We laughed.

'What's the matter, Skip?' asked Tim.

Skip just shook his head.

'When's this ship coming, Captain?' Gabriel was polishing the end of his spear. 'I thought it would have come by now.'

'I wish I knew. Could be tomorrow, could be the next ten minutes, could be a week or more for all we know.'

'Could be never,' said Simon.

'That's right, could be never.' The captain threw a quick look at him. 'But by my reckoning, we're well on course for the coast of Chile, so if the worst comes to the worst and no ship comes, we should make a landing there in about three weeks. Weather permitting, of course.' He looked round at us all and smiled in an encouraging way.

'Three weeks.' Simon drooped.

'It's nothing,' said Rainey sharply.

'In the course of your life, Simon,' the captain added, stifling a yawn, 'three weeks is a drop in the ocean.'

'It's my head,' said John. 'If I could just get rid of this headache.'

'Where is it?' I asked. 'I've got one too.'

'All over.'

'Mine's at the back of my eyes.'

'It's bloody awful,' Skip said in a sudden tearful voice. 'I can't stand it.'

'What do you mean by that, Skip?' Dan said. 'You *are* standing it. You have no choice.'

'*He's* standing it,' John said, 'it's me that's going mad.'

'It's *my* head too,' said Skip.

'And mine,' said Yan.

'It's the sun,' said Mr Rainey, voice chop-chop like a blade.

'True.' The captain squinted up at the blank blue sky. 'The sun goes down in an hour and a half.'

'Ten days it is now,' said Dag.

'Nine.' A rare word from Wilson.

'Ten.'

'Nine.'

'Ten,' said Simon, closing his eyes.

'Not if you don't count the day we stayed with the ship.'

'It's the thirst,' said Rainey, and his voice cracked like a schoolboy's, shocking to hear from a man like him. I tried to open my mouth, but it stuck shut.

'Water,' Tim said. 'Must be time.'

My tot of water. Silver on my tongue.

The captain looked up at the sky and down at the bottom of the boat where Pole lay on his side panting weakly in the heat. 'I think,' he said, 'it's time we killed a pig.'

Our hog was nameless, a stolid soul that took no notice at all when Pole began to scream. Nothing makes such a racket as a hog. Such exquisite terror. Wilson hauled him from his nook and got him over on his side. Out splayed his spiky little legs, trotters stabbing in spasm, kick, kick, kick. Wilson held him down while Simon and Dag grabbed and dodged and had the devil of a job getting him hobbled, but he was tied in a few minutes and they lay across his body to keep him still. Wilson cut his throat. The hog twitched on as his blood drained into the bucket John Copper held under his throat, and screamed on too, terrible sounds, vile, cutting. Blood filled the bucket and slopped over into the bottom of the boat.

'Here, Yan, pass the other bucket over,' said Captain Proctor.

The smell made my head light, the smell of the butcher's shop two doors down from our old house on Watney Street. The smell in the early morning of blood and brine, the pig's heads in a tub. The captain tipped some of the blood into the second bucket, dipped one of our tin cups in and hesitated for a moment before handing it sideways to Mr Rainey. Rainey took it, looked down into it, closed his eyes and drank. The captain filled the other cup and passed it in the other direction, to John Copper.

'Not too much, John,' Proctor said. 'Sip it.'

The cups went round in both directions and all of us drank except for Gabriel, who started heaving.

'Can't,' he said. His eyes streamed.

'It's all right, Gabriel,' Dan said. 'It doesn't taste of anything.'

It didn't, not really, but it was salty and warm.

'I know,' said Gabriel, closing his eyes. 'Give me a minute.'

Skip drank as if tasting good wine, tentative, thoughtful. His eyes closed as he drank.

The hog's dying went on.

'Knock its head in, for God's sake!' John Copper said.

'*You* knock its head in,' growled Simon.

'I will,' said John, but by the time he'd groped his way forward and shakily lifted the axe, the hog was gone.

Wilson had a few sips then set about his work. 'It's not the best knife for the job,' he said.

The cup came round again.

The blood was already changing colour, thickening like a roux. My body twitched with joy. I'd never been hungry like this. Wilson cut the hog's legs and head off, slit the hairy black back and put his big meaty hands in under the flaps. He pulled, and two great blankets of hide came away with a tearing sound. Dag hung them up on the sails for the sea to salt.

'Here, we'll make a fire here,' Rainey said.

'Jump to, Skip and John, get all this cleared up,' said the captain.

They were baling blood. Sea blood, salt blood. Skip's eyes were wide and his lower lip drooled from its centre. The chitterlings were in a bucket, plump and shiny, grey and pink. They smelled like shit. The liver was a wing, deltaed with fat. A soft balloon of a thing, the bladder, delicately patterned. Wilson tied its end off and squirted piss to wash blood from the boat. We cleaned up and made a fire on the top of Joe Harper's toolbox, up out of the wet, with wood from the ship. We'd been drying it in the sun but it was still damp. Wilson had managed against all odds to keep a supply of dry matches. God knows where he kept them. Up his arse probably, Tim said. Who cared? So long as they lit a fire. Now that we were doing something and had drunk, we were cheerful. Saliva returned to our mouths, thick and claggy. Dan whistled.

We kept the flames ticking along with a few bits of rag.

'What are you doing, boys?' said Dan, elbowing us aside. 'Don't you know how to light a fire? Useful knowledge, boys, useful knowledge. Just watch me.'

They passed over from the other boat a shoulder, a leg, some ribs. We stuck them with knives and tools and held them in the fire, and the juices ran down and made the flames spit and fed the fire. We cooked everything as well as we could, but we couldn't wait long enough. The smell was driving us mad. They'd started their own fire over there now and stuck the hog's head, eyeless, on a stick over it. The sun was beginning to go down and our fires were warm and lovely and made homely trails of smoke rise up above our boats. Among our sails hung wonderful hides, marbled pink and white with flesh and fat.

The ears cooked in no time. Wilson cut them off.

'Who gets these?' he asked.

'Cut them in half and let the lads have them,' the captain replied. That was Skip and John and me and Tim. Skip cried when he got his. Sat there chewing with a runny nose. My God, hog's ear is food for gods. It's tough, you can suck and chew and gnaw and it lasts for ages. Next came the tail, Simon got that, then the feet, and when at last I got my teeth into a real ham, it was pink in the middle and eating it hurt. Agony in the pits of my cheeks, sharper than the sting of salt in the sores erupting like volcanoes on my legs. We ate the lot, guts and all, apart from the hides and some strips of pork hung up to dry. It was glorious. The captain said we could have an extra ration of water, just for tonight, to celebrate the killing of the pig and our tenth day in the boats.

'We have done splendidly,' he said, his ringing tone restored. 'Splendidly!'

We have food enough. We have water for a good time yet, we have our spirits and we are sure of our salvation in God's hands.

He led us in a small prayer of thanksgiving.

We were at peace like big cats after feeding. There was a moon. The ocean was beautiful. Simon played his fiddle. We sang 'The Black Ball Line', 'Santy Anno', 'Lowlands Low'. Yan sang something from his country and Dag sang something from his. John sang the filthiest version I ever heard of 'My God How the Money Rolls In'. And we sang 'Blood Red Roses', a song of many moods. For every occasion there is a verse to suit. For the crashing storm and galloping wind, we would roar at the tops of our voices:

> Our boots and shoes is all in pawn
> Go down you blood red roses, go down!
> It's fucking draughty around Cape Horn.
> Go down, you blood red roses, go down!

And for now, a time of content and full-belly warmth:

> Oh, my dear mother she wrote to me,
> Go down, you blood red roses, go down
> My lovely son, come home from sea –
> Go down, you blood red roses, go down . . .

. . . sweet and teary, some of us thinking of the mothers they'd never had, some of the one they had or the one they'd had and lost. Even my memories of home and Ishbel and Ma and everything made me happy. All we lacked was a smoke.

Tomorrow, perhaps, a sail.

But we got no sail. Not tomorrow or the day after or the one after that, and it went on.

'Once,' Mr Rainey said, 'these seas were full of whale ships.'

The wind shifted to the north. We ate the marbled flesh from the hides till they started to turn a funny green and the captain said it was best not to take any chances, so we chucked them over and were back on the salty hardtack and warm water. The taste and smell of the hog stayed on the edge of sense, the warm slip of the blood down the gullet, the juices. Having drunk, I was drier than ever, my mouth a wretched, clamouring place. Ever east towards South America. Much talk of islands. There *should* have been islands. The captain and Mr Rainey often put their heads together and murmured over the quadrant.

'I can remember a time,' Mr Rainey said, 'when you couldn't sail more than a few days without there'd be another whale ship.'

There should have been islands and there should have been ships.

'True,' said Gabriel, 'the whaling's done for.'

'Jaf.' Tim's voice, careless. 'What if we've sailed into another world?'

'There'd still be islands.'

'What if it's a world without islands? What if it's a world where there's nothing anywhere except one great big ocean?'

By the fourth night after the hog, I was beginning to think he was right. We *had* sailed into another world, something running along next to ours, something that had always been there but invisible. It consisted only of ocean. It couldn't be our world. Everyone knew the Pacific was full of islands. Where were the whale ships? What use were the compasses and the quadrant and all of the captain and Mr Rainey's reckonings and consultations if they could not bring us in reasonable time to one of these islands or steer us into the shipping grounds?

John Copper woke us up screaming in his sleep, said he thought there were horrible wormy things with biting teeth running up his arms and sides.

'It's him!' he said, shuddering as if someone had just thrown a bucket of raw fish all over him like in the old story. 'Poking me. He's driving me mad.'

'Not this time,' said Skip, 'I didn't.'

'You did,' Simon said. 'I saw you.'

'No, you didn't.'

'My head's killing me,' John groaned.

'Skip, you're causing nightmares.' Proctor rubbed his face. 'For God's sake, man, pull along with the rest of us.'

Wilson Pride chipped in. 'This ain't fair,' he said, 'and it ain't wise. They should have him for a bit.'

'You're right,' the captain said. 'Yan, change with Skip.'

'Oh Jesus.' Gabriel lay down and covered his head.

'Beg pardon, Captain, I'm not so sure that's a good idea,' Mr Rainey said.

'Why not? The way things are carrying on, if he stays over here he'll end up done away with. We need respite.'

'Very well, sir,' Mr Rainey replied stiffly, 'but I won't answer for him.'

'No more need you, Mr Rainey,' the captain said. 'He can look to himself. Skip, I hope you're listening to all this. Pull yourself together.'

'Yes, Captain,' Skip snuffled meekly, raising himself up and groping his way towards us.

'Skip,' said Mr Rainey, 'if you poke one person – even *once* – do you hear? – I will personally throw you overboard.'

'It's my fault,' said Skip in a small voice. 'It's because I killed the dragon.'

'You didn't kill the dragon!' roared Rainey.

'I did. I set it free so it died.'

'How do you know it's dead?' said Tim. 'How do you know it didn't get home and it's sitting there right now on its little island with its grandchildren at its knee telling them all about its big adventure amongst the madmen?'

'Sit down, Skip,' said Dan. 'Don't open your mouth again.'

Mr Rainey came down with a bad head cold. His eyes watered constantly and his nose ran like a tap. 'I'll be coughing next,' he said, 'it always goes to my chest. You lot better keep away from me.'

Fat chance.

'Remember, lads,' Dan said, dispensing our water, 'for every day that passes we are one day closer to rescue.'

'Aye, by God,' Rainey agreed, wiping his nose on his sleeve.

We drank a little then baled some more, till Dag gave a shout and we saw dogfish between the boats. Gabriel reached for his spear. Shining fins, three, four, came and went. It was no good. We couldn't get anywhere near close enough. We stalked them as well as we could for the best part of an hour before they left us, heading west in a line. Darkness fell complete, no moon, no stars. It was Tim's watch, then Dan's. I slept. When I woke, Mr Rainey, coughing irritatingly, was talking with Gabriel.

'The boat's gone, Jaf,' Tim said in a wonderstruck voice.

'What do you mean?'

'Gone.'

'What? The other boat?'

'Yeah.'

'How?'

'It was just gone when the light came up.'

I sat up. The sea was empty. Skip woke up and raised himself slowly, blinking. No one spoke. There was nothing to be done. We drank our ration. Mr Rainey spewed his back up, nearly flinging himself overboard in the action.

'Lie down, man,' said Dan.

'How can they be gone?' asked Skip in a puzzled tone.

I tried not to think.

'I think I will,' Rainey said, blinking. His forehead was bright red, dripping.

'*Where* have they gone?'

'Hush, Skip.' Gabriel put a hand on his shoulder. 'There's no answer to it. It's not a question worth asking.'

'Give us your knife, Gabe,' I said, 'I want to cut my toenails.'

'Don't cut your toes off, boy.' He handed it over.

'Can't look for them,' Dan said. 'Nothing we can do.'

'They've got the quadrant,' I said, setting about my nails.

'And the matches,' Skip added.

'No matter. We can dead reckon.' Dan smiled bravely. 'Valparaiso, here we come.'

We would miss the fiddle. I concentrated on my toes. My eyes filled. Our friends over there, their faces always glimpsed sideways, the captain big and owly, Yan's handsome, slanted cheeks, Simon brooding, Wilson stoic, Dag's blond shock of hair. And poor, worried John Copper biting his lips. Never see them again? They weren't dead though, not like those other ones, and now I must number them again, for to forget is death. I laid the knife by. I was blind, full of tears. Billy Stock, Henry Cash, Martin Hannah, Abel Roper, Joe Harper, Mr Comeragh, Felix. Who else? Sam. How could I forget old Sam? If I closed my eyes he was there. If I closed my eyes anything was there: Ishbel, Meng's fireplace with its meerschaum pipes, the corner of Watney Street.

We sailed blind all day and all the next.

'How far away do you think it is to Chile?' asked Tim.

Dan laughed. 'A little way yet.'

'At least two weeks,' said Gabriel.

Mr Rainey had ripped his shirt open at the front and, still sleeping, was scratching fretfully away at three red sores the size of shillings that had formed a triangle on his hairless chest.

It rained. The weather at sea is like running paint. All the sky smudges. The shades of sky move in a dance, run along the curving horizon, take on form. The east was a shining slate and shimmered at us like a god. Mr Rainey slept in the rain. It cooled our sores. We held up our faces to catch the drops and it ran in our eyes and washed all sweat away, singing like a choir, millions of voices in perfect harmony. The boat began to buck and prance. Big waves rolled under us.

'It's coming. Down sails,' Dan said.

The gale raged all night and all the next day and all the night after that. There was nothing to be done with the boat. We lay low, all huddled together in the bottom. When darkness came we held onto each other, every man clutching a fistful of cloth, a hand, a shoulder, an elbow. Every few minutes sheet lightning flashed across the sky, and we'd see each other's ghastly lit-up faces, big-eyed and stark.

On the third morning the wind dropped and the sea calmed, and we raised the masts again and sailed no more than an hour, before a sound like a gunshot reached us from a great distance. It was on Tim's watch and he cried out: 'It's them! It's them!' and all of us rose and stared against the glaring sea.

I saw nothing.

'It is!' exclaimed Gabriel. 'I see them.'

Then we all saw the tiny dark stain very far away, west, and Mr Rainey took out his pistol and fired once into the sky. A faint roar was our reward.

We cheered, hurt our throats.

'Impossible,' Dan said. His hand gripped my shoulder, trembling. Though he smiled like a madman, he looked scared. His watery blue eyes, never blinking, were fixed with something akin to horror on what approached, and it jumped into my head that the boat would reach us and we'd see it was full of dead men still going about their business. Their sores would have run mad, covering every inch of them. Their eyes would be ghastly.

'Mr Rainey!' the captain hailed us.

We could see their faces now, their good old ordinary faces: Captain Proctor, Wilson Pride, Yan, Simon, Dag and John. All smiling.

Mr Rainey pulled himself together and called across that we were all fine and dandy over here and in very good spirits.

I was on watch one day when something hit the sail and fell into the boat.

Fish. Another. Another.

There was a scramble.

A whole host of fish. Beautiful things, flashes of silver leaping from the sea and flying like shearwaters, some the size of a finger, some as long as a foot, skimming close to the surface, touching down from time to time, only to take off again. They had bird's wings at the front behind their heads, and little finny ones vibrating at their tails. A dozen or so landed in our boat – three or four of fair size and lots of tiddlers. We gorged, raw. It was like eating the sea.

'See?' said Dan. 'See? Providence,' pulling bones from his teeth.

'Providence!' Gabriel laughed. 'Providence can go either way.'

'So it can,' said Dan. 'For now it's with us. Rainey, are you all right?'

'No. I'm bloody not all right. Do I look all right?'

He'd gone all bug-eyed. Since we'd eaten the other hog he'd been getting terrible headaches and spent a lot of time rubbing his forehead and the backs of his ears. Dan was pretty much our skipper now. A month had passed. Heat, sudden, heat by day, cold by night.

'I don't think I can take much more of this,' Gabriel said dreamily.

'My face feels funny,' I gobbed.

'It's all right, Jaffo,' Tim said.

'No.'

'It is. It *is* all right, you know.' He had a curious, stiff smile.

'Yes,' I replied. My tongue stuck to the back of my teeth with

229

a bitter, gummy slime, which gave off a vile stenchy taste as rank as a Bermondsey sewer.

'Ah, landlord,' he mugged, 'a flagon of your best!'

'You'll get your ration soon,' Dan said.

Our mouths would have dripped if they could.

'Do you remember when we caught fish under London Bridge, Jaffo?'

'Me, you and Ishbel,' I said.

'Fried in a bit of butter,' Tim said.

'Wonder what Ishbel's doing now?'

'She's washing her feet,' he said.

The thought of Ishbel washing her feet filled me with joy.

'Do you think so?'

'Oh yes. She wonders about us.'

'She'd have come if she could.'

'I know.'

Mr Rainey started sneezing convulsively, over and over again.

'He's for the chop,' Tim said.

Seemed likely.

'He'll be the first,' I said.

'Likely.'

I yawned till tears wet the corners of my eyes. Immediately they dried. No clouds.

'Can't swallow properly,' I said. 'I keep trying.'

'Don't try,' said Dan.

'I want to get off this . . . this . . .' Gabriel, a great sigh. 'Sick of the whole fucking . . .'

Rainey fell asleep and started snoring hoarsely.

'He's had it,' Dan said. 'Poor man.'

'Nearly time for the sun to sink,' said Skip.

'Where are the others?'

'There.'

A ghostly grey boat that dogs us always, bearing our shades, hollow-eyed.

Dan gently woke Mr Rainey. The captain's boat came nigh, the faces of Yan and John and Simon and Wilson and Dag. Dag's broad face was the colour of teak, his hair white as Lancashire cheese, his whiskers wild and wiry. The captain and Mr Rainey gave out our portions.

'Yum yum,' Tim said.

'Reached for a chicken, got me a goose,' sang Gabriel. The sores on his lips had cracked and were running into one another. His forehead shone.

'Here, get this in.' Dan trickled water from his fingers through my lips. My tongue unstuck.

'I'm going in,' said Skip.

'I wouldn't,' Dan said. 'You get salt in them sores you'll be screaming.'

'Can't make a difference,' Skip replied, 'I'm salt all over anyway. Long as it's cold I don't care.'

'Me too,' Tim said, 'I'll come too.'

'Don't let go the side,' said Dan.

So they went over, softly sinking in the cool sea, their heads bobbing alongside. It was funny. They didn't know whether to groan for the salt sting or sigh in ecstasy as the water cooled their blood. So they laughed instead, looking at one another and giggling like children.

'What's it like?' I asked.

I would have gone, but I had a feeling that if I left the boat, I'd never get back, so I just hung over and dangled my hands. Then Gabriel too slid over the side. Had to, he said, he was burning up. Not me, said Dan. The sun would soon sink, *then* we'd feel cold enough.

The boats came together. Soon after, up goes the cry from Skip

231

that there's shells under the boat, hundreds of them, and they start pulling them off and cracking them and stuffing their mouths with the flesh from inside. It went dark, sudden like it does, and all you could hear as the lanterns were lit were the splashes in the water and the shouts of excitement. Both boats were covered. We passed over the buckets, and when they were filled and not a single shell left under the boats, the boys were too weak to climb back over the side, struggling to raise a knee or haul themselves up with an arm, like kittens going upstairs, pathetic and funny, laughing at themselves. All of us laughing as we pulled them in like heavy nets, eating the barnacles or winkles or whatever they were. Beautiful, soft and succulent, plucked living by the white neck from the brown shell. We said we'd save some, but we ate the lot in one. All except Mr Rainey, who said he couldn't fancy them. Couldn't fancy them! Offer me a worm, I'd have given it a go.

'Come on, man,' Dan urged, 'they'll do you good. Just one, here, try.'

'Let me sleep,' the poor man said, laying his head against the gunwale, folding his arms and closing his eyes.

It's funny, the things you say when words are strictly limited. A word was a sacred, precious, much-laden thing.

'That was lovely fresh water,' Rainey croaked.

He looked peculiar, all puffed up around the face and neck. I saw Dan get his mouth ready for speech, working his tongue and lips several times before he could get a word out.

'Mad,' he said. 'Glory Lord.'

We'd had a norther for a while and got along at a merry old jog, but then it turned. We'd hardly moved since God knows when, crawling on like a snail on a pavement over the sea, which seemed mysteriously to have emptied itself of all life but ourselves. The birds had gone. I missed their squawking company. Fish too, scarcely one broke the surface.

'How long?' asked John Copper. Water.

The captain swallowed audibly. 'Hour,' he said.

'Can't be!

A nod.

Yan leaned over the gunwale and trailed his hand in the sea. He murmured something and scooped up a little in his palm and dashed it against his lips.

Proctor shook his head. 'Don't swallow.'

'Wait,' Dan said. 'Only an hour.'

'Can't.' John followed Yan.

'But if we don't swallow . . .' Tim said.

'No.'

Yan and John licked their lips. The gleam of moisture all too much.

'Drink piss,' Dan said thickly. 'Better.'

I'd been thinking about that. Saving it for when I felt bad enough. We'd even had a laugh about it, me and Tim and Skip. But a boat would come before that, or an island with streams. An island, a boat, a vision, an angel, the devil in person, anything at all, please come.

'Boys, boys, my boys,' I heard Dan, far away, 'I am proud of you. What a character I will give you when we get home. Only a little longer now, boys. Hang on.'

But I could no longer believe that this was anything but madness. We were quite out of the world, in a place like a dream, where terrors could harm and nothing was impossible. I turned away so I wouldn't have to see them with the water in their mouths, a tightening of pain in them as the salt touched ulcers.

'Nonsense,' I heard Rainey say. 'As long as you don't swallow, a mouthful can do no harm.'

I closed my eyes. Darkness on the face of the deep. I wanted to hear Sam singing. If I tried, I could. His peculiar gnat-like delivery that was sometimes unbearably pure. I got him singing and singing to me in my head, his old hymns: 'God moves on the water, God moves . . .' He sang it over and over and over till it started going funny, tripping along to the rhythm of the waves. God bring a boat, God bring rain, God bring manna, God this, God that. Words words words. In my heart there was only an aching, empty place like a lost tooth, that and the empty sky and sea, and eternity, and a presence that did not reassure.

'One mouthful then. One only.'

Dan held the cup to my lips.

One mouthful, hold, spit.

Wet mouth, for a second.

Do NOT swallow.

It's okay, better than piss. Piss came shortly after. It's hideous, but you can swallow it. It was worse than I expected and it looked so nice too, as if it would be sweet, but no such thing. It tasted the way it smells when it's been standing a day because someone's forgotten to empty the jerry. A stern, bitter, unfriendly taste, I thought, though some didn't seem to mind it at all. Maybe theirs was better than mine. Anyway, it didn't work, or it did, but not for long. It was a false quenching, like drinking hard liquor: wet, but in the long run thirst-inducing. So I never took to it, though you'd hear different from some, no doubt. Tim's piss was golden, of course, and he drank it with relish. Honey sweet, no doubt. Dirty brown, gold-haired Tim, with darker gold whiskers encroaching from his ears, and round brown hollows about the eyes. 'You know what, Jaf?' he said. 'I feel as if my mind's going funny.'

'Yes.'

'Yours?'

A nod.

234

'Tell Simon to play something.'

'Simon. Hey, Simon.'

Simon sawing away at the fiddle, a merry thing. He was good, Simon. Lovely player. Could make you cry, make you smile. But it was nothing, that poor little fiddle, a voice singing against the great waterfall at the end of the world, where our small boat plunges over and falls for ever. Mr Rainey's mouth was yellow all over. And still he would hold the salt water in his mouth because he couldn't bear not to. 'Long as you don't swallow,' he said. He did it more than the rest of us, more than he should have, that's why he went down so fast, I think, that and because he caught that terrible cold not long after we set off and it went onto his chest. It scared me to see so hard and big a man, a man I'd been scared of, go down. He couldn't swallow. His throat was closing over. His face clenched and grew naked in spasms. His feet swelled up like bladders. I went over to sit with him. The movement made me dizzy and for a few seconds grey clouds gathered in front of my eyes, and my heart went mad. I couldn't talk to him. I didn't know him at all. A very uneasy man he'd always seemed to me, and that at least was still the same. Tears were trickling from the corners of his eyes and gleaming in the crinkles there.

The wind dropped. Every now and then someone spoke, but I forgot what they said at once. Every now and then I got my portion. I kept feeling my chin to see if I was getting a beard, but nothing. Only the captain still shaved. Rainey was shaggy as an old dog. It made him look handsome and terrible, like an Old Testament prophet with his tormented eyes. Salt was drying us by degrees. Salt fish all of us, salt fish with wide open round eyes goggling at the sky. Our faces all had the same skinned, wild look about them and the bones of our skulls were cutting through. Wet hair curled on our shoulders. Our eyes gleamed. We were

235

hard brown and weathered, knobbled like branches, and our togs were rotting through.

The sails blew out their cheeks. On into sunsets and sunrises. They said we had to be very careful with the water, just in case.

'It won't last, will it?' Simon said in a matter-of-fact way.

'It will if we're careful.'

'It'll rain soon.'

'The rain won't help.'

'How long to Chile?' asked Dag.

The captain sighed. 'Depends on the weather. Perhaps twenty days.'

No one spoke. Twenty days.

'Don't fret,' the captain said, 'there's no need to cut the ration yet, but if nothing happens in the next – six – days,' he hesitated fractionally, as if he was making the decision on the instant, 'we may have to.'

'But we couldn't manage on less,' John Copper said.

Skip put his arms over his head and started moaning.

'What's the matter, Skip?'

He just shook his head and moaned on, a sing-song humming as he rocked.

'Oh, leave him if it makes him feel better. Moan away, Skip, only not too loud.'

'It's because I killed the dragon,' Skip said, looking up at us. 'That's why everything happened.'

'Mad.'

Rainey raised himself up from the bottom of the boat, set his hands upon the gunwale and stared ahead with glaring eyes. It was a blazing hot day and the sun was almost at its zenith.

'Cover your head, man,' said Dan, but Rainey silenced him with a stiff gesture.

'Shh!'

236

'What?'

'Listen!'

Nothing.

'What is it?'

'Can't you hear it?'

'Can't hear a thing.'

'Jaf, can you?'

I shook my head. The shaking of my head set up a humming in my brain.

We were all listening now.

'Poor thing,' Rainey said, his eyes filling with tears. 'Poor thing.'

'Where?' said Skip. 'Where is the poor thing?'

Where else could the poor thing be but there, in the sea? It wasn't here with us in our little boat. Nor over there, in the captain's. All there were well enough. What could be crying in the sea or the air?

Tears poured down Mr Rainey's cheeks. 'My God, my God, my dear God,' he said, 'let this thing pass.'

Mr Rainey was only a man after all. A very strong one up to a point, but he was going down. Dan got him lying down and wiped his face. 'You've been swallowing seawater,' Dan said. 'No more now. Here.' And he gave Mr Rainey his own ration of water there and then, and had only a tiny drop himself left for later. 'Lay off the seawater, man,' he said, 'it's no good. Kill you, man. Lay off it now and you'll be fine.'

'Yes,' said Mr Rainey, his teeth chattering.

'Now hold together. I mean it. You give up and let go and what happens? You get a boat over the horizon the very next morn.'

A storm came from the southwest and we were back at the baling, except Rainey, who remained at the useless place where the steering oar had been before some rough sea took it, weeping stoically and staring out at – what? A flash of lightning. The sky

237

growling. If he dies, I thought, we can have his portion. He turned away from the sea, his tears unanswered. He lay in the bottom of the boat, talking to himself. Sometimes he laughed joyfully, sometimes cried like a newborn and called on his ma. Horrible to see that big man in that state. 'Maria!' he called. 'Maria, Maria,' he groaned.

'His wife,' said Gabriel.

'Yes, yes, we all think on our wives,' said Dan. 'Are you a married man?'

Gabriel nodded.

In the evening, just before dark, Mr Rainey sat up and wiped his eyes and licked his gummy lips with his slow gummy tongue. 'Well,' he said, 'here we are.'

'So we are,' said Gabriel.

Tim put his hand in mine. 'The sky,' he said, looking up.

It was that second before dark. It glimmered.

'Where are you from, Mr Rainey?' Skip asked.

Rainey looked at him and thought for a moment, then smiled slowly. 'Norwich,' he said.

Said Tim:

> The man in the moon came down too soon,
> And found his way to Norwich.
> He went down south and burnt his mouth
> From eating cold pease porridge.

'Do you all eat porridge in Norwich?' asked Skip.

Mr Rainey laughed and tears came out of his eyes, trickling through the dirt on his face. 'No more than they all eat jelly in Delhi,' he said.

We all burst out laughing. The others in the captain's boat must have thought we were having a rare old time. But in the middle of us all laughing came the sudden throwing backwards of Mr

Rainey against the gunwale, as if a giant invisible hand slapped him there. Then he went mad, banging and flapping about horribly with his head twisting and thrashing enough to break his neck, and his mouth open and his tongue rushing out and in, and his eyes squelched shut, and his feet kicking and his arms flailing. He was so broken by it, it made me sick. I couldn't stand to see him like that, and yet he was there in front of me cracking himself to death, and with every smack of his head against the boards, I closed my eyes like you do at hammer cracks.

Dan and Tim went to him, but could get no hold.

His eyes rolled up and up and up, blue-white and bulging. Then the whites stopped flickering and he fell still and was dead.

11

I never saw anyone die till I saw Billy Stock die. Animals, many. Never a person, never a person I knew, a Billy Stock or a Mr Rainey.

The boats came together. We sewed Mr Rainey up in his clothes, me and Gabriel and Skip, not a word between us. The last glimpse of his face: open-lipped, frowning, the shadow of the shroud half upon it. Blue skin. Gabriel closed the cloth over it and sewed it up with his bone needle. The captain said the prayer. Dan and Tim slipped him over the side.

'Oh Lord, we are eleven souls afloat . . .'

Me and Tim and Dan and Skip and Gabe on our boat. Six over there: the Captain, John Copper, Wilson Pride, Dag, Simon, Yan.

Dan said to us, 'You know, he was at the seawater all the time. On the quiet. That's what did for him. Don't you do that, boys. We'll raise a good glass in Valparaiso.'

We were at our daily ration. A cup of water. A lump of hard-tack. I tried to spin it out. I wasn't hungry like I was at the beginning, this was different. The cramps had gone, but something remained like a ghost, like I suppose it feels when they've cut your leg off but you still feel it there stuck to you, itching and twitching and aching and doing all the other things a limb does. I scraped tiny bits off my hard biscuit and sucked them from my fingers. I was very good. Very sensible, I thought, not like Skip, who got through his in about five minutes and then, like a dog, watched me eat mine. Tim was quick with his too. He'd follow it up with an hour or two's nibbling and sucking peacefully and steadily on the leather of his oar.

'What's it like?' I said. 'That?'

'Nice.'

It made the time pass a little softer. My eyes roamed, looking for food. Wood? How about that? Wood was all around. Wood. I'll mention it to Dan, I thought. It's possible. Leather now, we're not so badly off. Still a few boots around, Proctor's and Dan's, and belts. And now the sea-soaked stuff was gone and it was nice dry tack, and there was still plenty of water. For now. What else? More barnacles. Must go under and look. But I was scared of going over. I felt weak, not sure I could get back in. Could be anything under there. I closed my eyes and saw scallops fat as puffballs, white and orange, already out of their shells, clinging all over the bottom of the boat, blowing there like flowers under the sea, sweet as the sticky Chinese fruit we ate in . . . where was it? Meat. The stew my ma cooked out of fat mutton and onions and barley, the grease that floated on top of the pan, quivering as it simmered. Fried fish, steaming layers of eyeball-white flesh. Mashed turnip with the butter melting in it. Bacon frying, singing in the pan, bacon and a fried egg, round orange dome, jelly, the rashers just beginning to burn. Barley soup, goose with gravy, liver and onions, wine, beer, gin, pig's feet, tripe, toast and dripping. Mrs Linver's milk pudding with a rich brown crust on top. Cream on my tongue. Raspberries, ruby, dusted, crushing their seeds between my teeth. Juices spurting. There in the street outside the pastry cook's shop on Back Lane again—

'It's my fault,' Skip said.

He said this so many times it became true. Yes, we thought. If he hadn't let the dragon free. So many dead and it's all your fault. Not that we were angry with him. No point. It was God everyone was angry at. The thunder and lightning. The stupid waves. We rode a monster.

'Will you shut up with that?' Tim said listlessly.

'Sorry,' said Skip.

It went on and on, a day and a day and another day, until the day Captain Proctor said we had to cut the rations again. Wilson Pride laughed. I never saw him really laugh but that once; a rich giggling laugh that just about cracked his face open, and got us all going as if it was a great joke, this cutting of the rations. Captain Proctor sacrificed his leather belt. Precious little to make a fire with. Wilson took a couple of leaves of Skip's sketchbook to help the flames along, and he boiled up the belt in one of the buckets and kept it bubbling there with a little water, very careful, very careful with the water now. It smelled like the tanning factory. Bermondsey on the ocean. He said we shouldn't eat the belt itself, but doled out the water it was cooked in, dark and roasty and bitter, the fire of a hot drink down the startled gullet. That and my portion and it was, all told, not a bad night that followed. I slept cosy. The good, hot drink stayed in my stomach, a wonderful hum of ease as I drifted in dreams of bright wanderings in strange worlds that spun on and on and in and out of each other, hundreds and hundreds of them.

I woke in the night and heard Dan talking to Yan. The boats were hooked together. They lolled each in their respective sterns, quietly conversing.

'Like fire,' said Yan.

'Whereabouts?'

'Here.'

243

'How are your ankles?'

'Terrible.'

'No better then?'

'Look.'

Dan shifted. A moment's silence then, 'Jesus,' he said.

'You see?' said Yan.

'We could do with Abel. He had a way with that sort of thing.'

'What day is it?'

'Day forty-seven.'

'Are you sure?'

'Sure.'

'Weather's on the turn.'

'God, let it rain.'

It did, but not till next nightfall, and we filled the buckets and drank. First sip, sip, then more, at last a time to drink.

'That's enough,' Dan said.

His hand on mine, gentle, decayed.

'There, see?' he said. 'Something always comes along.'

In the morning we awoke to the slow whining of the fiddle. Scrape, scrape, the sound was losing sweetness yet oddly lovely, the voice going hoarse. Something was getting at the fiddle. The salt I suppose, just like it got at everything else.

'Ach!' said Simon. 'No good.'

Dan shook me. 'Up, Jaf,' he said.

I felt light, as if I might drift up into the sky.

'Up, Jaf.'

He pulled my cover off. I couldn't see a thing. Blind in the full sun full in my eyes.

'Steady.' Dan's hand.

I knocked against Tim.

'Watch what you're doing!' he snapped.

I retched. Nothing came. Things cleared.

'Come on, Jaf,' Gabe said, 'take your oar.'

A huge yawn shook me. I dragged myself up. Skip was sitting next to me crying, his moon face gone beyond recall. He was the colour of liver. His skin clung to his skull, though his eyes were still bright.

'All right, Skip?' I said to him.

He nodded.

Yan was in a bad way.

'You're five and we're six,' the captain said. 'Take one more, will you? This man has to lie down, we need more room.'

So Dag came on our boat and we dipped lower in the water. In the captain's boat, Yan stretched out like a log. John Copper groaned and held his stomach, groping down his breeches and sticking his scrawny arse over the side to drip dark green goo into the sea.

Not even worth baling these days, it was so still. Nothing to do but lie and doze. But you keep on waking up, that's the trouble. There's always someone somewhere moaning or champing his mouth disgustingly, someone swearing or mumbling, waking from a dream with a cry. Always your own heart yattering on in your ears as if it'll burst. When evening came Yan refused his bread. Pushed it away. Wouldn't even drink. Simon tried to pour it in his mouth, but he let it run out. We ate our portions and drank our share, and all the time Yan never moved, though there was some kind of churning in his throat and his eyeballs switched about, eerily visible, as if his eyelids were transparent. After a while this stopped too, and then the captain put his hand over Yan's face, felt for the pulses in his wrist and neck and found nothing.

'Dead,' he said.

It didn't mean anything. We just lolled there a while with Yan lying dead, then Simon said, 'So what now?'

The captain sighed.

'We can use his belt,' Wilson Pride said. 'Come in useful.'

Another long silence.

'The custom of the sea,' said Simon expressionlessly.

'No.' That was Gabriel.

'Supposing,' Tim said, 'we could—'

'No,' said Gabriel.

'I don't mean—'

'No.'

'I mean bait. Bait for sharks, then we could catch—'

'No.'

'What sharks?' said Skip.

It was true, the waters were empty.

'We could . . .'

The captain stirred himself. 'Let's prepare him for the sea,' he said gruffly.

So Simon and Wilson took his belt for boiling up tomorrow and sewed him up in his clothes like we sewed up Mr Rainey, and we buried him in the sea. We'd miss Yan, but there was no spare water for tears and all of us were blank. None of us had any idea what kind of a service you should say for his oriental soul. No one knew how they did things in his country. So it was just a bit of a mumble from the captain again, and the bowing of heads and the closing of eyes, and I fell half asleep and scarcely noticed as they slid him into the sea. That night when prayers came, it was: 'Oh Lord, we are ten souls afloat . . .' and I nearly laughed. We are twelve, eleven, ten, nine, eight souls afloat . . .

At some stage this grisly countdown must stop.

Dag went back over their side so we were five apiece again. John Copper was coming down bad now, he kept getting the runs, and Gabriel wasn't looking too good. A light breeze blew up two or three days down the line, cheering us all up. Simon took up his fiddle and scratched away for a while, then we all started singing. Not that we really could sing, not that the fiddle could do more than croak these days, but we did our best. It turned into something, a great wake perhaps, a joyful wake. We were bobbing along together on a moonlit ocean and the world was beautiful. Tim and I held hands and sang as we could. Nothing like a song to bind the world together and bring on the best sort of tears. We sang, and Dan growled along with us, and so did Dag, in a voice still surprisingly pure. Gabriel laid his head against the pillow of a sucked leather oar and his eyes stared bright with weeping. We sang 'Oh, say was you ever in Rio Grande', and 'Reuben Ranzo' and 'Round The Corner Sally', and when our voices ran out we hummed on into the darkness of silence. Tim held onto my arm as he slept, gripping so hard it hurt. His mouth fell open and his head tilted back. He made me think of home. Me and him in the yard mucking about, insulting each other. Cold in the early morning, a grumble in the belly. Clumps of hair falling out. No, that's now. I'm glad Ma can't see this. She'd hate it, poor old Ma. She'd cry. What could I do about it? It was too big, it filled me up. So I put her away, not too far, not so I couldn't call her back any time I wanted. I went to Ishbel instead. The last I saw was cloud coming over, directly above, blackness coming over. Drifting black sleep, soft as cloud, warm in my bed boasting at the rain. I opened my eyes in darkness so complete it was like being blind. Some gigantic thing was beating the ocean out there, not far away, a great plunging and cascading and thrashing. Tim's hand was still on my arm, clutching. A voice chanted 'please God please God please God please God' endlessly.

'Tim,' I said, 'what is it?'

An arm came round me. 'I don't know.'

'Lie still,' Dan said, 'it'll go by.'

It sounded like mountains crashing into the sea. Not like a whale. Not anything I knew. Some monster come up from the deep, the dark deep underlying, some fearful malicious *thing*. It's true there are places of horror on the earth, falls with no end, cracks that open and breathe forth hell. It's true there are bad spots, sounds of crying above the waves, wild winds yelling with the voices of drowned souls. The crew of the *Essex* still sail these seas. I started snivelling. It was big and near, whatever it was, and the wash from its commotion was slapping the side of the boat.

'It's all right,' Tim said, 'it's going away.'

'Please God please God please God please please . . .'

Whose voice?

A great sucking of the sea took the creature down. A light flickered far away, the captain's boat.

'It's gone,' said Dan.

12

After that there was no more sense. What remained was brighter and realler.

The sea changed constantly. I could focus and unfocus at will, soften it here, sharpen it there, make it slide and swoop and shift. For days I drifted like this. Once I heard, faintly, a girl's voice singing far away. The sky? The sea? I don't know. It was sad and soft, and you couldn't hear it and not cry. Who she was I don't know. Love lost. Impossibly gone. I could have slipped over the side, swum to her, if I'd not been a weakling. She sang through the sound of the sea and the wind all morning, fell silent at noon. After which a shark, wonderful, came swimming between the boats, out of reach. Two sharks! Sharp black fins, cutting the sea in lines. Food. Us to them, them to us. We should have kept Yan for bait. It wouldn't mean anything to him now, would it? I saw Yan's face as I last saw him, the wide-parted lips, the look of a shrunken head beginning, because of the way his lips had retreated from his long teeth. His gums were white, like bone. The black fins accompanied us, stirring the sea all day, circling, approaching, retreating. Wilson Pride was getting sick now, and Dag. Poor old John was the worst though, pulling himself up, talking nonsense, falling down again.

He'll be next.

Gabriel gave me a prod. My watch. Dragged. Dizzy. Stood on Skip's foot. 'Fuck you to hell!' he snarled.

'Fuck you too!'

He kicked out with his bare foot but missed.

My watch.

I forgot why I was there. My eyes were very old by now, slitted, able to look into the brightness. I felt like a fly on a ceiling. As if I was upside down and the sky was under and the sea was up, and there was no difference between the two, and no beginning or end to each. I wasn't troubled, not then, not really, though I was starting to quiver, the small hairs pricking up all over my arms and the back of my neck. I couldn't say I was troubled, no such thing, too much for that, what was coming was bigger, for there *was* something invisible rising, resounding like the feeling in the air before lightning, bigger than the sea and sky and covering everything. There was a small, thin sound in the air, a living tone that came closer, moved palpably in my head, then flew far up and diffused, as if a crowd of children babbled beyond the sky.

'But true,' said Skip, 'there is something out there. You can hear it too.'

His breath stank.

Hearing isn't quite the right word.

But, 'Yes,' I said, 'I can.' I was feeling faint. 'What is it?' I asked.

He smiled mysteriously.

'You don't know any more than I know,' I said.

'Did I say I did?'

'I don't know. I thought you did.'

'I do know some things.'

He crouched by me, hugging his legs. His breeches were ragged and ripped and both his knees poked through, sharp and bony. As he spoke he picked cruelly at a hanging scab on the right one, sucking in breath through his teeth with a hiss. 'It's wild,' he said. 'Very, very wild, Jaf, very, very wild indeed.'

The sound was a hum now, changing, scarcely, slightly, all the time. Blood burst up out of Skip's knee, a shiny red bubble. He licked it.

'And very, very old.'

More blood came, a sticky ooze. It smelled like liver, like kidneys sliced ready for the pan.

'Old like millions and millions of years, and it walks on the tips of its hooves.'

My dream, the dragon walking on tiptoe on the sea.

'If it comes,' he said, 'try not to look. Some things you shouldn't see.'

'I'm scared,' I said.

He looked at me very closely. I started to cry because I was too scared and couldn't think anything straight through any more. He sucked his knee.

'I'm dizzy,' I said.

He went on sucking his knee, and I started drooling as well as crying.

'Dan,' Skip said, 'Jaf's not well, he shouldn't be on watch.'

Blood. Taste. That's a good thing to do. Better than leather. A tiny filling. If I pull at the raw bits in this elbow crack, I can make it bleed, and the hurt's nothing. But that's hard to get to. If this one here on the back of my wrist gets bigger. I don't care about the salt and sting and lurch of fear, all I want is food, there never was anything else, nothing else at all.

'It's all right, Jaf,' Dan said.

'Let him lie down.' Tim's voice.

I fell asleep. When I woke up it was cooler and I felt well enough to sit up. The two boats were together, absolutely still. I heard voices.

'What's he saying?'

'Fucked if I know.'

'Doesn't even sound like English.'

'Portuguese?'

'*Obrigado, obrigado, três senhora, tres, por favor . . .*'

In Horta, on the beach, the old beggar women holding out their hands.

'He's gone,' said the captain.

John Copper.

Dan put his face in his hand. The sun glimmered red on the water. We bobbed listlessly. Here we are – how many? – surely not – how many? – close your eyes and here we all are back again, Billy Stock and Joe Harper and Henry Cash and all, and nothing ever happened, it didn't, you can go back there, it's a strain and it takes every stretch you've got, but it surely is real and you can go back there.

'What now?' asked Dag, his eyes all a-goggle in the weird, jutting thing his face had become. But no one answered and no one knew.

The captain and Wilson Pride butchered him. I saw nothing of it. They rowed a little way away, and I lay with my head below the level of the gunwale and heard the sounds of severing and hacking, the trickle of liquid, the smothered grunts of effort.

Tim's breath, stale and rich, came on my eyes. 'It's all right, Jaf,' he said, 'it's all right, he's not there any more, he's nowhere near, he's all right.'

Behind me I heard the breathing of Gabriel, catching, halting.

I opened my eyes. Tim's face. Smiling. He spoke. Egg-white stretched between his lips. 'Not long now,' he said.

Running water.

My mouth burning and prickling, my throat closing.

'I *can't*,' said Gabriel harshly.

'You can,' said Dan.

They came near, we were rocked by their approach. Skip sniffed and gulped.

'They lit a fire,' murmured Dan.

'It's all right, Jaf.' Tim smiling.

It was going dark. Good to have smoke in the nostrils, and a small dancing light.

He held the cup to my lip. 'A sip,' he said.

Thickening blood, rich.

I drank and lay back with my eyes wide open, looking up at the sudden night sky. A hot cooking smell of meat rose upon the air and an exquisite pain burst under my tongue. The stars were low. When I lived in Bermondsey I used often to be hungry. I would walk along bankside to Southwark to smell the hot dinners roasting in the ovens of the Anchor. It's a kind of eating, standing in the street drawing in a thickening smell of juices. The river slapping bankside in Southwark, sweet grey Southwark across another sea, across a continent, across the distance between me and the blaring stars.

'It's just meat,' Dan said to Gabriel, but Gabriel shook his head. He was humming very low and deep in his throat, staring with huge eyes straight ahead. But he had to eat in the end. Who could not? He was a big man, but he'd turned into a stick. When he did eat, it was with fury and concentration and heavy breathing. Dan passed me a thick slice of charred meat, tender as thin jelly in the middle, running with pink juices. I sucked and my mouth overflowed. I was dripping, drooling, long trails pouring down the front of me as if I was a baby.

'Need a bib,' I said, and we laughed. All of us dripping and drooling, our stomachs cawing and churning.

We ate our fill and the captain ordered an extra ration of water for each man. He said there was more meat for tomorrow, they were stowing it in the boxes our tack had been in and it should do well enough for a little while. And then the lights were gone and we all lay down. I kept seeing John Copper's face.

Having eaten well, we slept well, a boatload of us snoring away, and in the morning I woke with his face still in my eyes and a snake in my belly, coiling. Bile in my throat. Still hungry as ever.

'Here,' said Dan, 'drink.'

The sun was already high. Simon was lighting a fire with a few bits of thin stick and some tightly coiled strips of rag. Had to cook what was left fast, he said, or it'd go off. Some already had. The captain was hovering over a pail of offal that was turning green.

'What do you think?' he said.

'Chuck it over,' said Simon.

Over it went.

'How long can you keep that going?' The captain nodded at the fire.

Simon made a wry face. 'Ten minutes. Longer but . . .'

'Hm?'

'Depends how many days.'

Wilson was feeling seedy and was lying down with a cold rag on his head, his dark brown face shiny with sweat. Dag, sitting up groggily in the stern of the boat, picked constantly at his swollen eyelids. His face was as gawkily skull-like as ever, but his legs and arms had turned into fat pink hams, and were spotted here and there with angry red boils. I had boils too, big flaming things that raged – one behind my knee, one inside my thigh and the worst one on the back of my neck.

'You know, it's funny,' said Tim, 'I feel hungrier than ever now.'

'Me too,' I said.

'That's the way of it,' said Dan. 'Don't fret, we've plenty for a good ten days.'

We got a strip of meat for breakfast, along with our tack. I made mine last a long time. Dan hummed a tune, lolling back against the prow, arms slung across the wood. When I caught his eye he winked. 'All's well, Jaf,' he said. 'All's fine and dandy.'

Sometimes still the captain and Dan would put their heads together and conference, as if there was anything to be done, but very little was going on any more in the way of navigation. Skip grinned and mumbled, sometimes laughed in a weary way. Tim cursed and swore. Gabriel muttered prayers, a wistful, rhythmic humming in my ears. Simon simply wasn't there. His body was, of course, but he never played his fiddle any more and hardly spoke or bothered to move unless he had to. He hardly looked up to see when a shark stalked us for a time, or when a crack of thunder sounded in the west, or when silent lightning clamoured in an empty sky. Dag chewed his nails though there was nothing left of them. I thought of Ishbel's awful hands. Poor Ishbel. What hunger she must have had to eat herself like that. Very painful it must have been. I saw her clear then, and another huge kick of home got me, the Highway, the Docks, me and she and Tim, street Arabs running about.

'Do you remember?' I asked Tim.

'Of course,' he said as if he could read my mind. Then he leaned forward and grinned and ruffled my hair. 'Little Lascar, is it?' he said.

Heat pressed down, making it hard to think.

'Hear that?' said Skip.

'What is it?'

Gabriel laughed shortly. 'Now we're all mad,' he said, and went back to praying.

'Listen.'

It wasn't really a sound. More the vibration in your ears when a thousand miles of emptiness presses on them. More a sense of the elements putting us in our place.

'Look out there,' said Dan. He put his arms round me and Tim. 'My boys,' he said, and tears ran from the brown corners of his small sad eyes. 'My boys, I'll take you home safe. One way or another. Didn't I promise old Jamrach I'd bring his boys safe home?'

Something's happening. The sea is changing. Strangeness, like twilight or weather, falls upon the earth.

'Children,' Dan Rymer said, tears in the wrinkles of his face.

'How old are you, Dan?' I asked.

He grinned. 'Sixty-two,' he said, 'last time I looked.'

'You're very old,' Tim said.

Dan laughed. 'The old man of the sea!'

The sea didn't care. We were nothing.

'What is it?' asked Dag.

'Shh!' The captain covered his eyes.

'Hold hands, boys.' Dan said. 'We face this thing together.' He was wings, we huddled under. I heard sound above the clouds, one voice or many, impossible to tell: a human, animal thing, many-stringed, childlike, wild as a crying baby. Nothing wilder than that.

'Hold hands,' he said.

Tim grabbed my hand. His face in mine, wild-eyed, smiling. 'Jaffy,' he said, 'old Jaf.'

'Together, boys,' Dan said.

The captain's boat drew close.

'Haul to, haul to,' a voice said.

The sound of timbers striking timbers.

'Mr Rymer!' the captain hailed, 'all's well with you?'

'All's well!' Dan replied.

'What's this coming in, do you think? Storm?'

Dan sniffed the air like a dog. 'Coming in,' he said.

The sound swelled in my ears and exploded. I was lying against Dan's arm. His lips were next to my ear.

'Good boy, Jaf,' he said. 'You lie down now and sleep if you can. Don't worry about a thing. Soon be home.'

He made me and Tim lie down as if we were infants, we had to close our eyes and pretend to sleep to please him. It kept him happy. Dan was singing sleepily, pissing over the side of the boat. 'When other lips and other hearts their tales of love shall tell . . .'

'What's happening, Dan? What's happening?'

'Nothing. It's all right.'

I remembered Skip. Turned my face. 'Skip,' I said, 'you still sane, boy?'

He smiled. 'Was I ever?'

'Here,' said Dan, and raised me up, put water to my lips. I peered over the gunwale. I saw the captain's boat, dark against a red background. Slumped forms there, all sleeping in a coming night. No one keeping watch. That cannot be right.

Skip gripped my arm, hard, the forearm just below the elbow, sharp on the inside.

'Look!'

It was getting dark.

'Nothing there.'

'Yes, there is.'

'I don't know. What?'

He saw things, of that there is no doubt. His claws, below the elbow. 'Now! Now!' he said. 'Now it's turning its face this way.'

'Get off me!' I shook him off.

'Shut your stupid gob,' said Tim furiously. 'It was you in the first place, Skip, you said it. You. What was it? You did? What?'

Skip covered his eyes.

'You did!'

'Boys, boys,' said Father Dan.

The captain's bread ran out, and the meat ran out. Boils erupted, our skin became volcanic. We waited for Wilson Pride to die. Yes, we did. We knew he'd be the next to go. That's what we'd come to now, wishing it, hoping, as he lay there burning in his dry sweat, his blue-black tongue pushing through between his lips. Our cook, who used to make us stew and duff and barley broth, and the rice and peas of his homeland, spiced up with whatever was to hand, or just a bit of salt, a radish, a few green plucked herbs of a strange island. A little fried fish. Small fish, innards and all, heads and tails and eyes and everything. Oh, my belly, the great hollow of the world. Broth. Hot broth, savoury steam. Bright green leaves, blush-orange roots, silky leeks a-simmer, dancing gold liquid.

'My ma,' I said, 'she used to make this broth. Ham bone if she could get it. Beans and peas. Turnips. Carrots.'

'You let the dragon out,' Tim was saying, 'that's what you did.'

'Well! So?'

'You did. You said. Let it out.'

'Leeks,' I said, 'leeks are very important. You need leeks.'

Wilson doesn't cook any more. Wilson's gone far away. His soul's gone a-wandering, knapsack over its shoulder. I have been trying to talk to Tim about how I have no sense in me of right and wrong any more, and how I'm stony and fire watery, turn and turn about, and how it seems I have many, many things to tell him, but can't speak, can't get the words off my tongue because it's too heavy and stupid.

Silently the captain removed the hot rag from Wilson's fore-head, dipped it in the sea and pulled it out freshly cold, gave it a squeeze, shook it hard and replaced it on the dying man's head.

Wilson was talking or rather chunnering, making no sense. His big lips had withered inwards, and his eyes, when they were not closed, stared at the sky with a look near to humour.

'I sailed with him twice before,' the captain said.

'Did you so?' Dan scratched steadily at the scurf around his neck.

'Simon, will you shift a bit and give him more room? It'll be over soon.'

Simon shifted, so Dag had to shift too, stiffly, wincing at his swollen legs, the colour now of cooked bacon. His face crumpled and he dry sobbed for a few seconds.

Dan called us to him like chickens. 'Here, boys,' he said. 'No point in looking.'

We sat with him in the prow.

'Look at me,' he said. 'Here is something we must do and it's very important. It's an order. You must remember all the words to "Tobacco's But An Indian Weed".'

'I don't know them!' Tim protested.

'Yes, you do. Think. You remember, that time by the Wapping Steps?'

'Yes, but I can't remember any words.'

'You must try. Jaffy, what about you?'

'I only know the first couple of lines.'

'Good. You begin.'

> Tobacco's but an Indian weed,
> Grows green in the morn, cut down at eve,
> We are but clay . . .

'Something else,' said Tim.

We are but clay, da-da, da-da,
Think of this when you smoke tobacco.

Tim looked at Dan. 'Go on, Clever Clogs,' he said.

'"The pipe that is so lily white,"' sang Dan softly, '"Wherein so many take delight; It's broken with a touch . . ."'

A short pause. Wilson's high-pitched breathing filled it.

'You, Tim,' Dan said, giving him a shake, 'your turn. Look at me. "It's broken with a touch." What comes next?'

'"Man's life is such . . ."' Tim continued, and we three in unison:

'"Think of this when you smoke tobacco."'

'Happy little souls, aren't you?' Gabriel, irritated.

'Skip? You know it?'

Skip shook his head. His eyes were big and glassy.

'Soft now, Wilson, good man, let it go,' the captain said tonelessly.

Wilson whimpered like a small baby.

'Look at his throat,' Dag said.

I turned my head.

'Jaf!' Dan pulled my face round by the chin. 'Next verse now, come on.'

'I don't know.'

'Concentrate. You do.'

'I don't.'

A sound like a pumping bellows began.

'I'll give you a start. "The pipe that is so foul within, shows how man's soul is . . ."'

Drowning. His throat squeezing. His voice forcing out from some abyss, a hollow animal bellow.

'Hold steady,' said the captain.

'Look at his throat!' Dag, panicky.

260

'Tim! Continue.'

'"Full of sin,"' said Tim.

'Good! Jaf!'

'Don't know.'

'Try.'

I don't remember. Something about smoke and all of us returning to dust, blah blah blah . . .

'"The ashes that are left behind,"' said Tim triumphantly, '"should serve to put us all in mind".'

'Oh yes,' I said, joining in.

> That unto dust return we must.
> Think of this when you smoke tobacco!

'Now now now, one more verse, come on, boys, think hard.'

'Smoke,' I said.

A horrible sound, a rattling choking vomiting sound, as if the lungs of the man were heaving themselves up his throat and out of his mouth.

'Smoke!' Dan snapped his fingers. 'Skip! You!'

Skip was crying.

A breath like the scraping of a nail on slate, exhaling into silent infinity.

'"The smoke",' said Dan gamely, '"that is so . . ."'

'No!' Tim. '"The smoke that doth so high . . ."'

'That's it,' the captain said.

13

T hey are now three in their boat and we are five. I counted on my fingers. We are eight. Should one of us move over to the captain's boat? But who should go?

'I want you boys here,' said Dan.

That leaves Skip and Gabriel, and neither wants to go. We all sit, stupid with the problem. Anyway, someone says, too late now, soon be dark. For God's sake, let's just sleep on it. We've eaten. That too has made us stupid. So we should say the prayers now as usual, but we just lie there like bloated sacks, none of us moving.

The dark night came down and there was nothing, not a star. No one lit a lantern or spoke.

After a while: 'Oh Lord,' said Dan in an odd tone, defiant, almost declamatory, a peculiar smile in his voice, 'here we are . . . here we are still. We are . . . we are . . .'

'Eight,' I said.

'Thank you, Jaf. We are eight souls afloat. What do you say to that, hey?'

And then there was laughter, I don't know who, me anyway, and Tim because he was next to me, trembling hard. And Dan, but I don't know who else. A few. The covering dark gave the feeling of giggling under blankets. When we stopped there was only the gentle sound of lapping waves, soothing. I yawned. Saliva ran again, bitter as lemon. Strips of meat hung in the darkness, salting steadily, drying out.

Some time later: 'Goddamn it!' cried a voice, Jehovah summoning fire and brimstone. It was Gabriel, lurching as if to stand up, making the boat pitch.

'Sit down!' we all growled.

He flopped heavily down again, roaring in a cracked voice: 'God! God! What fucking God? God's evil. That's what it is. God's evil and the devil's won. That's what it is!'

'Don't talk about the devil!' begged Skip.

'Calm down,' said Dan.

'How? Calm down?' Gabriel laughed, a humourless bark. 'Are you mad?'

'I may be,' Dan said. 'Calm down anyway.'

'Quite simply,' said another disembodied voice, very steady, the captain probably, though it didn't sound like him, 'it's possible all of us will die.'

A hand crept into mine.

'I don't want to die!' Someone whining, I still don't know who. Simon, I think, though again it sounded nothing like him and it was so long since he'd spoken that I'd almost forgotten him. Someone else started crying, a fierce ragged sound.

There was a lurch. 'Goddamn you, Skip,' Gabriel said, 'this is all your fault.'

'I know, I know.' Skip's voice, suddenly close by my ear, so close it made the small hairs there quiver, a pale whisper of a voice. 'Sorry. Sorry.'

'We should chuck you over.' Dag's voice, teeth chattering, hiccuping.

'That's enough now,' Dan said.

'Chuck him over!' Gabriel with a grin in his voice.

'Chuck him over!' Simon joined in.

'Chuck him over! Chuck him over!' Tim now too, and I was about to join in when Dan's stern voice cut through.

'Remember I have a pistol,' it said. 'The first person to lay hands in anger on any one of us gets first bullet.'

Silence. Then Captain Proctor spoke. 'I too have a pistol,' he said.

Silence.

'I too have a pistol,' he repeated thoughtfully, then: 'Mr Rymer, enlighten me please. Am I not still captain of this – this . . .'

'You are indeed.'

'If there's any shooting to be done, *I* decide.'

'Of course. I didn't mean . . .'

'You fools!' said Gabriel with a depth of scorn. 'What does it matter?'

No one spoke for a few minutes.

The waves were small and even, singing like a lullaby, up and down, up and down, lullullullullullulluuu for ever and ever and . . .

'You think I'm a fool!' the captain gritted out. 'I am not a fool!'

'No one thinks you're a fool,' said Dan.

Skip screamed, a long horrible madman's shriek that pierced my head, and the captain yelled: 'Shut him up, for God's sake!'

'Skip,' said Dan, 'come here.'

Then all hell broke loose, terror skipping from one to another, leaping between us, settling and enveloping us all, a suffocating cloud. I heard a whimpering very close to my ear. Then it was all around and I was in it and of it and falling horribly through it, a weeping and wailing and gnashing of teeth.

'Enough!' A pistol shot.

Silence.

The captain spoke. 'We are not animals,' he wheezed. 'Not one more sound or the next bullet finds more than empty air.'

A few moments of staggered breathing and snuffling and sighing faded away into nothing.

'Now,' the captain said, 'settle down, everyone, and go to sleep. Mr Rymer, keep that boy under control.'

'Come here to me, Skip,' said Dan softly, sounding very tired.

'Have him,' Gabriel said sulkily, 'I can't sleep for him.'

'Sleep?' said Tim. 'You *sleep*?'

Then we were all laughing again.

Skip trod on me in the darkness.

'Fuck you,' I said.

'Sorry,' said Skip.

'You think I'm a fool,' the captain said tightly. 'I am still in command of this enterprise. I must consider the welfare of us all.'

Skip flopped down somewhere. The boat quivered.

'For God's sake, sleep,' said Dan.

The silent length of night with no moon or stars. The sound of Dag's snoring. Tim's hand loose in mine, and me thinking about Ma.

'Ma,' I said.

'Yes. Shh,' said Dan. 'You'll see your ma again.'

Death was close. Sitting next to me. It hurt, if the others were anything to go by. And if them, why not me? How do you get there? Death, I mean, wherever it was the wild thing dropped you: you, breath-stopped, amazed. Will I fall there or drift? When would be the moment of knowing? What sound? What sight? The sky, dark or light? The side of the boat? Would I go hard or easy? What grief. More than anything else, what grief to leave the world.

I must have fallen asleep. Ishbel and me, same as ever, walking along the Highway. Everything clear and bright. She wore a white dress like a ballet dancer's, and was unpainted, as if she'd just got up. Then I was in our old house in Watney Street, our room with the curtain across and old Silky and Mari-Lou snoring on the other side of it. Then back on the sea once more, the lullullul-lullullull of the waves, the sound of Skip snoring. Someone was poking me.

'We didn't give him a send-off!'

'What?'

Tim's voice. 'We didn't give him a send-off!' His angry claw tight on my arm. It would leave a bruise.

'What?'

'It's wrong! It's wrong!'

'Who? What?'

'Poor Wilson,' he said. 'You should always give a man a send-off.'

'Ah!'

'That's us damned!'

Towards dawn someone in the other boat commenced praying in a deep belly voice: 'Plea-ea-ease. Plea-ease! Pleaseplease! Pl-ea-ea-ease oh please. Please please. Plea-ea-ea-plea-ease! Aaah! Plea-ea-ea-ease!'

'Shut up!' Another voice, weary.

Dan gave a long guttural sigh. He put a hand over my ear, a great flap to keep out sound. His belly was under my other ear going up and down, weird little creakings in it.

'I cannot do this,' I whispered. 'I don't want to die.'

'Take no notice,' he said. 'Go to sleep.'

When I slept I dreamed of groaning tables and feasts of plenty, and woke adrool to see Dan with his head tilted back, storm-battered face talking to the sky. 'Well, well,' he said, a low sing-song, 'my sore runs in the night and ceases not, indeed

267

it does. Oh indeedy.' His tongue, swollen and grey like a giant tick, flipped uselessly over his lips. 'I breathe therefore I am. Thinking doesn't come into it.' He sucked a little blood from his arm, a meditative look on his face. Caught my eye and cracked a v-shaped smile. His brows had dropped and grown fierce and hairy.

'You know you used to say, Don't worry, I've been in worse than this?' I said. 'Well, you can't now, can you? Not any more. You haven't been in worse than this, have you?'

Dan thought for a moment. 'No,' he said, 'that's true. But don't worry.'

Dag was half sitting up, propped against the gunwale, talking in his own language, a constant mumble pierced occasionally by a throaty yell like a boy hailing his dog.

'Look what's happening.' Sharp and cracked, the voice of Simon, rarely heard these days. 'Oh no!' He moved backwards.

The captain wrung out a filthy rag. 'Won't be long now,' he murmured.

'What is it?'

Dag was sweating blood. His jutty face and swollen neck, sun-blackened, oozed a fine rose-tinted dew.

'Here, Simon.'

The captain handed Simon the rag and he wiped Dag's face. The rag came away stained.

'Give him a drink,' the captain said, 'wet his lips at least.'

Dag's blue eyes opened wide.

'God!' cried Gabriel. 'God! He knows! He knows!'

'Ssh!'

They trickled water on his lips, poured it through his jaws. His tongue shot out. 'Mama,' he croaked. 'Mama . . .' then a torrent of words, another burst of pink sweat on his skin, a sudden horrible awareness in his eyes.

'It's all right,' said Simon, wiping away with the rag, 'it'll be better soon.'

But Dag knew, and he gripped Simon's wrist.

'It's all right,' said Simon, 'lie down now.'

What a day that was, the day of Dag's dying. He wouldn't stay down. Up and down like a jack-in-the-box. His voice came and went, sometimes silent for a whole hour at a time and you'd wonder if he'd gone, but no, then you'd hear his awful breath still scraping at the world like claws trying to hold on. Skip was going barmy too, snivelling sulkily like a big stupid kid, occasionally shouting about a thing that walked alongside us on the water, a hoofed thing like a goat and a man and a fish all at once. He said it grinned and was stalking us. Still, we were all mad in our different ways, sitting there helpless, with the sea still twinkling like eternity everywhere, with never a sail or an island or a rock or a bird even. Mid-afternoon, Dag's voice went peculiar. Not that we'd understood anything he was saying, but there'd been a human quality at least to it, but now he turned and became like the Minotaur in the myth, bellowing like an ox being dragged to slaughter. He shat himself. Then a terrible thing happened, an image that seared itself indelibly onto my eyes and into whatever I am. He was leaning up against the gunwale and Simon had just finished wiping his face. The captain was dipping the rag in the sea. Dag's eyes were open, looking out at the world with fixed interest, as if he'd never seen it before. Next second blood gushed out from his nose, then more, a great flood from his eyes, from his mouth, from his ears. As if all the blood of him was leaving through his face.

His head fell down on his chest and he was gone.

Whether it was the blood horror of it I don't know, but this death disturbed me more than all the others, more than I can say. I saw that sight as you see a demon in your worst nightmare,

269

but I didn't wake up. I palmed my eyes and pressed them hard, feeling sick. My eyes burned with wanting to cry, but they couldn't. There was nothing there. No spare. My bones rubbed against one another, against the boards beneath me. There was Tim's same old hand in mine, but they were poor things now, those hands: brown spindly sticks linked. The palms ticked with nerves.

The captain said, 'Let's just get on with it, shall we? We know what we're doing . . .'

'It's not fair,' Simon said, 'why's it always us has to do it just because it always happens on our boat? One of them should do it for a change.'

Oh God, not me.

'Next time,' the captain promised.

Close your eyes but you still must hear.

'Dan,' I said, 'what's a good way of doing yourself in?'

'Shoot yourself,' he replied immediately.

'Would you give me the gun if I wanted it?'

He looked at me for a long moment. 'Would I? I wonder? I don't know, Jaf.'

I could smell blood, a whiff on the breeze.

Here came the cup and I drank.

'Drink of this,' said Dan when it was his turn, raising the cup as if it was a chalice, 'for this is my blood, shed for thee . . .'

We had days of meat, and then days of no meat, and then more days of no meat. A change stirred in the sky. The sun dimmed and a chill came whispering on the air. Clouds piled up on every side, and rain fell in a soft blue-grey shimmer far away in the east. The east: coasts of the Americas. The American sailors have a song that goes: 'Oh, say was you ever in Rio Grande, those sweet señoritas they sure beats the band . . .' Black-haired bosomy girls welcoming weary sailors to soft feather beds. The wind got up. The sky flickered. We took in the sails and the wind spun us

270

round. Our boats drifted far apart, and the rain came down all at once in a drenching torrent, icy cold, and it was laughable the way from cursing the bloody heat we were suddenly freezing to death and soaking wet. We lay to. It was dark suddenly, and there was baling to do and Gabriel couldn't. He'd spread himself out since Skip had gone back to the captain's boat to even things up, and now could scarcely push himself up from the boards. A great shake had come over him. Every lightning flash revealed him lying in inches of cold water with twitching legs and grinding teeth. We didn't get to sleep till late next morning when the rain abated, and as soon as I woke I saw him sitting with his eyes closed and a look of concentration on his face. He'd gone a funny olive-green colour.

'He won't eat his tack,' said Tim.

'Gabe? You've got to eat.'

He didn't react.

He never ate again after that. Hardly a drop of water passed his lips either. The wind calmed from wild to merely boisterous and we drifted on, tossing up and down. He didn't eat, but he opened his eyes and started cursing God again.

We sang 'The Blind Man Stood on the Road and Cried' the night Gabriel died.

> The blind man stood on the road and cried,
> Oh, the blind man stood on the road and cried,
> Oh, my Lord save me,
> The blind man stood on the road and cried . . .

Round and round like that for ever. Round and round three or four times, the wispy hoary things that were left of our voices. Gabriel was singing too, his eyes closed, serene. He'd been good to me. For his life on shore and all before, I knew nothing, could remember nothing, whether I'd been told or not. But what a

271

strange depth of knowing of him I had, suddenly in that moment. He stopped singing, opened his eyes and looked right at me with shining eyes. My heart broke. He held out his hand to me and I took it, but he had no grip. His hand was crisp and salted like a kipper.

'Don't go, Gabriel,' I said with tears bursting out.

But he did. He just did, quietly, looking at me like that. He was there, then gone. No more Gabriel behind the glazing brown eyes.

'Please, Gabe,' I said.

I'd been light-headed for a long time, but somewhere here the feeling ran away, rushed up to the reaches of the sky. It was another world, brighter than the old, as if new-painted a second ago. Strange magic, spiriting away this one, that one, another, one more, one by one, pulling them out of their bodies. I got filled up, filled right up, all of it pouring out of my eyes and down my face. There was some beauty in it too. My shipmates. Their faces in my mind. Their voices raised in song. Their meat too, beautiful. Organ blood, thin. Clots, wonderful. Sticky, sweet and full. They were life to me. A bucket of red and brown. I can smell it, just. My nose is salted up. I have meat, my nose is running, the salt stings and I'm crying.

I don't know what day it was when the captain's boat went missing. Weeks anyway. Weeks. Weeks, weeks . . . must've been, because Skip had come back to us, gabbling how he had to stay awake all the time for fear they'd cut his throat.

'They hate me,' he said.

Over the water, the captain's face, haggard and sad. Simon's, empty, open-mouthed, burned near black.

'Ah, come on, Skip,' Tim said, 'you'll be all right with us. We're all jolly boys here. Don't bring your demons though.'

'Not *my* demons. Why's Jaf crying?'

'Can't think.'

It was after that, I don't know how long.

My mind goes. Falters, flickers. Stops. Dream unfurls.

The sea changed and changed. It rained a lot of the time. Sometimes the wind blew and we were tossed about. My sores had a life of their own, the salt sting hot and white. A rime formed about their heights. Dan talked to his wife. 'Alice,' he said, 'when are you going to cut my hair?' And: 'Do you think we should move back to Putney, Al?'

And one morning Captain Proctor's boat was gone.

The sea was empty. We four looked and looked and said nothing. It had been a very windy night. A great breath had blown them away.

The four of us drifting. Singing. Our arms round each other, all jolly boys. Me, Tim, Dan, Skip. If it threatened storm we huddled close together, tenting our backs to shelter our fronts and faces, breathing our combined breath of sour salt bile. We still had some meat, but we had no fire. We had ribs. When we finished the meat we still had some tack and a bit of water now and then. But you can't sing for ever. Your voice stops. You open your mouth and nothing works. A soft wheezing hiss, fragile as a dewdrop, is all, and no one hears because of the greater salt hiss of the sea. Your voice stops and your brain runs out of the top of your head and you soar very high and see from above the curving rim of the world, blue blue blue, far as the eye can see. One of Ishbel's old songs runs in your head, the mermaid with a comb and a glass in her hand, her hand, her hand, with a comb and a glass in her hand, and her face appears, a round pale moon, very solemn, and with it the sound of a knife grating against bone or hard sinew or something. I had nothing to do with it, any of it, I was far, far away above the clouds. Her face was the knife cutting. Her face was whatever it was I was in and couldn't get out of. At

273

the end there would be a straight line stretching both ways for ever, and it would be the end of the sea and the lip of the last waterfall, a fall into white nothing, the foam spray of it rising to meet you long before you could make out anything of the crashing impact below. That's where we were going, drifting, each one of us soaring high and always returning into our eyes and seeing what was there before us, facing each other. All without speaking, we four joined hands for the plunge.

One day I woke and my tongue was out of my mouth. It had turned into a creature I did not know, lazy and fat, swelling and oozing as it thrust its way out into the light through the slack hole of my mouth. My own tongue made me retch. This brought tears to my eyes, which I gratefully drank. Was then I think I saw Skip's demon, a cloven-footed grinning thing like a shadow on the sky, looking sideways at me with bright intelligent eyes full of mischief. The sky was dark, a morning of rolling black cloud, a quiver on the sky, the sea moaning. I saw it. I looked at Skip, but he was mad, sitting there grinning like his own demon and frightening me with his glare. His whole face had changed. His eyes stuck out painfully, big goggling balls above the sharp lines of his bones. When I looked back the demon had gone.

I asked for water. That is, I gestured at my mouth and made a noise with my throat, a kind of bark. But Dan said:

'Not yet.'

What followed was a tantrum of the soul, within and completely silent. It's not fair, I cried. It's not fair! I didn't do anything bad!

At last I got a little water, enough to wet my fat tongue. Dan trickled it on my lips from a cup. 'Come on, Jaf,' he said, 'buck up, boy.'

Water. For a little while we could speak.

'This is ridiculous,' Tim said.

'I want to go home.' Skip hugged his sides.

Home. Hope Ma's all right. She should be, Charley Grant's a good sort. Home, Ma, Ishbel, never get back, never go home, never again. A burning place in my chest. Something to hold against the terror, a blanket. I'm alive, burning brightly with a head full of everything that ever was, our Bermondsey home, the Highway, the tiger, the birds, the smell of lemon sherbet.

The night returned, darker than most.

In the morning we drank again, and ate a scrap. Dan showed us what was left of the food: a square of hardtack about the size of a matchbox. We laughed at it. 'This is ridiculous,' said Tim, in a tone of mild exasperation. 'Enough's enough. Look at us.'

'Oh, boys,' said Dan, 'we're still breathing.'

We four joined hands. Skip's face still had that gawk-eyed look on it, his tongue stuck between his teeth. Dan was a hunched brown leathery thing, shiny like a polished idol in Jamrach's shop. God knows what I looked like, and Tim was a bony brown elf with wide blue eyes and white hair falling down around his face. Smiling. 'This is no good,' he said, 'it can't go on. No more.'

Dan said, 'Something will happen.'

'Don't, please don't tell me.' Skip with his eyes on stalks.

Don't bulge at me like that, I would have said if I could. His hand in mine was spiky, returning to bone.

'Help me,' he said.

'Yes, yes,' said Dan.

'Help me.'

'Skip, it's—'

'Help me help me help me . . .'

His bones go crunch and I look down at his hand crunching mine, our bones together.

The sea threw us up high. The sky was muddy but white at

275

the edges. I was cold. I saw a fire in my mind, a fire somewhere blazing in a brown fug, a house, warm.

'Hold,' Dan said. 'Hold tight, boys.'

'Please,' begged Skip.

'Draw lots,' said Tim.

'What are you talking about?'

'You know.'

'No.'

'You know exactly what I'm talking about. It's how it's done.'

'No, no.'

'Only way. You know.'

'No.'

'It's sense.'

Skip on one side of me, Tim the other. Skip grips like a madman.

'What's happening?' he whispered.

'Nothing,' said Dan. 'Hold fast now.'

Tim laughed. 'It has a name,' he said.

'You mean lots,' Skip said. 'Straws.'

'We have to do something.'

'Not yet.'

'The way it is at sea,' said Tim. '*You* know. It's how it's always been done.'

'Where do you think they are?' I said.

'Who?'

'Simon. The captain.'

No answer.

'I think there may still be a ship.' Dan wouldn't give up.

'Too late for some,' I think I said. Thought it anyhow.

'It could bear down on us in a second.' He raised his grieving eyes.

'Or not,' said Tim, and grinned. His teeth were bleeding and his eyes were full of tears. 'Let's do it. Before we all go mad. We're dead anyway if we don't.'

Skip's teeth chattered loudly in my ear. 'Oh shit,' he moaned in a terrible deep voice that sounded nothing like him.

'Each of us equal—'

'Oh, God,' said Dan.

'. . . lots . . .'

'There'll never be a ship,' said Skip bleakly, 'never.'

'I can't stand this any more,' I said. 'I'm with Tim.'

'Wait!' Dan cried out. 'One more day.'

'What's the point?' Tim sort of laughed, his voice high.

'One more day.'

'Why have *you* got the gun? Ain't we equal?'

Dan put his head in his hands. The horizon soared high and dropped away. Soared high. Nothing happened for ages, just Skip's eyes getting bulgier and more terrible. 'There are demons,' he said, clutching me harder. I wrenched my hand from his and hit out at him. Tim put his arms round me, both his arms. He was a lot bigger than me and I got a funny feeling I can't explain, almost as if he was my mother or something. I didn't want to get tearful now, it would be too hard, so I put it away in the back of me.

'God send a ship,' Dan said.

Which was stupid because, one way and another, enough praying had gone on in that boat to sanctify all the holy places of the earth and it had long since become plain that God didn't answer. Not so's the average idiot could understand anyway. You could cry 'save me, save me' all you liked but it wasn't going to make any difference to what was going to happen. But we did anyway. Cried 'save me, save me' all in our own ways, with or without words, as you do, all morning and all afternoon, looking for a coast, a golden clime, till I felt my mind going again, and

Dan took the gun out and laid it between us in the middle of our circle.

'I don't care,' he said. 'You can shoot me if you like.'

All this time our mouths were steadily clagging up again. It was hours since our last drink. They frothed and gibbered revoltingly, gumming together, pulling apart with great effort to slobber forth the words. We were hideous. A light rain was coming on, silver and grey and very beautiful. Wonderfully cool on my forehead.

'There's rules,' Tim said seriously.

'*Rules*!' Dan threw back his head and laughed like his old drunk self.

'It has hooves,' said Skip.

Dan laughed harder. You'd have thought he was sitting in the gods at the Empire.

'Anyway, you've got a family and all that,' said Tim, and that stopped him laughing and had him suddenly all dissolved in tears like a big rock toppling. He hung his head and wept softly, mouth distorted in a monkey grin.

'Equal shares,' said Tim.

Dan wiped his nose on his sleeve, put his face down further till his shaggy head was resting on his knees, wrapped his arms tight round himself and shook hard, and that was it again for a while, as if we could only proceed in quick bursts and long vacancies. The sting brought me out of it. It had been constant and vile for a long time but for some reason in the past hour had reached the pitch of madness, specially in the cracks of my elbows, where it raged and groaned and made me yearn for claws to tear it with.

'Drink,' I whispered.

The rain had stopped. My tongue would go again soon. Puff itself up like a bladder and demand air.

'Yes, drink.' Tim touched Dan's arm. 'Have to.'

Dan raised his head and looked at us with something like humour. 'Of course,' he whispered.

'Equal shares,' said Tim, reaching for the old tin cup.

Things would happen. I'd lie here and watch. If I once closed my eyes I could sleep for years and years like Rip Van Winkle and return into some other place. When the water came my way I received it as a sacrament. I kept my eyes wide open. What a bright beautiful sounding world we were in, humming and shushing all around us, bobbing us here and there, cat's paws spinning us; what a weird violet sky. There was blood in the water from someone's mouth. Dan was still crying, and it was catching. It was the cool water on my tongue tipped me over, it was so lovely. Next thing we were all crying, but not in a bad way. It was good crying, refreshing and scouring. After we drank we put hand in trembling hand and made a circle again.

'We must all agree,' said Dan.

We four. We look about us, into each others' eyes, which are amazed and dancing. Skip's eyes are bleeding, or his tears are infected with blood, one or the other.

It's like the songs, the stories.

'Eight bits of paper,' Tim says. 'Put marks on two.'

'Two?'

'Has to be,' he says, 'second for who does the shooting. That's how it's done.'

'Jesus Christ!' I whisper.

'We must all agree,' Dan repeats.

'One goes,' Tim says, 'or we can all die.'

Skip smears his bloody tears. He is smiling as he takes what's left of his sketchbook from his breeches pocket. 'Use this,' he says. It is the last page, Horta, from inland, a whispery grey scene of rooftops, the flowers of Faial; I remember the lovely stew in the

279

tavern and a girl sitting on some stairs. He gives the picture to Dan. It's not large, only four or five inches square, but big enough. Dan folds it very neatly and precisely and tears it into eight small squares.

'Now,' he says, laying them out. 'We mark two.'

Smudges he puts on them. They sit there, eight little scraps, us looking at them. Not a sigh of air to move them.

'Sun goes down soon,' Skip says with a faint sob.

'It's all right, Skip,' Dan says, looking at him. 'You don't have to do this if you don't want to. No one does.'

'We do,' he replies, still smiling, reaches down and, one by one, folds each small square into a smaller one, and then a smaller and then a miraculously smaller, so that we all laugh. 'What shall we put them in?' he asks.

'We still don't have to do this,' Dan says. We haven't got any caps left so we're using the tin cup. He wipes it dry with his fist. Me and Skip put the tiny pellets of folded paper in the cup and then the cup just stands there like the Holy Grail in our midst, and we do it homage.

That moment. Life quivered in it, sharp as a raindrop. Our eyes, all of our eyes, constantly meeting, seeing ourselves reflected back.

'Are we agreed?' Tim picked up the cup, covered its top with his palm and shook it about roughly, then stopped. 'This is wrong,' he said, 'this is a cock-up. We should have just put four in. Now they're all mixed up and we may not get any.'

I was past it, couldn't understand a word he was saying. 'Oh, just do it,' I said.

'Are we agreed?'

'Fucking get on with it!'

'Dan?'

He nods. Yes. All of us nod. Who goes first? It's so stupid, we haven't worked it out, no one knows who's supposed to go first, but then Tim says it doesn't matter, we'll all open them together.

'Like Christmas presents,' Dan says.

'Exactly.'

We laugh.

'Do it by age,' Dan said. 'You first, Jaf, then you, Skip, then Tim, then me. No one opens theirs till we've all got one. Agreed?'

Nods.

It was Tim. Tim drew the bad lot. The rest of us drew blanks. He just looked at it. 'It's me,' he said, and laughed and yelled and wept all together, throwing the marked scrap of paper down in the centre. 'Fuck, oh fuck, oh fuck, lads, it's me.'

'You don't have to do this, Tim,' Dan cried, 'you really don't.'

'No! No, no, no!' said Tim. 'I do, I do.'

'No, you don't.'

We said nothing, me and Skip. It unfolded.

'We agreed,' Tim said.

Dan was still crying. He kept stopping and starting. 'We can't do this,' he got out. He coughed and went on coughing, and his eyes ran like mad.

'It's all right,' Tim said. 'All agreed. Next lot. You three.'

'We can't do this.'

'Get on with it, please.'

'Draw the next one, for God's sake! We agreed!'

'Jesus.' Dan gave a weird frantic kind of a whine and twisted his hands and arms together in a very peculiar way that made him look mad.

'Oh, for Christ's sake!' said Tim, picking up the cup and rattling it about and setting it down once more.

'Here, take one.' He thrust it under my nose.

I took one. Then Skip. Then Dan.

'Now open them,' he said.

It was me.

I shook my head.

Tim started to cry, just a welling of tears and a look in his eyes.

'Can't,' I said.

'Oh, Jaf,' he said, 'you got the worst of it.' But he was smiling.

'I can't take this,' Dan said. 'We have to stop now.'

'No. Do it quick. Now, Jaf.' Tim tried to push the gun into my hand but I pulled away with a shudder. I felt sick.

'I don't care,' Tim said. 'I don't mind anyway. I can't see any more point in hanging about. Come on.' I looked deep in his eyes. They were dancing, full of fun, magnified by tears. 'You got the worst of it, not me. I'd rather go. Honest.'

Me and him and Ish, up and down the Highway. Smell of it. I was all choked up. He put the gun in my hands, gently. I shook my head.

'Please, Jaf,' he said. 'Just do it.'

His eyes.

'Don't think about it,' he says.

'Can't do it, Tim.' My voice all cracked.

Dan says: 'No. No, no, no, no, no, boys, no. Please listen.' Bent and impossibly aged by the sea, he leans forward, pulling us all in. Skip's just there, wide eyed, scabby, watching. 'I'll take it. I'll take your lot, Tim. Then you two draw for who does it.'

'We agreed,' said Tim.

'Boys, I can't have you do this. I wouldn't live with myself.'

'Look, this ain't easy for anyone,' Tim said. 'Let's just fucking get on with it.'

He lumbered up, breaking the circle and drawing me after him with one bony bird of prey claw embedded in my shoulder. Dan crying, Skip staring, me with the gun and Tim to the other end of the boat, the mild grey horizon going up and down.

'This is just me and you now. Tim, I can't do this.'

Tim pulled me close then, and we hugged. 'It's all right,' he said. 'It's happening, that's all. We drew fair and square.'

'Aren't you scared?'

'I'm always scared. I'm fucking terrified if you must know. Best if we do it quick. We all agreed and we got to stick by it.'

We separate, awkward. A warm breeze blows in my face from the south. The gun is in my right hand, my left in his.

'All square between me and you, Jaf?' he says.

''Course.'

'You take care, Jaf. If you get back, say – I don't know, tell them not to worry, you know . . .'

'This is mad.'

'Mad.' He laughs.

'Are you sure, Tim?'

'No blame, Jaf,' he says. 'I'd do the same for you. You're my best friend. You know what to do?'

Of course I do. All of us do. He lays down with his head on a coil of rope, curls up and closes his eyes as if he is going to have a sleep. Nothing and everything is real. I cock the trigger and put the gun next to his right temple, not quite touching.

'Tell me when you're ready,' I say.

'When you are.'

I shot.

I had to look, make sure he didn't suffer. His eyes clenched as the pistol discharged. Nothing else moved. The red running all over his head, down his face and neck. Nothing else moving. Side of his head sticky and flat.

We got on well for a few days. There was a steady breeze to bear us on, a steady rolling sea, constant as a pulse. Always in my mind the sights I could never forget, never unsee. Still now, and as long as I live, always there. Dan told me not to look, but it had gone too far for that to matter.

My ears sing. His hands shake as he cuts off Tim's head, lets it fall, holds the body so as to pour the spouting blood straight into the bucket Skip holds. It's still Tim's body, arms out straight, shiny, hairless chest, graceful filthy feet. His head I can't see any more for the bulk of Dan. Then, still and headless he lies, bleeding into the boards. Dan gives a great sigh, turns aside and drops something over. I can't help it, I run see, but there's nothing, it's sunk like a stone.

They cut off what was left of his clothes. It wasn't him any more. Dan worked dispassionately, mouth a straight line, fallen cheeks ghastly under pebbly eyes. It was a lot for one man to do. We helped, me and Skip. No one spoke. We helped with the cutting up, that was hard, there were things like moles and scabs and small hairs on the skin that showed it was him. I felt my head begin to swim and Dan sent me away. I sat and hugged myself, watching the rise and fall of the waves and thinking how peculiar it would be if a ship now hove into view. If it did, I thought, that would prove that God was bad. To do a thing like that. I had lost all sense of what time it was or what day or anything at all. I was very tired and yearned for sleep as I had never yearned for anything, with all my body. I think in fact I did sleep. When I woke up it was all over, there was just meat, and a bucket of stuff and some things in a bag made of his old raggedy shirt. We gave it as nice a send-off as we could. It was light and floated along beside us for a while before going under.

We had no fire. Some things we had raw straight away, pink heart meat, other soft things. Go easy, go easy, we said. No fools us. We all had something to suck on from time to time, sensible. Meat hung drying, long ribbons adorning our tattered sails. Meat spread salting. I kept looking round for Tim. I could still feel him

284

in the boat with us. My mouth was wet once more. When I licked my lips my tongue did not cling like a grub. The cup had gone round three or four times: sip carefully, sip like a bee. Blood. What's this I feel? What is it? Not sadness, not sickness—

'He's given us a few days more,' Dan said.

Having eaten, we three were now, to some extent, serene. We lay rocked upon the bosom of the deep, alive yet, alive-alive-o. We three? We four.

'Feels like he's still here,' I said.

'He is,' said Skip. 'There!' and nodded towards the stern of the boat.

But *I* couldn't see him. Not fair, I thought, if he was here it would be me he'd show himself to, not him. Didn't show himself, but I felt him there all the same. It got dark and we just lay.

What is it I feel? Not sadness, not sickness. What I feel is a kind of lightness, a perverse sense of well-being. This is the funny thing: Tim and me, I feel we are closer than we've ever been. You go through a thing like that with someone – it's not like he's gone away, not like that at all.

I dream, I suppose. It's a soft pink dawn full of cloudy billows and murmuring distance. Peaceful. I have no pain, it's all fine, a lovely day. I can't remember how I came to be here. These my companions and I have been floating this many a year. All about us there is laughter on the sea. There are strange things out there, things it is forbidden to look on lest they turn you to stone. But when I fall asleep and see John Copper's head floating by the boat, face up, it's not stone but jelly I turn to, and I wake up.

14

End of a long wild watch, those two sleeping fitfully and me alone in the world, watching endlessness, falling in and out of it. Tags of flesh tied on the spars, a-flicker on the breeze, a thick smell like the tanning factory down the road. I have a bone. My tongue has turned into the long grey scooping tongue of a dog and will not cease until it has scoured out as far as it can reach every last life-giving suck of the honeycombed heart of the bone. It occurs to me that all the world's the same substance: a man's bowels are like the London sewers. Skip's red legs, swollen like sausages. Dag swelled up like that. I hug my bone. Its creamy smell tickles my nose. Why is Skip alive and Tim dead? *He* should have gone, not Tim. He's on the way out anyhow. Only have to look at him.

I woke him up.

'Your watch,' I told him, and lay down.

As for sleep, I don't know that I ever did any more. There were other worlds, for sure: hosts and hosts of them overlaying one another like troubled veils, ripples in a wild place. Where they existed I've no idea, but these dreams were nothing like the dreams of ordinary sleep. Soon as I closed my eyes they foundered against one another like the waves beneath. I could see through my forehead. Tim was in the boat still, sitting where he always did. Tim died: words words words. Now and then I sucked my sweet bone, the good smell, hugging and holding. My sores curdled.

I am a brother to dragons and a companion of owls. The bone lies across my chest and beats like a heart. The bone and I will go on. When I want to cry because I am afraid, I put the hard, shiny knob at the end of the bone in my mouth and suck with closed eyes and swoon away into sleep again and stay there for a long sweet time till it falls out on the pillow. I scream and it comes back. I'm in my cot in Bermondsey. The dark river washes against the pilings. Ma's there. Big Ben strikes ten. The tiger, the sun in glory, softly steps on kitten feet and turns his golden eyes on me, regards me as the sea does: I'll eat you by and by, no hurry. Don't take it personally.

The dark silhouette of a huge head has risen over the side of the boat.

Dan shakes my shoulder and I scream.

'It's all right, Jaf,' he says, sounding tired. 'You can go back to sleep.'

It was light. Dan was lying with his eyes half closed, smoking an invisible cigar. Skip was standing in the bow, gazing earnestly eastward. I couldn't see Tim, but I knew he was still there. I felt him. I felt him inside me also, as if he'd passed through and through in millions of channels smaller than anything a human sense could catch at. I closed my eyes and held on tight as I could to my bone. And all those worlds began to jangle again, the worlds on worlds, whispering and rustling together like millions of leaves shivering on one of those early autumn nights when the weather's just on the turn, just catching in your nostrils. 'Tobacco's But An Indian Weed'. Once on the Wapping steps.

Next time I woke it was dark. Skip was asleep and Dan was

lying on his back with his hands clasped behind his head, staring up at the night sky with serious eyes, as if something up there in all those stars might be revealed.

'Dan,' I said.

He didn't reply. I thought he might be dead, his eyes frozen for ever on the stars.

After a moment he said: 'Life made more sense in those days.'

'Dan.'

'What?'

But I'd forgotten what it was I wanted to say so I put my head back and watched the sky along with him. It was black and very starry. Starry out there is not like in London. There, starry is an observable impossibility, and looking up is a gaze into infinity.

'What is that bone?' Dan asked.

'It's an arm bone,' I replied.

White, criss-cross, other bones lay gleaming in the belly of the boat. Skip's arm, outflung, trailed across them.

'What do we do now?' I asked.

Dan began laughing uncontrollably, a tight, smothered creaking that went on and on till the tears rolled down his face. He wiped them off with his fingers and smeared them across the withered hole of his mouth.

'What will it be like for the last one of us?' I asked the sky.

Dan shook his head and sat up, blowing his nose in his hand and flinging it.

My mouth's been bleeding, my gums are all gone to sponge. I can taste blood in my teeth, sharp and good, and I swallow. My throat rasps. I don't hurt so bad at the moment. 'Cept for my eyes.

'Soon be morning,' said Dan.

When it came, Skip slept on. When we tried to wake him he wouldn't open his eyes. He hit out at us, shuddering and scowling, mumbling angrily, so we left him. He'll die soon, I thought. No point in drawing lots again, it's clear he's going first. What then? Me and Dan. *Who* then? Me or him. Alone. Will it be me? What then?

I laughed.

'What?' asked Dan.

'I was just thinking,' I said. 'When it's just you and me.'

After a while he laughed too, and made an attempt at song:

> Says Gorging Jack to Guzzling Jimmie
> I am extremely hung-a-ree . . .

I joined in:

> To Gorging Jack says Guzzling Jimmy
> We've nothing left, us must eat we.

You can see why people laugh, can't you? It tickled us both so much that our sniggering finally woke up Skip, who shot up like a revived corpse, turkey neck and staring eyes. I can't stand those eyes. What's in them is hard to look at.

'It was yellow,' he said.

'What was?'

'Look,' said Dan, spreading before us what was left of our supplies, enough to keep a rat alive for a day or so.

'It was yellow . . .'

'Look at it.'

'. . . like an eye.'

'Look at it,' Dan said. 'That's it.'

Such a ridiculous amount it set me and Dan off laughing like fools again, which only infuriated Skip. 'Throw it over!' he shouted. 'Have done with it!' and tried to stand up, but toppled over immediately and fell to feebly punching the side of the boat with red raw knuckles that left smears.

'Fuck this, I'm done with it, I'm done with it!' he spat out.

'What are you trying to do?' Dan put a hand on his shoulder. 'Stove us in?'

'Better that.' He pulled himself up onto his knees. A great heat was burning on his cheeks and forehead.

'What was yellow?' I asked.

Skip hauled his eyes onto me like heavy sacks. 'I know what you're thinking,' he said.

'No, you don't.'

'I know everything.' His eyes changed, made a sideways flip from anger to horror. It wasn't him looking out from his eyes. 'You want me to die,' he said.

'I do not.'

'Sit down,' said Dan, pulling on his shirt.

'You want to kill me.'

'I do not.'

I didn't. I wanted to smash his face in though for making me remember how I killed Tim.

I killed Tim.

Sounds stupid but I only realised it at that moment. It was like falling from a great height.

'I killed Tim,' I said, sick to my stomach.

'You didn't!' Dan tried to sit up but fell back.

I began to moan, a straggly lowing trail of a thing that meandered along absolutely separate from me like a ribbon proceeding out of my mouth. I shoved my fists in my mouth to stop it. It wasn't me, it was a thing in my body forcing its way out, I had no control over it. And as it keened on, lost in the slop and slap of waves, something invisible got into the boat with us. I tried to hide behind Dan. Blind bloody gut-cramp fear, not to be fought.

'Leave me alone,' sobbed Skip.

Dan struggled himself upright, a wild-looking thing, ragged old death's-head man of the sea. 'To me,' he said.

We three hunched in the bow.

'Don't think,' Dan said.

The sticky hold of fear. I was a fly trying to lift at least one of its thread-like legs from the syrup.

'Make it stop,' I said.

'Don't think.'

I looked up and saw Dan's face wet with tears. Or was it the rain that had just begun, a sweet English drizzle?

'I killed Tim,' I repeated. It seemed important I should acknowledge this as truth eternal, an irreversible fact to be absorbed by the universe. Dan's eyes closed and the water poured down. I couldn't say if he was laughing or crying.

'You'll have a long life, Jaf,' he said. 'Don't waste it on this.'

'Send a ship,' Skip cried, a shrill seagull's voice that echoed in my ear.

But it wouldn't make any difference, I had still killed Tim. For ever and ever amen I had killed Tim.

My moan was changing into a stupid childish crying, a miserable wipe-my-nose and pick-me-up sort of a grizzle. Clouds of grey and black boiled in front of my eyes. I went somewhere strange, somewhere far and lost as a rock on another world, and forgot how I got there or where I'd come from or what name I had or anything at all apart from a subtle and steady push towards some surface far above. When I got up finally from this and my head cleared I saw that Dan was praying silently, moving his mouth, leaning his head against the side of the boat, asking God to take care of Alice and the kids. Skip was lying down with his arms round his head. And there was the smidgin of hardtack and the couple of inches of warm water, and the gun, and the invisible fear thing was gone.

'Let's eat what's left,' I said.

292

So we did, breaking the tack into three and passing the cup round, sipping small long-held mouthfuls. It took about half an hour before it was gone. That's how long we spun it out. Then like old men by the fire after a good dinner we sat back in contemplative silence. The rain was like silver rods whispering and shimmering, piercing the sea. That was beautiful, soothing. Skip lay back down and said he wasn't getting up again. He said there was no point. He smiled and closed his eyes and put his arms back round his head and said he was going to sleep, but was up again immediately. Then down, then up, down, up, with his horrible eyes, down, up, like a dog with worms, standing in the heaving bow screaming he saw a ship, a ship, then, oh God, a low rumbling laugh because, oh hell, there's an eye pierced on every spar, all googling and bloody, and they're turning, every bleeding one, on us. 'You want me dead!' he screamed, whether to us or his big god or the sea or the demon I've no idea, but whatever it was it seemed to strike him down at once, for he spun about and dropped, holding his head and screaming at the top of his lungs.

We took hold of him and tried to hold him from thrashing too hard. He screamed and screamed, twitching all over his shoulders and arms, froth at the corners of his mouth.

'Nothing to worry about, Skip,' Dan said, 'nothing at all.'

He calmed down a little and we laid him down with a bunch of rags under his head.

'There, see, you're all right,' we said to him.

He called for water. Called for a candle, though it was light. He called for Polly-dog and his ma and pa. Three hours he chattered but made no sense, and he never again opened his eyes, though he said he saw tall things with horns approaching, smiling, on the restless sea. Late in the afternoon he died with his head on Dan's knees, bravely rambling till the very end, which came as a terrible convulsion that shook the boat as if we'd landed a shark.

I remember you a strange misty morning man in the yard, early life, early morning, Mr Jamrach standing in the light from his office door, and you there with a whiff of the ocean about you, the wild places that called. You sang 'Tobacco Is An Indian Weed' on the Wapping Steps. Where else could I go after that? Look at us now. Dan's my mirror: scooped hollows in his face, eyes like pits. I look like that too. Skin shrinks. Lips turn black, teeth stick out.

'Need to shorten sail,' he said. 'You do that while I get on with this.'

I did. I looked out over the rippling babble of waves and heard, as I had heard before, for Tim, for Gabriel, the cleft and slurp and rasp of the knife. For Skip.

Smash. Hatchet.

Dog's lick. Marrow.

Close eyes, suck.

Close eyes, suck.

I saw the thing Skip saw. It came striding and stalking with hoofed front legs on the sea, a creature of jovial reptilian cast, with the long, curled tail of a fish following proudly in its wake. When it got alongside the boat and a ship's length off, its eyes swivelled in its head and fixed me, its lip curling delicately to reveal the long, pointed teeth of a cannibal. Then again I saw spectral ships, and fingers of smoke that crept along the gunwale. I saw a tree dripping living colours that ran with kittenish joy into and out of one another all along its elegant branches, faces that flashed a million changes, questing eyes, water-dappled ceilings, a great lost city in ruins of pink and gold. I soared above the earth on vast bat wings, mighty and proud. But I went too high, couldn't stop myself. As if I was a balloon and someone cut my string, I went up and up and up, sucked at hideous speed, till there was nothing of me left but a thought that I was still me, whatever that was, and any second now would come the fall, inescapable. These terrible dream falls; always at the howling rushing point of no return I have woken safe: in bed, in *Drago*'s belly, under a table at Spoony's with a whore cradling my head. Always, the world has returned. Good old world. This time it would not. All lost: Ma's warm armpit, songbirds, moon over London Bridge, a small gold head in the crowd, the smell of sarsaparilla, all of it, and everything in a great surge of longing, a love I had been born to feel, and which was also required of me and the purpose of my life.

And then I fell.

Voices.

Corncrake groan of a rigging. Soft flapping of sails at peace. Sea-green, delicate little bones, white and creamy ones wrapped in my arms. We love our bones. We'll never part with them.

A great shadow falls. Faces look down at us.

It was the passenger steamer *Quinteros* sailing between Callao and Valparaiso that picked us up. We were not far from the Chilean coast. I can't remember how I got up on deck. I remember a sense of weary wonder, strange fear, a voice in my head crying out again and again as if it was angry with me. I remember a blurry gaggle of staring faces that moved gently as if some great hand was shaking them up and down. I remember a smell like frying onions, and tears pouring down my face so hard I thought they were my life blood leaving me. My legs would not stand. Arms caught me. Many voices murmured and one, strong above the rest, spoke words into my ear that made no sense. There was

295

tapioca in a bowl, and a spoon I dropped when they put it in my hand. We were more than half mad as we sailed for Valparaiso. We sat and shivered, staring like madmen. And Dan said to me: 'We say nothing about the Ora,' and I nodded, my teeth chattering in my head. And we never did. I don't know why. Felt like bad luck, I suppose.

PART THREE

15

'Don't look at me with those eyes, sailorboy.'
'What eyes? These eyes? They're mine. What other eyes should I look at you with?'

Red-haired. A little poxed but not much. Pretty face, chin too long. She has the faint remains of a scab in the corner of her mouth and I feel sorry for her.

'What's your name?'

'Faith,' she says.

'Pretty,' says I.

'Want a place to go?' says she.

I must have been grinning. She took my hand. 'What you laughing at?' she said. 'You laughing at me?'

'Have you got a place to go?'

'I have that. You come with me.' She led me good as gold through the streets of Greenwich in the rain. She'd picked me off the quay, from among all those sun-beat faces, those half-savage things that seamen are when they're coming in after long years at sea, pulled me from the heave and holler of those touts and crimps and runners all wanting a piece of me. But I wasn't green any more. I shivered as she led me through those glorious green and grey rain-sodden Greenwich streets, how beautiful and shining they were, how altogether heartbreaking. I started crying.

She noticed as we reached the tall dark house. Pushing me aganst the wall just by the doorway in the hall, seizing my head between her hands and staring in my eyes with blazing grey eyes. 'Go on then,' she said, 'have a bloody good cry, chicky.'

'I'm not green,' I said, 'I know you want to rob me. Just letting you know I know.'

'There we are then,' she said, letting me go. 'Glad we got that one straight. Come on.'

So up the stairs, one flight only, to a bare landing, where she lit us a candle from a cupboard on the left, then a door with spotted brown paint that opened onto a small room almost filled with a bed covered with an Indian cloth. The candle flickered on the ceiling and the walls, adorned here and there with sentimental pictures of violets and kittens, and there in the window was a linnet in a cage.

'Here, Faith,' I said, 'what's your charge?'

She smiled, lopsided. Her forehead was high, with mobile wrinkles that spoke as much as her eyes. I guessed her at thirty. Business done, she took off her jacket and sat down on the bed to take off her boots. It was nice, I thought. Cosy. Outside, the sounds of life. Footsteps that tocked along the pavement. I am home, I thought. Home.

'Did you get this from Jamrach?'

The linnet.

'I don't know,' she said, 'it's not my room.'

I put my face up against the bars of the cage and looked at the linnet.

'Linnet,' I said, 'linnet, hello, linnet.'

'Is that what it is?' she said.

I cried again.

'You lay down,' she said, getting up and leading me firmly to the bed. 'You got half an hour, have a nice lie down and a little weep.'

So I did. I was very drunk. I was drunk before I left the ship. It's all fady, through a veil. I'd paid her for half an hour, had a bit more cash in my breeches and knew she might try and steal it, and knew my head was full of whirling clouds and that I could no more stop crying than the rain could stop pouring till its true time was up; and that made me feel the rain against the window-pane, its glowing drops moving leisurely, its song, its soft lullaby. My head hit the pillow, a poor, hard, straw pillow softer to me than rose petals and goose down. How could I save my money, now I was going out like a candle?

'Here,' I said, 'I've paid for you.'

She lay down next to me and I took her in my arms.

'You rob me I kill you,' I said.

'No, you won't,' she said indulgently, "cos you got no need to.'

Couldn't stop the tears. She wiped my nose with a small hand-kerchief perfumed with lavender. That made me cry more.

'What's this?' she asked.

Bruises on my upper right arm. They had not faded.

'Nothing.'

'That's enough,' she said, 'calm yourself down now. Here's a nice deal: you give me one more guinea and I promise not to rob you.'

'Done,' I said.

No more did she. She chucked me out when my time was up and I walked along the river way to the bridge in the light silvery sifting rain, passing where we used to live in Bermondsey all those years ago. It was no better. Still stank to high heaven. The fore-shore by the bridge was filthy as ever. I sat on the steps for ages, looking across to the other side. To Ratcliffe Highway. She let me off, that woman, I thought. But then I think she knew me for a native.

I put off going home, wandered aimlessly, crossed the river eventually, the day nearing noon, stood for half an hour watching them landing the sugar. As yet I'd seen no one I knew, which suited me. The news had flown before. Long before we docked they'd all have known our story. It would be in their eyes when they looked at me, their knowledge of what had passed. Maybe we should have lied, but we didn't. God knows how I'd face Ishbel and her ma. Impossible. Part of me thought I should never have come back, should have buried myself away in some lost, forgotten corner of the world, but it wouldn't have been fair on Ma. So I dawdled and fooled about, and it was two before I reached Ma's. She'd been expecting me since yesterday afternoon and was out on the corner looking up the street. Same old Ma, just a bit greyer. I saw her before she saw me. Her face could have been taken for hard but I knew she was just worried. When she saw me she relaxed, mouth flexing into a twisted line of grim joy. She took a couple of steps towards me and gave me a quick hard hug.

'Are you all right?' she asked.

I kissed her on the cheek. 'You've not been standing there all day, have you?'

''Course not, you silly creature,' she said. 'I've been in and out.'

We stood back. I was grinning rather foolishly, I thought. Her eyes were pained.

'Are you all right?' she asked again, looking closely at me.

'I'm not so bad.'

'I never thought I'd see you again.'

'Well, there you go.' I laughed, a pointless snigger.

'Come on.' She took my arm and led me into a court with a long flagged drain down the middle and a blacksmith's shop at the far end. The sound of metal hammering rang from the eaves,

302

and a tall black horse stood tethered at the gate, head in its nosebag. Their house was on the left, a half door, a bucket of suds, a deep windowsill on which shells were distributed, a large scallop and a few scotch bonnets. It was bigger and cleaner than their old place, and smelled of laundry and fish and Ma's old broth that I used to dream about on the boat. Charley Grant stood straddle-legged with his back to a blazing fire, above which a kettle on a hook vibrated and hummed quietly. His face was pink as a ham and he'd fattened up since I last saw him.

'Jaf,' he said, coming forward and gripping my shoulder warmly but awkwardly, 'very, very good to see you home.'

'It's good to *be* home.'

A lad of about eighteen months sat in a high chair at the table, a wooden spoon clasped in one porridgy fist.

'Looks nice, don't he, Charl?' Ma said proudly, prodding me into a chair opposite the child.

'That he does.'

'Who do you think this is, eh Jaf?'

The child had a snub, broad face and a surprisingly luxuriant growth of brown curls right on top of his head. He looked at me appraisingly, and I winked at him.

'That's your little brother, Jaf,' Ma said briskly. 'His name's David.'

'What!'

'There's a surprise for you! David! Say hello to your big brother, Jaffy.'

David and I regarded each other with interested suspicion.

Of course, it wasn't that surprising. She wasn't so old. Looked it though. Ma had aged. Not yet forty, I supposed. She was young when she had me. Strange it was, all this. I felt very far away. After all my time at sea, this steamy room, the child, the smiling man with his ham face and braces, the heat, the bowl of broth she placed before me, the hunk of bread, the unmistakeable air of the river beyond these walls – everything a fancy in my head, something flashing in front of my eyes at the moment of faint.

The broth was food for gods.

I found myself crying.

'There now, it's all over,' Ma said, bending and putting her arms round me, swamping me with her old familiar smell. 'Everything's going to be all right from now on.'

'I know, I know.'

She showed me my room. It was tiny, but the window looked out over rooftops towards the river, where the masts of tall ships traced the sky. A lovely bed she'd made up for me, with a silky counterpane patterned with red flowers, and beside it, on a squat four-legged stool, a spray of honesty in that old green jug we used to have on the mantelpiece in Watney Street. My bed. All I wanted to do was get into it and sleep and sleep. But when my head touched the pillow and Ma drew the curtains and kissed me goodnight and went out closing the door softly, my mind ploughed uneasy billows in the darkness. All the things I had to do: go see Ishbel and her mother. Get that over with. Sleep. A lot. Everyone said I needed it, the doctor on the ship, the doctor in Valparaiso. What else? Get myself back, my mind, that is – reel it in from these far chasms and boiling seas, think about the future that might never have been. What to do now? Go out and meet the eyes. Everyone knows. Nothing was hidden. These people of the docks have lived so long with the sea and heard so many mariners' tales, nothing surprises them. They won't look askance at me. Still, there'll be something in their eyes, a knowing.

I slept at last, but sleep was not restful and tossed like the sea. This was when I started to fathom these deepest deeps, and conclude nothing.

Mr Jamrach came to see me next morning. I heard his voice, he was talking to Ma, saying he'd had a long talk with Dan Rymer,

304

and that Dan had said he would not ever go back to sea. Ma said, well, it was about time he settled down, wasn't it? A man his age with such a young family. 'He wants to stay at home now and enjoy what he's got,' she said. I could hear David chuckling in the background. He was like that. He'd sit and play with his fingers and chuckle and chatter to himself, quite wrapped up in some happy world of his own for ages.

I didn't want to go down. I wouldn't. No one could make me. Not yet. It was all too much for me at the moment, I'd just stay in bed for as long as I possibly could. Days even, if they'd let me. While I worked out what to do next. Sleep. That was the thing. Life now would be simple: fish, soup, warmth, sleep, baccy, beer. My head was spinning: all the sounds, the smells, the endless proliferation. Yet so many gone. So when she came in and said Mr Jamrach's come to see you, I said I was feeling too tired to get up, and he called out not to worry, another time would do, and I turned over and tried to get back to sleep, tried hard, hard, with the light seeping in the window.

Next day though she made me get up and she shooed me out of the house. First I went to the barber's then to see Mr Jamrach. Cobbe was still in the yard, looking just the same as ever only balder, which gave him the look of a convict. He put down his bucket and came over and embraced me gruffly, a thing I never could have imagined in a million years.

'Hello, Cobbe,' I said.

He grunted and walked away.

Something in the yard was changed but I couldn't work out what it was. Jamrach's fat Japanese pig was eating cabbage down the far end. Mr Jamrach saw me through the window and came out to greet me. He'd thickened and widened and reddened since I last saw him. 'At last!' he cried, beaming from ear to ear. 'Jaffy boy! Feeling better?'

305

'Very much better,' I replied, feeling nothing of the sort. I had no idea why I was out of my bed and couldn't wait to get back to it.

He clapped me on the shoulder, man to man. 'This business, Jaf,' he said, looking me in the eye, 'a terrible thing.'

'Yes.'

'Terrible.'

I nodded.

'Come into the office.'

There was a new boy in an alcove all of his own, scrabbling about with a pile of paperwork and whistling cheerfully. Not as messy as the old days when Bulter lolled about behind the desk. Charlie the toucan was still going strong, but the old parrot Flo had fallen prey to tuberculosis and departed this life. Mr Jamrach sent the boy away and poured coffee from a pot on the stove. It was cold outside and cosy in here, smoky as ever. Charlie sat in my arms and nibbled my ear.

I asked how things were going.

'Not bad, not bad,' he said, putting back his head and blowing smoke towards the ceiling. Then he told me he'd got his son Albert in with him now and was training him up to run the business. Only Albert was at home today with a bad cold.

'Shame,' I said.

Mr Jamrach offered me a pipe, relit his own and sat back.

It was an awkward meeting. For a while we sat and smoked, saying nothing.

'Coffee all right?' he asked. 'Not too strong?'

'No, just right.'

'That's the ticket.'

'You know, Jaf,' he said, leaning forward, his sad old eyes blinking, 'I can't begin to find the words—'

'It's all right, Mr Jamrach.' I disengaged Charlie's claws from my jacket. 'I know it's awkward.'

'No, I mean to say . . .' He gestured with one hand. 'I mean to say . . . what you suffered is beyond my imagination. I want you to know that . . .'

'I know,' I said.

'. . . anything at all that I can do . . .'

'Of course.'

'You know Dan's retired?'

'I know. He told me in Valparaiso.'

Such a curious feeling. As if Tim was standing in the room with us.

'You're still very young, Jaf,' he said. 'You mustn't let this blight your life.'

'I know.'

'There's not a spot of blame on you.'

'I know.'

'People understand.'

'I know.'

I could have sworn I'd see him if I looked around.

'Of course, no one expects you to do anything yet, but you know there's always a job here if you . . .'

'I know.'

But he and I both knew there was no hurry. Mr Fledge had proved generous to me and Dan. Anyway, I don't know where he thought he could fit me in. Clearly I could no longer be a yard boy, and a desk job would never do for me. I had no idea what I was going to do, to tell the truth. Still had a swirling sea in my head.

'I really don't suppose I'll come back here,' I said.

'No.' He nodded thoughtfully. 'I can see why.'

'Anyway,' I said, looking around, 'it's nice to see the old place again.'

'Not so much changed, eh?'

'A little.'

'It's a bit neater the way it's laid out now. That's Albert,' he said.

We sat for a while longer, then he said, 'Well, when you decide what it is you want to do with yourself, come to me, won't you, Jaf? Because whatever it is, you know that . . .'

'Thank you very much, sir,' I said.

I had to go. We stood up. Charlie flew onto Jamrach's shoulder. The lobby was full of finches waiting to be moved into one of the bird rooms. Newly come from the docks, the birds hunched neckless in their tiny boxes, sullen with the change. A wave of nausea weakened me but I don't think he saw it.

'You take care of yourself, Jaf,' he said, 'and come straight to me, you know, if there's anything you want. Promise?'

Suffocation was on the air. I couldn't wait to get out of there.

'Sure,' I said.

He shook me firmly by the hand, looking at me hard with pained, watery eyes.

'You want to get yourself an aviary, Mr Jamrach,' I said.

He smiled, looking sadly at the birds for a long moment. 'It's not ideal,' he agreed, 'but, there you are, there isn't the space.'

He opened the door. Charlie had slid down onto his chest and nestled there like a newborn deer, casting up his round ridiculous eye.

Out in the street I stood for a while breathing the ripe air and considering. Had to go see Tim's ma. I walked along slowly, dreading, thinking I'd just go home instead. Have to get it over with, though. Ishbel might be there. The thought of it made me hollow. Tell me, just what do you say? Look at it this way, Mrs Linver. At least *I* came back.

Come on, let's get it over with.

Not yet.

I slipped into the seamen's bethel. Nothing changed. Jephtha and his daughter still there. Old Job and his boils. What a homecoming! I went into a kind of dream in there. I had money in my pocket so I just about wiped them out of candles. Now! Here's fun! Trying not to forget anyone. I decided to start with Ishbel's brothers, remembering that day when she and I came in here – that day – where had we been? Was it the day she fell out with Tim after we'd been on the swingboats? Anyway, one each for those brothers, tall, upstanding, side by side, for ever faceless. Next, count: Joe Harper making the cage on deck, his sliding toolbox. One and two: Mr Rainey with his sneer. Three: the captain, of course, more like a big schoolboy than the captain of a whale ship. Four: ah now, Martin Hannah, pudding. Abel Roper. And are you? Are you that, Mr Roper? Ha ha ha! That's five. Six. Each one a light coming into being, quivering, standing tall and straight in the quiet chapel. Gabriel. My friend. Yan holding my sick bucket. Billy Stock, outraged. Where am I? Let's see, one, two, three, four, five, six, seven, eight? Nine: oh, Mr Comeragh, he was a nice man. Poor Mr Comeragh got bitten by the dragon. What a wild, ancient thing that was. Did he get back to his island? Is he walking with weird rounded steps along his sandy beach, flick-a-tongue, low swaying of the head? Nine: Wilson Pride, flat-footed, bloodshot eyes. Ten: Henry Cash, head like a seal, going under. Eleven: Felix Duggan, mouthy, nuisance. Twelve: Simon, of course, playing his fiddle. We never found out what became of the captain and Simon. And Sam, thirteen. Sam Proffit, whose voice was a silver thread. Dag. Dag Aarnasson, who hunted the dragon with me. Fourteen. Fifteen . . .

I went blank. There was, of course, we last four, me and Dan and Tim and Skip, which still left two more. It was horrible, not remembering. As if by losing them in my mind I was consigning them to outer darkness for all time.

John Copper! How could I forget?

I've missed someone. Or have I miscounted? Start again. One, two three, four . . .

In the end I got it. I wouldn't have left there if anyone was missing. I looked back from the door. My twenty candles burned steadily.

It was Saturday. Mrs Linver lived in Fournier Street now, so I wandered in that direction, hands in pockets, collar up. I passed by Watney Street and walked past our old house and looked out for a sign of Mr Reuben or Mrs Regan or anyone else, but the door was closed and there was no one sitting on the step. Three times I bumped into people I knew and had to stop and talk, stand and get clapped once more on the shoulder, my face searched nervously, congratulated on my survival. I pushed on through the Saturday Highway of whores and drunken sailors, mulish laughter, shrieking hilarity, screeching fiddles beyond doors. The pot man, a short dirty man smoking a short dirty pipe, leaned in the doorway of Spoony's. He wasn't there in my time. I thought about going in and having a drink, in fact getting filthy drunk and falling asleep on the floor till some woman came and hauled me off somewhere soft to sleep it off. But this cloud, hovering: go see Tim's ma. Got to be done. Ishbel might be there. I hear she's gone into service but still, she might be there. Her face like his. There's no forgetting Tim. The taste of a raspberry puff. Push on, Jaf, push through. Go down to the docks and get on the first ship that'll have you.

Till I ended up on Fournier Street, searching for her door. Sadly unnumbered some of these houses were. She had a black door at the side of a cooper's yard, with three steps up to it and a poster in the downstairs window for tonight's show at the Gunboat.

310

Ishbel opened the door. Dressed in black, bright brown eyes, pale face, fair hair pinned back behind her ears. A glance and then I couldn't meet her eyes any more and looked slightly to one side.

'I wondered when you'd come,' she said.

'Hello, Ish.'

She stepped forward and embraced me formally, her silky cheek one moment against my new stubble. Dear God, let me not be a fool. She used to be taller than me. We've evened out. When she steps back I see that I am actually three inches or so above her and she's wearing heeled boots. She's changed. Is it the simple black making her more stately than before? What is she to me now? I have no idea.

'Well, look at *you*,' she said, 'you've grown up.'

'So've you.'

She led me along a dark hall and into a room at the side.

'I hear you're in service.'

'That's true.' She looked over her shoulder. 'Mr Jamrach found me a position in Clerkenwell.'

'Do you like it?'

She shrugged, opening a door.

It was grander than the old place, high-ceilinged and bow-fronted, with a large fuchsia plant in a white pot in the bay, a fine black range covering one wall, and polished brasses about the fireplace. Mrs Linver sat in a rocking chair with her slippered feet up on the fender.

'Look who's come to see us,' Ishbel said cheerfully.

Mrs Linver jumped to her feet and stared. A tortured ball of handkerchief fell to the floor. 'How dare you come back without him!' she cried.

'Don't be stupid, Mother,' Ishbel said, 'it's not Jaffy's fault.'

'I'm so sorry, Mrs Linver,' I whispered. I couldn't stand this. 'I'm so, so sorry.'

311

'Sit down, Jaffy.' Ishbel pushed me into a chair. 'I'll make some tea,' and she was gone.

Her mother took a few frantic steps towards me with her hands clenched hard down by her sides. Raddled, she looked. Dark hollows in her face. She stopped, shaking, a foot or so from me, then fell to one knee in front of me, the better to look in my face. It was a terrible thing to look in her eyes. 'I know it's not your fault, Jaffy,' she said urgently. 'I know it really, but it's just a very very hard thing.'

My eyes burned.

'It's a very hard thing,' she repeated, staring.

I felt as if my head would burst, tried to speak, but found my throat blocked.

'There, that'll be ready soon,' said Ishbel, coming in and drawing up a small table, pulling her mother to her feet, thrusting her back into her chair and handing her the dropped handkerchief, all, it seemed, in one continuous movement. Every inch of her, every movement was familiar yet profoundly different, the reality of her more dreamlike than her memory.

'It's been very hard for our Ishbel,' Mrs Linver said, still looking at me. 'She's had to take her father's place, you know, really. What with her brother gone. We're so grateful to Mr Jamrach for finding her such a good position.'

'Yes, of course.' Ishbel drew up her own chair and perched there very stiff and straight like a lady, with her hands in her lap. A woman's bosom had replaced the two small lemon-shaped breasts I remembered. Her hands were as bad as ever, and I watched fascinated as they picked at and played with each other. 'Strangely enough,' she said, 'we're not doing too bad. How's your ma, Jaf?'

'She's well,' I said. 'Have to say though, I got a bit of a shock when I saw this sprog sitting there.'

'Oh yes.' She smiled. 'We thought about that. Little David. Sweet, isn't he? He reminds me of you.'

I chanced a look, but she was watching her mother.

'So tell us then, Jaffy,' Mrs Linver said, sitting forward, 'tell us what you have to tell us.'

'Mother, leave him,' she said in a strained voice. 'Let him have his tea at least.'

'It's all right,' I said, 'I don't mind telling you anything, only it's hard for me to talk about. You must understand.'

'Of course,' said Ishbel.

'I just want to know,' his mother said, 'that he didn't have too terrible a time, and I want to know if it was quickly over. You know. At the end. That's all I want to know. And I want you to tell me the truth.'

'He went before the worst,' I said. 'I'd be lying if I said there was no suffering; there was, for all, but he went before the worst.'

There was a long and painful silence. I couldn't look at them.

'They said it was his idea to draw lots,' his mother said.

'It was. But we all agreed.'

I raised my eyes. Both of them were staring at me and the blood sang in my ears.

'He kept going, you know, Tim,' I said. 'I never saw him lose his spirits.'

His mother's eyes grew huge.

'He told me to tell you both he was all right. I know it sounds funny, but it's what he said. Tell them I'm all right.'

Ishbel shrieked, 'Oh! Idiot!' and threw her hands up to her face.

'Said he's all right and you're not to worry.'

She was laughing. We all did, for a second.

'Oh!' she cried. 'Ain't that just like him?'

So there we were, the three of us with tears streaming down our faces.

'He was steady,' I said. 'He really was. Don't think I could've been so steady. He was . . .' My voice gave out.

Mrs Linver blew her nose.

'I'm so sorry, Mrs Linver,' I said, and there was nothing I could ever do to make it better. I was here and he was gone, and between us all for ever the shared horror of what had become of him, what I had done. It came back to me still, the pressure of my finger on the trigger.

Ishbel wiped her cheeks with the palms of both hands. 'I'll get the tea,' she said, bobbing up and dashing out. I sat in agony, wanting to run, stiff like a bug in amber.

'Really,' I said, 'he was very, very brave.'

Silly words.

Mrs Linver nodded, knitting her brows into jags and turning her face away to look into the fire. The coals shifted. The sounds of people passing in the street came as if from dreamland, echoing like sounds in a shell. For a moment I believed I might faint.

'That's a nice plant,' I said desperately. 'Does it flower in the summer?'

'Oh yes, very beautiful,' Mrs Linver said sadly, 'lovely pink flowers.'

Ishbel came in with the tea tray, walking backwards as she pushed the door open. I jumped up and took the tray from her. Her face was flushed.

'Now,' she said, 'just put it down there, Jaffy. Thank you.'

Did they expect more of me? All the things I could tell, the things I have tried so hard not to dwell upon. Could I soon go?

'Mind you,' Mrs Linver continued thoughtfully, 'it's getting leggy.'

'What is?' Ishbel sat down.

'That plant.'

'Oh yes, I must give it a trim.' Ishbel smiled at me brightly as if this was just an ordinary visit. 'Thanks for coming, Jaffy.'

'That's all right.'

'I can't imagine how terrible it was for you.'

'At least he's here,' her mother said.

'Well, thank God for that.'

Ishbel poured the tea. 'Did I tell you I was engaged to be married?' she said, not looking at me. 'Me? Can you believe it?'

Of course.

'Really?'

She handed me a cup.

'He's a lighterman,' she said, 'works on the Surrey Dock.'

'Oh! Congratulations!'

'Thank you.' She gave her mother a cup and saucer. 'He's a good sort, is Frank,' she said, sitting back down and stirring her tea. I felt like a stone. 'So what about you, Jaffy? What will *you* do now?'

'Me? I haven't decided yet.'

'Oh well, no rush.'

There was a long silence while we sipped our tea. I had to get out.

'What's it like where you are?' I asked, and my voice came out harsh.

'Oh, it'll do.' She set her cup down. 'That's too hot.' She frowned.

'Hard work?' I asked.

'I don't mind hard work.' She glanced sideways at me, half smiling. I looked away. 'Trouble is, it gets very tedious.'

'Things do.'

The fire hissed.

'I'm not sure I can see myself keeping onshore,' I said, surprising myself.

'Are you mad?' She laughed.

'Possibly.'

'I suppose you've every right to be.' She picked up her tea again and blew on it. 'Oh, it's not so bad where I am, but I'll go off my head if I stay too long.'

'Don't you dare leave there!' her mother exploded. 'How would that look? After Mr Jamrach spoke for you!'

'Oh, Mr Jamrach knows me,' Ishbel said airily and turned to me. 'Do you know, I had a regular slot at the Empire?'

'Really?'

'Really.'

For a moment our eyes met. There was puzzlement in hers. As for me, I don't know what she saw.

'We've been ever so well taken care of,' Mrs Linver told me, nodding gratefully, nursing her cup under her chin.

Fledge's money.

'Yes, we have.' Ishbel smiled prettily. 'Isn't it funny?' Then her face broke up, just like it used to when she tripped up and scraped her knees years ago. She put her cup down so clumsily hard that it cracked the saucer. 'Oh shite!' she hissed.

Tea spilled on the cloth.

'Oh, Ishbel!' her mother chided.

'It's only a saucer,' she said.

I leaned forward to help with the mopping up but she slapped the back of my hand. She was shaking with tears, they came in a feverish rush. 'Shame you never even found the dragon,' she said, the words catching in her throat.

Damn that thing. Damn it to hell for calling up demons. Our superstition.

'Let me help,' I said, reaching out once more towards the mess on the table.

'Oh, leave it!' Ishbel tossed herself back into her chair.

'There you are, love, don't cry like that,' her mother said, but the saying of it set *her* off too, and I couldn't stand it any more. I stood up.

'I have to go,' I said desperately.

'Yes,' said Ishbel, 'this is very hard.'

Eyes tight closed, Mrs Linver sucked her knuckles, clicked her throat.

'I'm so sorry, Mrs Linver,' I said again lamely, but she waved me away.

Ishbel stood. 'I'll see you out.'

In the dark hall she threw her arms round me and squeezed me and kissed my mouth hard. 'It's so good to see you again, Jaffy!' She was laughing and crying at the same time. I couldn't see her face. I grabbed her again and pulled her close.

'God, Ishbel,' I mumbled. Her soft warm breast pressed against me.

'I know,' she said, 'it must have been hell.'

'God.' I wouldn't let her go. She was all things good I'd longed towards when I was in the boat. I could have crushed her.

'Poor, poor Jaffy,' she crooned, swaying about with me and stroking the back of my head. It lasted a few long seconds, till we drew clumsily apart and bumped giddily towards the door as if drunk.

'Come and have a proper talk with me, won't you?' she said as she opened the door for me. 'I'm back at work tomorrow and I won't get a chance to breathe before Friday week at least. Will you go in the Malt Shovel on Saturday?'

'I couldn't say.'

'Well, I'll see you soon,' she said, smiled and gave me one last kiss, tears still running from her eyes, and there I was out in the early evening, reeling, down towards the Highway where the sailors and colliers were beginning to whoop it up. I went into a tavern and got very drunk with a sailor from Naples, who swore and scratched his bug bites savagely for the entire duration of my stay, making his arms bleed. Filthy lodgings, he said, spitting. Filthy food and filthy girls.

317

'I agree,' I said. 'Filthy, all filthy,' and spent some more money. I could never go back.

'I killed my friend,' I said to the Italian.

He waved an arm forgivingly as if to say, don't we all? I opened my mouth to tell more but was dumb. Never go back. She was engaged. No point at all. Just rub salt in the wounds whenever she saw me.

The touts and whores had noted my carelessness and circled round, but I was wise to all that. Around midnight I went home in a cab, and to bed, with spinning head and dry mouth, heart as sick and bloated as a tick.

They tell me I was afloat for sixty-five days.

You don't easily get back from a thing like that. Dark in the night I'd lie awake and know I'd never really returned, that I was lost still and always would be. I floated in a stream of babbling time. I went to ground. Never went to see Ishbel. She sent a letter, but I ignored it. Said sorry she'd missed me at the Malt Shovel, she hoped I was well. Well, she was a kind-hearted girl, she would say that. I went back to bed and wouldn't get up. I stayed upstairs at Ma's. Slept and slept, sat and sat, drank and drank, scribbled my testament and tore it up, again and again. The sounds outside my window soothed me. My bruise ached, a permanent bruise on my upper right arm, from Tim's grip on the boat. I should have shown her that. I should have shown Ishbel. Now and then I looked out over the wintry rooftops. Dream and life and thoughts, darks and lights, coalescing, my head no more than a bubble about to burst. My mind walked on cloud tops, soared in trances of killing delight. My head was a chasm. The universe pressed down on me.

Ma kept coming in and nagging. I kept sending her away. One day she said she'd bumped into Mrs Linver, and Mrs Linver had

318

said she hoped I was well and that Ishbel sent her love. How could *she* know that? It was just something people said to be nice. Anyway, I didn't even have Ishbel's address, so it was up to her to come round here if she wanted to see me. But she didn't bother, and I didn't bother and anyway I was too tired to do anything or even think about anything. Here in this world, all that I'd gone through counted for nothing. No one could know me now. Only Dan, and he'd gone back to his family. We had a dragon between us, never to be mentioned. Still now it seemed as if the thing's unleashing caused it all. What was the point of explaining? Pointless. How was I supposed to go back to work as if nothing had happened?

David kept coming in and messing about with my things. Would you believe I had souvenirs of my grief? A piece of twine, a scrap of sailcloth, a few knuckle bones. One was from Tim, the others could have been anyone's. It didn't matter. The rest they took from us when we were taken on-board.

'Piss off out of here, you,' I told him.

'David, leave him alone.' My mother's voice.

Voices downstairs. The normal sounds of life.

A stone crushed my chest. I did not leave my room unless it was very quiet. Ma brought my food up and I picked at it, stuff I'd cried for in the boat. It upset my stomach. She kept on at me to come down, came and sat on my bed and stroked my hair and said everyone was enquiring after me and sending good wishes. 'I've done you a lovely chucky-egg,' she said.

'I'm not a baby,' I replied, floating back into the stream of time, day and night, dark and light, sound and silence, my room and the boat lapping along together, nothing between them. I lay in it like a hedgehog in the winter, huddled warm, the world above persisting beyond my care, like the heavens above the sky or the world of air above the undersea. I saw the wisdom of cats and old dogs that sleep time away. Whenever I came up it was to sink back again. I was in this state even when up and walking about, as I did to please Ma every now and then, appearing bashfully, sitting at the table to play with my food, bringing the coal in, minding David. That was easy. He was a placid child and he found me fascinating. That is, he took great satisfaction in studying my face with close attention, a thoughtful frown on his brow. When he wasn't doing that he was talking happily to his train, a long red wooden thing called Dob, knocked up by Charley Grant. A few words were coming through, not just Ma and Pa: he was coming out with 'trousers' and 'cot' and 'doggy', and 'baby' and 'drink' and 'raining'. And 'no', which he said a lot. The rest was babble. I could gain a lot of points with Ma by minding David, and I could do it pretty much in my hedgehog state, so that became my occupation for a lot of the time as I drifted, protected by the soft blanket of slothdom, thoughtless, maddeningly boring, tepid. Panic stirring like a whale in the deeps below.

One night I went out. I went to old Spoony's and was greeted as a returning son. Bob Barry sat at my table and bought all the drinks, old faces smiled into mine, new ones picked up the story and turned my way. I was quite the toast. God knows how I got home, I drank a skinful. They had a big dirty pot man and a new little pot boy, about nine years old, couldn't get enough of me. I remember him in all the bright head-spin of that place, me sitting at my solitary centre, his eager snubby nub of a face looming into mine, grinning wildly. 'Hello, mister!'

'Hello,' I replied.

'You want me to fetch you a pipe?'

I considered. A pipe. That would be nice.

He ran away delighted, returning with a well-packed meerschaum carved in the likeness of a lush naked woman, which he put solicitously to my lips and carefully lit. It drew beautifully and filled my lungs with warmth.

'Thank you,' I said.

'Mister.' He stood back. 'What was it like?'

I took my time, leaning back and blowing out a thin stream of smoke.

'What?' I asked. 'Which bit of it?'

'I don't know. Everything.'

'Everything?' I laughed.

Much later he got round to telling me that what he really wanted to know was what it tasted like. Was it like pork? He'd heard it was like pork.

'A bit,' I said. 'Not quite.'

'How not like?'

'I dunno.'

'Was it nice?'

I didn't answer.

'Won't you tell me?'

'No.'

He wanted a story. A thing of horror. I have a story, a terrible one. But I'll tell no tales. He doesn't understand at all: it's not *that* kind of a story, not horror but grief I have to deal with. Too much to tell. What shall I do with it?

Live with it.

So I rolled home and went back to bed, and if anyone came round I hid upstairs. They let me. There's freedom in madness, I didn't need to justify anything. The world owed me a little peace. I put my head back down under and let the sweet fishes nibble my nose. Oh, sweet sleep, sweet, sweet, sweet . . .

For about eight months I went on like this. Somewhere in the middle of it all Dan came to see me. I was lying on my bed dozing, and he walked in and kicked my foot. 'Shake a leg, Jaf,' he said.

I got up on one elbow.

'Stinks in here,' he said. 'Look what I brought you.'

A bit of scrimshaw, the likeness of a parrot carved on it.

'It's walrus,' he said. 'I thought you'd like it.'

'Nice.' I turned it over and over in my hand.

'How are you, lad? Your ma says you're not up to much these days.'

'True. Still tired, I suppose.' I was yawning as I spoke, and he laughed. There wasn't a chair, so he sat himself down on the floor under the window, his coat hunched up about the back of his head. He fished out a pouch of sweet tobacco, and we sat and smoked as the darkness in the corners of the room turned blue. Little and old and twisted he looked sometimes, but the way he sat and smoked still carried a curious quality of youth in it, and his hair was still vigorous. Had a nasty cough though.

I asked him: 'How is it? Life ashore?'

And he smiled and said, 'Precious.'

Half an hour did we sit? I don't think it was longer. We didn't talk much. He said from now on he would devote his life to watching his children growing up, and to the study of natural history, and he asked me what *I* would do. I didn't know.

'I'd say we have a duty, we two.' His face was indistinct, but I could see the smoke spuming out of his nostrils.

'Don't give me that,' I said.

He laughed. 'I know,' he said, 'I know what it's like. But I'm older than you. It makes a difference.'

'Wisdom? Huh!' I said. 'When I look around me, Dan, I don't see a lot of old wise people.'

He laughed again. 'Who's claiming wisdom? I'm only saying being old makes a difference. We came through, we have a duty to make the most of it.'

I was sick of people telling me how lucky I was. I didn't feel lucky. If there was a God, I thought, he must be a twisted sort. All of them gone and all that pain and fear, and not a one of them deserved it.

'Listen,' I said, 'there's no meaning in it. Just chance. Random, pointless. There's no other way of seeing it.' My anger grew. 'I might not have gone. I nearly didn't. Some other boy would have got my place. Remember George? Jumped ship at the Cape? Chance! He's alive and they're dead. That's all it is. Blind chance.'

It was the longest speech I'd made since my return.

Dan's head was now completely obscured by smoke. 'You're right,' he said.

We sat in silence for a while. The room grew darker and the smell of stew rose up from beneath.

'So, what are we to do?' He was invisible. 'Shall we die?' A spasm of coughing. 'Or shall we live?'

A longer silence.

'A hand is dealt,' he said. 'You take it.'

I felt I ought to speak: 'And *that* is my duty?'

'It is.'

I was tired, so I lay down and closed my eyes.

'I'll be going,' he said.

I didn't open my eyes. He groaned as he pushed himself up from the floor. 'These old bones.' He heaved a sigh.

He stood for a moment as if waiting for me to say something, but I didn't. Then he said: 'I know what it's like. I have it too. The melancholics.'

I still didn't speak.

'You should come to dinner at our house, Jaf,' he said, 'when you're feeling up to it.'

'Thanks. I will,' I said.

But I couldn't see it happening soon.

*

323

It was one morning, the sound of a concertina playing 'Santy Anno'. Over the rooftops. Towards the river, towards the Highway. Winter and spring had gone, and the summer was full-blown. I went for a walk, following the sound, but I never found it or it took another direction, I don't know. I just wandered about, stopping now and then to loll about and watch the river. I could still hear 'Santy Anno' in my head, and it came to me that I must get myself a concertina and learn to play it. It came as something more than an idle thought, more like a kick, so that I almost jumped up there and then and ran for home to get some money and off to Rosemary Lane to pick up an old concertina. But it was so nice by the river watching a big clipper sailing in like a swan that I didn't move. I could see the sailors moving about their business on the decks and in the rigging, and it seemed to me I could feel the deck beneath my feet, real as ever. There flashed across my eyes then, bright and startling, first a bleeding sunset more beautiful than a heart could bear; then an explosion of pink heart muscle throbbing in a bucket as the boat lurched high; and last: Tim, just as he always was, my daft friend. He was horrible to me sometimes, but I think he loved me. I was dreamy. I drifted home. I don't know where the day went. The lateness of our yard surprised me. Ma's shells were tidy on the windowsill, and David stood full in the window, smiling snot-faced at me. It was a lovely smile. It brought back that great wave of love I'd felt out there in the boat when I thought I'd never get back. Filled me right up. Terrified me. Oh, my London. All wasting. I am still here. I went in and straight upstairs and got into bed with all my clothes on and pulled the covers over my head and lay down in the dark. My heart was beating loud and scared in my ear that lay against the pillow. Long as I live I'll never be wise. Never understand why it happened as it happened, never understand where they've gone, all those faces I see clear in the darkness. There's no way out of this, it's stark: live or die. Every given moment a bubble that bursts. Step on, from one to the next, ever onwards, a rainbow of stepping stones, each bursting softly as your foot touches and passes on. Till one step finds only empty air. Till that step, live.

There was a movement in my room, a little mouse creeping. I opened my eyes and stuck my head up from under the covers. It was Ma with a candle, half in and half out the door. 'You coming down for a bite, Jaf?' she said.

I was going to say no, but said, 'Is it ready?'

'Just about.'

She put the candle down and went away, leaving the door open. I sat up and put my feet down on the floor and yawned till tears forced out from my eyes. I was cold. I went down to the fire and the food.

'Lovely bit of herring, that is,' Charley Grant said as I sat down. 'Here.' He pushed the bread board towards me.

The herring was crusted with oats, fried brown.

'We were thinking,' Ma said, 'you ought to start going out with Charl on the market some of these mornings. If you're not doing anything else you might as well learn the ropes here.'

'Fine,' I said, but oh my God, that night lying awake in bed, thinking: got to do something or I'll end up living with Ma and Charley for the rest of my life and die on the fish stall. What's the choice? Fish. Pot boy. I'd be quite a draw. The cannibal pot boy. Work at Jamrach's again. Go back to sea.

Back to sea, I suppose.

Next day I went to see Dan Rymer. He must have done well over the years, one way or another. He had a big house in a fine terrace in a nice part of Bow, with a black railing at the front and steps going down into an area, where a fat black and white cat sat meditating. The door was opened by a girl of about fourteen, aproned and bedraggled. 'You're Jaffy Brown,' she said.

'How do you know?'

'I'd know you anywhere,' she said, 'never stops talking about you, he don't. Curly hair, dark skin. 'Course it's you.'

'Never stops talking about me?'

'Oh no! Best man he ever sailed with! Here, you'd better come in.'

I stepped into a hall with walls covered in hangings and clocks and masks from all over the world, and an open door with kids running in and out.

'In there,' she said, so I went in. There were tiny tables and big stuffed chairs, a wall full of books, roses all over the carpet and a large solemn dog not deigning to get up out of its comfortable sprawl in front of the fire. In the window, two caged lovebirds sat breast to breast, eyeing the room. There were children, noisy, I can't remember how many or who, but they took no notice of me at all till Dan appeared, clasping me to him like a long-lost son, and then they crowded round, curious, and even the dog got up. It was funny seeing Dan at home. Quite the seaman's beard he was growing for himself these days.

'Alice!' he shouted. 'Jaffy's come!' and she came, that tall woman from a far-ago morning at the Greenland Dock (the smell of the morning air, tar, sweat, ale, me and Tim standing together and Ishbel waving, red shoes, black shawl), and stooped, smiling, to kiss my cheek.

'At last,' she said warmly. 'Thank you for bringing him home, Jaffy.'

'Other way round, ma'am,' I muttered. 'It was him brought *me* home.'

She had wide, thin lips, hard angles in her face, lines growing in the corners of her eyes. Very friendly, she was. Her dark brown eyes were steady and intelligent. 'Say what you like,' she said, 'you brought him home.'

326

One of the girls brought in tea, and I felt myself the centre of attention. I was getting used to that, me being the cannibal boy. All of Dan's eight children were there, the biggest a slow straw-haired boy of fifteen, the youngest a slobbery tot that chomped on its fist on a big sister's knee. They gathered, standing and sitting, just staring. I winked at one of them, a small boy, who turned coy and looked away. Dan shooed people about, made me sit in the biggest chair by the fire and sat himself down opposite me. He leaned forward, grinning madly, to strike a match on the side of the fireplace. The dog nosed his knee thoughtfully and was rewarded with a rough scratch on its sable loose-skinned neck. His wife poured the tea.

'Sugar?' She stood poised with the spoon.

'Three please.'

'Sweets for the sweet.' She smiled. When she sat, the way she drew her skirts about her, straightened her back and lifted her cup to her lips in one long elegant movement reminded me of dancers I'd seen, girls at Paddy's Goose and the Empire.

I wanted to say to her: he never stopped talking about you. It was a bit of a joke, him and his Alice. But it was all strange. I couldn't. Something was awkward. She asked very kindly after my ma and the family and if I'd had time yet to think about what I was going to do next, and I laughed and said I was spoilt for choice. We sat for a while talking of this and that and nothing much, till she got up and herded all the others out before her, saying she was sure we two had things to talk about.

'Shall I send in more tea?' she asked from the door.

'Brandy,' said Dan.

'Brandy it is.'

The brandy was good. We sat by the fire, smoking and sipping, serene. I remember little of the conversation.

'She's very nice,' I said, 'your Alice. She's lovely.'

He nodded. 'Fell on my feet, there. God knows how.'

'You've got a lot of books.'

He turned his head and looked at them. 'Natural history,' he said.

I got up and had a look. There were the works of Charles Darwin, Alfred Russel Wallace, Charles Lyell and Thomas Huxley, although at that time I wouldn't have known the names of any of those people apart from Darwin, a great tome of whose had had a permanent place on the bookcase in Mr Jamrach's office for years. One whole shelf was stuffed with Dan's own scrapbooks and memos from his travels, and for the rest it was all animals and birds and fish and plants, and books about the sea. I picked out this and that one. Audubon's *The Birds of America*. Beautiful pictures.

'Take it,' Dan said. 'Go on.'

It was a wonderful book, the smell, the very feel of it. It rested on my lap for the rest of the visit, my hands smoothing its cover. When I stood on the doorstep taking my leave, the sun, appearing suddenly, shone on the cover.

'I'm going back to sea,' I told him.

He nodded. 'Probably the best thing for now. The sea gives a man time to think.'

I held up the book. 'I'll treasure this.'

'Go on with you,' he said, and gave me a shove.

I went down to the Victoria Dock and looked around and found a ship bound for Spain, and signed. Ma slapped my face when I told her.

'How dare you!' she cried. 'How dare you do this to me!'

'Ma,' I said, tears springing to my eyes, 'lightning don't strike twice.'

'How do you know?'

328

'Look, Ma,' I said, 'I could get run down by a cab tomorrow. Think about it sensibly.'

'Don't you talk to me about sense,' she said, and for a moment I felt sorry, but it was too late. I had two days.

'Ma,' I said, putting my hands on her shoulders, 'I have to do something. It's only Spain. The sea gives a man time to think.'

'Oh,' she said bitterly, 'you didn't get any of that done up there all these months then?' motioning with her eyes to the ceiling.

But she calmed down as she always did, and I let her bustle around me bringing soup and bread. She didn't say anything any more about not wanting me to go.

> Our Captain calls all hands
> We sail tomorrow
> Leaving these fair pretty maids
> In grief and sorrow.
> It's in vain to weep for me
> For I am going
> To everlasting joys
> And fountains flowing.

Funny how sad that sounds.

Then began my ramblings again, and there were adventures and girls and good friends and I got myself a concertina and learned to play 'Santy Anno'. The whaling was all washed up and I was through with it anyway. It was traders and clippers for me from now on, no more of these long voyages. I shipped to Spain and Holland and the Baltic shores, and once to Alexandria, and was home fairly regular. Once or twice I saw Ish and we were civil but strange with one another. Once I saw her with the fiancé, a good-looking sort, taller than me. I hated seeing her. Sent me home and back to bed with my head under the pillow and an aching mind. And I was well on the way to being one of those salty types who can't abide the land for more than it takes for him to spend his cash, only I discovered a liking for learning.

16

There are turnings and twistings, a tangle of wool that needs sorting out and winding into a ball, but I ain't doing it. It's broth, all sorts thrown in and floating, the things that don't fit, lost things, offshoots. In and out we roll, waves of time and impression, rolling forever on the shore, waves and waves becoming ripples and ripples, smaller and fainter till sleep comes.

Sometimes we walk along by the old places. It's changed, the Highway, like a face changes, till you see the face beneath the face beneath the face.

There's a song, you probably know it:

> Oh, I am a cook and a captain bold,
> And the mate of the *Nancy* brig,
> And a bosun tight, and a midshipmite,
> And the crew of the captain's gig.

God knows how many verses it's got. I once heard a man sing the whole thing on stage at the Empire and you should have seen the audience falling about. Funny, isn't it? You'd bring the house down if you got up onstage and made an act of that, someone once told me. Probably true.

> 'T'was on the shores that round our coast
> From Deal to Ramsgate span,
> That I found alone on a piece of stone
> An elderly naval man.

Of course, you know his story. You find a naval man with a story on just about every other stone around here. They've seen a lot, these people of Ratcliffe Highway. They don't mind me.

One of my shore runs I met Mrs Linver coming out of the stale bread shop, practically knocked her over in fact. A funny old woman she'd become with those wild staring eyes and her frizzy hair gone thin and tarnished.

'Oh, Jaffy,' she said, 'you never come and see me!'

So much time had passed. Her greeting surprised me.

'I'm not home much,' I said, shifting awkwardly. Actually I was very glad to see her. God knows why. She was just like the old days, that's why.

'Well, you could make the effort now and then,' she said, 'it's not hard.'

'I don't know, Mrs Linver,' I said, 'I thought you might not want to see me.'

'Don't be stupid.' She shifted her basket to the other arm grumpily. 'You've got to get over that,' and stomped off.

My God, that brought a tear to me. I ran after her. 'How are you, Mrs Linver?' I said. 'Can I carry that for you?'

'Too late now,' she grumbled, but I persisted and walked her home to Fournier Street, and went in and built up the fire for her and made tea, and sat and drank it with her for a while. I felt curiously fond of her, painfully grateful that she could bear to be with me.

'*She* never comes to see me either,' she said. 'Always the same, ain't it?'

'I don't suppose she gets much time,' I said.

'She does, she just don't come. Too busy getting her beauty sleep. She's gone back to the singing.'

'Has she? Where at?'

'Oh, I don't know. The Goose, I think.'

'Still engaged, is she?'

'Oh yes,' she said, preening as if it was her own beau she was talking about. 'He's a lighterman, he is. Very steady.'

I didn't mean to but I went to Paddy's Goose. My feet just took me, and there she was sitting at a crowded table, soft and tipsy, in tears, giggling. I hadn't seen her since that time, so stiff and awkward, when she kissed me in the hall. I walked straight over and pushed in next to her.

'Saw your ma,' I said.

She turned to me smiling, her face shiny, sleepy eyed. 'It's Jaffy,' she said, leaning on my shoulder and putting a knuckle in her mouth, 'my dear old Jaffy.' The way she slumped, the peculiar fixed stare. Drunk off her silly head. Now I was here I didn't know what to do.

'I'm away tomorrow, early,' I said.

'Lord,' she said, her head rolling back, 'isn't that always the way?'

I put my arm round her. 'Where's your Frank?' I asked her.

A crowd jostled our shoulders, making the curls on the back of her head bob.

'Somewhere around.' She glanced vaguely about. 'My lovely, lovely Jaffy,' she said. The kiss she gave me was hot and heavy, blunt and heedless as a child's. 'Don't worry, Jaf, he won't mind if I kiss you,' she said, crying all the time, pulling away and wiping her cheeks with her palms.

'Why are you crying?'

'Me?' She laughed. '*I'm* not crying. I'm doing very nicely, darling. Packed my job in,' she said, 'Couldn't stand it. Fool's game, I can make more down here. Look, sweetheart, watch me,' and she grabbed and drained her drink straight down, a practised passage, then jumped up and joined the dancers. The fiddler, a less skilful man than Simon Flower, played a waltz. What a show that girl was, smiling her way throught the bright smoky room. I wasn't sober. How much I remember is true I don't know, but it seemed to me she never actually took her eyes off me while she danced, even when the fiancé came and put his arm round her waist. But I waited and she never came back to our table. In the end I lost her in the crowd, and went home half hating her.

I steered clear of her after that. She was too unsettling. I went back to sea, and at night in the fo'c's'le by candlelight I'd look at my Audubon birds. Somewhere I picked up a drawing book like the one Skip used to have, and whenever she came creeping in my head I set to copying the pictures as carefully as I could. It cleared my head, dropped a curtain between me and my ceaseless bloody mind. I didn't know if my drawings were any good. *I* liked them. I went mad raiding Dan Rymer's bookcases when I was home, grabbing any book with pictures of birds in it. Mr Jamrach gave me *Cage and Chamber Birds* by J.M. Bechstein. My drawings multiplied: lark, linnet, lovebird, woodcock. I loved the detail. Siskin, nightingale, goldfinch, waxbill. Still she wouldn't go away. I'd draw every known bird in the world. Avadavat, turtle dove, chaffinch, bullfinch. It would be something to do and it would take care of time and give me some pleasure. I'd do all the different varieties of all the different birds. I'd have to learn to paint. It could take the rest of my days.

In the silent bird room at Jamrach's I sat and drew. The birds on my pages were free. I gave them backgrounds: lakes reflecting castles, cauliflower forests, mountains like volcanoes. I'd seen the bamboo houses of songbirds on Flores and the Sumban coast, a cage like a doll's house in Patagonia and one like a diamond in Alexandria. I'd seen a cage of ivory, one of glass. Temples and palaces, barrels and bells, hexagons, octagons, domes.

Jamrach's cages were prisons. I imagined those poor feathery scraps inside, flying wild in my pencil's dove-grey depths, and remembered the man with the milky eye crafting his bamboo palaces, patiently tapping in the little wooden pegs. Poor things, I thought, you're here now and there's no going back. I'll make you some nice houses. And I drew cages with tops you could lift off, and ones you could open by a door in the side. Space. Lofts for roosting. You could have a ladder between, they'd like ladders.

Then I thought: why can't you have a shop where all the birds fly about? Like an aviary? An inside garden, with a pergola, and plants that grow indoors, and a glass roof. Like rich people have, only it would be a shop and people could come in and buy a bird. You could make a wild. You could have rocks and streams and rivers and fish and birds and even a few small animals, voles and dormice and such, all living free. Waterfalls and pools. *Trees*.

People would pay to come in and wander in Eden for half an hour. Everlasting joys and fountains flowing. Bowers for sitting. A treetop walk. Green and yellow parrakeets flitting here and there.

'You'd never make money like that,' Jamrach said when I showed him my sketches of the wild.

A cartload of canaries had just come in from Norwich, spangles and lizards. The boys were stowing them, stacking up the waxbills a level or two higher to make room.

'Nice cages though,' he said, turning the pages. 'You could sell those.'

A little laudanum suits me. Now and then. A little absinthe with sugar. It brings a little dream sense now and then. Dreams are not real, but have a very weighty seeming, and spawn feelings, and change the way things look the next day. So, for instance, as I was rapt in the soft shading on a siskin's throat, suddenly I saw Skip's face, and knew I'd dreamt him last night and this was why I woke so strange and frail this morning.

Clear as day, he was. First time I ever saw him, first day out on the ship. Mr Rainey clouted him on the head. I was scared of Mr Rainey. The story begins again its endless repetition. Then, dreamlike, I was at Jamrach's smoking a cigar and idly sketching Charlie the toucan and Mr Jamrach was telling me business was good. Mr Fledge gave up on the dragon idea. Said he fancied a polar bear now. 'Fancy a jaunt to the Arctic, Jaf?' Jamrach asked, and we both laughed. Rossetti the artist wanted an elephant, Jamrach said, to clean his windows, but couldn't stretch to the price. He settled for owls instead, owls and a laughing jackass, a marmot, a wombat. And that was the day he told me about this place that Albert had been using as a warehouse but didn't need any more, and said he'd help me with the deposit.

I had money put by, I was able.

So I came here, and went to sea no more. But the sea never left me. It called and moaned and dreamed in me day and night, beat like a heart at the back of everything, even when I slept, even as I created my wilderness. I had two storeys with a ladder connecting, and a yard out the back. I lived upstairs and had my workshop below. I discovered an aptitude. First thing I made was a round cage on eight legs, five feet tall and domed, with a carved eagle on the top, and a zigzag trellis. I put in twigs and perches and mirrors, blue-patterned china feeding bowls that slid in and out, a pull-out tray at the bottom. Ten green linnets moved in and seemed content. I tamed a jackdaw. That's easy enough. Guess what I called him? Jack. He took to sitting on my shoulder picking at my ear while I worked. I made cage after cage after cage, all kinds, bells and squares and lanterns, none too small, and soon enough I was getting a trade.

I sold the cages in the front of the shop and worked in the back. I made a cage that was completely spherical, and another like a huge pumpkin. I made a loft for turtle doves, an aviary for larks and goldfinches, and the whole yard I covered with wire work and laid with turf and planted with shrubs.

I became another sort of recluse.

I read Darwin's *The Variation of Animals and Plants under Domestication* and Haeckel's *Natural History of Creation*. I continued with my birds of the world. In the evenings the doves sighed in the loft. At some point I heard that Ishbel was fancy-free again and living towards Aldgate, but our paths hadn't crossed in a long time. She was far away, part of a life that was gone. I'll go and see her, I thought, but I did nothing, kept making plans and finding ways out of them. She'll come if she wants to, I thought. Me and my birds, we'd found a kind of peace. I was scared. I'd see her and all the old pain I'd tamped down would rise up. I'd look at her face and see her brother, and the great fact of what I'd done, the unthinkable, would fall between us. We were grown-ups now, different people. It was all too hard, too dangerous. My thinking consisted only of a toiling moil of impressions and didn't stretch to making decisions. My brain hurt. Anyway, I couldn't stop working on my wilderness. If I stopped something terrible would happen. I carried rocks, chopped eggs for the nightingales, mixed pea meal and moss seed, treacle and hog's lard to make paste for the skylarks. My heart hurt, and at night I'd look up at the sky and remember the stars at sea and ask: am I forgiven?

You should hear my nightingales. Here in the seedy depths of a Ratcliffe Highway night, they carol like angels. There are no words for that high sweetness. They carol to me that all shall be well and all shall be well and all manner of things shall be well (Jaffy Brown, see, became quite well-read), yet I know the tiger's mouth awaits. Come what may, whatever we may say, the tiger's mouth awaits. Every little second is the last chance to savour the time that remains. How I swam here to this rock I'll never know. A canary lands before me on a cherry branch, a jonquil, pure deep yellow.

She had a spangled-back canary on her shoulder next time I saw her, I remember. It was at Jamrach's, funnily enough, because she never went there. I'd gone to pick up some flax seed and some rape, and there she was sitting in the office with a canary on her shoulder and a wombat on her knee. She was all made up as if she was on her way to work and she looked at me and smiled. 'Hello, Jaffy,' she said, and something lifted like a veil.

'What are *you* doing here?' I asked her, cheerful as I could sound.

'I came to see the wombat,' she said, looking down at the furry brown creature.

Mr Jamrach got up from his desk. 'Poor thing won't last,' he said.

'Why, what's wrong with it?'

'Nothing yet.' He chuckled and poked it in the stomach.

'I like wombats,' Ishbel said.

'Doesn't have luck with his animals.' Jamrach fiddled with the blinds. 'Rossetti. The last one ended up stuffed in his hall.'

'Well, this one won't. Will you, cherub?' She lifted it up in front of her face as if it was a baby, an amiable round bear of a thing with a very large head and beady black eyes, gave it a kiss and deposited it once more in her lap, where it sat like Buddha, staring out at the world.

'You've got a canary on your shoulder,' I said. My mouth had gone dry

'Just grew there.' She smiled, rocking the wombat. Her bonnet was shabby. 'Mr Jamrach,' she said, 'could you move this little birdie, please? I don't want it shitting down my back.'

Jamrach leaned across the desk and took the bird onto his finger. 'Nice little batch, this lot,' he said.

I went out and filled my sack. I felt a little frantic. I even thought about not going back into the office, just walking out and going home and pretending nothing had happened. But my feet walked right back in and I licked my lips and said, 'What are you doing these days, Ishbel?'

'Same old thing. Bit of this, bit of that.'

'Ah.' Dumb.

'So . . .' The wombat nuzzled under her arm. 'How are *you*, Jaffy? I hear you've got yourself a lovely little bird place.'

'It's coming on,' I said.

'A haven of tranquillity!' Jamrach announced floridly.

'Can I have a look at it?' she asked. 'Are you going back there?'

'If you want,' I said. There was a faint, pounding beat inside me: take care, take care, take care.

'Oh good!' She smiled, jumped up and handed the poor wombat over to Mr Jamrach. We left it to its fate and she walked back to the shop with me. 'Isn't this funny?' she said. 'You're taller than me.'

'By a head at least.'

She put her arm through mine just the way she used to sometimes, just as if we were back all those years ago and nothing had ever happened. Why is she doing this? Does it mean anything? I was walking fast. Every now and then she ran a few steps to keep up with me and the sight of her old scuffed boots when I looked down filled me with such tenderness I could have cried.

'Is it far?' she asked. 'I'm supposed to be at work in twenty minutes.'

'Not far. See the yellow sign?'

Jack flew to my shoulder as soon as I opened the door. She jumped away with a little scream as his fierce black face flapped towards us.

'So this is it,' I said proudly.

She laughed. 'All this is yours, Jaffy. All this!' And I was guilty all over again for being alive and having all this. But she meant no harm. She flitted about admiring it all, the cages, the parrakeets, the parrots, the Java sparrow, my pictures stuck all over any bit of spare space. '*This* is nice,' she kept saying, and when we stepped into the yard she clapped her hands. 'It's so beautiful,' she cried, running up one of the gravel paths, turning, running back. I'd planted a rockery and the campanula was running everywhere. The linnets were in song.

'What's it like where you are?' I asked her.

'Horrible,' she said. 'Stinks.' She was standing next to me by the door. 'Look at you,' she said, 'you with the bird on your shoulder, matches your hair. What a pair you are.'

'Can you bear to see me?' I hadn't meant to say it.

She became very serious, put her hands on my shoulders and stared in my eyes. 'Is that what you think?'

'I don't know what I think.'

She went on staring and my eyes started to water. 'I thank God every day that you survived,' she said very quickly, then turned away and walked briskly back to the front door.

'Where are you going?' I dashed after her.

'I have to go to work.' She turned with the door open. The street outside was settling into its evening.

'But you're coming back?'

'What do *you* think?' she said. She was smiling. Then gone.

At midnight she returned, unpainted, like the girl who ran about the docks with us, like her brother. She never went away again.

17

All this was a long time ago.

Things are very different now. You can buy fruit in a sealed can, and meat from America; and the Highway's going up in the world. St George's East they call it nowadays, but people around here still call it the Highway and I daresay always will. They've closed down a lot of our familiar haunts, and they've cleaned up all from here down to the docks. The bridge of sighs, where people used to chuck themselves over – that's gone, and Meng's with the old Chinaman on the door. Spooney's went years ago. Still a good few of the old dives and dens left though. Not that I'm in them much these days. Too many responsibilities. My fifth decade gathers on the horizon like weather at sea. There is a place on my arm which is eternally bruised. The other night I caught a glimpse of my face in the glass and it pulled me up short. Didn't look like me. And when I look at the faces of my friends I see that they're all changing too, as are the streets outside.

Sometimes, waking, I forget where I am. It's the sounds that bring me back. There's an alehouse not far away. When I float through to consciousness its sing-song ding-dong comes to me from afar through the void, like a ship through fog. It reassures me to hear its sentimental din still merrying up the dark reaches of the night no matter how far I've sailed in dreams. You'd think after all this time I'd know I was back, wouldn't you? But sleep still scrambles me. When my head falls down that great gulf it crashes like a bauble into a million fine shards, and all of my beings fly out: the bawling babe, the sewer boy, the yardboy, the boy who went to sea, the boy who came back, the man. Takes a while to get back to this: me, now. Sometimes in that halfway place I don't know where I'll be when I emerge. I float in a murmuring womb, helpless, waiting to find out. The mermaids take my hands, kiss my lips. My tiger takes me up in his mouth, comes for me one more time, carries me from here to there, casually drops me. Here a drop, there a drop. Anywhere will do. Carried. That's me. Carried. Still a babe.

I'm often dreamy. When I dream I feel the sea under me, and sometimes I think I hear it too, sounding away behind the distant music of the Highway. It never goes away. It's what I always loved about this place, though I wasn't aware of it when I first came. Stand in Ratcliffe Highway and you'd swear there was salt on the air.

Night sounds steal into the garden where I sit watching the smoke from my pipe rise up to the stars. The nightingale sings. I close my eyes and trace with my fingers the outline of a parrot carved into a piece of scrimshaw lying on the palm of my left hand. It was a gift.

Rossetti and Darwin died two years since. At that time too there was another passing, unremarked, my good friend Dan Rymer, nearest thing I ever had to a father, who died of a swelling on the brain at the age of seventy-six. Still, a good age. His widow still lives in Bow. She's remarried and still has the youngest two of her children with her. She was twenty years his junior. Mr Jamrach long since retired and Albert's got the old business, but

342

these days it's me the real bird-fanciers come to, people from the Friendly and the Hand in Hand. Our shop's on the right-hand side as you go towards Limehouse. You can buy a parrakeet or a pair of lovebirds and a decent cage to put them in. Or you can walk through the shop and pay your penny to go and sit as long as you like in the bird garden, by the fountain, or the statue of Pan who plays his pipes all day to the chaffinch and the bullfinch, the golden carp in the pool, the honeysuckled pergola.

Her ma likes to go in there with her knitting. Her ma lives with us now. Peace and quiet, she says, though you can still hear the sounds of the Highway. It's a good old place, the place where late of night I go with my pipe, look up at the stars and roll away on billowy waves, hear the ocean's roar, and the sky all thunder, feel the swell, hear the voices of the demons of the deep howling into it all. One way or another I suppose you could say that voyage was the making of me. I'd have been a yardboy. Is that what it was all for? To make of me the man I am now? Is God mad? Is that it? Stuck between a mad God and merciless nature? What a game.

I don't fit the world of everyday things, the people going about their daily routines, bed on time, up on time, dinner on time. I don't want to be a part of it. Sometimes I long for a monk's cell, a hole in the rock, a bower in the woods, so my mind can flood all directions like water, the sea.

Time to gaze. On waves. Rise and fall, the breathing of the world.

This hurly-burly palls. Ishbel, of course, has to live with it. I've told her most things over the years, even about the dragon. 'Poor thing,' she says softly, meaning me and the dragon both. She'll never understand, but how could she? Understanding doesn't matter, it's the constancy that counts, so: I must go back to sea, she won't let me go back to sea. We argue about that.

343

'You'd manage.' I say. 'It wouldn't be for long. David could help out.' But she won't hear of it.

'Sorry, Jaf,' she says, 'me and Ma can't take it no more.'

So I go out in the garden. I'll never go back to sea. My eyes are closed. The children have been in bed for ages. I take from my pocket a piece of scrimshaw with the likeness of a parrot carved on it, turn it over and over between my fingers. Walrus. Dan too had his solitudes, these unaccompanied places. What I've seen and done and weathered is eternal, as much a part of me as my blood and bones. I saw skies of angels, heard laughter from the deep. The nightingale sobs. I rub the place on my arm where Tim used to hold onto me on the boat. Still aches. He comes to me sometimes. How could he not? He isn't angry. He's my friend. We are still in this together.

I open my eyes and see upon the violet-blue sky, moonbow, peerless, singing in the east. Very far away still on my journey, very far away and more beautiful than you could ever imagine.

Acknowledgements

This is a work of fiction that borrows from history. The only character in the book who actually existed is Jamrach himself, all the rest are made up.

There are two true stories:

Firstly, a Bengal tiger escaped while being delivered to Jamrach's menagerie near Ratcliffe Highway. An eight-year-old boy who walked up and patted it on the nose was knocked down and carried away in its mouth, but escaped unhurt after Jamrach jumped on the tiger's back.

Secondly, after the sinking of the whaleship *Essex* in the early nineteenth century, a sixteen-year-old boy called Charles Ramsdell shot his childhood friend, Owen Coffin, after the drawing of lots. Owen Coffin insisted on the lot being honoured. Charles Ramsdell survived, went back to sea and lived to a ripe old age.

There are several survivor accounts of the *Essex* voyage, all of which can be found in *The Loss of the Ship* Essex, *Sunk by a Whale* by Thomas Nickerson, Owen Chase and others. The classic book on the *Essex* is Nathaniel Philbrick's *In the Heart of the Sea*.

Many thanks to the Civitella Ranieri Foundation who gave me six wonderful writing weeks in Umbria, also to The Authors'

Foundation for their generosity in awarding me a grant. Thanks to Nina and Dave Bleasdale and to Frances and Tim Whittaker, who gave me quiet places to work. Thanks to Richard Butler for his invaluable technical help, and also to Martin and Joe, Emily Atherton, Mic Cheetham, Simon Kavanagh, Francis Bickmore and all at Canongate who have given their help and support.